THE *Best*
OF TIMES

THE *Best* OF TIMES

a novel

ANITA STANSFIELD

Covenant Communications, Inc.

Cover images: *Large Victorian House in Winter* © Gary Buss, Courtsey of Getty Images. *Blank Sign* © xyno, Courtsey of iStock Photo.

Cover design copyrighted 2009 by Covenant Communications, Inc.

Published by Covenant Communications, Inc.
American Fork, Utah

Printed in Canada
First Printing: November 2009

16 15 14 13 12 11 10 09   10 9 8 7 6 5 4 3 2 1

ISBN-13: 978-1-59811-848-3
ISBN-10: 1-59811-848-X

*This book is dedicated with deep admiration and respect to
the greatest fiction writer of all time—
Charles Dickens—
whose work as well as his life have been a great
inspiration and comfort to me,
and to all who have been touched by the great work of
this great man.
"God bless us, every one."*

CHAPTER 1

Anaconda, Montana — The Sunday before Thanksgiving

Chas Henrie rushed frantically to make certain everything was under control at the inn before she checked on her grandmother and hurried off to church. She was pleased when she managed to get to her usual seat five minutes before the meeting started, which gave her time to take a few deep breaths and shift the gears of her mind from her responsibilities in temporal matters to her desire to improve in spiritual ones.

Chas was used to sitting alone at church, but it still made her feel lonely. People were kind and good to her, but everyone else had family members to sit with. She'd often been invited to sit with a number of families, but she preferred her solitude over pretending to fit in with a family that wasn't her own. Granny was her only real family, but she was not a member of the Church. She'd always been completely respectful of Chas's decision to join The Church of Jesus Christ of Latter-day Saints, even though she'd thought it was a bit strange. And they had a firm mutual respect regarding each other's opinions and beliefs. Chas didn't criticize her grandmother for drinking coffee or having her warm brandy at bedtime, and Granny didn't criticize Chas's decision to not join her for coffee or brandy. A cup of cocoa maintained their social rituals without compromising Chas's standards.

As the meeting progressed, she found it difficult to focus during a couple of talks that were decidedly boring. They were good people and she admired them, but many of the speakers who ended up at the pulpit were not necessarily good at it. Still, she readily recognized that the spirit of the meeting was strong, and she was grateful. And yet her mind wandered. The lessons in Sunday School and Relief Society were good, but her mind continued to meander around in territory she preferred to avoid. After all these years, why did it still have to feel this way?

It was starting to snow when Chas left the church building, and by the time she had returned to the inn, it was coming down heavily. The storm was destined to be bad, and her thoughts focused on the guest who was flying into Butte this afternoon from Virginia and making the drive to the inn. As she quickly went to check on her grandmother, she said a silent prayer for him that he would arrive safely.

"You okay, Granny?" she asked, making the old woman's bed now that she'd moved to the big chair with a book.

"I'm dandy," Granny said with her usual enthusiasm while focusing on her reading. Chas chuckled while she automatically tidied the room. Her grandmother could barely walk from the bed to the chair to the bathroom. She was old and weak and tired. But at ninety-three she had the most positive attitude of anyone Chas had ever known. She was always "dandy," even when she clearly wasn't. No matter what happened, Granny—as Chas had called her from the cradle—always saw the glass half full. Chas consciously tried each day to do the same, but it was harder for her than for Granny, and she wished she'd inherited more of an ability to be positive from this great woman who had raised her.

Chas's father had never been around. Chas didn't even know who he was, and preferred it that way, since she was well aware that her conception had been a crime. Her mother had been—according to Granny—so emotionally and physically traumatized by the event, that her health had been tenuous throughout the entire pregnancy. But she had been determined to keep her baby, and had loved it long before it was born. Chas's mother had died bringing Chas into the world. And Chas had been left to be raised by her grandmother, a widow with no family to speak of and nothing to her name but a rotting family home that was more than a hundred years old. But Chas had loved growing up in the huge, old mansion. And she'd never wanted for anything, especially love and a sense of belonging, something she suspected other people born under such circumstances might not feel.

Granny had worked most of her life in a bakery, which had provided sufficient income for their needs since the house had been inherited free and clear. It had been a good childhood, and Chas had felt certain the goodness of her life would continue when she'd married her high-school sweetheart. She believed that she had loved Martin since kindergarten. He'd always been around, always been a playmate, and they'd always felt drawn to each other. For as long as she'd known him, he had talked of becoming an Air Force pilot. When he'd asked Chas to marry him, she'd known he was joining the military, and that she would spend her life moving from place to place. But she loved Martin and committed her life to him and to his military career. Granny had been heartbroken to think of Chas leaving Anaconda, but she never would have stood in the way of Chas's happiness. Granny had always liked and respected Martin. It had all seemed perfect.

After being stationed a thousand miles away with her new husband during his training, Chas had returned to Montana the week before Thanksgiving to finish out her pregnancy and have her first baby in her hometown, with her Granny there to help her. Martin would have a few days of leave during the holidays, and more when the baby came. Then on the Sunday before Thanksgiving, everything changed. The glass had spilled, and she'd been trying to get it half full ever since.

"How are *you?*" Granny asked, setting her book on her lap.

"I'm fine," Chas said with a smile, telling herself that it was more an attempt to be positive than it was a lie. "What are you reading?" she asked for the sake of distraction. Chas took the book to see the cover, already knowing it would be a Dickens novel. Granny rotated through them regularly, and rarely—if ever—read anything else. She practically had them memorized. *Martin Chuzzlewit.* She chuckled. "You love the way Dickens makes fun of Americans in that book, don't you."

"Yes, I do!" Granny said and actually clapped her aged hands together. The light in her eyes and her smile contradicted her frail appearance. "But I especially love the part when young Martin comes home from America."

The words stung Chas. *When young Martin comes home.* It took all her willpower to not let her chin quiver or her eyes water. But she was even more determined not to let her emotion show when she realized that Granny was watching her closely, waiting for a reaction. "You said that on purpose, you old goose!" Chas said and put the book back in her grandmother's lap before she turned away to pretend to watch the snow falling.

"Of course I did. I had to say something to get you to acknowledge what day it is."

"I don't have any trouble acknowledging what day it is, and I don't want to talk about it."

"Maybe you should," Granny said, and Chas marveled that a tiny, shriveled old woman could have such a voice of authority.

"There's nothing to say that we haven't said a hundred times. It's been twelve years."

"And you're still hurting over it."

"I'll get your lunch, Granny," Chas said and hurried to the kitchen, stopping first to shut herself in the bathroom and cry just enough to relieve the pressure of her grief.

"You know what your problem is," Granny said when Chas returned with the lunch tray.

"*You do,* apparently," Chas said and situated the little portable table in front of her grandmother so that she could eat her meal.

"You need to find someone else, someone to love, someone to replace the memories."

Chas was momentarily stunned. She'd heard her grandmother say it before, but not for about five years. That's when Chas had issued a firm decree that her need to find a man would no longer be discussed. She'd said then and she said now, "If God has a man out there for me, I'm sure He'll send him my way."

"So you seem to believe, but do you think any man could get through that armor of yours, even if God gave him a big shove in your direction?"

"I'm not talking about this, Granny," Chas said. "Is there anything else you need right now? Do you need to get to the bathroom before you eat?"

"No, I'm fine. Thank you for the meal, honey. Remember that I love you."

Chas sighed. Granny said it frequently, like a disclaimer to counteract any hurt feelings between them. And it always worked, because Chas knew she meant it. "I love you too, Granny," Chas said and kissed her grandmother's forehead before she went to check on the progress of the day's business of the inn. Chas didn't like working on Sundays or having other people do it for her. But that was the nature of the business. She had long ago settled the issue with the Lord, and knew with confidence that He approved of her profession, and she took very seriously the task of creating a different atmosphere at the inn on Sundays. Only the bare minimum of work was done to care for guests coming and going. Rooms that didn't have to be cleaned for Sunday night arrivals waited until Monday. And Chas considered her role as innkeeper to have deep meaning for her.

Once she knew that everything was under control, Chas fixed some lunch for herself, then sat to write in her journal. More and more it had become her best friend. She didn't know if that was good or not. She had friends from church, and friends outside of the Church. In fact, she'd been blessed with many friends. But only one came close to being what she could call a best friend. That was Charlotte. But as much as she and Charlotte enjoyed each other's company and helped each other through a variety of tasks and situations, their values were dramatically different, and Charlotte simply didn't understand the most important aspects of Chas's life. Therefore, her journal was truly her closest friend, and she poured her heart out, especially on this difficult anniversary. She shed tears again as she recalled so clearly the day when the news had arrived. The Sunday before Thanksgiving.

Chas was startled from her grief by a thought that urged her to go to the office to look at the reservation roster. There was only one guest arriving tonight, the man flying in from Virginia. It was her standard policy to get detailed information when reservations were made, so she knew where he was coming from, when his flight was scheduled to arrive, and that he would be renting a car. And she knew his cell phone number. She smiled to recall their phone conversation when he'd called to make the reservation, confirming the fact that she would rent rooms by the week according to what he'd read on her website. She'd asked him all the usual questions, and he'd said in a voice that was facetiously sarcastic, "Is this some kind of background check? Would you like me to fax over my fingerprints?"

"You can if you want," she'd replied in the same tone, "but it's really not necessary. I just want to know when to expect you and how to get hold of you if I need to. I make it a policy to take very good care of my guests."

"All I need is peace and quiet," he'd said with the barest hint of an edge to his voice.

"Now, that's not true," she'd countered lightly. "You need a bed, a bathroom, and a good meal now and then—or you wouldn't be talking to me."

"You got me there," he'd said and gave her his credit card information, adding a crack about blood samples and DNA testing.

Chas looked out the window at the deepening snow and said another prayer on behalf of his safe arrival.

* * * * *

Jackson Leeds watched from the plane window as the runway of Butte, Montana, came closer and closer through the flurry of snowflakes. The jolt of the wheels hitting the ground startled him, even though he'd been waiting for it. He was still wondering if he'd made a mistake, running away like this, hiding like some scared rabbit. But he didn't know what else to do, or where to go. There was nowhere familiar to him that might keep him safe from the varying degrees of well-meant concern and consternation of everyone he knew.

It took far longer than he'd hoped to get his luggage and pick up his rental car. By the time he was on the road out of the city, he felt exhausted and just wanted to sleep, even though it was still daylight. He glanced at his watch and estimated his time of arrival. Less than an hour from the airport, he'd been told. He was counting the minutes until he could be in bed.

Jackson hadn't been driving for long when the snow suddenly worsened. He had to slow down considerably, and he cursed under his breath as a simple drive turned into a stressful ordeal. His frustration grew as he was forced to keep driving more slowly, and it became difficult if not impossible to see the lines on the road, or the signs. When the car clock showed him that he had passed the time when he should have been taking a nap, he hit the dashboard with a fist and cursed more loudly. He was actually beginning to feel nervous about getting stranded or lost when his cell phone rang. He glanced quickly at the caller ID, then back to the road. *Dickensian Inn* it read, and he flipped the phone open, wondering if there was a problem with his reservation. The very idea *really* ticked him off.

"Yeah?" he said, then reminded himself that he wasn't talking to one of his coworkers.

"Mr. Leeds?" asked the same person who had helped him make his reservation a few days ago.

"Yes."

"Forgive me, but . . . I just wanted to make certain you were okay. The weather's gotten really nasty."

"You think?" he said, then cleared his throat as if he could cancel that. "Sorry," he said. "Yes, the weather is nasty and I'm beginning to wonder if I'm lost. It was very kind of you to call. Thank you. I'm on my way, but I'm not sure when I'll get there."

"Where are you?" she asked.

"I have no idea," he admitted, and she began asking questions about signs and landmarks. When he told her that he hadn't seen anything for many minutes because of the snow, she offered him kind reassurance that she'd come and find him if she had to. He laughed, then had to say, "You're serious."

"Yes, of course." She sounded surprised that he would doubt her.

"And what makes you think you wouldn't get lost yourself?"

"Because this is my hometown, Mr. Leeds, and I can get whatever help I need from the people around here to make certain my guests arrive safely."

Not certain how to acknowledge something so surprisingly kind, he was relieved to be able to say, "I just passed a sign." He told her what it said, and she told him to watch his odometer, and exactly how far it was to the turn.

"Okay, thank you," he said, but she didn't hang up. "You really don't need to talk to me until I get there."

"I just want to know you're safe."

"You don't even know me."

"But I'm responsible for you."

"No, you are not!" he said, wondering why he sounded so defensive.

"Mr. Leeds, if you—" The call cut off, and an annoying buzz replaced her voice. He flipped the phone closed and tossed it onto the passenger seat, paying close attention to the odometer, unable to deny his gratitude for this woman's intervention. He shook his head and told himself that he really needed to be a nicer person. He admitted being in a foul mood, as he had been for many days now. But even in the best of times, he knew he wasn't necessarily known among his peers as being warm and friendly.

Right after he'd made the turn, there was a sudden letup in the storm, and the visibility improved long enough for him to find his way to the street where he knew the inn was located. Then the visibility decreased again, worsened by the fact that it was dark now. He suddenly realized it was unusually dark. He couldn't see a light anywhere, and he knew he was in the middle of town. The phone rang again and he grabbed it. His navigator.

"Hello," he said, proud of himself for his friendly tone.

"Hi. Sorry about the cutoff. The power went out and I was on a cordless phone. Now I'm on the landline. I've got two kerosene lanterns burning on the porch so you can find us. After you pass the lights, turn left into the driveway and park on the side. Are you close?"

"I think so. I . . . oh, I see the lights. Thank you. I'll see you in a minute." He ended the call and took a long glance at the huge Victorian mansion barely visible through the snow, and the two glowing lights on either side of the wide porch. He found the driveway with no difficulty, and once the car was in Park, he let out a weighted sigh, blowing out the stress of the drive with a long, deep breath. He grabbed his bags, locked the car, and hurried through the snow and up the walk toward the lights that guided him. He realized a path on the walk had been recently scraped with a shovel because the snow wasn't as deep there. The same with the steps. He'd barely put a foot on the porch when the door came open and another light appeared, a lantern being held by a woman that he didn't get a good look at while he was more focused on getting through the door and out of the storm. He heard the door close behind him and immediately felt surrounded by an unexpected warmth, not just in the absence of the wind and snow, but in the many oil lamps and candles burning in every direction. The Victorian decor looked exquisite and inviting, and now that he was here, he felt like maybe he'd actually made the right choice to run away.

"I'm so glad you made it safely," the woman said, and he turned to look at her, the lamp she held illuminating her kind eyes and pretty face; very pretty, in fact. Her hair appeared to be dark brown and hung a little past her shoulders, with more fluff than curl. She was dressed in jeans and a heavy white sweater.

"Yes," he said, "so am I. Thank you for your help. I would likely still be out there if you hadn't called."

"I was praying for you," she said with a smile, and he felt taken aback. Religion was not something he'd encountered personally in his life. He'd met and worked with many people who lived it in varying degrees and beliefs, but he couldn't recall anyone ever saying they had prayed for him. He felt touched and had to visually assess her again. Her kindness and concern took on a whole new level of meaning; he just wasn't quite certain what to make of it.

Chas had been wondering during their brief phone conversations what this Mr. Leeds might be like. She'd had no idea of his age or what he might look like, and he wasn't at all what she'd expected— even if she hadn't known at all what to expect. He was average height, which made him about five inches taller than she. He had nice features without being so handsome that he might turn heads on the street. She guessed his age to be fortyish, although he had a youthful look that wasn't deterred by hair that was going prematurely gray. It was cut short, almost military in appearance, more salt than pepper, which told her that he'd once been quite dark. He wore a long wool coat, dark brown, expensive, and a cream-colored wool scarf that hung around his neck. He had brown leather gloves on his hands, and a brown leather bag on his shoulder. With his other hand he held a black case that she guessed held a laptop.

"Do you have baggage?" she asked. His brows went up, and one side of his lips did the same.

"Undoubtedly," he said. "Is this part of the psych evaluation you require for admittance?"

Chas chuckled and glanced away long enough to break eye contact. "Is that all of your luggage?" she clarified, recalling that he had reserved the room for a week.

"I have another bag in the trunk, but I can live without it till morning."

"Let's get you settled in, then," she said and started toward the stairs.

"Don't you need to . . . swipe my credit card . . . take a blood sample?"

Chas chuckled. "We can take care of the technicalities in the morning. You must be exhausted. If—"

"Did he get here all right?" Granny called from her room on the other side of the parlor.

"Yes, Granny," Chas called back. "He's here." Mr. Leeds again showed the barest hint of a smile, and she added, "Sorry. That's my grandmother. She adds character to the place . . . quite literally."

Chas started up the stairs, and he followed. "How is that?" Jackson asked, surprised by his own intrigue, but not by his curiosity. He was always curious. That's what made him so good at what he did. He just didn't like people *knowing* he was curious.

Chas gave an explanation that she was accustomed to giving when new guests arrived. "My grandmother inherited this house, which was built by her grandparents in 1870. The renovation was completed about ten years ago, and that's when we opened the inn. Granny is sort of an abbreviation for Grandmother Fanny. Yes, that's really her name. And even though I'm her only grandchild, she likes everyone to call her Granny, so feel free."

"Okay," Jackson said, although he didn't have any intention of hanging out with anyone but himself while he stayed here. He'd come for peace and quiet, to sort out everything that had happened, and hopefully come to terms with it—or at least make some progress in that direction.

They came to a landing at the top of the beautiful staircase, went down a hall, then up more stairs. He was fine with that. The higher the room, the less noise and interference. His innkeeper continued her explanation as they went. "It was my idea to turn the place into a bed-and-breakfast, but Granny insisted on the Dickensian theme. She loves Dickens. In fact, she was raised on Dickens; it's practically a religion around here. She has his novels memorized and will be able to offer advice on any given matter in relation to one of Dickens's characters."

"I'll be sure not to ask for any advice," he said, and Chas laughed.

"Very wise. She wanted the rooms to have themes related to Dickens's works, but I took a stand on that. I didn't think guillotines and prisons would go over very well for romantic getaways." She remembered that he was alone and added, "Or just getaways."

Chas was surprised when he chuckled and said, "So, you don't have a blacking factory suite?"

Chas turned to look at him. "You know Dickens?"

Jackson enjoyed the expression on her face. She'd asked it as if the writer were alive and well and they might be mutual friends. When he didn't answer right away, she added, "I mean . . . not many people know that he worked in a blacking factory as a child."

"Did he?" Jackson asked. "I was talking about David Copperfield."

She smiled and moved on. "So, you've read Dickens."

"A long time ago."

"Well, Granny and I settled on a compromise. The rooms are named after characters. You'll be staying in the Dombey. We also have the Copperfield, the Florence, the Nickleby, the Chuzzlewit, the Dorrit, and the Little Nell. And then there's the Carol."

"Is there a character named Carol?"

"No, of course not." She laughed softly.

"Then—"

"As in *A Christmas Carol*. It's the Christmas room. Of course, anyone is welcome to rent it anytime throughout the year, and they do. It's a wonderful room. And who couldn't use a little Christmas anytime? But the reservations in December fill up fast."

"How quaint," he said, not even wanting to think about Christmas.

She stopped at a door and turned a key in the lock. Not a plastic card with a magnetic strip, he noticed, but a key that looked as old as the house. "I'm Chas, by the way."

"Just Chas?" he asked, curious over such a name.

She hesitated with her hand on the doorknob. "Chas Florence Henrie. I loathe being called Mrs. Henrie. Florence is a deplorable name, but according to Granny I have to respect it because it was after her favorite Dickens character."

"And Chas?"

"The abbreviation for Charles," she said with a sly smile. "I was supposed to be a boy, according to Granny, because she wanted to name me Charles. Since I was a girl, she settled for Chas. It is my legal given name, and it's the name you need to know if you want anything around here."

She pushed open the door to the room, and Jackson felt like he was in some old movie. There was a fire blazing in the fireplace, with a healthy woodpile beside it, and there were three different oil lamps burning in the room. The room itself was simple but tasteful, with dark green paint on the walls, and authentic Victorian decor, including a four-poster bed and a beautiful wood-carved mantel over the fireplace.

"The furnace isn't running because of the power outage," Chas explained, "but the firewood and extra blankets should keep you from freezing to death. I'll have more wood brought up in the morning if you need it. I think the rest is self-explanatory. You should have everything you need, but if I can do anything for you, just . . . well, I was going to say call, but . . . well, when the power is on, I keep a cordless phone with me all the time and you can push zero to get me. Until then, you might have to come down the stairs and find me."

"Fair enough," he said. "Thank you."

"Any questions?"

"Nope. I'm good," Jackson said.

Chas almost left, then turned around to say, "Oh, I'll bring you up something to eat in a little while."

"I thought it was just a bed-and-breakfast."

"And where were you going to go to get any supper tonight?" she asked with a smile that matched the kind voice that had guided him safely here. "It might not be real great without a stove, but I won't let you starve."

Jackson was still trying to figure out how to respond to such perfect kindness when he realized she'd closed the door and was gone. He put down his bags and explored the room further. There was a little desk with a chair, perfect for using his laptop—had it not been confiscated as part of the investigation. Instead it would do nicely for the books that filled his laptop case. There were two wingback chairs facing the fire. He could use one for his feet. The bathroom had an old-fashioned tub and fixtures that were obviously new but made to look old. The bed had lots of decorative pillows, but they looked soft and inviting. On the bedside table were two books with leather bindings. One was a room journal where guests had written comments during their stays. The other was an old edition of *Dombey and Son,* by Charles Dickens. He smiled and glanced around. Everything was elegant and perfect. A good place to hide. He opened the blind to watch the snow falling and found some peace in feeling safe and cared for. He couldn't remember the last time he'd felt that way. Yes, it was a perfect place to hide.

CHAPTER 2

Chas went carefully back down the stairs, then hurried outside to get the lanterns off the porch and lock the door. She checked on Granny and found her dozing beneath a blanket in her big chair that Chas had moved closer to the fire when the power had gone out. Chas put another blanket over her, touched her silver hair, and went to the kitchen with an oil lamp to figure out what might be presentable to serve a guest. Fortunately she had some of Charlotte's homemade whole wheat bread and the makings for a good sandwich. Chas prepared a lovely plate with a thick sandwich, some old-fashioned potato chips, a pickle spear, and a sprig of parsley. She added a bottle of water and a tall glass of milk, figuring that one or both would work. She would have preferred to take the discreet elevator that had been installed during the renovation, but with the power out she had to take two flights of stairs in order to deliver supper to the door of the Dombey, knocking lightly.

Jackson pulled the door open to see Chas holding a tray against her shoulder with one hand, and a lamp in the other. "Your supper," she said, and he hurried to take the tray to relieve her of her burden.

"Thank you," he said, setting it on the little desk. "You're very thoughtful."

"It's not much, but . . ."

"It's great. It looks great. Thank you. Um . . . do you have any liquor available?"

She didn't look surprised by the question, which meant it was likely a common one, but he was surprised by her answer. "Only my grandmother's brandy, and she'll fight you for it. Sorry. You're on your own." More facetiously she added, "Besides, I don't allow drunken behavior at my inn."

"Don't worry," he said. "I'm a quiet drunk."

He felt her attempting to measure the degree of his seriousness versus humor. It was a character trait he prided himself on. The fact that people who didn't know him well didn't know whether or not he was joking held a certain fascination for him. He liked to see their reactions, and he'd found that he could learn a great deal about a person by how they responded to his humorless humor. Some people ignored him. They usually had no backbone. Some people argued with him. They were usually insecure. Some people sought to clarify. They were the ones he respected. And when they did it with eye contact, he respected them more.

"Good night, Mr. Leeds," she said. No backbone? That didn't seem to fit.

"Call me Jackson, Chas."

"Not Jack?" she asked, and he wasn't sure whether or not she was teasing him. Was she beating him at his own game? Did she know it was a game for him to figure people out and keep them from figuring *him* out?

"Not Jack," he said. "I'm not a pirate; just FBI."

She let out a one-syllable laugh. "You're joking, right?" She was trying to clarify. He liked her more with that one question.

"About what? Being a drunk, or being—"

"FBI."

"I thought you would have figured that out with my background check."

Chas remembered then his jokes about fingerprints and DNA. Was that it? He thought like an FBI agent because that's what he was? She was quick to retort with an even voice, "The database was offline due to the power outage."

Jackson let out the same kind of laugh he'd just heard from her. She was good. Any doubts he had about her having backbone disintegrated when she said, "Prove it."

Jackson snapped his wallet out and opened it as he'd done thousands of times to show the badge and ID in order to be allowed to enter places most people couldn't go. She didn't just glance at it, she took the wallet from him and held the ID close to the lamp she was holding. "Jackson T. Leeds. Federal Bureau of Investigation. Very impressive . . . Jackson." She handed it back to him. "What's the T for?"

"Tobias," he said.

"Serious?"

"Serious."

"Almost as bad as Florence."

"No, much worse than Florence."

They watched each other for a long moment while Jackson attempted to figure out if he was attracted to her, or just to her kindness.

"FBI, huh," she said, looking away. "A lonely job, apparently."

"How do you figure?" he asked, and she looked at him again, making eye contact in a way that was almost unnerving. And it took a lot to unnerve him.

"For a man who came here for peace and quiet, you certainly seem to enjoy having company and conversation." Jackson straightened his shoulders and lifted his chin, the same way he might if he were wondering whether or not to draw his weapon. Without flinching, she added, "I can tell when people want to be left alone, and when they want to talk." It felt like some kind of accusation until she added with perfect kindness, "If you'd like, you could bring your supper downstairs and eat with me and Granny. I'm afraid we're the only company available, since you're the only guest in the house. Most people leave on Sunday."

Jackson quickly figured how to save face and not be unkind. She was sharp enough to see through him, and he had to soothe his defensive impulse with a reminder that he respected her. "Thank you for supper, Chas . . . and everything else. You've been very kind."

"I told you I take very good care of my guests."

"And I can see that you are a woman of your word."

She left the room asking, "What time would you like to eat breakfast?"

"What time will it be ready?"

"You're the guest. You can choose. Seven, eight, nine, or ten."

"Nine," he said, hoping to sleep in a bit.

"I'll see you in the dining room just off the entry hall at nine. Good night . . . Jackson."

She left and closed the door. Jackson let out a long sigh, put some wood on the fire, and ate his sandwich. He wondered if it was the atmosphere or the hands that had prepared it that made it taste like the best sandwich he'd ever eaten. Or maybe he was just hungry. He stopped trying to analyze and just ate the sandwich before he went to bed, wondering why he felt lonelier than he'd felt since he'd left the home of his childhood more than twenty years ago. And yet, somehow, he felt less alone. Chas and Granny were in the house. The thought made him chuckle. They *both* added character to the house.

* * * * *

Jackson slept well but woke up early. He knew snow was still falling since he'd left the blinds open last night. The clock on the bedside table was flashing numbers, which meant the power was back on. Since the fire had long since gone out, he concluded that the only reason he wasn't freezing was due to the furnace running. He laid there for a long time, comforted somehow by his surroundings. The room was even more amazing in daylight. He loved the Victorian details of woodwork and plaster that held no hint of modern architecture. And it had been restored so beautifully! He gave himself credit for good instincts when he'd picked this place out of the list on Google when he'd been searching for a remote bed-and-breakfast. Thinking of the breakfast part, he hurried to shower and get dressed in order to get to the dining room by nine.

Jackson lovingly stroked the polished wood banisters as he descended the two flights of stairs and quickly found the room where six little tables with two chairs at each were aesthetically arranged, with a sideboard against one wall that he suspected would display a buffet on mornings when there were other guests. Today it had little more than a pot of hot coffee and a pot of hot water, side by side on a hotplate that kept them warm. He heard some noises from the kitchen where he could only see a refrigerator and a counter. While he was pouring himself a cup of coffee, he heard Chas call, "Good morning. Have a seat and I'll be right there."

"No hurry," he said and sat at one of the tables where he could see the snow falling. On the table were cloth napkins and dainty silverware and goblets.

"There are some newspapers over by the window if you're interested," she told him from the other room.

Normally he would have wanted to look at a paper. Today he felt like it would encroach on his hiding from the world. "Good coffee," he said when she walked into the room with a tray.

"That's what Granny says." She set a china plate with a muffin and a tiny dish of butter in front of him, along with a pretty little bowl of fruit.

He looked up at her. She was wearing an apron in the same deep green shade as the napkins, and he was startled by a little quiver in his stomach. It was a sensation he'd not experienced for years, but again he asked himself if he were attracted to her, or her kindness. Or perhaps simply to her company and conversation, as she had pointed out last night. Focusing on the food, he said, "Thank you. It looks delicious."

"Would you like milk, juice, or both? I've got orange, apple, grape, or white cranberry peach."

"Um . . . juice would be great. I'll take that . . . white kind; whatever you said."

She came back while he was buttering the warm muffin and poured juice into the goblet from a pretty carafe. Everything in this place had class, especially Chas Florence Henrie. Then he recalled that she'd said that she loathed being called *Mrs.* Henrie. He scolded himself for jumping to conclusions, but then . . . she was alone here with her grandmother and she wasn't wearing a ring. Did that necessarily mean what he thought it meant? And what was he thinking, anyway? It would be nothing but foolish—for both their sakes—to even consider making something romantic out of his intrigue with this woman who represented nothing more to him than a temporary refuge from another kind of storm that raged many miles away. Still, he couldn't help being intrigued. He'd never met anyone like her. She wasn't tough and hard like the women he worked with, and yet she had backbone. She wasn't simpering or tawdry like the women he encountered in everyday life. She was refreshingly tasteful, and she glowed with a depth of genuine kindness that he'd never encountered.

"Now," she said, "what else would you like to eat? We have—"

"This will suffice," he said, motioning toward the fruit and muffin.

"Oh, that's just to get you started. We take the word *breakfast* in our title very seriously. So, there's bacon, sausage, hash browns, eggs any way you want them, pancakes, and waffles."

"And who's cooking? You?"

"Yes! I'm a *great* cook."

"I'm not disputing that. I was just wondering if there's anybody else who works around here, or if you're a one-woman show?"

"You're getting awfully personal, Agent Leeds," she said facetiously. "I have maids that come in to clean as needed, and Polly, who is basically the office manager and covers for me here and there so I don't have to be on duty all the time. But *I* am the cook. Now, what will it be?"

She looked as if she would be personally insulted if he didn't eat a hearty breakfast, so he chuckled and said, "Okay, I'll take bacon and scrambled eggs. That should be more than enough. Thank you."

"It'll be about five minutes."

"No problem," he said. "I'm not going anywhere."

"Good thing," she called from the kitchen. "Even the snow plows are having trouble getting through this morning. It's good you got here when you did."

"Sure is," he said more to himself and took a long sip of coffee.

Chas came back with his bacon and eggs and set the plate in front of him. On the plate was also an artistically cut strawberry and a mint leaf. "Thank you," he said. She smiled and went back toward the kitchen, but he stopped her. "Aren't you going to eat breakfast?"

"I already did," she said, looking surprised by the question.

"Then why don't you sit down and have a cup of coffee with me . . . unless you have something else you have to be doing." She said nothing. "What?" he asked when she just stood there, looking confused.

"I've just . . . never had a guest ask me to eat with them before. It's a little weird."

"I figured since you were such a great detective and figured out that I'm apparently starved for company and conversation, you could indulge me a little."

"Okay," she drawled, "but first I need your credit card."

He lifted his brows. "You charge extra for conversation?"

"No," she laughed, "but I do need to swipe it for the room you've rented."

"Of course," he said and took his wallet out of his jeans pocket.

"Everything is included in the price I told you over the phone. There're some snacks and sandwiches in the little fridge right there." She pointed to it. "You're welcome to anything there, anytime. If you want dinner, that's extra."

"I thought this was a bed-and-breakfast."

"And I thought you were here for peace and quiet. Were you planning to go exploring the town with that much snow on the ground? I fix supper every night for me and Granny. Fixing for one more is not a big deal, as long as I know ahead. And then I'll add it to your bill." She smiled. "But I'm a great cook and reasonably priced."

"How far ahead do you need to know?"

"Breakfast time for that particular evening. That would be now."

"I'll be here for supper."

"Very good," she said and left the room. By the time she came back with the credit card and a paper for him to sign, he had finished eating. He put the card back in his wallet and wondered if she would accept his invitation to join him for a cup of coffee. She *did* sit down across the little table from him, but it was cocoa in her cup.

"So . . . what can I do for you, Jackson?" she asked, entirely business. "What do you need?"

"What makes you think I need something?"

"You asked me to join you. I run this place. You're a guest. My first assumption is that you need something."

"And I already told you I would like some company and conversation."

"And why is that?"

"Why do you ask so many questions?"

"I'm making conversation. But I'm still wondering why a man who comes here with the firm declaration that he wants peace and quiet, wants to talk."

"Maybe I just want to listen," he said. "I like listening to *you* talk. If you were annoying or got on my nerves then I'd be hiding in my room reading the books I brought with me."

"So, what would you like me to talk about, Jackson? Although we should probably avoid anything too personal, since . . . this is purely professional. Right?"

"Sounds fair. Tell me more about this place." He looked around. "I love it. I've stayed in a lot of B&B's, but I don't think I've ever been in one that . . . affected me like this one does."

"Ooh, that's very good. Maybe you could let me put that quote on my website. Great endorsement."

"Fine, as long as it's anonymous."

"Oh, that's right. FBI. Can't be too careful." She looked suddenly alarmed. "Hey, you're not hiding from the mob or something, are you? Because if you're in danger and you're here to—"

Jackson stopped her with an abrupt chuckle. "No worries, Chas. I'm not hiding from the mob. There are no bad guys after me."

"Then what are you running from?" she asked with a lift of her eyebrows as she took a sip of cocoa.

"Nothing personal, remember. You were going to tell me more about this place."

Chas felt puzzled by this man as she took another sip of cocoa and pondered the course their conversations had taken. He wasn't really her type, but she couldn't deny enjoying *his* company and conversation. Perhaps even more so, she was fascinated by his mysteriousness. She wondered why he was *really* here, and what kind of life he lived when he wasn't searching for peace and quiet. She was glad for a slow morning with no other guests, which allowed her the time to indulge in spending some time with him.

She reminded herself that like every other friendly guest who had come here through the years, they always moved on. Sometimes they came back; some were practically regulars to some degree. But they always moved on. They all had their lives beyond the Dickensian Inn. This was just a way station, a temporary reprieve from life. Of course, most of the people who stayed here were couples looking for romantic getaways. A small percentage were business people needing to be in the area for a few days. Guests had only used the weekly rate on a few occasions, and they usually spent long hours away from the inn doing business. On rare occasions, someone came alone just to get away, perhaps following a divorce or a death in the family. But they had never stayed more than a few days, and those people had never been prone to wanting anything but to be left alone.

That's what Chas had expected from Mr. Leeds when he'd made his reservation. But she'd never had a guest behave like this before, and she wasn't sure what to do with him. While she couldn't deny enjoying his company, she had to stand firm in the understanding that it was temporary. For her to become dependent on his company—even a little bit—would set her up for a letdown when he inevitably moved on. And she just wasn't up to any more letdowns in life.

Jackson cleared his throat unnaturally in order to bring her out of her thoughts. She offered an apologetic smile for allowing her mind to wander, then took another sip of cocoa.

"You said that your grandmother inherited the house. When was that?"

"Oh, she's always lived here. Her grandparents built it in 1870—which is the year that Charles Dickens died. That tidbit of information will help you impress Granny when you meet her."

"Okay," he said, showing the barest hint of a smile. She realized then that he never really smiled. He just hinted at one, as if humor threatened to crack the stone of his visage. Even when he chuckled, it kind of seemed to slip through without his expression changing much.

"Granny's grandparents came to America from England with a fair amount of money. Apparently they both came from well-to-do families, but wanted to make a fresh start. So they built this house with the plan to raise a large family here. The Dickens tradition apparently began with them, since they had both lived in London while Dickens was still alive. They had both read his works, had grown to care for each other while discussing their common love of his stories, and there's a rumor that they actually met the great writer after attending one of his public readings."

"Amazing," Jackson said.

"Yes, it is."

"So, they got married and came to America and built this house."

"That's right. Due to medical problems, they were only able to have one daughter who lived. That daughter grew up and married a local banker, and they all lived here together in the house, since it was obviously more than ample. Their daughter also hoped for a large family. But she and her husband also only had one daughter who lived. There were five births of babies that didn't survive."

"That's dreadful. Do you think it was something genetic?"

"Most likely," Chas said, and Jackson noted for the first time since he'd met her that he'd made her uncomfortable. Her confidence had discreetly crumbled.

He wondered whether to ask about that or change the subject, but the "nothing personal" rule convinced him otherwise. "And the daughter who lived is your grandmother."

"That's right," Chas said with a brightness that completely erased her previous glimpse into something painful. "Granny married young, a fine man named Walter. They started dating because she totally hooked him with the fact that Walter was a great character in a Dickens novel."

"Of course," Jackson said, that minuscule smile appearing again.

"Fanny and Walter had much the same experience. They had one daughter who lived, and three babies who did not."

"So, it *is* something genetic?" Jackson asked, wanting to go back to the subject *without* getting personal.

He expected her to answer the question cryptically and once again show vague discomfort. Instead she looked at him with a hardness in her eyes that he never would have expected from the woman he'd gotten to know so far. "You're very sharp, Mr. Leeds," she said. Her terse formality apparently came with her mood. "That *is* what the doctor told me when *my* baby died. She lived less than forty-eight hours. Heart defect. The pattern in the family was apparently fascinating to one of our local doctors who had a friend who worked in the field of genetics in some big city. He came and talked with me and Granny. Apparently, with what she could remember about her own babies and her siblings, and the autopsy they did on my baby, that's the conclusion they came to."

Jackson allowed silence to settle the words around them. He heard her blow out a long, slow breath just before he said, "I'm sorry. I didn't mean to bring up something difficult—and personal."

"It's okay. You didn't know. Now you do."

"But obviously *you* are very healthy. And so is your grandmother."

"Obviously. It's just hit-and-miss, apparently. My mother lived to adulthood, but she never had a strong heart. She died giving birth to me. That's why Granny raised me. It's just been the two of us for a very long time. Walter died before I came along. Granny worked at a bakery nearby for many years. Since the house was free and clear, it was plenty for us to manage on, and we've had a good life." She chuckled tensely. "Which brings us back to the history of the house, and—"

"The history of the house and the history of the family are closely intertwined, are they not?"

"Yes, but . . . I've given many guests the history of the house without ever bringing *that* into the conversation." She pointed a finger at him. "It's because you're an FBI agent, isn't it. You're trained at getting information out of people."

"I can't deny the training—or the practice. But my intentions were entirely sincere, I can assure you."

"Sincere, how?" she countered.

Jackson leaned his forearms on the little table. "I'm genuinely interested, Chas. I'm not trying to prove that you're guilty of a crime. There *is* a difference."

Chas smiled and tipped her head. "Fair enough."

"You *aren't* guilty of a crime, are you?" he asked facetiously to lighten the mood.

Completely straight-faced, she answered, "Nothing for you to be concerned about; it wouldn't fall under federal jurisdiction." For a long moment he really thought she was serious. Then he had to laugh—at himself—to see how thoroughly and naturally she could beat him at his own game. She smiled. "Crime is against my religion, Jackson Tobias Leeds. And if nothing else, I am a woman who lives my religion."

He noted that she used his full name in a tender voice when she was sincere; moods of sincerity could be variable. "And what religion is that?" he asked.

"I thought we were talking about the house."

"The house," he said and leaned back, motioning with his hand.

"I was raised in this house, and loved every nook and cranny."

"Have you ever lived anywhere else?"

"You keep asking personal questions, Agent Leeds," she said. Apparently her use of his professional title was meant to put him in his place.

"Sorry," he said. But he wasn't. Especially when she answered it.

"I lived away from here for a little over a year after I was married. I left at eighteen and was back before I turned twenty." He hoped for more explanation, but she avoided anything more that was personal and gracefully went back to the house. "At that point Granny was still working at the bakery and doing okay, but she was starting to show some signs of health problems due to aging, and I knew she couldn't do it forever. I also had no idea what I wanted to do with *my* life."

Jackson suspected that the death of her baby had probably occurred in there somewhere, and he would guess that her leaving here had had something to do with becoming Mrs. Henrie, and since she now loathed being *called* Mrs. Henrie, he guessed there had been a divorce.

"The obvious answer was in the house. It was free and clear. Neither Granny nor I had any debt. So, we mortgaged the house to provide the funds for renovation. The project took a couple of years, and here we are. For a while Granny helped with the cooking, but gradually she just couldn't do it. My friend Charlotte used to work at the same bakery as Granny; that's how we became friends. She now bakes at home in order to be with her kids; she's a single mom. And she provides all the baked goods we use here."

"You like it here, then," he said. "You like your work."

"I love it!" she said with even more enthusiasm than he'd expected. "I am grounded to this house. I can get away when I need to, but this is my home port. It's a part of me; I'm a part of it. This house is generations of my family. I can't even imagine living anywhere else. And I *do* love the work. It's perfect for me. I like taking care of people, helping them get some good R & R. I can afford to hire enough help that it makes my workload pretty light. I have a good life."

Jackson glanced around, as if his surroundings represented the life she spoke of. "I can see that," he said, then looked at her again. "But it's just you and Granny?"

A flash of anger came into her eyes so quickly that he was afraid she'd get up and leave, but she only said, "Now you're getting *way* too personal, Agent Leeds."

Neatly put in his place, he nodded and said, "Forgive me. I'll try to be less personal . . . Mrs. Henrie." He wanted to add a snide "touché," but he could tell by her eyes that she'd already gotten it. Then they were saved by the bell.

The ringing of a phone startled Chas, then she realized it was on Jackson's belt.

"Sorry," he said and stood up as he pulled off the phone, glanced at it, and answered, "Agent Leeds here." He moved into the hallway, but certainly not far enough away to be out of earshot. Apparently he didn't care if she overheard. Discreetly listening was a great distraction from the gamut of emotions she'd just gone through during their little chat.

"What do you need?" Jackson said into the phone in a voice that made it evident he likely held some position of significance; he was accustomed to giving orders. "Or did you just call to shoot the breeze?" Long pause to listen. "No, I *do* know you better than that." Another pause. "No, I'm not all right. Did you expect me to be?" Short pause. "Then you're a bigger fool than I took you for." Very long pause, then his voice became gentler, more concerned. "How are Mary and the kids?" Long pause with occasional grunting noises to indicate that he was listening. "I'd ask you to give them my love, but I don't think it would go over very well." More silence. "No, I'm not going to tell you where I am, and if you trace my credit card or the GPS on my phone, I'll have you fired." Forced chuckle. "I still have enough clout to get you fired, so mind your manners. Thanks for calling." Silence. "No, I don't know when I'll be back. Maybe I *won't* come back." He hung up the phone without saying good-bye.

"Sorry," he said again as he sat back down.

"Why are you apologizing? It's not like we're on a date or some-thing, and even if we were, I wouldn't be offended by your taking a phone call."

"*Would* you go on a date with me?"

"No," she said without even looking at him, and he knew that she knew he was teasing. "Did you *want* to go on a date with me?"

"No, I was just wondering."

"Glad that's settled," she said and finished off her cocoa. The silence made it simply too tempting not to say what she was thinking. "I couldn't help overhearing."

"And what did you figure out about me . . . Detective?"

Jackson expected to hear summary and speculation over the entire conversation, when he wasn't certain *he* could even remember what he'd said. But she looked at him squarely and said, "That you're not all right." He looked away abruptly, not wanting her to see the echo of her words in his eyes. Then she added gently, "You obviously weren't trying to keep me from overhearing."

"Maybe I should have," he said and stood up and left the room, taking his coffee with him.

CHAPTER 3

Jackson hurried up to his room and paced for twenty minutes. He could always think better when he paced. He couldn't think of a single logical reason why he felt so utterly fascinated with and drawn to this lovely little innkeeper. But he could think of a great many practical reasons why she was a woman worthy of spending time with. She was smart, but not just smart—she was sharp. She was funny, practical, interesting, and she could see right through him. That was perhaps the part that created the greatest enigma. That was the oxymoron. The very thing that left him frequently off balance and defensive was the very thing that made him want so badly to figure her out. Maybe that was it. Maybe he just saw her as a mystery, and for him, a mystery always needed to be figured out. And yet, just figuring her out didn't feel like enough. He wanted to *know* her, and he hadn't been confronted with a desire to really *know* a woman since Julie had left him. How long had it been? More than twenty years. Beyond that, he'd lost count. He was obviously out of practice in communicating with a woman who could hold his attention. The women he worked with didn't count. They had brains and brass. He respected them, but they weren't the kind of women he would ever want to go home to.

Jackson gasped over that last thought. *Go home to?* He'd not even known Chas Henrie for twenty-four hours. Had he lost his mind? This was surely some part of the post-traumatic stress he'd been warned about. What was he doing? Latching onto some obscure comfort to compensate for some deep-seated, unfulfilled need? Maybe he *did* need a shrink. Recalling how angry he'd gotten about insisting that he *didn't* need one, prior to leaving the office, he felt a little foolish.

"Okay, Leeds," he said aloud, then groaned. Now he was talking to himself. He finished the rest of the statement silently. *You're just exhausted and traumatized. She's a nice lady. Quit trying to analyze it and just use the vacation for what it's meant for. Get some peace and quiet.*

Peace and quiet was a good theory, but what he really needed was to expend some energy. The thought appeared at the same moment as he looked out the window to see the walks and driveway piled deep with snow. He didn't know who was *supposed* to remove it, but it looked like just what he needed to clear his head and release his pent-up energy.

* * * * *

Chas checked on Granny, then cleaned up the kitchen, wondering if Jackson Leeds was all right—or more accurately, how *not* all right he was. And why? She tried to tell herself he was just another guest and it was none of her business. But there were too many implications laced through their conversations to ignore. He needed a friend, and if she was any kind of a decent innkeeper, she could be that friend while he was around.

She heard a scraping sound outside and wondered what on earth it could be. If the snow removal guy had arrived, she would hear the small engine of his ATV with the snow blade. Peering out the window, she checked the accuracy of her vision, then chuckled, then felt a deepening level of respect for Jackson Leeds. He was shoveling the snow off the walk with a great deal of vigor. And she knew it was a heavy snow from the little bit she'd scraped off the steps earlier with the shovel that was always left on the porch. She grabbed her own coat and dug into the chest of miscellaneous cold-weather gear before she went out to the porch. He turned for a moment when he heard the door close, then he went right back to his work while she walked down the steps and stood behind him.

"If you keep this up, I'll have to give you a discount."

"Not necessary," he said with a subtle terseness that made her wonder if he was still angry over what she'd overheard—or more accurately, what she'd said about it.

"Okay, but you could pause a moment."

He stopped and turned to face her. She held up two choices of thick knit caps. "Your coat and gloves aren't bad for Montana, but your head and ears are going to freeze. Black or green," she said like a game show host.

He took the black one and pulled it onto his head. "Thank you," he said and went back to work.

"I have someone coming to clear the snow. They're just backed up, for obvious reasons. You really don't need to do this."

"I need something to do," he said.

"Fine, shovel the walks. But leave the parking lot for the snow guy. He'll feel cheated if he doesn't have anything to do when he gets here."

Chas went back in the house and hovered in the parlor, not close enough to the window that he could see her, but close enough that she could see him. She'd never met anyone like him, but she wasn't quite sure what to make of it.

Jackson shoveled all the walks and enough of the main drive so that a car could get in or out without getting stuck. He left the rest for *the snow guy*. The falling snow had slowed to a light sprinkle of white glittery dust, which meant that the results of his efforts might actually last a while. He went through the back door this time, where he discovered that the office was located just off the hall. While stuffing his gloves into his coat pockets he noted a rack for coats, a little bench to sit on, and a place for shoes. Since his shoes were very wet, he sat down to unlace and remove them. He hung up his coat and the hat she'd loaned him. He peered into the office and found no one there, so he took a moment to absorb its details. The large desk showed evidence of much paperwork, and a lot of busyness taking place there, but it was tidy. There was a phone with lots of buttons that obviously connected to every room in the house. The desk itself was likely a period piece, as were the chairs and the large sideboard that had a plate of pastries beneath an elaborate glass cover, and stacks of pretty paper napkins. On the shelves above were copies of novels by Charles Dickens for sale. On the opposite wall were several elaborately framed photos of the famous author at different stages of his life. *How very Dickensian,* he would have said to Chas if she were here.

Jackson wandered up the hall to the front of the inn where he'd come in the night before. The staircase rose from a beautiful entryway. To one side was the dining room, and off of that was the kitchen. On the other side of the entry was an inviting parlor that was obviously intended for the use of guests. There were magazines on a coffee table, and a computer on a corner table. Of course, the furnishings were all authentic or at least excellent imitations. Then his eye caught something completely out of place, but it made his heart quicken before he fully realized what it meant. On the ornate wood mantel of the fireplace was a military American flag, folded and preserved in a triangular wood and glass case that housed it perfectly. On one side of the flag sat a framed set of two military medals that he knew well. And on the other side was the framed picture of a man wearing dress uniform. Air Force. He noticed then a tiny gold plaque at the bottom of the flag case. *In loving memory of Lt. Martin Henrie.* He let out a weighted sigh and felt his heart tighten on behalf of this woman he was just getting to know. He cursed under his breath and shook his head as he picked up the framed pictured of Chas's deceased husband. He wondered what kind of man he was, and how it had happened. He hadn't expected to get caught.

"I see the two of you have met," Chas said from the doorway, and he turned, still holding the picture.

"How did it happen?"

Chas sighed and stepped a little farther into the room. "I wish I could say he had died defending a life or fighting for freedom. But it was meaningless. A training exercise."

Jackson reverently set the picture back on the mantel. "He was still fighting for freedom," he said firmly.

Chas heard an unexpected conviction in his tone and guessed with some degree of confidence, "You have a military background."

Jackson was surprised by her perception. She had gotten that out of six words and his body language. So much for thinking he was unreadable. "Marines. Twelve years."

Not wanting to talk about Martin, she said, "Great experience for an FBI agent."

"Yeah." He looked at her and wondered for the hundredth time what made him want to speak his thoughts as opposed to his habit of keeping them to himself. Instead of trying to figure out why, he just said, "I'm afraid both have given me a lot of experiences I'd rather forget."

Chas thought about that for a moment and got a hint of why Jackson Leeds seemed so troubled and dark. She hoped she wasn't being *too* obnoxious to ask, "Is that why you're here? Trying to forget?"

"Something like that."

A thought occurred to her, and she asked with mild alarm, "You don't have a gun here, do you?"

"No," he chuckled. "Are you afraid I'll freak out and kill you in your sleep?"

"No, I was hoping you could protect me if the house gets invaded."

"I can throw a mean left hook."

"Oh, well, then, there's nothing to worry about. Do you *usually* carry a gun?"

"Yes."

"Why not now?"

"I'm on vacation."

"I know, but . . . I thought . . . FBI was like . . . always on duty kind of stuff."

"You've been watching too much TV. But yes, I usually carry a firearm. I feel naked without it."

"Then why don't you have it?"

"Why do you ask so many questions?"

"When I start asking more questions than you do, then you can ask why I ask so many questions."

"Once I figure out what that means, I'll let you know."

"Why no gun?"

"How long since your husband was killed?"

"I was asking the questions."

"Fair is fair. How long has it been?"

Chas sighed and couldn't dispute fair being fair. She answered, if only to give her more leverage in satisfying her own curiosity. "I was notified twelve years ago yesterday. I don't remember the date as much as I remember that it was the Sunday before Thanksgiving."

Jackson was surprised at how long it had been, but not by the evidence in her eyes that it was still hard. Some things were just that way. He thought of how young they must have been, and it stirred memories of his own. They were more alike than she realized, but he wasn't sure he wanted to point that out. Not yet, at least. He chose instead to point out the obvious. "Then yesterday was a difficult day for you."

"The Sunday before Thanksgiving is always a difficult day for me."

"Men in uniform came to your door."

"That's right," she said, then silently waited for clarification of this statement.

"I used to be one of those men who showed up at the door. I'm sorry for your loss."

"Is that what you always said?"

"Yes, and I always meant it. I mean it now."

"Thank you," she said and looked down. "Does being an FBI agent also include such deplorable duties?"

"It does, actually."

She looked at him. "Maybe you should consider a profession that isn't so depressing . . . or dangerous. It is, dangerous, isn't it?"

Jackson hated the way his mind flashed instantly through a hundred moments that verified the statement, the worst being the reason he could hardly bring himself to look in the mirror. "I suppose it is," he said nonchalantly, "but after being a marine, danger becomes relative."

"What you mean is that you get used to putting your life on the line."

"I suppose that's what it means. I've never really thought about it. I just do it." Wanting to get the conversation back to *her*, he added, "The way your husband did it." Her eyes turned sad, and she looked down. "You still miss him."

"I do. We grew up together. I've loved him as far back as I can remember."

"I've often wondered why it's the good ones who get killed." His words had a bite that increased when he added, "Why can't more of the idiots and jerks get killed in training exercises?"

Rather than pondering how that bit *her* emotions, she chose to say to *him,* "Ooh, that sounds personal."

"You bet it's personal, but I'm not going there with someone I only met yesterday."

"Fine," she said and put up her hands. "Why don't you have your gun with you?"

Jackson sighed, hoping she might have forgotten where the conversation had been leading. "I'm compulsively honest, you know. My coworkers said it wasn't always a good thing. I've been told I should be a little more tactful and a little less honest."

"Is that relevant to this conversation?"

"I either have to change the subject and avoid the question, or I have to tell you the truth."

"So, tell me the truth."

"I'm on administrative leave." He checked her expression for a reaction, and couldn't keep himself from finishing the explanation. She had that effect on him. "When a shooting occurs, the firearms involved are taken by the department until the investigation is complete." When she only responded with silence, he asked, "Have you watched enough TV to know what I'm talking about, or do I need to spell it out for you?"

She thought for a minute. "You fired shots, and there're some questions over what happened exactly, or there wouldn't be an investigation."

"Very good, Detective," he said, only mildly sarcastic. While he was questioning his wisdom over getting into this conversation, he had to admit he was glad he'd done it. There was something liberating in having her know the truth, just as he felt better knowing what had happened to her husband. Even though both stories were ugly. But she didn't know it all yet. Her questioning gaze let him know she soon would.

"Administrative leave? Do they think you did something wrong?"

"It's under investigation."

"Did you do something wrong?"

"I don't know, Chas. I've gone over it in my mind a thousand times. I'm not sure what I did, or how it happened. All I know for sure are the results, and I'm not sure I can live with them."

"That's why you're here. You needed distance from it."

"That's right."

"How long has it been?"

"One week, three days, and nine hours."

Jackson was thoroughly amazed at the stark compassion and understanding that appeared in Chas's eyes, with no hint of judgment or skepticism. And she didn't even know him. "What were the results?" she asked in a hushed whisper.

Jackson turned away. He couldn't look into her eyes when he said it. He sighed, then he coughed. "I shot a man."

Chas measured her words carefully. She felt sure it was far from the first time he would have needed to do such a thing with his career history. But she knew she had to ask, "Did he die?"

"Yes."

"Did he deserve to?" she asked, and his surprise made him look at her.

"Yes," he said again with firm resolve. "He was a horrible person. He'd taken many innocent lives through his own greed. And he was a split second away from shooting *me*. It was either me or him."

"I'm glad it was him."

"I'm not so sure," he said and looked away again.

"Are you giving your life the same value as such a horrible person?" She wanted to add that she knew all human beings were children of God, and she hadn't meant her question to sound judgmental. But that wasn't really the point of the conversation.

"No, I'm giving my life much less value than the man on my team who died while I was killing someone else. Maybe if I'd done something different, the whole thing wouldn't have gone down the way it did. And if somebody on the team had to die, I think it should have been me. I had no one to miss me, and nothing to lose. Dave left a wife and three kids. It's just not right."

Chas was so stunned she could hardly breathe. She wanted to just cross the room and hug him, but she didn't know what to say. She saw him searching her eyes, waiting for a reaction. She hurried to come up with one, if only so he wouldn't have any reason to believe that she thought less of him for what he'd just admitted. "I think," she was surprised at the tremor in her own voice, "that if you're still alive, there's a reason. If you believe that you did the best you could under the circumstances, then you've got to accept it and move on."

"Like you've moved on from your husband's death?" he countered.

"I *have* moved on," she said. "I miss him, but I'm happy. You're still in shock. You need to give it time, Jackson."

He shook his head and put his hands on his hips. "How do you do it?" He put his hands in the air then back on his hips. "I don't even know you, but you just . . . stand there and make me spill my guts like you're some kind of psychotic shrink, or something."

Chas chuckled, then bit her lip to try to remain serious. She reminded herself that the conversation was no cause for humor.

"What's funny?" he demanded.

"I'm hoping you meant psychic, as opposed to psychotic. Because if you really think I might be psychotic, then . . . we've got a problem. I mean . . . I'm not psychic *or* psychotic, but in the context of our relationship, I really don't want you to think I'm psychotic."

He chuckled too. "Not only are you like a *psychic* shrink, you have a way of . . . making things funny when they aren't but they should be, and just . . . putting everything into perspective. How do you do it?"

"I'm just being the same person I've always been, Jackson Tobias Leeds. You're just the only person who's come along that doesn't fall into the usual two categories of people in my life."

"And what are those?"

"The people who have known me so long that they already know what I'm like, and the people who come and stay here who don't share enough conversation to notice that I might be a little weird."

"In a good way."

"But not psychic, or psychotic."

"No, neither. Just a little weird . . . in a good way."

"So . . . maybe we should stop trying to analyze it and just appreciate having a friend . . . for a few days at least."

"A few days? Didn't I warn you that I would be staying longer than a few days?"

"You asked about a weekly rate."

"I think it's going to take longer than a week to be ready to go back to what I left behind."

Chas smiled. "As long as you pay your bill and mind your manners, you can stay as long as you like."

"Fair enough."

"And look at it this way. I'm a good person to talk to because I don't know you and I don't know any of the people you know. Once you've had your time away, you can go back to your life, and all of your secrets will be safe with me."

"Sounds reasonable," he said, but it didn't *feel* reasonable.

Neither of them moved or spoke, even though it seemed the conversation was over. He wanted to tell her that he didn't just want to be her friend. He wanted to say that he felt more intrigued with her than he'd felt with any woman in more than twenty years. But he'd already babbled more about himself to her since he'd arrived here than he had confided to people he'd worked with for years. He decided to simply take her sound advice and stop trying to analyze the reasons for this bond they had developed so quickly, and just enjoy having a friend. He only wished that he knew how to get out of the room graciously, or to find an excuse to be in the same room with her.

For the second time that morning, he was saved by the bell—literally. "What is that?" he asked when he heard a tinkling sound.

"It's Granny," she said and turned to leave. Now what was he supposed to do? Go up to the Dombey room and read the stupid books he'd brought with him? She disappeared into the hall, then popped her head back around the corner. "You want to meet her?" she asked, and he wondered if she *was* psychic.

"Sure, why not?" he said, trying not to sound as enthused as he felt. When he'd first arrived, the idea of putting up with an eccentric old lady had made him want to steer clear. But now that he'd gotten to know Chas, he figured her grandmother could be very entertaining, especially to a man so lost and bored.

Jackson followed Chas down the hall just a short way and through an open doorway into a room decorated as beautifully as the rest of the house, but it looked more cluttered and lived in. The bed was not made, as if it had only recently been used, but the old woman was sitting in a comfy-looking recliner with a little table next to her. The table had everything she could possibly need within reach. Water, telephone, coffee cup, two remotes, ChapStick, hand cream, and salt and pepper shakers. It was evident to Jackson that Granny obviously spent most of her time in this room; that she rarely left it, if ever. She took her meals here as well. Sometimes his habit of paying attention to details was just annoying. But that habit allowed him to take notice of the careful attention that Chas paid her grandmother, tucking a lap quilt around her, and asking her quietly what she needed. And the tiny, elderly woman's eyes lit up at the appearance of her granddaughter. What they shared could make him envious. He usually avoided thinking of the fact that he had absolutely no tender relationship in his life, no family connection whatsoever.

Jackson hovered discreetly in the doorway while the two women shared some quiet conversation that he couldn't hear. Chas went into a bathroom that was private to the room and came back with a pill, which her grandmother took with water. Chas then looked up at Jackson while she said, "I brought someone to meet you, Granny. This is our only guest at the moment." Granny looked eagerly toward him, and Chas added, "Meet Jackson Leeds. Jackson, my grandmother. She'll insist on your calling her Granny, so don't try calling her anything else."

"I wouldn't dare," Jackson said, stepping forward to take the old woman's hand. Chas saw something different in this man as he warmly greeted Granny—a genuine smile. Even when she'd heard him chuckle, he hadn't really smiled. Yet he was so genuinely warm with her grandmother. Granny loved to meet the guests, but most went in and out quickly and had no interest in visiting with an old woman. Jackson, however, was not just being polite; he seemed sincerely pleased to meet her even before he said, "It is such a pleasure, ma'am."

"Oh, you are a nice young man," she said, patting his hand. "Are you the one who almost got lost in the blizzard?"

"That's me," he declared proudly. "Thankfully your granddaughter is a pretty good navigator, and she takes very good care of her guests."

"That's what she tells me, but it's nice to hear it from somebody else." This comment came with a wink toward Chas. She winked back, then saw Jackson slip his hand out of Granny's, but only long enough to slide a chair closer, which he sat on, then took her hand again. Granny was clearly pleased. "Tell me about yourself, young man." Granny leaned forward a little to focus on him more closely. "Tell me everything. You look like the type who could be the hero in a good book."

"Granny!" Chas scolded. Then to Jackson, "She spends way too much time reading novels."

Jackson just chuckled. "I'm no hero, ma'am, I can assure you. I'm just an ordinary guy with a pretty pathetic life. I'm probably more boring than Chas."

"That's not possible," Granny said, and Jackson couldn't tell whether or not she was kidding. Apparently she was a lot like him. "Chas tells me you're in the FBI. I've never met a real FBI agent before, but I've watched every episode of *Without a Trace*."

"At least twice," Chas said, sitting across the room.

Jackson chuckled. "I don't think my job is nearly as exciting as what you see on TV."

"But it *is* a dangerous job," Granny told him as if she was more aware of that fact than he was.

"That's what *I* told him," Chas said.

While Jackson was trying to think of a way to take the emphasis off of his *dangerous* job, Granny patted his hand and said with genuine concern, "When you go back to work, you need to take good care of yourself, young man. We don't want anything bad happening to you."

"I'll do my best, ma'am," he said. Chas noted his repeated use of the word *ma'am,* as if he were speaking to a superior female officer. For a man with his background, it surely showed a great deal of respect.

Jackson glanced around the room, then back at Granny, saying, "You grew up in this house, I hear. Your grandparents built it. Is that right?"

"That's right," Granny said, and Jackson spent nearly an hour hearing stories from this woman who had seen a lot of life. She'd lived through the Depression, two world wars, and the introduction of space travel, computers, and nuclear weapons. She was sharp and bright, and Jackson liked her. He wondered what it might have been like to grow up with a grandmother, or rather, a decent and likable grandmother. At the very least, he was enjoying his conversation with this one.

Chas felt thoroughly entertained by watching Granny tell Jackson stories she'd heard a hundred times. It was more Jackson's reaction and responses that intrigued her. He was definitely a unique individual. She heard Polly come in and excused herself to go to the office and greet her. Granny was clearly in good hands.

"Hey," Polly said as they exchanged the usual quick hug. The secretary-slash-office manager-slash-assistant was slightly plump, shorter than average, and had a head full of thick, red curls cut short. She looked like Little Orphan Annie and had the energy of a pinball machine.

"You shoveled the walks and drive?" Polly asked. "I know the snow guy hasn't been here yet because he's still at the bank. But I thought I wasn't even going to be able to park my car or get in the door."

"One of our guests did it, actually," Chas said, and Polly made an astonished noise while she hung up her coat, then threw her purse into a desk drawer. "Our only guest at the moment."

"Is this the weekly-rate guy who called last week?"

"That's him. He barely made it in through the storm, but he's proven to be fairly tolerable company."

"Company?" Polly asked, at the same time looking over papers on the desk. She was the best multitasker that Chas knew.

"Yeah." Chas chuckled.

"So, having him here for a week won't be too annoying?"

"No, I don't think so. He's entertaining Granny now."

Polly looked up. "Wow! And he shovels walks, too. Is he cute?"

"Cute? Not really the type anyone would call *cute*. He's at least a decade older than I am, and not my type. So don't go there." Polly was incessantly trying to line her up with any unattached male she could think of. It had become a regular joke between them.

"Sweetie, you don't have a type. A woman who hasn't gone on a date in twelve years does *not* have a type."

"I have too gone a date; several, in fact."

"Yeah, okay. Several first dates."

"Why should I waste more time than that on a loser? Maybe I don't know what my type is, but I know what my type is *not.*"

They went over some business, and Jen, one of the maids, came in while they were talking. They all chatted casually for a few minutes before Jen took the usual printed list of rooms that had been used Saturday night and needed cleaning. Jen glanced at it and said, "So, there's a stay-over in the Dombey?"

"Yes, he'll probably be here all week. He's talking to Granny right now, so do his room first."

"He's talking to Granny?" Jen asked, astonished.

"Yeah, and he shoveled the walks," Polly added.

"Wow!" Jen said the same way Polly had said it. "Is he cute?"

"Oh, get to work," Chas said with a laugh.

A few minutes later Michelle, the other maid, came in to say hi before she went upstairs to help Jen get the rooms in order.

"I think I'd better go rescue Mr. Leeds," Chas said and left Polly to her work. But when she left the room, she found Polly following her. "What?"

"I want to meet him."

"Okay," Chas drawled skeptically, and together they entered Granny's room just in time to hear Jackson and Granny laughing loudly.

"Everything okay in here?" Chas asked, and they both turned toward her.

"We're doing dandy," Granny said.

"Okay, but don't monopolize Jackson too long, or he'll never come back."

"You don't need to worry about me," Jackson said to Chas. "I can defend myself."

"I'm sure you can," Chas said, then Polly cleared her throat to remind Chas that she was there. "Oh, this is Polly." Not wanting Polly's presence to look conspicuous, Chas added, "Polly handles the business, so if there's anything you need and I'm not around, she can help you."

Jackson stood up and held out a hand to shake hers. "Nice to meet you, Polly," he said.

"And you," she replied. Then to Chas, "I'll just . . . get back to work now." Jackson sat down again and turned his attention back to Granny. Polly whispered in Chas's ear, "Not your type?" Chas shot her an astonished glare, and Polly added, "Sweetie, if Martin had lived to be *that* age," she nodded toward Jackson, "he would be *exactly* that type."

Polly left the room, and Chas could only stand there and look at Jackson Leeds in the context of Polly's statement. Was it true? The idea didn't instigate any thoughts of attraction or romance. But it *did* spur a sudden ache for Martin that created a physical pain in the center of her chest. She wanted him to be here, sitting in that chair, laughing with her grandmother. The fact that he wasn't made her angry, and she had to leave the room, wiping a few stray tears as she went to make certain the kitchen was in order. Why, after all these years, did she still have to miss him so deeply?

CHAPTER 4

When Jackson could tell that Granny was getting sleepy, he asked her if she needed anything, and she assured him she was fine. She apologized for her sleepiness, and he assured her that it was not a problem; she'd earned the right to rest, and he promised to come back and talk to her later. He went up to his room and found the bed made and fresh towels in the bathroom. He wondered if Chas had done it, then remembered that she'd mentioned maids coming in to clean the rooms. He tried to read but felt restless. He heard noise outside and looked out the window to see an ATV with a snow blade clearing the little parking lot. The snow guy had finally arrived.

A while later, Jackson was glad to feel hungry because it gave him an excuse to go downstairs. He thought of trying to go somewhere to get something to eat, thinking it might be good to expand his horizons here in this town a little. But his car was covered with snow—along with the rest of the town and he felt content to remain in the safety and coziness of the Dickensian Inn. He'd managed to get the rest of his luggage out of the car and up to his room, but that was all the ambition he'd been able to muster in that regard.

Recalling what Chas had said about sandwiches and snacks for guests, he went down and found them. He sat in the dining room to eat a sandwich while he looked at yesterday's copy of *USA Today*. He wondered where Chas was and what she was doing, and he reminded himself that he hadn't even known her for twenty-four hours. Perhaps that was why he almost felt frightened when she found him there, and his heart quickened to see her come in the room.

"We should call it *USA Yesterday,*" she said, motioning toward the paper. "We're always a little behind in getting them delivered."

"Old news is better anyway," he said. "In a house like this, you wouldn't want to be too up with the times."

"True," she said with a chuckle and went into the kitchen where he could hear her working. He glanced at his watch and realized it was later in the day than he'd realized. She was probably fixing supper. He felt a little giddy to recall that he'd arranged to eat supper here, but he wondered if that meant being able to eat across the table from the innkeeper.

Suddenly too distracted to read, he put the paper back where he'd found it and went into the kitchen. Chas glanced up in surprise when he entered. "Is it okay if I come in here?" he asked.

"Of course, but . . . it lacks the ambience of the rest of the house. This room was designed for practicality."

He looked around and saw signs of Victorian architecture and coziness. "Still, it has ambience," he said. "Is there anything I can help you with?"

Chas stopped working and looked at him squarely. "You're a guest here, remember? A *paying* guest. And my services don't come cheap."

"Very reasonable I'd say for such a nice place—and great service."

"You're still paying," she said, "so stop asking if you can help."

"Sorry," he said, but he didn't leave.

"Are you really that bored?" she asked and continued with her work, dipping pieces of chicken in something before she put them into a sizzling pan.

"Yes."

"You're used to being pretty busy."

"Too busy to think."

"So having time to think is the problem?" she asked.

Recalling all he'd confessed to her earlier, he had no trouble saying, "That is *exactly* the problem."

"Well, maybe it would be good for you to think. That is part of the point of this leave you're on, isn't it?"

"Maybe, but I don't want to talk about that."

"I can respect that," she said. "I know there was something I was going to tell you, but now I can't remember, and . . . oh, now I remember." She stopped working and held up her hands that were covered with whatever was on the chicken. "Since your check-in wasn't typical, I forgot to tell you that there's Internet in the parlor you're free to use, and the inn is open for tours between one and three in the afternoons, except for the rooms that are being used. You're welcome to look around, but I'd keep your door locked—especially between one and three. Although, it's past that now and there are no other guests here tonight. We have a couple coming in tomorrow, and they will be here for three days, and three more rooms are reserved for the weekend."

"Okay," he said.

"So, if you're bored, maybe you should look around. Supper will be ready at six."

"Do you eat with your grandmother?"

"Not usually. She likes to eat in front of the TV, and my eating schedule doesn't normally coincide with when she gets hungry. I tend to eat in snatches while I'm doing other things."

Jackson felt like a teenager asking a girl on a date when he said, "Does your eating schedule make it possible for you to eat with me?"

"Sure, why not?" she said, coating chicken again. Obviously his company didn't have the value for her that hers had for him. But as long as he didn't have to eat alone, he could live with that.

The sound of a door opening startled him, and he turned to realize that an outside entrance led directly into the kitchen.

"Sorry I'm late," a blonde woman said as she entered holding a large tray covered with a white towel. When Jackson saw how she was trying to hold the door open with her foot while a young boy came in beside her, he hurried to take the tray, noting her surprised expression.

"Thank you," she said, and their eyes connected for a moment. She was somewhere between his age and Chas's, he guessed. Very pretty, he couldn't help noticing. "Who are you?" she asked, closing the door.

"Oh, this is Jackson Leeds," Chas answered for him while she washed the goo off her hands. "Jackson, this is Charlotte."

"Hello," they both said at the same time while he felt her appraising him. He couldn't deny appraising her too, but likely not for the same reasons.

Chas explained, "Jackson's a guest who likes to hang around the kitchen because he's bored out of his mind."

"Well, he makes a nice addition," Charlotte said in a voice that was a little too coy, which immediately rubbed Jackson the wrong way. While he'd prefer for Chas to flirt with him a little more, the fact that this woman was flirting with him at all was annoying.

Chas discreetly observed the exchange between Jackson and Charlotte and felt a little mischievous, wondering if she could manage to line them up. Charlotte could be great at easing a man's boredom, and she wasn't interested in any long-term relationships, which made his temporary presence something that would appeal to her. Chas and Charlotte were as good of friends as it was possible to be without sharing any of the same values. Charlotte had integrity; she was charitable, trustworthy, and kind. But she lived a worldly life according to Chas's standards. They accepted and respected each other, and had found a comfortable place somewhere between their lifestyles where they could be friends. And Chas would bet money that Jackson Leeds's standards were likely a lot more in the category of Charlotte's standards, as opposed to her own. The way they were looking at each other now made her smile.

Jackson turned his attention to the little boy shedding his winter clothing near the door. Wanting escape from a moment that had become far too awkward, he asked, "What's your name, big guy?"

"Clark Kent," the boy said, and Jackson chuckled.

Charlotte explained, "He's having a Superman fixation. Humor him." She whispered too loudly for the boy not to hear, "His name is actually Logan."

"It's nice to meet you, Mr. Kent," Jackson said as the boy's coat came off to reveal a little red cape underneath that was obviously homemade and well worn.

"Jackson is with the FBI," Chas announced, and Jackson gave her a little glare that only made her chuckle.

"Ooh," Charlotte said.

Superman asked, "What's FBI stand for?"

"Funny Big Idiots," Jackson said with a straight face. The women both chuckled. Superman obviously believed him. "How old are you, Clark?" Jackson asked.

"Four. I go to preschool on Tuesdays and Thursdays."

"That's great."

"But today is Monday so I helped Mom bake."

"Speaking of which," Charlotte said, turning her attention to the tray she'd brought in and removing the towel, "here's the quiche for tomorrow's breakfast." She put a dish in the fridge. "And I've brought the usual. I'll put it away, and then I've got to scoot. Karlee will be done at dance lessons in ten minutes."

"Okay, thank you," Chas said.

"Put your coat back on, buddy," Charlotte said to her son.

"Mom," he groaned.

"I told you we couldn't stay today. Put it back on."

Charlotte took a plate of cookies out of the room, and Chas noticed Jackson squatting down to help Logan put on his coat, saying softly, "If you put this on, people won't know who you really are while you're out fighting crime."

Chas smiled to see the boy eagerly put his coat on. "One crime fighter to another," she said, but Jackson kept his focus on the boy. She wondered then if he had children somewhere. For that matter, she wondered if he had a wife, or at least a significant other back home. She felt stupid for not having thought of it. Just because he didn't wear a ring didn't necessarily mean he wasn't attached. She'd do well to get more information before she started lining him up with her friends. His interaction with Logan seemed so natural and patient that she felt sure he'd had experience.

Charlotte came back into the room and put some baked goods out on the counter, then she hugged Chas, and offered Jackson a coy farewell with an added, "Hope to see you again before you leave."

"I'll be here a while," was all he said.

"Bye," Logan said to him. Jackson waved and was once again alone with Chas.

"Charlotte does all the baking for the inn," Chas said. "She's amazing! I'm not bad with using the top of a stove, but most things that have to be done in an oven don't cooperate with me. For Charlotte it's the other way around, so we make a great team."

"You're friends?" he asked.

"Yes, actually. I mean . . . practically speaking, we don't have a lot in common, but we do stuff together. We watch out for each other. She's a single mom and a good woman."

"That's good, then," Jackson said, implying that it was good Chas had a friend.

Chas smiled to herself, certain that Charlotte and Jackson might enjoy each other's company if she could just manage to do a little discreet finagling.

"Well, if you can't find any work for me to do, I guess I'll go entertain Granny."

"She'll love it," Chas said, and Jackson went to Granny's room, where he found her sleeping in the chair with the TV on. He decided to just sit down and wait for her to wake up, and he quickly realized that she'd been watching a DVD. It was an old version of the Dickens classic, *Great Expectations*. Jackson knew the basic premise of the story from having read it decades ago, and he quickly became intrigued enough with the film to lose track of the time. When Granny woke up she was delighted to find him there. Their visit centered around stories of her life, which he found much more satisfying than talking about his own. Chas checked in on them a couple of times, then she brought Granny her dinner and insisted that Jackson come to the dining room to eat his.

"Jackson might be back to see you tomorrow if you haven't talked his ears completely off," Chas said to Granny.

"Oh, I'll be back," Jackson said and squeezed the old woman's hand. "You take care now."

"You do the same, young man," Granny said.

Jackson went to the dining room to find one of the several little tables set for two. There was water in the goblets, rolls and butter on little plates, and salads. "Have a seat," Chas called from the kitchen. "I'll be right there. And don't ask if you can help."

"Fine," he called back. A minute later she appeared with two dinner plates, which she set on the table before sitting across from him. The chicken, rice, and vegetables in front of him looked more appetizing than any dinner he'd had in months.

"Thank you," he said.

"It'll be on your bill."

"Thank you for not making me eat alone."

"No problem. That works both ways. I could take my food into Granny's room, and I do sometimes. But a lot of what she watches on TV makes me crazy."

"Great Expectations?"

"Dickens I can handle, but she's not *entirely* obsessed with Dickens."

He picked up his fork, and she said, "We need to bless it. Do you mind?"

"Not at all," he said. He'd certainly eaten in homes where prayers were said prior to meals, but it hadn't happened very often. He set down his fork and listened while she said a brief but sincere prayer. He added his amen, and they began to eat. "It's wonderful," he said.

"Thank you. And thank you for shoveling snow. You come in handy, Agent Leeds."

"No problem," he said, imitating the way she'd said it a minute ago. "This really is good. I live on a lot of fast food, and it gets really old. Your cooking is a great bonus."

"I'm glad you like it," she said and found the perfect opportunity to ask, "So, you live alone back in . . . where was it you come from?"

"Norfolk. You should have known that from the background check."

"I knew it; I just forgot. You live alone in Norfolk?"

"I do. And the answer to your next question is that I've never been married, and I have no children."

"Why not?" she asked as if she were asking why he hadn't become a doctor.

"I've only loved one woman, but she didn't love me enough to commit to a military lifestyle. I asked her to marry me and she told me no."

"When was that?"

"We were high-school sweethearts. We'd known each other all our lives. I joined the Marines at eighteen." Chas set down her fork and became suddenly solemn. "Did I say something wrong?" he asked.

She sighed loudly but wouldn't look at him. "I told you earlier about me and Martin, that we grew up together. It just . . . sounds so much the same."

"Yeah," he said, "I thought the same thing earlier. It's too bad someone like me couldn't have been killed in a training exercise, and someone like Martin couldn't have come home to his wife."

Chas looked at him then, but she didn't know what to say. She'd shared more deeply personal conversation with this man in the last twenty-four hours than she'd shared with anyone else in years. And what they had in common was beginning to feel eery.

Jackson couldn't help but ponder the coincidences stacking up between them. The conversations they'd shared felt as dreamlike and strange as his being in this house, buried in snow and at a safe distance from the realities of life. How could he not consider the similarities they shared? Feeling a little sorry for himself, he wondered how his life might have been if Julie had agreed to marry him. He found it easy to say, "It must have been very difficult for you to marry a military man and leave all of this."

"I loved him," she said with a forced smile. "I think it was harder on Granny than on me. I would have gone anywhere just to be with him." She paused and tilted her head. "Is that an insensitive thing to say to a man like you?"

"No," he said. "I like honesty, even when it's brutal. If Julie'd married me, she probably would have eventually divorced me."

"What makes you think so?"

"I don't think I would be very easy to live with."

"How could you know when you've always lived alone?" She felt a little alarmed to think that maybe she was being presumptuous. In today's world, admitting he'd never been married didn't mean he'd always lived alone. *"Have* you always lived alone?"

"Yes," he said. "Since Julie left me, I've had only a few brief and meaningless relationships."

"So your life is your work."

"Pretty much. And the people I work with make it clear that they're glad they don't have to live with me."

"Do you have anyone in your life beyond the people you work with?"

"Not really," he said. "I found friends among my coworkers, but now . . . all of that's become . . . awkward."

"Since the shooting."

"That's right."

Chas picked up her fork again and began to eat. "And what about family, Jackson? Where did you come from originally?"

Jackson let out a partly facetious groan. "Now you're treading into taboo territory."

Chas was surprised. "You can tell me about the woman who left you and a shooting that's turned you inside out, but you can't tell me about your family, your hometown?"

"That's right," he said again.

"Why not?" she demanded as if they'd known each other for years and she had a right to know. "You know practically *everything* about me."

"To put it in less than a hundred words, Detective, my childhood was a nightmare. My grandparents were always arguing or drunk—or both. My father was a violent drunk, and my mother probably would have liked to keep him from beating us kids as much as it suited him. But he took it out on her, too. And she just passed it on. She smacked us around herself now and then. They gave me life and kept me fed—barely. I left the minute I turned eighteen, and I've never been back."

"Not once?"

"Not once."

"Do you call . . . write?"

"I send a Christmas card every year to let them know I'm still alive. I do *not* include a return address. I have no desire to hear from any of them, at all."

"What about your siblings?" she asked with an astonishment that surprised him. He'd admitted to shooting a man, and it hadn't phased her. But his avoidance of his family was apparently a felony.

"I have one sister who ran away from home before I did, with a guy who was way too much like our father. There's no hope for her. Could we change the subject?"

"Why?"

"Because it's none of your business."

"Maybe not, but I would at least think you could call your own mother. At least you *have* a mother."

Jackson leaned farther over the table. "You, who were raised by that amazing woman down the hall, have no right to tell me what I should or shouldn't do. Your telling me that I should live my life differently than I live it sounds awfully judgmental to me."

"Your telling me that I'm judgmental sounds judgmental," she countered, then softened her voice. "I'm not judging your decision. I just think a mother—even a bad mother—deserves to hear from her son once in a while."

"I send her Christmas cards."

"Okay." She put her hands up. "I surrender. Don't shoot."

"Not even a little bit funny."

"Sorry," she said, and he could see that she meant it. "I wasn't intending that to be connected to anything you told me earlier."

"Apology accepted. Now, can we change the subject to something a little less . . . volatile?"

"Okay," she said, and neither of them said anything for several minutes. "Wow," she finally interjected. "We've known each other for one day and we're arguing."

"You make it sound like that's a good thing."

"A little stimulating disagreement over matters of principle keeps people on their toes, don't you think?" She didn't add that she hadn't shared any such stimulating disagreement with anyone but Martin. She *did* say, "Granny and I disagree on a lot of things, but we don't talk about most of that stuff. We only argue over things like . . . what color to paint the walls . . . which Dickens book is the best . . . which American Idol should win. Stuff like that."

"That sounds stimulating enough."

"So, what are the possible outcomes of this investigation?"

Jackson sighed. "Is that your idea of a topic less volatile?"

"I just figured it was something you should be prepared for, right? And maybe you should talk about it."

"Funny how you have everything figured out about me after twenty-four hours."

Chas noticed that he looked very intense—even mildly angry—and she couldn't hold back a chuckle. "We're arguing again."

"And you're enjoying it."

"Yes, actually."

"You are a strange woman, Chas Henrie."

"Yes, but since you'll be gone in a week or two, you really don't need to concern yourself with that." Jackson wanted to contradict that comment, but just the thought of doing so was ludicrous. "So, what's going to happen?" she asked, sounding genuinely concerned. "Tell me."

Jackson sighed. "If they conclude that I did something wrong, I will be without a job. I think my record will work in my favor. I suspect they'll just ask me to resign, and they'll give me an early retirement."

"And then what?"

"I don't know what. That's the problem, Chas. I'm too old to start over. I don't know how to do anything else."

"You're not *old.*"

"I didn't say I was old; I said I was too old to start over."

"Granny would disagree with you, and she's ninety-three."

"Really? She doesn't seem that old."

"She tells me she doesn't feel that old, even though her body is failing her in many ways."

"She's lived a good life, which is more than I can say for me."

"I'm sure you've done many good things in your life." He looked skeptical, and she added, "But if you feel that way, then maybe this would be a good time to start over, and make a better one."

Jackson let out a wry chuckle. "I'm pushing toward fifty."

"Ooh. The ancient mariner. Oprah says that life begins at fifty; that's when you finally get it all figured out and know what to do with what you've got."

"Is that right? Well, I don't have it figured out; not even close."

"Maybe you should ask Granny's advice on the matter. You might not get any sound advice, but it could be very entertaining."

"Maybe I will."

"She'll probably tell you what Dickens would say."

He chuckled. "And what would Dickens say?"

"Oh, he loathed getting older. His heart was too young for his aging body, it seems. I guess that gives him something in common with Granny. But he died at fifty-eight, and looked much older than that. I think he worked himself to death. You could take a lesson from that."

"I'm sure I could."

"How old are you really?"

"I'll tell you if you tell me."

"Okay, I'm thirty-two." He looked surprised, and she added, "What? Do I look older than that?"

"No," he said, "your eyes look older. The rest of you could pass for twenty-six, easily. I'm just surprised that a woman would admit so readily to her age."

"Age is what it is. I've never understood this lying about your age thing. But then, I don't lie about anything. I'm compulsively honest." Her eyes showed enlightenment. "Oh, you admitted that you're the same way earlier."

"Yes, I did, didn't I."

"So, how old are you, Agent Honest?"

"Forty-four."

"That's not pushing fifty."

"It's getting there."

"Granny would tell you that you have a whole lifetime still ahead of you."

"I think I'll ask Granny myself instead of taking your word for it."

"You do that," she said and went to the kitchen to get the dessert.

CHAPTER 5

The following morning, Jackson woke up to a dazzling brightness in the room. The snow had stopped, the sun had come out, and the effect was brilliant. He felt motivated to indulge in his usual morning habit of a good run and didn't see anyone on his way out of the house. It felt good to get some exercise, even though it was cold. Given the temperature and the change in elevation, he wasn't able to run as far or as fast as he would have at home, but it still helped clear his head and get his blood pumping. It also gave him a chance to get a look at this town in daylight. He couldn't remember the last time he'd been to a town this small—at least since he'd left home more than twenty years ago—and then it had only been on business.

Jogging up the road toward the inn, he was able to see its full effect in sunlight. He was surprised by the way just seeing it made him smile. Once inside, he left his wet shoes near the back door and went upstairs to take a shower. When he went down to breakfast, Polly was in the kitchen. She explained that Chas had gone to do some errands and to keep an appointment.

"I don't know when she'll be back, but if you need anything, I'll either be here or in the office."

"Thank you, Polly," he said. "I'm certain I'll manage just fine." He added to himself, *I've managed fine for decades without Chas, why not now?* He couldn't come up with an answer that made any sense. Polly was kind, and they shared a few congenial words, mostly out of necessity. If nothing else, she proved that it was not just his desire for *any* company that kept him gravitating to Chas.

After he'd eaten, Jackson went to Granny's room and found the door open, but she was sleeping in her chair. He decided to take that personal tour of the house Chas had suggested. He remembered her saying that a couple would be arriving today, but until then he was apparently still the only guest. He found the door to every room not only unlocked but open, and he enjoyed exploring them, examining the fine details of the decor and architecture. He noted how some rooms were designed more romantically, and some more practically. His was practical. She had known he was coming alone. The only room in the house he hadn't seen that had a locked door was right next to Granny's, and he logically concluded that it was Chas's room.

Satisfied with his tour, he found himself some lunch in the guest refrigerator. While he was eating in the dining room, Charlotte came by with baked goods and sat to talk to him for a few minutes. He had to admit being more impressed with her than on their first meeting, and he could see why she and Chas were friends. He asked about her kids and got far more detail than he'd ever hoped to hear, but it wasn't like he had anywhere to go. After she'd left, he got on the Internet to check his email. Most of it was junk. There was one from a coworker that simply said, *Are you okay?* And he answered, *I'm fine. Thanks for asking.* Another from a different coworker said, *Where are you? We're worried about you.* He replied simply, *No need to worry. I'm fine.*

Jackson went again to Granny's room and found the door open and Chas reading a newspaper. She'd come back without his realizing it. Granny was reading from a Dickens novel.

"Oh, hello, Jackson," Granny said, noticing him before Chas did. "Come sit down, sit down."

"I don't want to intrude," he said and took a chair, noticing a quick glance and a smile from Chas as she set down the paper.

"I welcome intrusion, young man. Chas gets awfully boring."

"Oh, thanks, Granny," Chas said, mocking hurt feelings. Then to Jackson, "Did Polly take good care of you?"

"Polly gave me a lovely breakfast. Beyond that I've been taking very good care of myself. But thanks for asking." He resisted the urge to ask her impertinent questions about her errands, and turned his attention to Granny. "So, how are you today?" Jackson asked her.

"I'm dandy. How are you, young man?"

"I'm managing well, thank you," he said.

"Jackson has some questions for you, Granny," Chas said, and the old woman's eyes lit up. Even more so when she added, "He needs some advice about his life."

"Chas is teasing us both," Jackson said.

"Either that or you're trying to avoid whatever it is you need advice about," Granny said.

Jackson chuckled. "You're a shrewd old woman."

"I should have something to show for all these years," she said. "So what do you want to know?"

Chas didn't give him a chance to answer. "He wants to know if he's too old to retire from his job and start something new."

"Why don't you let the man speak for himself?"

"Yeah, why don't you let me speak for myself?" Jackson asked, sounding more facetious than annoyed.

"Because he was just going to keep skirting the issue."

"You think you know me so well," Jackson said.

"Weren't you?"

"Probably."

"There you have it, then. You're transparent, Agent Leeds."

"You're not exactly opaque, Detective."

They both stopped when it became evident that Granny was watching them as if she were waiting for the final point of a tennis match. Then she smiled. Jackson turned his attention to her and scooted his chair closer. "So, tell me, Granny. Give me some advice. Give me any advice you think I could use, and I'm sure I'll come away more wise."

"Oh, he's very diplomatic, isn't he," Granny said to Chas.

"Not always," Chas said with a mischievous smirk.

"I think," Granny said, "that you're never too old to make a fresh start and try something new."

"What did I tell you?" Chas said smugly.

"And what new profession would you suggest I take up?" Jackson asked, just curious to see what she might say.

"What about innkeeping?" she asked without missing a beat. "You could take care of me and give Chas a vacation."

"What a great idea!" Jackson said. "I'll have to give that some thought."

"Now," Granny went on, "I believe Charles would tell you to travel. He really loved Niagara Falls. Have you seen Niagara Falls, young man?"

"I have," he said. "Have you?"

"Oh, I have. Nothing like it! How about Mt. Vesuvius?"

"Can't say I've been *there*," Jackson said. "And you?"

"Never made it to Mt. Vesuvius. But Charles did. He was very impressed with that as well. Fire and water. Grand extremes. He was like that."

Jackson knew her husband's name had been Walter, so he asked, "Who is Charles? Your brother?" He saw Chas roll her eyes discreetly.

"Heavens, no!" Granny laughed. "Mr. Dickens, of course."

"Of course," Jackson said with some hesitation.

"You need to understand," Chas said to him, "that Granny has trouble with the line between reality and fantasy. She's spent so much of her life reading everything by and about this man that she's lost touch with reality."

"She's joking," Granny said.

"No, I am not!" Chas said, but she laughed when she said it. "I can assure you, Agent Leeds, that the ghost of Charles Dickens resides in this house—or at least he visits occasionally."

"*That's* not boring," Jackson said and turned to Granny. "So, what is it that Mr. Dickens would tell me to do?"

"When he was alive I think he would have told you to travel and take in the world. Now, I think he would tell you to follow your heart, and be true to it. I think he would tell you not to worry about silly things like money, but to find joy in the simple things of life. I think if he could do it over, that's what he would do."

"I'll give that some thought as well," Jackson said.

Chas left the room to check in with Polly and get her grandmother a cup of coffee. She knew she'd be asking for it soon. She returned to find Jackson and Granny still chatting. Chas handed Granny the coffee, and the old woman said to Jackson, "I like it with just a little cream and lots of sugar . . . to keep life sweet."

"Granny likes sugar in lots of things," Chas said. "I have to nag her to eat her vegetables . . . and her fiber."

"Tell you what, Granny," Jackson said, "if you promise to eat your vegetables and fiber, I promise to eat more sugar."

"Good boy!" she said as if he'd just gotten an A on his math test. "You look like you could use a little sweetening up."

"I'm sure I could," Jackson said.

"He likes his coffee black," Chas said to her grandmother. Then she reminded Granny that one of her favorite shows was on TV, and she told her that Jackson would come back later. He hovered in the doorway until Chas had Granny settled, then he followed her down the hall when she came out.

"Did Polly tell you that I'll be having supper at the inn again tonight?"

"She did. Are you sure you can afford it?"

"I'm sure. Six again?"

"I'll see you then," she said, and he forced himself to go in a different direction.

Chas noticed Jackson leaving in his rented car, and she wondered where he might have gone. Probably just to explore the town a little. He probably had cabin fever. When she heard someone come in the door, she poked her head out of the office to see who it was, not entirely surprised to see Jackson. "Hi," she said, pretending not to notice the brown paper bag he was carrying that obviously had a bottle of liquor in it.

"Hi," he replied and went up to his room.

Jackson had enjoyed his little exploration of the town. Now he was actually glad to be alone for a few minutes and have a drink. He didn't want to admit how it calmed his frazzled nerves that were sometimes difficult to keep in check when the echoes of gunshot were still ringing in his ears, and the associated images were always in his mind. He felt relaxed enough that he laid down on the beautiful Victorian bed and gazed at the intricate plaster moldings around the edge of the ceiling before he took a short nap and got up just in time for supper.

Chas served sirloin tips in a mushroom gravy with mashed potatoes. It was delicious, and he told her so.

"I hope Granny isn't driving you crazy," she said.

"Not at all," he insisted. "I'm sure I could avoid her if I wanted to. She can't very well chase me down." They both chuckled. "I think your grandmother is a hoot."

"Yes, she certainly is. I would bet that the only people on the planet who know more about Charles Dickens than her are the people who run those museums in England."

"That's not a bad thing, is it?"

"No, of course not. *He's* not boring; that's for sure."

"But . . . Granny doesn't really have trouble with the line between fantasy and reality, does she?"

"Granny is sharp as a tack. She knows exactly where she is and what's going on."

"So . . . this ghost of Charles Dickens thing is . . . what? A joke?"

"What do you think, Jackson Tobias Leeds?" Before he could answer, she added, "Do you believe in angels?"

"Angels? I thought we were talking about ghosts."

"It's all relative, isn't it? Can't ghosts be good and angels evil sometimes? Aren't the two terms really synonymous?"

"As in they're both the spirits of dead people?"

"Something like that."

"Are you trying to tell me you think this house is haunted?"

"No," she chuckled, "the house is not haunted."

"But you believe in ghosts?"

"I believe in angels. I believe they're all around us, even if we cannot see or hear them. And I believe that some people are more sensitive to such things than others."

"You?"

"No, Granny. She talks to my mother and her husband all the time."

"And Charles Dickens."

"Yep."

"But you're convinced that she is *not* out of touch with reality."

"I just say that to tease her," Chas said, and Jackson looked at her as if he were considering a phone call to an asylum. She leaned over the table and said more softly, "Listen, I can't tell you whether or not my grandmother just has a vivid imagination or a remarkable gift. Whether she simply wants to believe it, or knows it's true, she's happy and she's well adjusted. For myself, I believe in angels, even if I've never seen or heard one personally. And if you want to get technical, who's to say that Charles Dickens—dead as he is—wouldn't pop by to check in on Granny once in a while, since she is probably one of his best friends still living on the planet?"

Jackson chuckled and shook his head. "I have no idea why, but I think that actually made sense to me."

She smiled more widely than he'd ever seen, and he decided he liked her smile. "There may be hope for you yet. And while we're on the subject . . ."

"Of hope for me?"

"That too, but I meant . . . the subject of angels. I believe in miracles too, Mr. Leeds. Do *you* believe in miracles?"

"Define *miracle.*"

"An event that defies any logical explanation or coincidence; an event that blesses people's lives."

"Like the parting of the Red Sea? That kind of event?"

She chuckled. "That's clearly one of *the* greatest miracles of all time. However—"

"You believe that really happened, then?"

"Of course it happened!" Chas said with vehemence. "It's in the Bible. Don't *you* believe it?"

"I've never thought about it, to be truthful."

"Maybe you should."

"Maybe I should."

"However, as I was going to say, I believe there are little miracles that take place in the lives of everyday people . . . well, every day. Things that happen that are wonderful and precious, even though they may be simple and happen quietly. Those are the things that we should stop and take notice of, be grateful for."

"Have you had such miracles in your life?"

"A few," she said. "Nothing terribly grand, but enough to make it evident God's hand is in my life. I've often found that gratitude to Him is one of the great sustaining factors in my life. It balances out the hard stuff."

"So you're saying that, in your mind, a miracle would only occur if God were responsible?"

"Can you think of any other reason an event would completely defy logic or coincidence?" He thought for a long moment and couldn't answer. She pointed a finger at him and chuckled. "See, I got you there."

"Are you trying to ask me whether or not I believe in God?"

"Do you?"

"I'm not sure. I've never really given it much thought."

Chas leaned forward. "How does a man reach your age and not even wonder if God really exists?"

Jackson shrugged. "If you put it that way, I suppose I have to admit that I believe there is some kind of Supreme Being. I think I've just probably taken that one point for granted, and my life has been too busy for me to really think about it or care."

"Religion has never been a part of your life then, obviously."

"Obviously. But it's a part of yours?"

"It wasn't early on, but it is now."

"Then . . . your grandmother didn't raise you with religion; you found it later."

"That's right. Granny firmly believes in God . . . and angels and miracles. But she never figured that she actually had to go to church to believe those things. And that's fine. God knows her heart, and so do I."

Granny's bell tinkled, and Chas came to her feet. "Speak of the angel," she said, and Jackson chuckled at the play on words—and the timing of the comment. "I'll see you at breakfast, Mr. Leeds," she added on her way out of the room, and he felt disappointed to realize she was closing their conversation. "Nine o'clock again?"

"I'll be there," he said, then sat where he was for several minutes before going upstairs to his room, where he gave more than a moment's thought to the concept of angels and miracles. Then he picked up *Dombey and Son* from the bedside table and read until he got sleepy.

* * * * *

The following morning Jackson went out again for a run and took a shower before he went down to breakfast. Chas was there to serve the meal, but he'd only been there a few minutes when a couple came into the dining room, and he had to adjust to not being the only guest at the inn. Observing Chas's friendly interaction with these people as she served them breakfast, he felt a little deflated to realize that she was just that way with everyone. He wanted to believe that their conversations had been more than just something to pass the time. But he wondered if he was deluding himself. Long after he'd finished eating, he sat where he was, sipping a cup of coffee and reading *USA Yesterday*. The couple left, both of them saying good morning to him as they passed by. He returned the greeting and turned the page of the paper. Then he heard something and tipped the top of the paper down to see Chas sitting across from him, holding a cup in her hands. Cocoa, he suspected. Apparently she wasn't a coffee drinker.

"Good morning," she said brightly. "How's my favorite guest?"

Her question assuaged his ego a bit, but he pointed out, "There's not a lot of competition."

"Ah," she shrugged, "they're nice, but boring. You, on the other hand, are not always nice, but definitely not boring."

"I feel exactly the same about you, my favorite innkeeper." He folded the newspaper and set it aside.

"How are your accommodations?"

"Everything is dandy," he said.

"You have definitely been spending too much time with my grandmother."

"Or not enough."

They each took a long sip from their cups, and he waited, knowing there was something she wanted to say. "I have something to ask you," she finally said.

"How convenient that I'm sitting right here, waiting for you to ask me something. You need the walks shoveled? Help in the kitchen? Is one of the maids sick? I could fill in."

"Thank you, but no. It's all covered."

"Then what? I'm on the edge of my seat."

She looked at his chair and said, "No, you're not. You look pretty relaxed to me."

He chuckled. "Just get on with it."

"So," Chas said, "Thanksgiving is tomorrow."

"Yeah?" Jackson responded, bored.

"And you're staying all week."

"At least one week; that's what I said, wasn't it? Or do you have some limit on the amount of nights a paying customer can stay?"

"No limit as long as he behaves himself," Chas said with a smile. "I'm just wondering what you're going to do for Thanksgiving. It *is* a holiday, you know. Technically we're closed tonight and tomorrow night, but of course there's no problem with your being here, or I would have told you so when you called. I'm just wondering if—"

"Okay, let's just get to the point. I have no intention of infringing on your holiday celebration. I brought some great reading material, and I'm very good at remaining invisible. I'm also sure there is some eating establishment in town where I can get a turkey dinner. Enough said."

As much as he enjoyed being with her, Jackson stood up to leave the room if only to emphasize the conclusion of the conversation. He had really hoped that it wouldn't even come up and he could have just discreetly avoided showing his face on the day in question. But Chas stopped him. "Wait a minute. I haven't said what I wanted to say yet."

"And what's that?" He stood looking down at her while she remained sitting.

"First of all, for as long as you're here I'm just going to plan on your eating supper here every evening unless you let me know otherwise. And I'll put it on your bill."

"Fair enough."

"And also, I was trying to invite you to have Thanksgiving dinner with us."

Jackson was so taken off guard he didn't know how to respond. "Um . . ." he said to give him another few seconds to think. "That is . . . kind and thoughtful, but . . . I will really be fine. I'm certain my being at dinner would be more awkward for all of us than my just remaining invisible. I'm not going to intrude on your celebration because you . . . feel sorry for me, or something."

"I *do* feel sorry for you, if you must know. It's pathetic for a man to be alone someplace like this on a holiday. But that's not why I'm inviting you. If you were annoying and got on my nerves, it would probably take more charity than I'm normally capable of to endure your company through Thanksgiving dinner. As it is, Granny and I would really like to have you join us. And there will be a few other people, too. But they're always around, so you will make it more festive."

"Me? Festive?" He snorted a laugh.

"I'm sure you have it in you. Consider it a favor to us. It will feel more like a holiday if we have company. And my guilt would kill me if I thought of you pining away alone on Thanksgiving."

"How guilty would you feel if I were annoying and got on your nerves?"

"That's between me and God. Dinner will be at two. We'll see you there." She stood and left the room before *he* could.

"You talked me into it," he said only to himself, since he was the only one there.

That evening Chas apologized for not sitting down to eat with him because she had a lot to do. He offered to help, but she adamantly refused, which was probably good since he had no idea what he might do that would have any value. After taking two bites, he took his food with him to Granny's room where he found her watching some stupid crime drama on TV. He hated TV, but he hated eating alone even more when there was too much to think about.

"Oh, hello," she said. "I'm just waiting to see if that horrible terrorist is going to get caught."

"You go right ahead. I just didn't want to eat alone. Have you had your supper?"

"I have, thank you. Chas makes a great chicken stew."

"So she does," he said and took another bite.

After he'd eaten, he took his dishes to the kitchen, where he found Chas doing something with a raw turkey. "Thank you. It was delicious," he said. "Are you sure I can't help?"

"You're starting to annoy me with such questions. Go read a book or something."

"Since I'm annoying you, I could just skip out on dinner tomorrow."

"Sorry. If you're not there, I'll raise the price of your room."

"Ooh," he said, feigning fear. "Who else is going to be there?"

"Does it matter?"

"Just curious."

"Charlotte and the kids always share Thanksgiving with us. They don't have any family around, and the kids for all their noise do make holidays more entertaining. And Polly. It's the same for her. No family around. We're all like family. It'll be great. You'll see."

"I'm looking forward to it," he said and meant it. Setting aside his pride, he couldn't deny a deep relief in not having to spend the holiday alone. He'd always had multiple invitations to choose from for Thanksgiving and Christmas, from coworkers who had families and didn't want him to be alone. He'd become accustomed to such celebrations, where he could be a part of it, but in a passive, spectator kind of way. But with everything that had happened, the thought of trying to celebrate anything with the people he worked with would have been torturous. Still, he hadn't wanted to be alone. "Thanks for taking such good care of me," he added to Chas.

"A pleasure, Mr. Leeds," she said, like the innkeeper of the year.

"I'll see you in the morning," he said and went upstairs and poured himself a drink, then he walked back downstairs to enjoy it while he visited with Granny. He found her still awake and alert and thrilled to see him. And the TV was now off. She asked questions about the FBI that made him chuckle, things that no one but she would have ever thought to ask, such as, "Are all the agents as handsome as you are?" or "How many bullets are in your gun at one time?" He really laughed when she asked if FBI agents wore any special kind of shoes, and she asked if he had met any of the local police officers of her small town while he'd been in training. His personal favorite, however, was when she asked if any of the female agents he knew were as sassy as Chas.

"Not quite," he said, which made them both laugh.

"I gave her that name, you know."

"So I've heard."

"I thought she was going to be a boy. I don't know why I thought that, but I did. I'd told her mother she should certainly name him Charles, but she wanted to name him Daniel. I never liked that name. I knew a boy named Daniel back in school; set my hair on fire once, he did. Why would I want to name my grandson after him? Of course, my Agnes died giving birth to Chas. It was wretched." She shook her head. "Truly wretched."

"I can't imagine how difficult that must have been for you," Jackson said and took a sip of his drink.

"I can't imagine myself, but she did leave me that beautiful baby girl. Being a girl though, I didn't know what to name her. Of course,

Charles would have been ideal, because you know how fond I've always been of Mr. Dickens. And it just seemed like using the abbreviation for Charles was the right thing."

"It certainly suits her."

"Yes, it does. She's as stubborn as any man."

"Are you calling me stubborn?"

"Yes, I am. And don't try to deny it."

He chuckled. "Never!"

"Of course the same thing happened in *David Copperfield;* the same but in reverse, I suppose."

"What happened in *David Copperfield?"* he asked.

"The aunt wanted the baby to be a girl, and she was going to name it after herself. When a boy was born, she stormed away and didn't come back. She hadn't wanted a boy. I don't know why I thought Chas would be a boy, but now I'm sure glad she wasn't. No boy would ever take care of me the way my sweet Chas does."

"She does have a gift with that, doesn't she."

"Yes, she does. What are you drinking there, young man?"

"Scotch whiskey. You want some?"

"No, I'll stick to my brandy. Thanks just the same. You want some brandy?"

"Perhaps another time. Thank you."

When Granny started getting sleepy, Jackson went upstairs and *did* read a book until he got sleepy himself. After having another drink he slept fairly well and woke up to pleasant aromas. With the thought that this could actually be a really nice day, he had to admit that maybe he *did* believe in miracles.

CHAPTER 6

Jackson went for his usual morning run before showering, then he found Chas busy in the kitchen, with Polly helping her.

"Good morning," they both said at the same time when they saw him.

"Good morning," he replied.

"Did you sleep well?" Chas asked.

"I did, thank you."

"Comfy bed? All that?"

"I bet you say that to all the guys around here."

"I do, actually. Your breakfast is on the sideboard. Simple and boring this morning, I'm afraid." Then she added with the facetiousness that he'd grown to like about her, "I don't have time to be a short-order cook for you when I've got Thanksgiving dinner to fix."

"I *like* simple and boring." He chuckled and corrected, "Or let's say, I'm used to simple and boring. I'll be more than all right. Thank you."

"Dinner's at two," Chas said as if he might have forgotten.

"I'll be there," he said as if he were a child being nagged, and the women both laughed.

After breakfast Jackson visited with Granny for a while. When she asked him to help her with something, he was glad to comply, as long as it didn't cause a problem for Chas. He slipped out to the kitchen first to ask. "Hey, Granny wants to be here in the kitchen with you for a while. She's in a rather nostalgic mood, apparently. Do you have a problem with my bringing her in here?"

"No, of course not," Chas said, "but I can—"

"I've got it covered," Jackson said and hurried back to Granny's room. According to her directions, he found a wheelchair folded and tucked in a large closet and got it ready for her to use, including a blanket that would prevent the chair from feeling cold to her. He liked the way she didn't have any problem telling him *exactly* how she wanted things, nor asking for help with details like helping her into her sweater and putting her slippers on her feet. He figured a woman who had reached her age ought to know what she wanted and not have any qualms about expecting it. But of course, she did it kindly. He told her—not for the first time, "I want to be like you when I grow up."

After lifting her carefully into the wheelchair, she said, "Oh, it's nice to have a strong man to help. Chas and I manage, but we're a bit awkward. We only use the chair for special occasions, because quite frankly I like my room."

"And what constitutes a special occasion besides Thanksgiving and Christmas?"

"A doctor appointment, usually."

"How exciting," he said with sarcasm and tucked a blanket over her lap. "All set?"

"All set!" she said with enthusiasm.

"We could see how fast this thing'll go up and down the hall, if you like."

The old woman let out a delighted laugh. "That sounds very exciting, young man, but probably a little too exciting for me. It would likely stop my heart, and you'd have Chas crying over her dead Granny instead of fixing the turkey."

"Perhaps another day, then," he said and wheeled her into the kitchen.

"Perhaps for Christmas," she said just as they entered.

"I'm afraid I won't be here for Christmas," he said, but the statement became lost as Chas and Polly expressed their excitement at seeing Granny out and about, so that she could make certain they did everything right. Jackson was tempted to hover in the kitchen with them, but he already felt like he was intruding on family time, and he didn't want to make a nuisance of himself. He went to the parlor to check his email and found simple Thanksgiving greetings from a number of people, mixed with evidence of concern for his absence and his well-being. He responded with holiday greetings in return, and assurances that he was fine and that he'd been invited to have dinner with a lovely family. He received two invitations for Christmas and just wrote that he'd get back to them. He knew he'd be back home long before then, but he wasn't certain yet what he wanted to do. So much had changed among the dynamics of his friends and coworkers—or rather, his friends who were his coworkers, because other FBI agents were the only people who could tolerate him. After he returned to Norfolk and was able to gauge the temperature and mood a little better, he would be better able to decide what was best. He couldn't help thinking that it would be nice to just keep hiding here through the holidays, but the idea was ridiculous. If he felt like an intrusion for Thanksgiving dinner, being here for Christmas would feel like a travesty.

Jackson hid in his room with *Dombey and Son,* finding some odd form of comfort from the memories that reading it stirred for him. He put on a nice button-up shirt that he'd hung in the bathroom when he'd showered, in order to steam out the wrinkles. He added a tie, glad that he was in the habit of never traveling without one. At exactly two o'clock he went down the stairs, inhaling the sweet aromas of a holiday meal into his soul as well as his senses. He was surprised to come to the bottom of the stairs and find a wide doorway open, when he hadn't realized a room was there. A closer examination made it evident it was an envelope door, and draperies that had covered it had been pulled back on each side. He entered to find no one there, but a long dining table was set elegantly, including candlesticks lit in the center. A fire was burning in a fireplace across the large room, and he noticed a couple of comfortable chairs placed strategically near the fire. What a great room! He almost felt as if he were in some kind of dream. The dreamlike sensation was enhanced by Chas coming through a different door that swung in from the kitchen.

"Oh, hi," she said, setting pretty little dishes of cranberry sauce on the table. She was wearing a festive apron over a black dress, and he was glad he'd put on a tie. "We're just a *little* behind schedule. Make yourself comfortable."

"Can I help?" he asked.

"Stop asking that. It's all under control. We're mostly waiting on Charlotte. She's bringing the pies and the rolls. She likes the rolls to be hot so she's probably pulling them out of her oven at this very moment. Oh," she said, "I take it back. I forgot. You *can* help. Granny's back in her room, but she made it clear that *you* would be escorting her to the dining room for dinner."

"A pleasure," he said and found Granny wearing a nice dress, which was an entirely different experience than seeing her in her usual loungewear. Her hair had also been given more than the usual attention, and she was wearing a string of pearls around her neck. In the midst of preparing the meal, Chas had obviously spent some time helping her grandmother get dressed up. He told her how lovely she looked, and she told him that he looked snazzy, which made him chuckle.

He pushed the wheelchair to the head of the table where a place was set without a chair. Charlotte and her children had arrived, and the food was being set out on the table. He noticed Charlotte putting a bottle of wine out, and Chas brought in a glass pitcher with some kind of juice that was a similar color. She told him to sit down at the end of the table, across the corner from Granny. Charlotte got her children seated, then she and Polly took their chairs. Chas brought in the turkey, and they all cheered as she set it in the center of the table.

The children were obviously impressed with the way Chas carved beautiful slices off the side of the turkey, but Jackson was more impressed with Chas. He wondered if what he was feeling was mostly due to the ethereal surroundings and storybook circumstances of the moment—or if it was because of her. He tended to believe that he would have been drawn to her under any circumstances. All he knew for certain was that he'd never felt this way before, and he didn't know what to do about it. There was only one woman he'd ever claimed to love, but when she'd broken his heart, he'd closed it off. He'd never had trouble admitting that his heart was more frozen than warm, and he'd learned to invest any emotion he might feel into his job and the people with whom he worked. But Chas was cracking the ice without even trying. He couldn't come up with one practical reason to think that she would ever see in him what he saw in her, or that they could share anything that wasn't temporary. But right now he could only see them wrapped in this magical cocoon with scenes that had been grossly absent in his childhood.

When there was enough turkey cut to get the meal started, Chas sat down next to Granny, across the table from Jackson. She smiled at him before saying, "It's tradition for Granny to say the blessing." He nodded, but was surprised when Granny took hold of his hand on the table. Everyone joined hands, and this sweet elderly woman offered a sincere prayer, offering thanks for all the good things in their lives. She asked for blessings upon those in the world who were suffering, and for those serving in the military, as well as their families. She thanked God for the beautiful meal and for the effort that had gone into its preparation, and she specifically thanked Him for Chas and all that she did for her and for everyone else who knew her. Jackson added his firm amen along with the others, and the feast began.

The food was as delicious as it was beautiful, and Jackson mentioned it more than once. He couldn't deny that Charlotte's rolls were heavenly, and he told her that as well. He was relieved at how relaxed he felt with these people, and to find that he was really enjoying himself. Charlotte's children, Karlee and Logan, were just childish enough to be entertaining, and well-behaved enough to not be annoying. He noticed that Chas and the children drank the juice that was in the pitcher, while the rest of them enjoyed the wine Charlotte had brought. But they all used the beautiful goblets.

When they were finished eating, Chas actually let Jackson help carry things back into the kitchen, but when the table was cleared, she insisted that he needed to let the women hurry and do the dishes, and then they were going to play some games. Noting that the children were impatient for the games and in the way, he offered to entertain them. His only experience with children had been in the homes of coworkers, and in dealing with those who had been affected in one way or another by a federal crime. Unfortunately, he'd had way too much experience calming down and communicating with traumatized children. In comparison, this was easy.

It was Logan's idea to build a snowman on the front lawn so that people coming to the inn would see it, but Karlee was equally enthused, and Jackson helped bundle them up. While they constructed

Mr. Frosty beneath sunny skies, Jackson learned that Karlee and Logan had different fathers and different last names. He was amazed at how much they knew about the divorces, the child support, and the truth about their parents that only children could see. He told them conclusively, "You guys should work for the FBI."

At this Logan said, "Hey, I asked Mom, and she said it doesn't stand for funny big idiots."

"She's absolutely right. I was just making fun of myself. Do you know what it stands for?"

"Federal something," Karlee said. "What does federal mean?"

"It has to do with the country. I'm like a policeman that looks for criminals who are a threat to the United States or its people." The children looked confused, but he was used to this conversation. It came up all the time. "City police are responsible for protecting people in a city. There's county police, and state police, and federal police."

"Oh, I get it," Logan said. "You're like Superman, 'cause he can fly anywhere to get the bad guys."

Karlee rolled her eyes. Jackson chuckled. "Not exactly. Besides, *I* can't be Superman. I thought *you* were Superman."

Chas came out for just a minute to check on their progress, then a few minutes later Charlotte came out with a carrot, raisins, buttons, a scarf, and a hat. She stayed outside while Mr. Frosty—as Logan had dubbed him even before they'd begun—was completed. While the children started throwing snow at each other, Charlotte got chatty with Jackson about the kids. Then Chas hollered out the door that it was time for cocoa and Bingo. She held the door open for everyone, and he came in last. She smiled at him and said, "Try to contain your excitement, Agent Leeds. Cocoa and Bingo at the Dickensian Inn are pretty exciting stuff."

"Yes, they are," he said, pulling off his gloves.

"We have prizes," she added with feigned enthusiasm.

"Woo hoo," he said in the same tone.

He found everyone in the dining room where the table was now covered with Bingo paraphernalia, and Granny was there, looking as excited as a child. He found the game more enjoyable than he'd expected when the kids were as funny as Granny. He won a bottle of bubbles and a cinnamon-scented candle.

"It will make your room smell nice," Chas said.

"My room already smells nice," he replied.

After Bingo they all had pie, which was truly the best he'd ever tasted. Then they played another game, which Jackson was also enjoying until he realized that something didn't feel right. When it connected in his mind with little pieces of evidence that had been accumulating through the day, he felt so angry he nearly bolted out of his chair and left the house. He reminded himself to stay calm, but then Chas made another comment about how wonderful Charlotte was, while at the same time giving him a sly smile. He remained disciplined enough to not appear angry as he excused himself and left the room. In the hall he had the choice of going upstairs or outside. Right now, cold air seemed like a good idea. He needed cooling down. He was neither surprised nor disappointed when Chas came out to the porch only a minute behind him.

"Is something wrong?" she asked.

As he turned, Chas watched his face closely when it came into view under the porch light. She'd tried to tell herself that it was only her imagination that he was angry. But he really *was* angry.

"You bet something's wrong," he insisted and took a step toward her. "What are you trying to do in there?"

"Nothing," she said, pretending she had no idea what he was talking about.

"Don't tell me 'nothing.' You're as transparent as that window. You're trying to set me up with her, aren't you." She didn't answer. "Aren't you!" he shouted in a whisper, not wanting to be overheard.

Chas swallowed and came clean. "All right, I am. Is that criminal?"

"Yes!"

"Oh, don't be such a ninny. I think the two of you are a lot alike. I think you could enjoy each other's company. There's nothing wrong with that."

"There is if I don't agree." He took another step toward her and put his face close to hers.

Hoping to divert her embarrassment over being figured out, she said, "I take it you're accustomed to intimidating people."

"It's my job. That's how I do what I need to do."

"Well, you're not on duty here, so stop it. Your intimidation doesn't impress me, and it certainly won't work on me. Just chill out or get out."

"Are you kicking me out?"

"I have the right to refuse service to any customer that I consider to be a harassment to me or my guests."

"Oh, now I'm harassing you?"

"No, just annoying me. I can tell the police whatever I want."

"But you wouldn't because you don't lie. Besides," he smirked, allowing humor to calm him, "FBI outranks local police."

"So, we're back to intimidation."

"Don't be ridiculous. If anyone is guilty of harassment, it's you. You're making a fool of yourself in there."

Again she attempted to steer him away from her own guilt. "Are you saying you don't like Charlotte? That you—"

"Charlotte is a wonderful person. I *do* like her. I like her the same way I like the guy who sells me coffee every morning, or the neighbor's dog that always runs to lick my hands when I get home from work."

"Are you comparing Charlotte to a dog?"

"I like Charlotte, but I don't think you want your friend to be lured into some meaningless relationship with a guy like me. *You* like Charlotte more than that."

Chas looked down and sighed. "I thought she might . . . inspire you."

"To what? Stop drinking so much? To open my heart and spill my burdens so that I can be a happier man and go on my way? Is that it?"

She lifted her eyes to look at him, feeling more than a bit sheepish. "How is it that you can see through me so easily, when I've never considered myself easy to read?"

"It's my job to see through people, Chas. I know in my gut when I'm being manipulated or used or lied to, with a one-percent failure rate. But since you seem to have trouble reading *me,* let me make something perfectly clear. Charlotte does *not* inspire me. And when I find a woman who means more to me than a good drink, I'll send out a memo or something."

"Okay," she said, "I apologize. I was wrong."

Jackson only saw one way to respond when it was evident she meant it. "Apology accepted." He sighed. "I know you meant well, and it's nice to know somebody cares. Let's just . . . drop it right here and go enjoy the rest of the holiday, shall we?"

Chas nodded, glad for the opportunity for a graceful escape. She went inside and waited for him to follow before she closed the door. "For the record," she said, "I may have misread that you might be interested in Charlotte, but that doesn't mean I can't read you . . . some of the time, at least."

"How's that?" he asked in a voice of challenge.

"How did you know that I know you have a drinking problem?"

Jackson regretted his challenge when he felt so caught off guard. "How *did* you know?"

"I didn't," she said. "But I do now."

She started to walk away, but he grabbed her arm and turned her to face him. Again he put his face close to hers, and she was ready to accuse him again of using intimidation when he said softly, "Read me now, Detective. This is me; that's all there is. I've told you practically all there is to know about me. You know more about me than some of the people I've worked with for years. Look into my eyes. Study my countenance. Assess my body language. Put together dozens of pieces of evidence that you've accumulated since I arrived Sunday evening. And tell me what inspires me."

"I have no idea what you're talking about," she said, dropping her eyes.

"Look at me," he insisted, and she did, amazed at how his intimidation tactics worked.

"I'm not afraid of you, you know," she said.

"I know. You're afraid of how you feel, because to feel anything at all would force you to feel the reality that you're almost as alone as I am."

Jackson saw the flicker of shock in her eyes, quickly covered by a strong will to remain firm and in control. He was expecting her to throw something back at him, but all she said was, "I thought I was supposed to read *you.*"

He wondered if that was an admission that he was right. Either way, he smiled as he said, "So, read me. Look for the truth, Detective. Don't look for what *I* want you to see, or what *you* want to see. Find the truth."

Chas pondered his words while she kept her eyes connected to his. She thought of how he lived his work, how he thought and talked like the man she had come to know him to be. She thought of his comment about her being afraid to feel, and being alone, and she felt more angry—or unnerved—with a moment to think about it. Then she heard herself gasp before she consciously realized that it had worked, just as he'd described it. She *could* see the truth. She not only saw it, but she knew it. Her heart began to pound, her stomach flipped over, and her palms went sweaty. She wondered how she could have missed it, then realized he'd already answered that question. *She'd been afraid to feel.* Was she feeling now? If so, it was much more complicated than fear. In an instant everything changed, and she felt like such a fool. She gasped again and stepped back, recalling that he still had hold of her arm. She glanced to where his hand was, and he let go.

"We should get back in there," she said. "It's um . . . your turn, and . . . they'll be wondering where we are." She couldn't look at him. "Again, I'm sorry . . . for making assumptions, and . . . creating an awkward situation." She hurried back to the dining room before the *present* situation became any more awkward.

Jackson stood in the hall for a minute before he followed Chas to join the group. He wondered if what had just been exchanged between them was good or not. He felt relatively certain that she *had* seen the truth in his eyes. He'd made no effort to hide it, but he had no idea how she might have perceived it, or what she might do with it. He felt vulnerable and exposed, and he hated it. His wifeless, childless life combined with the Marine Corps and tracking hardened criminals were all entirely contrary to being exposed and vulnerable. He reminded himself that being here was not his job; this was life. And maybe it was time he started actually *having* a life. He felt a little hesitant to be in the same room with Chas, not knowing what she was feeling or thinking. But he'd never find out if he avoided her. Considering how strong his feelings for her had become in so few days, he far preferred the idea of having the issue out in the open— especially if it would avoid having her line him up with her friends. As he went back to the dining room, he tried not to think about what Charlotte might think of the situation. As he'd told Chas, he liked Charlotte, but he really didn't care what she thought about anything.

Everyone appeared completely relaxed when he returned, as if they'd just assumed he'd taken a bathroom break, or something, and Chas's reason for leaving the room right after he'd left had been equally practical. He sensed no awkwardness between him and Chas, but she wouldn't make eye contact with him, which made it difficult—if not impossible—to read her.

When the game was finished, they all went to the kitchen to make turkey sandwiches and eat more pie, then Chas said it was time to help Granny get ready for bed. She'd had a long day. Granny hugged each of the children, as well as Charlotte and Polly, telling each of them how much she appreciated all they did for her and Chas, and for being as good as family. Then she turned to Jackson and held out her hand. "Come here, young man," she said, and he slipped his hand into hers. He squatted down beside her so they could talk face-to-face. He was relieved when the others became distracted elsewhere and weren't paying attention to the conversation. "I'm so glad that you could join us today."

"It was a privilege I will never forget," he said.

She patted his hand while she continued to hold it. "I want you to stay as long as you need to, young man. If you can't afford it, we'll work something out. I don't want you going back to that job until you're really ready. Do you hear me?"

"I hear you, Granny. Thank you. I assure you that I can afford it, but your offer means a lot to me, nevertheless. Maybe you should consult with Chas on such things, however."

"I already have. Besides, I'm still her Granny. For all her sass, she'll still do what I tell her. After all, it's still my house as long as I'm alive."

"Don't let her forget that," Jackson said with a chuckle.

"Oh, I won't," she said and laughed as well. "Now give me a hug, young man, before I fall asleep talking to you."

Jackson put an arm around her and was surprised at the strength he felt in the embrace she returned. How could he have grown to care for this old woman so thoroughly in so few days? Chas offered to wheel Granny to her room. They exchanged a brief smile, and he knew the answer to his question. The two women were so much alike, and he was growing to love them both. *Love?* Had he actually acknowledged the word? Even in silence it felt so unlike him, so vulnerable and frightening. But he couldn't help it. Of course, loving an old woman who had become a grandmotherly figure to him wasn't so scary, but to acknowledge such feelings for Chas frightened him more than having to draw his weapon to forcefully enter a home when a search warrant had been issued. There was a similar kind of adrenaline, and a sense of imminent danger, as if he were treading into unknown territory with no idea what might happen or who might get hurt.

Jackson said goodnight to Polly and Charlotte and the children before he went up to his room to have a drink. He waited until he knew the guests had left, then he went downstairs, still carrying his drink, and found Chas sitting by the fire in the family dining room. He felt that sense of danger again, even if he only feared having his heart wounded.

"Granny sleeping?" he asked.

"Yes," she said and looked up. "I was just thinking how quiet everything is now. Most of the time I like the quiet; sometimes it's hard."

"I understand that feeling," he said, then motioned to the other chair. "Mind if I join you, or did you prefer being alone at the moment?"

"Have a seat. I get way too much alone time. Company is nice."

"Yes, it is." Jackson took a tiny sip of his drink, which was the way he could habitually make one last for an hour or so. He wondered what she was thinking, or if anything might be said about their exchange earlier. Neither of them were the kind of people to avoid an issue just because it was awkward. But he didn't know what to say to bring it up without sounding like a fool. He *felt* like a fool. Choosing a different—and obvious—topic, he said, "I want to thank you for a lovely day. It's the best Thanksgiving I've had in a long time."

"You're welcome," she said. "It really was nice to have you here. You helped balance the group out a little. There's not nearly enough male influence around here."

"There's Logan," he said and took another sip. They both chuckled, then an awkward silence settled around them.

Chas was wondering how she should react to what had happened earlier, and how she felt about it. How could she respond at all when she hardly knew what to think? She felt afraid to even look at him, but then her fear of spending a sleepless night wondering if she'd read him correctly overrode her fear of facing him. She found him looking at her and didn't turn away as she'd been doing since their encounter in the hallway. In her mind she could hear herself saying, *So you're attracted to me? What do you expect me to do about it?* But the words wouldn't come to her lips. Instead she asked, "So, what are you drinking?"

"Are you asking out of curiosity, or because you want some?" He already knew the answer, but he wanted to see how she'd respond.

"You know very well I don't drink," she said. "You're just testing me."

He shook his head. "You can see right through me . . . sometimes."

"Sometimes," she said, looking away.

"Why don't you drink?" he asked. "Forgive me, but . . . it just seems strange for an adult to not at least have some wine with dinner or—"

"It's not good for you. I don't believe in it; not even a little."

"But you were raised by a woman who has brandy every night."

"And now we respectfully honor each other's wishes in that regard. I have my reasons for not drinking, but the biggest is that I just don't think it's good for you. It's the same reason I don't drink coffee."

"But you don't mind if the people around you do? You don't mind being the odd man out, so to speak?"

"I don't mind at all. Granny's lifetime habits are her decision, not mine. The same with my friends. It's not my place to judge or criticize others for having different views."

"Even though you believe it's not good for you."

"Well," she chuckled, "I just can't seem to convince them of the error of their ways. But I love them anyway."

Jackson smirked and couldn't resist the opportunity to crack open a door that had been opened earlier and then slammed shut. "Are you including me in that statement?" She looked confused. "You love me, too?"

Chas felt unnerved by the question and knew that he sensed it. But she kept her voice and expression steady as she gave a reasonable answer. "I think you're a fine man, Mr. Leeds, and—"

"Oh, so now it's Mr. Leeds."

"I think you're a fine man—Jackson Tobias Leeds—but I don't know you well enough to love you, except of course in the general sense of the way that God loves all His children, and He tells us we should have love for all men—and women, of course. But beyond that . . . . well, I like you—Jackson. I like you enough to invite you to Thanksgiving dinner." She considered for a moment whether to add a clarification to the end of that statement, and decided she might not get a better chance to say what needed to be said. "But don't go getting all mushy on me. I don't intend to be one of your meaningless relationships."

Jackson fought for his poker face. He didn't play poker, but he used it a great deal in his line of work. He didn't know whether or not he should feel insulted, but he did—even though he respected her for saying it, and he knew she was right. He'd admitted to her that his relationships had been meaningless. How could he expect her to think anything more or less of him than that? He cleared his throat and said, "But it's okay for me to be a meaningless relationship for Charlotte?"

"She likes meaningless relationships. I figured that gave the two of you something in common. Again, I apologize for being presumptuous. I was wrong."

"How do you know I haven't changed?" he asked. "Maybe I've come to set a higher priority on meaningful."

"It's readily evident that you can be a hard man to read, Agent."

"Not always . . . Detective." She shot him a skeptical glance, and he decided to just stop skirting the issue. This was challenging enough without infusing it with ridiculous games that only led to assumptions and misconceptions. "Now why don't we just stop avoiding what we're both thinking and clarify what's going on here?"

He was surprised at how eagerly she responded to his breaking the ice. She looked at him firmly and said, "Why don't we?"

"What did you read in my eyes that made you gasp and run off like a scared rabbit?"

"I wasn't scared!" she insisted. "I was . . . I needed time . . . to process it."

"And have you processed it?"

"A little."

"And?"

Chas took a deep breath and just said it. "You're attracted to me."

"You inspire me," he said, not as a correction but as an addition. "You make me want to be a better man. That's not so difficult to process, is it?"

"No, but . . ."

"But?"

"I don't know that the way we feel has any practical application. This is temporary, Jackson. We lead separate lives."

"Point taken. But did I hear you say 'the way *we* feel'? I must confess that I have no idea if you feel anything at all, or if you do, I wonder if you'd admit to it." He paused and clarified, "Martin's death hurt you very deeply."

"Yes, it did."

"I understand that feeling, Chas."

"I believe you do . . . maybe . . . to some degree."

"How *do* you feel, Chas?"

Their eyes connected firmly. "Truthfully, I'm not sure. Mostly I feel confused . . . and cautious."

"I understand that feeling, too."

She looked away. "I also feel exhausted, and I think we should continue this conversation tomorrow."

"Promise?" he asked.

"I promise," she said, wanting some time to think—and process.

Jackson came to his feet, figuring he'd been pushy enough for one day. And maybe tomorrow he would regret having brought it up at all. For now, it seemed they both needed a good night's sleep and some time to think. Impulsively he bent over and pressed a quick kiss to her cheek. "Thank you for a memorable day, Chas."

"You're welcome," she said again, and he left the room.

CHAPTER 7

For all of Chas's exhaustion she had difficulty sleeping. When she finally managed to doze off, she kept drifting in and out of sleep, mixed up in onslaughts of crazy dreams and hazy thoughts and memories. When dawn appeared, she lay staring at the ceiling, trying to come to some kind of conclusion, some understanding of how she really felt and what to do about it. She could feel a little angry—or at the very least defensive—to think of Jackson's accusations that she was afraid to feel. But she had never been a person to be hurt or offended by criticism. She'd always just taken it in, sorted it out, decided whether or not it was valid, then either discarded it or applied it respectively. She *was* afraid to feel. With the exception of the children, everyone else present at Thanksgiving dinner knew that about her. As sharp as he was, why wouldn't Jackson know that as well?

Once again she recounted her conversations with Jackson since sharing turkey and stuffing yesterday. Then she recounted every other conversation she'd shared with him since his arrival. Had she simply been so preprogrammed not to feel, or to think in the future tense, that she had closed herself off from seeing the incredible depth she'd seen in this man in such a short time? Especially when she considered the evidence she had that he was not normally so open. Then Chas took a deep breath, said a little prayer that she might be honest with herself and be guided by the Spirit, and asked the question she truly was afraid to ask. But not asking it felt out of character for herself. She felt troubled at the thought of having been in some degree of denial, and she didn't want to stay there.

"Okay, Chas," she said out loud, knowing the question would have more impact if she spoke it, "are *you* attracted to *him?*" She'd expected to have to ponder the answer for *some* length of time before the answer came. But it came with immediacy and force. Her heart began to pound, her stomach flipped over, and her palms went sweaty—just as they had yesterday when she'd been looking into his eyes and had been able to see the truth. Now she could see it in herself. "Heaven help me!" she muttered, then began an internal argument of all the reasons that being attracted to Jackson Leeds was a bad idea.

At the top of the list were the obvious ones. He didn't share her religious beliefs, he lived in another state, and he lived a completely different lifestyle. She thought she might as well stop there. With such things to overcome, it would surely never work out. And *attraction* didn't necessarily mean a blasted thing. That was right there in the mix with infatuation. Or at the very least, attraction was only prerequisite to the possibility of seeing if a relationship had any substance to it. Then it occurred to her that their relationship *did* have substance. She was startled by the sting of tears in her eyes to think of his tenderness with Granny and his interaction with the children. And his compassion regarding Martin. She considered herself a fairly discerning person. She'd been watching people come and go from this inn for years, and she prided herself on figuring people out. She hadn't known Jackson long enough to know what he was *really* like beneath the parts of himself he'd chosen to expose to her. But she could still see that he was a good man with a good heart.

Considering him through new eyes and new perspective, she found it hard to believe that he had such a personal interest in her. That *was* what she'd seen in his eyes, right? She had to recount that to be sure. He'd as much as admitted to it later. "Heaven help me!" she said again, clutching her covers tightly as the room became lighter. Scared and confused, and at the same time almost giddy, Chas slid out of bed and onto her knees, offering up a lengthy prayer on behalf of handling this correctly and remaining appropriate for the circumstances. She wanted to behave as a righteous daughter of God, and she also wanted to be smart enough to avoid any personal disasters in her life—like falling for a man who would only leave her life and never come back.

When her prayer was finished, Chas remained on her knees, just trying to clear her mind of its noise in order to listen. It was something she usually found difficult to do. There were always thoughts bouncing around in there of one sort or another. But she figured her efforts had to be worth something. Getting no obvious answers, she made the bed and got into the shower. She was getting dressed when she heard footsteps on the stairs and knew it was Jackson coming down—for his morning run, no doubt. She heard the outside door open and close and peered through the curtains to see him jog onto the street. Her heart and stomach did that thing again, but that didn't necessarily mean anything in regard to what she'd been praying for.

Chas went to check on Granny and helped her with her typical morning routine, but before going to the kitchen she had an urge to go back to her room and take just a couple of minutes with the scriptures. She normally did this every morning, but today her mind had been caught up in other things. She saved her more serious study for bedtime since it was a relaxing activity, and her mornings were always her busiest time of day. In the mornings, it was her habit to just let the scriptures fall open somewhere, read a verse that stood out, usually one that she had previously highlighted, then take it with her in her thoughts as she went about her day. Most of the time the scriptures she encountered held no specific meaning for any present situation, but once in a while she'd felt led to something that had really helped her through a difficult moment.

She wasn't consciously thinking of Jackson when the book fell open to Alma, chapter thirty-six, but as she read the words, thoughts of him burst into her mind, accompanied by a warmth in her chest that made the message clear and undeniable. The Spirit wanted her to take notice of this scripture in regard to Jackson. She read it again, having to blink away tears to be able to read. Rarely had an answer come with such distinct clarity. *And now, behold, when I thought this, I could remember my pains no more; yea, I was harrowed up by the memory of my sins no more. And oh, what joy, and what marvelous light I did behold; yea, my soul was filled with joy as exceeding as was my pain!*

Chas pondered for several minutes what this meant, and knew in her heart that she could somehow make a difference in Jackson's life, that perhaps by her example and her connection to him, she could help bring him to a place where his pain could be replaced by joy. She knew things that he didn't know. She'd been blessed with opportunities that he'd never had. If she could plant even some tiny seeds in his heart about the gospel of Jesus Christ, that was surely a good thing.

Noting the time, she hurried to the kitchen to fix breakfast. She worked first on putting something together for Granny, while her mind still considered a tornado of thoughts. Recalling that she'd admitted to being attracted to Jackson, she wondered how that could possibly fit in with doing her part to help bring him to Christ. She could do that by being his friend. She couldn't deny that they *had* become friends. They'd shared some pretty strong and sensitive conversations. But now it seemed to be evolving into something beyond friendship, or at least hinting at it. All she could think of was the futility of such a relationship—to any degree. Then quiet thoughts appeared in her head with more subtlety and less fanfare than the answer she'd gotten while reading the scripture verses, but no less undeniable. *Find joy in this time. Open your heart. Remain steadfast and immovable. God will take care of the rest.*

Chas sat down to take in this new and very clear answer. She'd gotten more direct personal revelation in the last twenty minutes than she'd gotten in a year. Apparently the situation was important to God, so it was obvious that it needed to be important to her. In that moment she knew that Jackson had not ended up at this place accidentally. And she just needed to follow her feelings and trust them—as she always had—with the confidence of knowing that she did her best to live a righteous life, and therefore the Spirit would guide her if she was in need of guidance. Connecting the dots, it occurred to her in a way that felt completely right and natural that it was not only okay to acknowledge that she was attracted to this man; it was a good thing—even if she didn't fully understand why, or if the end results were not what either of them might want or hope for. As long as she stayed true to her values and remained appropriately cautious, it was good and right for her to find joy in this time. She could almost imagine Martin saying to her, "It's high time you started opening your heart. I approve." Chas chuckled at the thought of Martin talking to her, but if she repeated the notion to Granny, the old woman would have been certain it was true. Chas didn't know whether or not it was. She only knew that she felt happy and positive with the prospect of the day. Jackson Leeds was a guest at the inn, and she was the innkeeper. How great was that!

Chas hurried to take Granny her breakfast and see that all was well, then she started working on breakfast for her and Jackson, smiling when she heard him coming down the stairs.

Jackson entered the dining room and heard Chas call, "The coffee is hot. Make yourself comfortable. I'm a little behind schedule."

"I don't have any appointments to get to," he called back and picked up *USA the Day before Yesterday*. But that was okay, since he hadn't read it yesterday. He heard dishes being set on the table in front of him but kept reading and said, "Thank you." He wasn't sure what to expect from Chas after what had been said between them last night. All he knew was that he'd probably been way too bold and way too open. The vulnerability and exposure had almost made him sick in retrospect, and he was determined to be a little more disciplined in her presence, and spend a lot more time reading—as he'd intended to do when he'd first come here.

"We should bless it," he heard her say, and he folded the paper down to see her sitting across from him, and breakfast for two ready to eat.

"Go for it," he said and set the paper aside. She smiled at him before she bowed her head to pray. He hadn't known what to expect, but it wasn't this. She seemed cheerful and bright—which was actually typical for her, except that he'd expected her to be more cautious, reserved, perhaps afraid after what had been said. Perhaps she was only deeper in denial.

After the prayer, they both began to eat. Fresh fruit of one kind or another was always present at breakfast. But today it accompanied crispy hash browns mixed with ground sausage, and scrambled eggs on the side. "It's good," he said. "Thank you."

"You're welcome," she said. "Breakfast *is* included with the room, you know."

"So I've heard. But you haven't told me how much extra it's going to cost me to have the innkeeper dine with me."

"Oh, that's just good luck on your behalf." She smirked and added, "Or mine."

Jackson studied her eyes, and his heart quickened. He was expecting her to be put off by his prior admissions. But there was no denying the meaning in that look. He wanted to find a way to comment, but she went on to say, "How do you usually spend your Thanksgivings?"

"I usually have at least one invitation to choose from . . . to spend it with the family of a friend."

"But no family of your own?"

"No, I've already told you that."

"Just clarifying. So . . ." she drawled and twirled her fork a little, "are these really *good* friends, or just . . . friends."

"When I figure out what that means, I'll answer it."

She chuckled. "Are they the kind of friends you'd tell every secret to and go to for difficult advice, or are they people you just know well enough to eat Thanksgiving dinner with?"

"Like you, you mean?"

"Would you say that we're friends?" she asked.

"Absolutely."

"But not the 'share secrets and advice' kind of friends."

"I don't know." He leaned back and took a sip of coffee. "I've told *you* more about my life than most of the people I might have Thanksgiving dinner with."

Chas looked astonished. "What does that make me?"

"One of the best friends I've ever had," he said, figuring he was past any concern for making a fool of himself, and it just wasn't in him to play games about stuff like this.

Still, he was relieved when she responded with casual reticence, "If that's true, then your life truly is pathetic. That is sad."

"That all depends on how you look at it." He took a bite of food, then waited until he'd swallowed to finish. "As I see it, that makes the past sad, and the present pretty good."

"And the future?"

"I think that sometimes you need to gather more information about the present before you can determine any outcome."

Chas took that in and felt comfortable—and comforted. They were thinking the same way. That was a good sign. She smiled and said, "That sounded terribly scientific and practical to me."

"For all of my feeling out of my mind most of the time since I got here, that's the kind of person I usually am. And I think that's the way you are, too. You far prefer practical assessment and logical analysis to anything too emotional." She didn't argue, and he added, "Which is why we're both avoiding what we talked about last night. The issue is way out of the comfort zone for both of us."

"At least we're in the boat together."

"What?"

"It's a figure of speech, Jackson. You know, being in the same boat."

"Yes."

"And this boat is sailing away from our comfort zones. But at least we're in it together."

"Are we?" he asked, just needing to hear her say it.

She smirked and sipped her cocoa. "Are you challenging me to prove that I can handle being in the boat? Are you wondering if I can talk about it?"

"Can you?"

"Can *you?*" she countered.

"I asked first."

"Fine. I can talk about it. You admitted that you're attracted to me."

"I didn't admit that. It's what you said you could read in my eyes."

"You didn't deny it."

"No, I didn't deny it, and I won't." She looked taken aback, and he smiled. "See, I can talk about it, too. What I said was that you *inspired* me."

"I make you want to be a better man?"

"That's right."

Chas leaned her elbows on the table and looked at him more closely. The subtle awkwardness of the conversation vanished behind a new intensity that made Jackson wish he would never have to leave this place—or this woman.

"How is that possible?" she asked. "I'm just an ordinary woman, Jackson. I live a simple life. There's nothing exotic or exciting about me."

"That's why you inspire me."

"I don't understand."

"I've never met anyone like you."

"That's not very likely in the criminal business—at least the side of it where someone like you might meet people. I don't think my type is generally prone to being associated with federal crimes. But that doesn't necessarily mean I'm as unique as you might think. If you lived in Alaska and you'd never seen a pineapple before, you might think it's pretty unique, but if you went to Hawaii, you would realize that to people in Hawaii, a pineapple is just a pineapple."

"You're comparing yourself to a pineapple?"

She shrugged, then chuckled. "Kind of prickly on the outside, and mostly sweet on the inside. But the core can be a little tough."

"That's very good. Did you come up with that just now?"

"Yes, I did, actually."

He smiled, but Chas's mind went far from pineapple metaphors. Until now it hadn't crossed her mind that a man who lived in a tough world and had never bothered to wonder whether or not he believed in God would likely have no comprehension of the standards and values by which someone like her lived. She didn't even have to think about whether or not she should address it head-on, and she didn't have to wonder if she should do it now or wait. "There's something I need to say," she said and saw his brow furrow.

"Say it, then."

"It's something I would say to any man who had admitted to being attracted to me, so don't think I'm picking on you, or anything. It's just that . . . I've never dealt with this since I lost Martin, and—"

"There's been no one?"

"No one who's . . . inspired me enough to go on a second date. And attraction was never an issue; at least not for me. I'll just get right to the point. I'm a religious woman, Jackson, and my religion has very strict guidelines on certain matters. There is nothing or no one that will make me compromise those standards."

"What are you saying?"

Chas just said it. He was a worldly man. He could handle it. "I'm saying that if your being attracted to me is connected to any hope that during your stay here we might end up in bed together, you need to know that it will never happen."

She could see that he was stunned, but she didn't know if it was because of her standards or her boldness. "Are you saying that you're . . . some kind of nun?"

"No," she chuckled, "in my religion there is no such thing. The intimate relationship between a man and a woman is considered sacred and one of the greatest gifts from God. Celibacy is only applicable outside of marriage, and all members are encouraged to be married."

"I see," he said, and she found him difficult to read.

"Of course," she said, filling the silence, "although Granny doesn't share my religion, she always had strict rules about that. She made it clear that in this regard it was best to always be an old-fashioned girl. Whenever I'd go out with Martin she'd say, 'You keep all four feet on the floor and keep your hands to yourself.'" She looked at his astonished eyes and let out a tense chuckle. "I can't believe we're talking about this."

"No, it's good. It's good to know where you stand."

"Are you . . . disappointed?" she asked, wondering how much she could gauge about his character from his response. But then, he was like a man who had never encountered pineapple. He'd probably never had a serious conversation with a Mormon in his life. She certainly couldn't be critical of him for that.

Jackson wanted to admit the depth of his disappointment. But how could he when she was once again proving herself to be unlike any woman he'd ever known? Now he was all the more intrigued— and inspired. Rather than make himself sound like a cad, he simply said, "I've just never met a woman who preferred marriage over sex. Usually it's been the other way around."

"Let me assure you, Agent Leeds, in spite of your sheltered life, there are a great many women like me out there, who would hold to such convictions. Several million, actually."

"Members of your church?"

"Member of the women's organization associated with the Church. See, it's just like that story I told you. Just because you've never seen a pineapple, doesn't mean they don't exist in abundance."

Jackson felt struck dumb. There were a lot of things he'd felt in his life. But it had been a good many years since he'd felt naive. "Point taken," he said, which was what he always said on the job when it became evident he'd been wrong and someone was trying to correct him.

She nodded and said, "Are you still inspired by me?" What she really wanted to know was if he still had any interest in her now that he knew he wouldn't be getting what most men would want.

"Oh, yes," he said. "And more so."

"Still attracted?"

"You tell me," he said, a silent challenge in his eyes. Chas looked into his eyes and saw it so clearly she wondered why she'd been too blind to see it before. She chuckled to avoid letting on to how his gaze affected her.

"How about you?" he asked as if he'd read her mind.

She felt tempted to skirt the question if only to continue bantering with him, but she just skipped past all evasions and implications and said, "If I weren't attracted to you, Jackson, I wouldn't have felt any need to have this conversation."

She stood up to take dishes to the kitchen, and he smiled. She'd left those lines wide open for him to read between. He picked up some dishes and followed her to the kitchen. While she was rinsing plates and putting them into the dishwasher, he asked, "So, is there anything else you feel the need to caution me about? Anything you don't like about me?"

She turned to look at him firmly. "Are you sure you really want me to answer that question? Because I don't think I'd want you to tell *me* what you don't like about me."

"There isn't anything I don't like about you."

"You have not been here long enough to know whether or not that could be true."

"Touché. Given what I know about you, there isn't anything I don't like about you. But there's something you don't like about me. I can sense it. And I'd like to know what it is."

"So you can change it? Prove something to me?"

"I'm not the kind of person to change for someone else. I am who I am."

"I'm glad to hear it, because I wouldn't want a man who felt any other way."

"Just tell me."

Chas focused again on the dishes. "I think you drink too much."

"But you don't drink at all. Wouldn't someone like you think that anyone who drinks at all, drinks too much?"

"I don't agree with drinking, but I don't inflict my standards on other people. My boundaries are my own. When I joined this church,

Granny was eighty-three. She supported me completely in my decision, but it would have been ridiculous for me to think that she would change her life to embrace *my* beliefs. She likes her brandy and coffee. I prefer not to drink those things. We love and respect each other."

"You don't think Granny drinks too much?"

"Granny doesn't drink to calm her nerves. That sounds like borderline addiction to me."

"I don't *need* liquor, Chas."

"Maybe not every day. But I think you need it when you need to dull pain or hide from reality. Maybe that's why you can read me so well—because you're afraid to feel, too."

"Is that what this is about, Chas? Feeling even with me?"

She wiped her hands on her apron, more disgusted than astonished. "I don't need to feel even with you, Jackson. I don't do competitions in any aspect of my life. You asked me a question and I answered it. I'm concerned. That's it."

"Fair enough," he said then wished he knew what to say to ease the strain.

He was relieved when she went on in a lighter voice. "Maybe you should reconsider."

"Reconsider what?"

"Being attracted to me."

"Is that something I'm supposed to have control over?"

"No, but you can control whether or not you suppress the feelings, or encourage them. You might consider the former, now that you can see how ridiculously different we are."

"Or maybe we're not."

She tipped her head. "Has it occurred to you that maybe it's not *me* you're attracted to?"

"That makes absolutely no sense. I know attraction when I feel it."

"But you said I'm not like anyone you've ever known. Maybe it's not *me,* maybe it's the way I am, the way I live my life."

"I have no idea what you're talking about." He tipped *his* head. "Are you talking about pineapples again?"

"Maybe." She smiled. "Only metaphorically speaking of course. There's a book in your nightstand. Read it. Then we'll talk."

"*Dombey and Son*?" he asked, even more puzzled.

Chas chuckled. "Not *on* the nightstand. *In* it."

"The Bible?"

"The other one."

Jackson thought about that a moment. He was an observant man with a trained eye and a keen memory. He knew what book she was talking about, even though he'd done nothing more than simply observe its presence and wonder why it might be there. The pieces came together, and he tried not to show the astonishment he felt. "You're a Mormon?"

"Yes. Is that a crime, Agent Leeds?"

"No, it's just . . . weird."

"You're saying I'm weird?"

"No, not at all. That's just it. You don't . . . seem like a Mormon."

She chuckled. "Then you have obviously never met a Mormon before. Don't tell me. Don't tell me. Polygamy and pioneers come to mind. You've figured we're something between the Amish and the Quakers."

Jackson thought about that and had to admit, "I guess I can't deny that."

"Well, welcome to the real world, *Detective*. Do some research. Figure out the facts before you jump to conclusions. Isn't that how it works at the Federal Bureau of Investigation?"

"Touché," he said again and tried to imagine this woman as a Mormon. Obviously he *was* misinformed, or at the very least he'd just assumed that the stereotypes were true. He would feel even more stupid if Chas knew how much he hated stereotypes.

Granny rang her bell, and Chas eased past him to leave the room, saying only, *"Now* maybe you should reconsider."

Jackson went to his room to be alone with his thoughts. He considered reconsidering. He added up everything he knew about Chas and decided that he liked her more—not less—than he had before breakfast. He just wondered if she would ever like *him* half as much as he liked her.

* * * * *

The next few days were typical for Jackson according to the routines he'd developed since his arrival at the Dickensian Inn. The weekend was very busy at the inn, however. In fact, every room was full both Friday and Saturday nights. The place was noisier, and Chas kept very busy. Jackson spent time with Granny, explored the town a little more, and saw Chas occasionally at meals where they talked as if they'd known each other forever, but not at all like people who had admitted to feeling mutual attraction. He finished reading *Dombey and Son*, after which he and Granny talked about it for a couple of hours. Then she was happy to loan him *A Tale of Two Cities* when he'd admitted it was his favorite. But he didn't tell her why. It was easy to avoid any further discussion on that topic when she became so enthused about showing him her favorite coffee mug, although she liked it so much that she never used it. It was in a cabinet with a glass door along with a number of odd things that obviously had meaning for her. She told him where to find it, then told him to take a good look at it. On the mug was a simple drawing of Charles Dickens sitting with his head beside him. Macabre at best, he thought. But since the man had written a classic novel about the French Revolution, with one of the heroes going to the guillotine, it was an image that made sense, in a strange sort of way. Then he read the words beneath the picture. *Mostly, it was the worst of times.* He laughed so hard his stomach started to hurt, and Granny laughed with him, as if she'd never heard it before either.

"I knew you would get it," she said, and they laughed some more. When they'd calmed down, she said, "I'm sure you know, young man, that most people have times in their lives that feel like Mr. Dickens without his head. Some of us have more times like that than others."

"I know *exactly* what you mean, Granny," he said.

"I'm sure you do." She winked as if she knew a lot more about his life than he'd ever told her.

On Sunday morning the inn was very busy, but Polly was helping in the kitchen, and he noticed that Chas was wearing a dress. And then she was gone. He didn't even have to ask to know that she had gone to church. He thought of last Sunday and wondered how it was possible that he felt like he'd changed so much in a week. But at the same time, thinking of the life he'd left behind—and the dramas at the center of it—he felt as if he hadn't changed at all.

By Sunday evening the inn was quiet again. One couple was staying in the Chuzzlewit, but they slipped in and out discreetly while Jackson read in the parlor until he ate supper with Chas, and they talked about *Dombey and Son* and *A Tale of Two Cities.*

"You sound like you know Dickens," she said.

"Not as personally as Granny," he said matter-of-factly, but she chuckled. "I didn't choose this place for the snow."

"So . . . you chose this place *because* of Dickens?"

"It intrigued me, yes. I googled Victorian bed-and-breakfasts. The name of this one caught my attention. And here I am."

"Yes," she smiled, "here you are."

After supper she invited him to watch a movie with her and Granny. She didn't have to talk him into it, even though she'd warned him that it was a chick flick. Still, he wasn't terribly bored. It did have a good plot, and for some reason he was feeling more romantic and sappy than usual these days.

On Monday Jackson went into town again. He bought more liquor, almost feeling a little unnerved to recall what Chas had said about it. But not unnerved enough to not buy it. Then he found the right store where he could purchase the right Christmas card. Looking through other cards just to pass the time, he found one that made him almost laugh out loud because it was so perfect, or at least it would be with a minor adjustment. He kept looking and found another that would do well, even if it was a bit gutsy. Maybe something gutsy would stir things up a bit. So he bought three cards and went back to the inn. Preparing the card to send to his family, he was once again haunted by Chas's words. Instead of just signing his name, he wrote below the printed message, *I hope you are all doing well. Merry Christmas, Jackson.* He wrote the address on the front from memory and took it down to the office where he found Polly working.

"You know where I can buy a stamp?" he asked.

"Just one?"

"One will do, yes."

"Oh, just put it in the pile," she said, motioning to several pieces of mail that were not yet stamped. "It's bill day."

"How fun," he said with sarcasm.

"I'll make sure it gets mailed," she said. "It's on the house."

"Thank you," he said.

He then went to Granny's room to find her awake and reading. "I got you something."

"A present?" she asked like a child.

"Not exactly," he said and handed her the card. "You'll either laugh or hit me, but I just had to buy it."

"I might do both," she said, breaking the seal.

He waited expectantly and hovered where he could read over her shoulder while she was reading it. On the front it said, *This could be the beginning of a beautiful friendship* . . . And inside, *If you weren't so old.* Granny didn't disappoint him when she laughed even harder than she had when she'd showed him her favorite coffee mug. It had originally said *Happy Birthday,* but he'd written a big "un" before the second word, then wrote, *Thanks for all the good times. Jackson.*

"I was hoping you'd like it," he said.

"I love it!" she insisted. "It's dandy; just dandy."

"What's so funny?" Chas asked, appearing in the doorway.

"Jackson gave me a card," Granny said as if she'd won the lottery. She handed it to Chas, who gave him a skeptical glance, and he shrugged. Chas read it and chuckled. Then she chuckled again, handing it back to Granny.

She looked at him, her eyes far more serious than they should have been for the humorous moment. His eyes questioned her silently, and she said, "Does that mean you're leaving?"

"Did I say I was leaving? I would really mess up the weekly rate by leaving in the middle of a week, wouldn't I?" Was that relief he saw in her eyes? He hoped so. Pulling his hand out from behind his back, he said, "I got one for you, too."

"What's the occasion?"

"I went card shopping and got carried away. It had your name on it."

"This was already here?" she asked, pointing to where he'd written 'Chas' on the envelope.

"Funny," he said with no humor. "Open it. I can't stand the anticipation."

He watched Chas as closely as he'd watched Granny when she'd opened her card. He didn't want to miss even the slightest evidence of how the implications of the message affected her.

As Chas broke the seal, her heart quickened. His countenance and body language were not anticipating humor. She felt Granny watching them like they were a couple of mice in a maze, and she wished they were somewhere else. She held her breath and read, not knowing what to expect. On the front was a watercolor picture of a beautiful house with a white picket fence, and it read, *I never believed in storybook endings* . . . And inside, *Until I met you. Happy Anniversary.* In his handwriting it said, *Thanks for a great week! Sorry I'm a day late. I'll try to do better next time. Jackson.*

Chas looked up at him, surprised at how much she was hoping that he'd not intended it to be funny. His seriousness was comforting. He really had intended it to be sentimental. "Thank you," she said, "it's very nice." In one moment she felt so overjoyed she wanted to throw her arms around him, and in the next moment she was terrified at the thought of him leaving. In order to push away both feelings, she added facetiously, "I'm sorry I didn't get you anything. I was thinking you'd come in on Tuesday, for some reason."

He smiled and she returned it, then they both looked at Granny who had that look on her face, as if she knew something they didn't, but she wasn't going to tell.

CHAPTER 8

At the very moment when Chas thought she had her emotions completely under control, unexpected tears stung her eyes, and she hurried out of the room before Granny—or, more importantly, Jackson—could see them. She opted to go upstairs where it would be easier to find a place to hide until she could figure this out. But she'd barely put her foot on the third stair before she felt a hand grab her arm, and she hadn't even known he'd followed her.

"What's wrong?" Jackson asked, but she kept her face away and couldn't answer without letting on to the growing threat of tears.

"Did I do something wrong?" he asked. "Was it something I said?"

"No!" she managed to get the one syllable out in a fairly steady voice.

"Then why are you trying so hard not to cry?" She turned farther away, like an ostrich digging deeper into the sand. He let go of her arm and leaned on the banister. "Come on, Chas," he said gently. "Let's just stop trying to pretend that we're not falling in love with each other." Chas's heart quickened, and she sucked in her breath. But she still couldn't look at him. "Talk to me. Don't tell me what you think you should say, or what you think I want to hear. Don't try to find some other point of reference in your life that will help you know how to handle this . . . or how to feel. There isn't one. Face it. Neither one of us have tasted pineapple before—not like this."

A little laugh jumped through her lips, but it also set the tears free. "Look at me, Chas," he said with perfect kindness. "I've seen women cry before. I just need to know why *I* made you cry."

Chas wiped her hands over her face before she turned to look at him. He smiled, and his words echoed in her mind. *Let's just stop trying to pretend that we're not falling in love with each other.* "Is it true?" she asked.

"Is *what* true?"

"That you're falling in love with me?"

She perhaps expected him to try to negate what he'd said, or worm his way around it. But he made eye contact with her, at the same time shrugging. "Falling, fallen, fell." His voice lowered, his eyes intensified, his countenance became firmer. "Hard and fast. And I'm done trying to pretend I don't feel this way." He shook his head. "It's just too exhausting to pretend, Chas." He wiped a thumb over her face that was still wet from tears. "I don't know what it is with you. I'm usually the man who can't say anything if it doesn't need to be said. But when I'm with you, I turn into a babbling idiot. It's like you have some magnetic force that won't let me keep my mouth shut." She smiled, and he wiped the other side of her face. "If I'm going to babble I hope to be able to say something that will make some sense. I just want you to know that this doesn't have anything to do with whether or not I was hoping to sleep with you, or how long I'm staying, or that you're a Mormon, or that I might have a criminal record, or—"

"You're babbling, Jackson. Just tell me what it *does* have to do with."

"I'm not sure I know," he said. "All I know for certain is that I just want to be in the same room with you, and I want to do anything that would make your life easier or better. I feel like I could . . ." he actually clenched his fists, and then his teeth, as if the sentiment would devour him, ". . . like I could stick my head in a guillotine if it could make you happy."

Chas widened her eyes and tilted her head. There was only gentle wonderment in her voice when she said, "What a very Dickensian thing to say."

"Yes, I suppose it is."

"And it's probably one of the most romantic things anyone has ever said to me."

He chuckled. "Only a woman who runs a place like this would ever say such a thing."

"You know the story well," she said.

"What story?"

"You tell me. Only a man who knew the story well would be able to put its principal point into an emotional metaphor—*and* know the title of the book it came from."

"A Tale of Two Cities," he said with no hesitation. "And yes, I know it well. 'It was. . . .'" He said only those two words before she joined him and they quoted the beginning of the book together perfectly. " . . . the best of times, it was the worst of times. . . ." He added, "Yes, I know the book well. What I need to know now is . . . whether I'm Sydney Carton or Charles Darnay."

She offered a slight smile. "I only have one man in my life, Jackson." She sighed and touched his face in return, surprised to realize she'd wanted to for a long time. "I just don't know if I want to feel this way about a man who will inevitably be leaving my life."

"Is that why you were crying?" he asked.

She nodded. "I guess that about covers it. More than anything, I'm just . . . confused, Jackson. Afraid, maybe."

When it became evident this conversation wouldn't be over quickly, he urged her to sit on the stairs, and he sat close beside her. "I'm not even certain yet *when* I have to leave," he said, "or if my staying away will be permanent. Surely we can enjoy what he have here—now—and not be so concerned with the future; at least for the moment."

"I know you're right," she said, sniffling. "It's not just that; it's more complicated than that."

"Which is exactly what I'm afraid of."

"What do you mean?" She looked nervous.

"It's probably about Martin, and the baby, and growing up without a father, and—"

"What does *that* have to do with anything?"

"Don't get all defensive on me. It's a part of my job to put people together based on what I learn about them. It's a cold, hard fact that children who grow up without a father in the home are more likely to struggle in life than those who do. And then there are abusive fathers, who are worse than no father at all."

Chas heard the personal reference laced into his words and felt a little more on even ground with him. To know he was making a point that included both of them didn't leave her feeling quite so vulnerable.

"All I'm saying," Jackson went on, "is that . . . your father left you . . . Martin left you. It would be ridiculous to believe that you wouldn't find it difficult to form any kind of attachment to me—or any man, for that matter—especially when it all seems so temporary."

Chas paused to check her own emotion and the context of the conversation. Was this really happening? Should she be doing something to try to stop it? In a split second all of her prayerful questions and the answers she'd been given in return came back to her. It was easy to say, "I agree with you on at least one point, Jackson."

"And what would that be?"

She took a deep breath, tested the temperature of her gut instinct, and just said it. "I'm tired of trying to pretend that I'm not falling in love with you." He smiled, and his eyes sparkled with something hopeful and warm. She almost expected him to kiss her and wasn't certain she felt ready for that. Instead he gave her a tight hug, the kind that a dear friend would offer after being parted for a long time. At first Chas felt reserved, then the reality of his closeness began to sink into her, draining away the loneliness she had been battling for so many years. She tightened her hands against his back and just held to him, never wanting to let go. Her mind went again through the high points of the conversation, and got stuck on one word in particular. She eased back just enough to see his face when she asked, "Does it *have* to be temporary?"

Jackson sighed and looked down. "That depends on a lot of things, Chas. Once we get to know each other better, you might prefer that I leave. We don't know each other well enough, or for long enough, to know if we might consider something permanent. If we both come to a point where we agree on a future together, then we would have to consider all the facts and decide how to compromise enough to overcome the gaps between our lives."

Again Chas checked what she was hearing and her own sanity. She had to ask, "You really did just say that to me, right? I'm not hallucinating or anything, am I? We've only known each other a week, and . . . you really did turn this conversation into speculations over sharing a future together."

He chuckled and shook his head. "If you knew me the way the guys at work know me, you would think I was completely out of my mind. No one is more well-known in Virginia for being a confirmed bachelor." He touched her face again. "But, yes . . . I really did say that."

She smiled and sighed. "It's nice . . . to know you feel that way. It's nice to know I feel that way, too."

"Yes, that *is* nice."

"Were you worried?"

"Yes, actually. As far as I knew, I was just another guest at the inn; someone to practice your charity on."

"No, it's much more than that, but . . ."

"But?"

"These feelings are wonderful, but not very realistic in the grand scheme of life. This inn *is* my life, Jackson. I don't know that I could ever leave here."

"And you shouldn't. This isn't just a job, or a house. You're right. It's your life. Your history is here. I would never ask you to give it up."

"But when this investigation is over . . . and you're no longer hiding . . . then what?"

"If they'll let me have my job back, I'll have to decide whether or not I want to take it."

"Why wouldn't you? Your work is your life. I've seen how antsy and lost you are without it."

"I can't deny that. But it's a young man's work, and I'd like to retire before I have no choice but to remain behind a desk. I don't think I could take it. I think retirement is getting closer for me. I suppose I just need to be sure that I get out when it's right, because it's something I'll have to live with the rest of my life. I have to know I did my time."

"And if the investigation finds something against you?"

"The only way that's possible is if somebody in the Bureau is doing something illegal, but then *that* is the heart of the problem."

"I don't understand."

Jackson sighed and pressed his fingers together, setting his forearms on his thighs. "The shooting . . . I told you about. I can't share details with you; I wouldn't even if I could. But it all went wrong; my gut told me there was something wrong even before the bullets started flying. The people over me concluded that there was only one way it could have gone the way it did. They believe there's a traitor on the team."

"As in . . . one of the people you work closely with . . . and trust . . . is a mole?"

"A mole?" He chuckled. "You watch too much TV."

"I spend too much time with Granny."

"Yes," he said, "a mole; somebody taking money from some scumbag who's trying to avoid the FBI, and putting our lives in danger in the process. *I* know that person isn't me, but nobody else knows it. I'm the quiet, mysterious one, so a few bigwigs have naturally assumed that means I have something to hide. I wasn't surprised when they took my gun. They always inspect the weapons after they've been fired in an incident. But when they asked for my ID and showed me the warrant, I was thrown off a little."

"The warrant?"

"I hadn't even gone home since the incident. I still had blood on my clothes from being so close to . . . Dave." It had been difficult for him to say the name ever since the shooting had occurred.

"The man who was killed?" she asked with compassion and took his hand.

He looked into her eyes and squeezed her fingers with his. "Yes," he said. "They had a warrant to search my apartment, my computer, everything. I could only go home accompanied by an IA officer to pack a few things, and those were thoroughly searched. I spent a few nights in a hotel and came here."

"So, you felt violated *and* betrayed, without even a moment to grieve for the loss of a friend."

"That's right," he said, his voice turning gruff.

"And what if they believe it's you?" she asked, feeling afraid.

"I don't have anything to hide," he said. "I didn't do anything wrong."

"What if someone is trying to frame you. What if they planted evidence to make it look like—"

"You *have* been watching too much TV."

"Isn't it possible?"

"Possible but not very likely. Someone in the Bureau would have to be awfully smart to frame someone else in the Bureau—because they're all really sharp, and figuring those things out is what we all do for a living. Besides, nobody can keep a secret forever, and the people I work with all know that. I'm not worried about being framed; I'm really not. It's just . . . the principle of the whole thing. It's knowing that Dave is dead, and it feels like everything I knew and thought I could trust died with him. They'll find out I had nothing to do with it, and they'll find the person responsible."

"You think they will?"

"I *know* they will. It won't be easy, but they will. *I will.*"

"What do you mean?" she asked, sounding panicked.

"I mean that they'll probably find out I'm innocent before they find out who's guilty. They'll need *me* to figure it out. And when I do . . ." He didn't finish. Instead he took a deep breath. "I'm not worried about job security. Even if I were, the very worst thing that could happen would be an early retirement, and that might not be so bad."

"But you want to work long enough to find out the truth."

"Yes. Yes, I do."

"And what will you do when it *is* the right time to retire from the FBI?" He gave her a smile that came with a sparkle in his eyes. She smiled back and added, "What would you have done if you'd never met me?"

"I have no idea. It's not like I need to work—at least not for financial reasons. Of course, I want to always stay busy and active. But I stopped working for the money a long time ago. I don't spend what I don't need, and I've made some good investments. Money is not the issue."

"That's nice then," she said and chuckled. "I look forward to that day around here."

"It'll come," he said, glancing around with overt fondness for the inn.

Chas glanced at her watch and was startled. "Oh, I need to cook dinner!"

"Is it an emergency?" he asked when she jumped to her feet and moved toward the kitchen.

"There are guests eating here this evening, so yes. An anniversary party; three couples. And no, you can't help . . . except for helping with Granny, if you don't mind." She turned around to find him following her and took both his hands into hers, squeezing them tightly. "Thank you, Jackson . . . for the card . . . and the conversation, and just . . . everything."

"It's a pleasure, Chas," he said and resisted the urge to kiss her. "I'll look out for Granny. You let me know if there's anything else you need."

"Thank you," she said. "I'll just bring you some dinner along with hers, if that's okay."

"It's more than okay. Maybe I can talk her into watching *A Tale of Two Cities* . . . since I'm reading it again."

Chas smiled. "Get her to show you her favorite mug."

"Oh, she already has."

She smiled again and hurried off to the kitchen.

Chas remained busy throughout the evening, but Jackson enjoyed his time with Granny. They *did* watch a movie version of the Dickens classic, which took the entire evening since it was long. Chas brought in two trays with food. Jackson took them and told her he'd see to the details.

"Thank you," she said and kissed Granny's cheek. Then she kissed Jackson's cheek as well.

"That's progress," Granny said.

"I'll never wash my face again."

"If you start to smell bad, she probably won't want to kiss you."

"Good point," he said and helped situate her dinner on the little table that he moved closer to her chair.

They watched the movie while they ate, then Granny asked if he could help her to the bathroom. "I can take care of everything once I get there," she said. "I promise not to embarrass you. I can just get there a lot faster with some help."

"It's not a problem" he said. "And remember, I've been in the Marines. It would take a lot to embarrass me."

"If you find me dead one of these days, you won't be too shocked, then."

"Not shocked, perhaps. But I'll probably cry."

"Don't waste too many tears on me, young man. I've had a good life. Yours is just getting started."

While Granny was in the bathroom, Jackson pondered her words. *Just getting started?* It felt mostly over and basically pointless—or at least it had until he'd met Chas. But he was older than she was, and sometimes he felt just plain old. He chuckled at the thought of how Granny would respond to such a comment. She was nearly fifty years his senior. When she was his age, Chas hadn't yet been born, and Granny had given a lifetime to raising her. Maybe he *was* just getting started. He'd like to think so.

After Granny was settled back into her chair, they finished the movie, but Granny dozed off toward the end, and he had to elbow her to remind her to watch the best part. "Come on," he said, "you can't miss Sydney facing off the guillotine."

"No, I wouldn't want to miss that," she said somewhat seriously. "It's a very Christian story, isn't it."

"Is it? I'd never really thought about it that way."

"There's a lot of things you should think about, young man," she said. "Since you're reading it again, take notice of what a Christian story it is. I believe Charles was very purposeful with the way he filled it with Christian metaphors."

"Such as?"

She looked at him as if he didn't have a brain in his head, but her expression made him chuckle. "One man giving his life for another, with the only motive being love and sacrifice."

"Okay, I can see that," he said. "I've just never been very . . ."

"What?"

"Religious."

"Neither have I, but that doesn't mean we're not Christians."

"How exactly would you define being Christian?" he asked.

"Believing in Christ, living in a way that coincides with what He taught, which is simple: to be kind to other people; have integrity. All the good things we can be in this world came from His example." She tightened her gaze on him. "So are you or aren't you?"

"What?"

"A Christian?"

"I . . . um . . ."

"You've never really thought about it?"

"No, I haven't."

"Well, maybe you should. Charles was a Christian; still is, I'm sure. It's evident all through his books what his beliefs were. That gives us something in common. You do celebrate Christmas, don't you?"

"I do."

"And you do know *why* we celebrate Christmas?"

"I do."

"That's something, then," Granny said.

"Is Chas a Christian?" Jackson asked.

"More than most people," she said as if she'd already given the matter a great deal of thought. "She not only believes it on Sundays, she lives it every hour of every day."

"So she does," he said quietly.

Granny fell asleep, and Jackson found Chas still busy in the kitchen. When she refused to let him help her wash dishes, he went up to his room, had a drink and read, watching for telltale evidence that Charles Dickens was a Christian. He fell asleep with the book in his lap and woke in the middle of the night. Once he was in bed, he thought of his conversations with Chas and couldn't wait to see her again. He slept again and woke to daylight. When he was ready to leave the room, he found a note that had been slid under his door. The piece of paper folded in half was stationery from the inn. On it was written in Chas's handwriting, *I had to leave early and won't be back until very late, so I'll see you tomorrow. Have a good day. Chas. P.S. Your anniversary gift is in the dining room behind the coffee maker. It has your name on it. You can't miss it.*

Jackson smiled and read it all the way through three times before he set it aside and hurried downstairs to see what she had left for him. He was disappointed to think of not seeing her today, and wondered where she might have gone. But the evidence that she'd been thinking of him helped immensely. Just behind the coffee maker was a large white mug. He picked it up to see that someone had written his name on it in permanent black marker. In Chas's elegant hand it said, *Agent Jackson T. Leeds.* He imagined it on his desk back at the office and smiled, but he wasn't sure of the point. Then he turned it around and laughed out loud to see that it was just like Granny's favorite mug. He glanced around to make sure he was alone and that no one had heard his outburst. Then he just had to say it aloud. "Mostly, it was the worst of times." Oh, the perspective it put on having a bad day once in a while!

Jackson left the mug there, certain no one else would use it when it really *did* have his name on it. After his run and a shower, Polly served him a lovely breakfast. Then he went into town to look around. Anaconda was a quaint place with a lot of character, and he liked the look and feel of it. He wished that he'd thought to ask Polly where Chas had gone. He thought, however, that he probably shouldn't appear too nosy; but when he returned and Polly was in the office, his curiosity was far stronger than his concern about looking nosy.

"She's gone to Idaho Falls," Polly said, keeping her attention on her paperwork.

"Idaho Falls?" he repeated as if she'd said Afghanistan. "Isn't that an awfully long drive?"

"Four hours each way," she reported.

"Why?" he asked too much like an FBI agent. "Does she have a friend there, or—"

"It's a religious thing," Polly said, finally looking up. "I don't understand it. I just know it means a lot to her. There's a Mormon temple there. She goes once a month. Drives over and back in one day. She'll probably be late."

"How late?"

"Way past supper late. But don't worry, I've got you covered."

"You don't have to cook my supper, Polly. I'm certain I could manage."

"It's okay. I have to take care of Granny, anyway. Chas left everything ready. It'll be a cinch. Is there anything you need in the meantime?"

"No, thank you. I'm fine. If you need any help with Granny, let me know."

The day dragged for Jackson, even though he spent some time with Granny more than once. He wondered what on earth Chas would drive to Idaho Falls for that had to do with her religion. He couldn't help being curious, but he wondered if this was the kind of religion that disapproved of people marrying *outside* of their religion. That would certainly complicate the possibility of their ever ending up together. And yet, here he was, contemplating marriage. Two weeks ago if someone had told him he'd be contemplating marriage, he'd have laughed—hysterically. On top of that, he was pondering religion, or at the very least, wondering if he was a Christian. He really had *never* thought of it before. He understood the dynamics of celebrating Christmas; and all that stuff about peace and good will was something he appreciated and respected, but not any more or less than he appreciated and respected the fact that Jewish people did *not* celebrate Christmas. It was certainly food for thought.

Throughout the evening, Jackson almost felt a tangible cloud gathering around him. He started feeling crazy for even considering that he could have a future with someone like Chas, certain that she deserved far, *far* better than he could ever be. He began to wonder if he should just pack his bags and get back to Norfolk before he and Chas became any more attached to each other. He knew the searching of his premises had long since been completed, and he could go back there now; but he wasn't sure if he was ready to face the creepy feelings he knew he'd have just thinking about people in his agency going through his every belonging. As he'd told Chas, he wasn't terribly concerned about the outcome. He just hated the ugliness of the situation. And that, too, added darkness to his mood. He thought of Dave's wife, Mary, facing the holidays alone with her children, and he felt nauseous. He started hearing the shots go off in his head, and those shots triggered other shots that took him back to moments during his Marine experience that he wished he could permanently erase. Emptying his glass and pouring more into it, he thought of Chas telling him that he drank too much and felt certain she was right. And she'd nailed it right on the head. It wasn't so much the quantity that he drank, or the frequency. It was his *reasons* for doing it that were a problem. *Everything* seemed to be a problem, he thought and went down to the parlor, wanting to be sure that Chas made it home safely. He'd never be able to sleep until he knew she was okay.

* * * * *

Chas pulled into the inn just after eleven, glad to be home and to know that everything was all right. She'd talked to Polly on the cell phone a while ago and knew that Granny was asleep, Jackson had been given a nice dinner, and all was well. Polly was going to sleep in one of the rooms, as she did on occasion. It was something they'd done many times for different reasons. Tonight it was just easier for Polly to go to bed as opposed to waiting until Chas got home.

Sometimes she slept there so she'd be available early if Chas needed extra help with breakfast for several guests. And Chas had decided back when she'd opened the inn that she would never spend the night alone in the house with only one male guest there. It was simply her policy for Polly to stay if that were the case. The only exception she'd ever made was having Jackson in the house, but of course, Granny was there. And Jackson made her feel *more* safe, not less.

Chas got out of the car and opened the back door of the inn with a key. As was her habit, she walked up the hall to make certain everything was as it should be and to peek in on Granny. She set her things down just outside her bedroom door, then she noticed a glow coming from the parlor. Creeping closer, she could see that there was a fire in the fireplace, and Jackson was sitting in front of it, his stocking feet up on the cocktail table.

"Hello," he said without looking in her direction when she entered the room.

"Hello," she said, noting that he looked a little dazed while he stared into the flames, holding a glass of liquor in his hand.

"You're home safely." He took a long sip but still didn't look at her.

"I am. Were you worried?"

"Maybe. I knew you would be late, but I wasn't sure I could sleep until I knew you were safe."

"That's very sweet," she said and sat down across from him, but still he didn't look at her. Certain the liquor had affected his brain, she felt mildly angry and intent upon getting his attention. She prayed silently that her wonderful day wouldn't be ruined by coming home to something that might mar it. Without giving him any warning, she took the glass from his hand and threw the contents into the fire where the flames let out a brief burst of exuberance from the added fuel. "Do you see what that stuff will do to you?"

Her tactic worked when he looked up at her, astonished, and snapped out of his daze. "You can take the cost of that stuff off my bill."

"Gladly." She slammed the empty glass on the table. "Although I think it'll balance out the extra charge for babysitting. Is this what you do when you're at home alone?"

"Usually," he had to admit.

"Well, if you think I'm going to let you just sit around here and drink yourself into oblivion, you're very, very, *very* mistaken."

"What difference does it make to you, Mrs. Dickens? As long as I pay my bill and don't cause you any trouble, what I do is what I do."

"Then do it in your room. But don't lie around in my parlor like an unmade bed, holding that booze like some kind of teddy bear." He said nothing, didn't move, and she added with a fair amount of confidence, "If you ask me, you *wanted* me to find you and dump it out. If you *really* wanted to be alone and get drunk, you would have stayed in *your* room."

"Fine, I'll stay in my room," he said and came to his feet. She noted that he couldn't have been drinking *too* much. He didn't have any trouble moving around her and walking briskly toward the stairs. She heard his footsteps on the stairs, and the distant sound of his door closing two flights up, then she sank into the chair where he'd been sitting and cried. It had been such a good day—until a couple of minutes ago. The feelings that had come to her with thoughts of Jackson and their blossoming relationship had been so warm and positive. She had really believed that they were on a good course, even if she didn't know what the outcome might be. And then she'd come home to this.

She sat there until the fire burned down, praying and pondering the situation. She finally came to the conclusion that she was tired, and this issue needed to be addressed once she'd had some sleep.

CHAPTER 9

Jackson came awake and recalled the conversation with Chas just before he'd come up the stairs. He groaned and wondered what he'd been thinking. If he was trying to convince her that he wasn't good enough for her, he was doing a good job. But that's not what he wanted, and he had to figure out a way to reverse it. He went out for his usual run, hoping that brisk air and exercise would help him find the answer. By the time he got back it was snowing hard, and the answer *had* come. He knew what to do as clearly as he'd ever known which person was guilty of a crime and needed to be arrested. When it was right, he just knew it. Still wearing his running clothes, he looked at the partially full bottle of expensive whiskey, and the other one that hadn't been opened. It took him a minute to gather the courage, and then he just did it. He opened them both, dumped their contents down the drain, and threw the empty bottles into the waste basket. He'd told Chas she inspired him to be a better man. Whether or not he could ever measure up to a woman like Chas, he was surely capable of becoming a better man.

He showered and went down to breakfast, drinking coffee from the mug with his name on it, and reading *USA Yesterday*.

"Good morning," he said to Chas when she appeared with the first part of his breakfast.

"Good morning," she replied, sounding only mildly cool.

He tipped down the paper and looked at her. "Thank you for the mug. I love it. If I ever *do* go back to the office, it will be greatly coveted."

"You're welcome," she said, seeming a little more relaxed. But she hadn't gone back into the kitchen.

"Listen," he said, needing to get it over with, "I behaved badly last night, and I'm sorry. It'll never happen again."

"Apology accepted," she said.

"Are you going to join me?"

"If you like."

"I would like that very much," he said and set the paper aside.

"Did you miss me?" she asked as she sat down.

"I did. Did *you* miss *me?*"

"I did."

"What did you do, exactly?"

"I already know that Polly told you where I went." She paused and studied his expression—and her feelings on the matter. She knew that now wasn't the right time to bring up religion with him. In that regard she needed to move slowly and with caution, relying on the Spirit to guide her. Only the Lord would know when the right teaching moments might come up with this man who had lived a hard life and would likely not be impressed by someone even appearing to push religion on him. "I'll tell you more about it some other time," she concluded and started talking about the weather. A taut silence ensued, and she decided that she just had to clear the air. "Forgive me," she began, "but I can't skip over what happened last night. It's really bugging me."

"Are you saying that you can't live with a man who drinks?"

"Whether or not we end up living together—only if we were married, of course," she added with panic, not wanting him to get the wrong idea.

"Of course."

"That issue is secondary to the fact that you're drinking, and usually alone, and more when I'm not around." Her voice softened. "I'm concerned, Jackson."

He set down his fork and folded his arms. "Okay, why don't you just say what you feel like you need to say and get it over with."

"Okay, I will. I'd wager you're dependent on alcohol and you just won't admit it." She ignored the way he glared at her. "It's nothing to be ashamed of. With the way the world is today, a lot of people are dependent on liquor to get through a day."

"So, you're saying I can't go without it?"

"That's what I'm saying."

"Okay," Jackson said, "I'll take you on. What's your wager?"

Chas grinned like a Cheshire cat. "If you can go a week without drinking any liquor at all—not a drop—I will take you out to dinner at the finest restaurant in town and buy you a meal you will never forget."

"And if I don't make it?"

"You have to do the same for me."

"I just see one problem with this," Jackson said. "What makes you think I'll be here another week?"

Instead of letting the question rattle her, Chas chose to sway in the direction of being positive. "Where else are you going to go? What motivation do you have to go out in this weather and get yourself to the airport where you can sit in a cold chair and wonder if your flight will get off the ground? You don't want to leave, and I know it." She saw him smile, that barest hint of a smile that rarely showed, even with short of bursts of laughter. And she couldn't resist adding, "Sometimes you're just a little more transparent than you think you are."

"Fine," he said, his smile going a little wider. On a scale of one to ten, he might have almost hit a three. "You've got yourself a deal, Mrs. Dickens. I assume this means you and I will be spending a lot more time together."

"You're assuming to the point of being presumptuous, Mr. Leeds."

"What else am I going to do to distract me from my supposed alcoholism?"

"Read a book."

"All day every day? Come on, this was your idea. You've got to help me out here. Consider me a charity case. I know how you feel about charity."

"*How* do you know how I feel about charity?"

He pointed to a stitched wall hanging to his right that read *Charity Never Faileth.*

Chas chuckled. "You got me there. Okay, charity case, after breakfast you can go down to the cellar and bring up some potatoes and carrots, and then you can check on Granny."

"Do you want me to read to her, too?"

"Wouldn't hurt. They say charity is the best way to stop feeling sorry for yourself."

"Is that what they say?" he asked and finished his breakfast.

Chas finished first and left him there while she hurried up to his room to make the bed and change the towels. On the nights when he was the only guest, she usually took care of it, and generally managed to do it while she knew he was busy elsewhere so he wouldn't catch her at it. Not that it would matter, but part of the etiquette of cleaning rooms at an inn was to avoid the guests. She usually got it done when he was out for his run, but this morning she'd barely gotten started when the phone had rung and she'd had to leave. The only thing she'd actually learned about him from being in his room was that the computer bag he'd brought hadn't held a computer, but books instead. Of course, she'd noticed the liquor, but they'd already addressed that issue. And that was the very reason she gasped when she saw two empty liquor bottles in the garbage. It took her a moment to assess the absolute indisputable evidence that he had emptied the bottles before he'd come down to breakfast. She'd been in the room earlier this morning, and there had been more than one and a half bottles left. He obviously hadn't consumed it. He'd dumped it out! He'd dumped it out *before* their conversation over the breakfast table. She put a hand over her heart and felt a little teary. He really was a good man. The positive feelings she'd felt about him yesterday came back to her, and she was looking forward to spending as much time with Agent Jackson Tobias Leeds as she could possibly get away with.

The next few days were slow at the inn, and Polly was happy to get in some extra hours. Chas took Jackson on a special personalized tour of her hometown and the outlying areas. They talked and laughed and held hands. She was amazed at how thoroughly comfortable she had come to feel with him, and how utterly she had fallen in love with him. At times their conversations were silly and trivial, at others deep and poignant. When he asked some specific questions about her religion, she answered them matter-of-factly without getting pushy. She knew him well enough to know that if a man like this was to ever embrace religion, it had to be on his own terms and in his own time. She could live with manipulating him into going without liquor, but she would never do the same with religion. If he couldn't come to it on his own, she could never make it an issue in their relationship.

Interspersed with their time out and about, she also got him to help her decorate the inn for Christmas. She had hired someone to put little lights all over the outside of the house and in the trees, and now that Thanksgiving was over they were always on after dark. In the house, she enjoyed doing the decorating on her own. But never had she enjoyed it so much as she did with Jackson helping her wind garlands on the stair rails, decorate every mantelpiece in the house, and put up a Christmas tree in the parlor. She started burning scented candles that filled the house with the smells of Christmas, and made sure that music of the season was often playing. She loved this time of year for the spirit that permeated her home. And having Jackson at the center of it just added to a sweetness surrounding her that she could never describe. She refused to even think about the possibility that Jackson might not actually be here for Christmas.

On Friday morning while Chas was cooking breakfast, she smiled to hear Jackson's familiar footsteps coming down the stairs. "Hello, Jackson," she said brightly when he entered the kitchen. "You're a little early for breakfast. What can I do for you?" When he just stood there, she asked, "You want some coffee?" She kept her focus on the goblets that she was drying by hand.

"Nope. But thanks."

"You hungry? I've got some—"

"Nope, I'm not hungry. Thanks."

"Then what *do* you want? *Anything* for the FBI."

"Anything?"

"Well," she chuckled, "within reason."

"Perhaps we should define your definition of reasonable."

"Perhaps you should give me a category," she said as if they were going to play charades.

"I'm not very good at this stuff, Chas. I'm just not a romantic guy, but . . ." Chas stopped at the word *romantic* and turned to look at him. Once they had established eye contact he added, "I want to kiss you, Chas. I've been thinking about it for so many days that I just had to say it."

Chas set down the towel and the goblet and turned her back, if only to conceal how his declaration was affecting her. She closed her eyes and put a hand over her heart. Trying to keep this a matter of practicality—however hypocritical that felt—she spoke with a level voice. "Now you've said it. What did you think would happen now?"

"I have no idea. If I could have predicted your response, maybe I wouldn't be so blasted . . . fascinated with you. I guess . . . the outcome . . . would depend entirely on . . . how you feel about . . ." His sentence drifted into silence.

"How I feel about . . . what?"

Jackson wanted to say *me*. Instead he said, "Being kissed . . . by me." She said nothing, and the awkwardness was killing him. "Um . . . I know you have these strict boundaries about such things . . . no hanky panky without marriage, and all that stuff. I respect that, Chas. I do. I wish I had been more that way. I wish I had even bothered to think about something like that before now." Hearing his own rambling he groaned and muttered, "I'm doing it again."

"Doing what?"

"Babbling like an idiot, analyzing the whole thing before there's anything to analyze. I just want to kiss you, Chas. I'm asking your permission because I don't want to do anything stupid. I don't want anything to . . . change between us. I mean . . . I guess I do; I want it to be better, to be more. I want it to be meaningful. I care about you . . . a lot. And I believe you care about me. I think what we share . . . warrants a kiss, but . . . I don't want to offend you, or upset you, or . . . oh, for heaven's sake. I'm doing it *again!* Will you at least turn around and look at me? I have a hard enough time reading you when I can see your face, but this is impossible. Please."

Chas turned slowly, and he let out a strained sigh. Her countenance was soft, her eyes warm. That was a good sign. But she said nothing.

"Talk to me," he said.

"I haven't been kissed in a very, very long time," she said. "I've wondered sometimes if I even remember how. I loved Martin and he loved me. We were high-school sweethearts. There was never anyone else, not before . . . or since. I was never impressed enough with any man to actually believe that a kiss would be worth the possibility of tainting what I'd shared with Martin."

When she put it that way, Jackson felt so utterly unworthy of her that he wanted to just say "never mind" and leave the room. He felt sure she was going to diplomatically tell him that for all their mutual attraction, he still fell into the category she'd just described. And he couldn't blame her. His life had been less than exemplary in most respects. He'd never imagined putting so much value on a kiss, and marveled that this woman had changed his perspective on so many things. What was valuable and what wasn't had been altered so many ways for him since he'd come here. He took a deep breath as their eyes connected. Eye contact was good. Whatever she had to say, at least she would be straight with him and do it with respect and kindness. That's the way she was. That's what he loved about her.

"So, what now?" she asked, and he wished that he could read her half as well as he'd been able to read most of the criminals he'd put behind bars.

"I'm just wondering if I should have never brought it up, or if I should have just skipped talking about it and gone with my gut instinct."

"And what's that?"

"That I should have just kissed you because I know you're putting off vibes that you want me to, and I want to, and I—"

"Shut up," she said, at the same time closing the distance between them. She put her face so close to his that he could see every fleck in her eyes, hear her breathing. "Just shut up and kiss me," she whispered and closed her eyes, tilting her face more toward his. Jackson took another deep breath and closed his own eyes as he touched his lips to hers. Never had a kiss been so easy, or so hard. Their kiss was lengthy but meek, unassuming but full of meaning. He felt startled by the depth of its meaning. He'd expected it to be good, simply because he'd thought about it so much, and he knew how he felt about her. But he never could have predicted that a simple kiss could bathe his spirit with such perfect peace, or warm the ice crystals in his heart—that could be the only explanation for the heat in his eyes and the tightness in his throat.

"Chas," he muttered close to her lips, as if she might have some explanation for all he was feeling. They both opened their eyes at the same time, but neither of them moved, as if they were equally hypnotized. Her lips parted slightly to draw breath, and she lifted them just enough to make her invitation unmistakable. As he kissed her again, every sensation became more enhanced, more intense. He felt wrapped in a warm blanket and refreshed by a cool breeze at the same time. She took his face into her hands, and he did the same in return. Their kiss gained fervor and warmth without relinquishing its innocence and fineness. Again they looked into each other's eyes, and he wanted to just savor this moment and relive the experience in his mind, while it was still close and fresh. She sighed and smiled. He did the same. Then she wrapped her arms tightly around him and put her head on his shoulder. He returned her embrace, and she pressed her hands tightly against his back.

"Oh, Jackson," she murmured and adjusted her head slightly as if it were searching for the perfect resting place.

"What?" he asked in a whisper and pressed a kiss into her hair.

"This is what I've missed." She tightened her arms around him, and he did the same.

"What, tell me," he urged when she seemed hesitant to explain. "You can tell me anything."

"It feels so good to just . . . have strong arms around me, the closeness of a man who actually cares about me, and who I really am." She chuckled. "And you smell really good; like a man."

He chuckled and pressed his face into her hair. "You smell like . . . fruit . . . and flowers . . . and spices."

"That's shampoo, soap, and what I was cooking."

"I know. That's why I love it."

They were both startled when his cell phone rang. He always carried it on his belt, but she'd only heard it ring three times before, and two of those were calls he'd ignored, saying they could leave a message and he'd return the call later. He kept his arm around her while he took hold of the phone to look at the caller ID, then he took a step back and turned around, as if he were steeling himself for something. But he didn't leave the room. She leaned against the counter and folded her arms as he flipped open the phone and said, "Leeds here." Following a short pause, he said, "Yes, sir. Thank you. It's good to hear your voice, also." Another pause. "I'm doing as well as could be expected. Thank you for asking." Through a very long stretch of silence, Jackson turned to look at Chas, then he looked away as if he couldn't concentrate on the call if he didn't. But she sensed that whatever he was hearing had to do with the investigation that was going on. She reached a hand toward him and he took it, squeezing tightly.

"Yes, sir. I understand," he said, and listened some more. She saw his eyes widen and felt his hand tighten in hers. "*Should* I be sitting down?" he asked, then he let go of her hand and moved to a chair as if he'd been ordered to do so and he knew how to take orders. Chas wondered what was coming, and how it might affect him, but she was entirely unprepared to see the horror that filled his countenance, even though he didn't make a sound. "Yes, I'm still here," he finally said, his voice barely steady. The only other thing he said before he closed the phone was one more faint, "Yes, sir." With glazed eyes he absently set the phone on the table beside him, and his breathing became noticeably audible.

She didn't know how to ask, or if she should say anything at all. Had they found the traitor? Was this his reaction to knowing who it was? Or had he been personally implicated? She'd almost gotten up the nerve to ask when he groaned and dropped his head to his knees, as if he feared passing out. He groaned again, then rushed to the sink where he threw up. She knew he hadn't eaten anything yet this morning, but he still heaved painfully. She knew that feeling well from her pregnancy. But she couldn't fathom what news he'd been given that would make him so physically ill. He kept his face lowered into the sink until he'd gained control of himself, then he turned on the faucet to rinse out the sink and his mouth. He splashed water on his face, then reached for a towel that he pressed there for a full minute. Chas put a hand on his arm, and he tossed the towel to the counter before he took hold of her as if he were sinking into quicksand and she was the only hope for helping him avoid suffocation. She returned his embrace with all the fervor of concern she felt, finding it ironic that not so many minutes ago they'd shared an equivalent embrace that had been nothing but tender and romantic.

"Tell me," she finally whispered.

"I don't know if I can even bring myself to say it."

"You have to say it," she said, taking hold of his shoulders to look at him closely. "You can't hold it inside. It will eat you alive."

He hesitated, then nodded, then moisture pooled in his eyes before he turned away, ashamed of his tears. He cleared his throat and muttered, "Sorry about the sink. If you show me where you keep the cleaning stuff, I'll—"

"Don't worry about the sink. I'll take care of it. I've puked in the kitchen sink more times than I can count." He looked confused. "When I was pregnant," she clarified. "You can't avoid this, Jackson."

"Okay," he said, looking at her again, his tears gone. "But . . . I think I need to sit down."

Chas nodded and guided him across the hall to the parlor, insisting that it would be more comfortable there, and no one would be around for hours yet. Granny had been given her breakfast and was taken care of for the moment. With her hand on his arm she guided him to the couch. He sat there for just a moment before he kicked off his shoes and laid down, putting a hand over his eyes. She didn't want to leave, but felt she should ask, "Do you want me to leave for a while and let you—"

"No," he said. "Please stay. Unless you have something you need to be—"

"Nothing more important than being here with you," she said and moved a chair closer so that she could hold his hand while he kept the other one over his eyes, as if the light hurt them. She prayed silently that she would be guided in helping him get through whatever had happened, and that he would be given comfort and strength. When she couldn't think of anything to say, she figured silence was probably best for now. Then she saw a tear trickle from beneath his hand, sliding down the side of his face, into the hair above his ear. She wiped away the trail it had left, and he moved his hand to look at her, almost alarmed, as if he'd been caught doing something he shouldn't.

"It's okay," she said, and tears rose in her own eyes.

He noticed them and showed surprise. "Why are *you* crying? You don't even know what happened."

"I know that you're in pain," she said, and he touched her face.

Jackson wondered for a moment what it might have been like to be dealing with this moment at home—alone. He couldn't even imagine! He'd never once in his life thought to thank God for anything, but he had to thank Him now for this. If Chas was never more a part of his life than she was right now, he would forever be grateful for having her there for him now, and to be comfortable enough with her that he truly felt that he could share this burden. He just didn't know how to say it, how to even consider accepting that it was true.

"You need to tell me," she said, as if she could read his mind.

"I know," he said. "I've given a lot of bad news to a lot of people in my life, but I don't know how to say this."

"How do you give bad news to people?"

"I just have to detach myself. It can't be personal."

"So detach yourself enough to say it, and then you can let it be personal."

Jackson nodded, amazed at her wisdom. Her theory made so much sense, but he still had trouble forming the words. He was relieved when she said, "Do you want me to ask you questions?"

"Yes," he said.

"You look terrified."

"I am. I feel like . . . I've been hit in the chest with a bullet, and the thought of repeating it is like knowing another bullet is coming."

Chas had to ask, "Are you speaking metaphorically . . . or from experience?"

"I've taken a few bullets in the chest," he said, and she gasped. "With a bulletproof vest on, of course, or I wouldn't be here talking about it. But it still knocks you flat, and it still hurts."

Chas appreciated the analogy and nodded to indicate that she understood. She prayed for guidance and sought for the right questions to ask him. "Did they figure out who was leaking information?"

"Yes," he said.

"Was this person responsible for Dave's death?"

"Indirectly, yes."

"Has your name been cleared?"

"Yes."

"So, there's no concern for your job?"

"Not technically. Whether or not I can ever go back to work remains to be seen."

"You feel betrayed." That wasn't a question; she already knew.

"Yes," he said, his voice growing deeper.

"Angry."

"Yes. And horrified. I've seen a lot of horrible things in my life, Chas. Things I would never want to repeat aloud, mostly because I don't want other people to be plagued with those images." Chas nodded, glad that he'd gained some momentum. He was talking. "You can't serve that many years in the Marines . . . or the agency . . . without seeing horrible things. But when it becomes personal. . . ." His voice trembled and his chin quivered.

"Like when you saw Dave get killed?"

"Like that. But this is worse."

"Worse than Dave getting killed?" she asked, hearing a hint of panic in her own voice.

Jackson knew he just had to say it and get it over with. He needed her to know because he needed her to hold him together, and he could feel himself crumbling from the inside out at this very moment. "They figured out who it was, and it's evident he knew they were closing in."

"You worked with this man? It was a man?"

"Yes. But I didn't work with him directly, even though I've known him for years. Our paths have crossed on the job countless times. I've met his family. I never liked him much, but I just figured that was a personality difference. I never would have believed him to be capable of this."

"He'll go to prison, of course," Chas said, startled by how quickly Jackson put his hand over his eyes, then over his mouth, as if he preferred holding back the sound of his sudden sobbing as opposed to the tears that came with it. He sat up abruptly and put his head down, resigned to not being able to hide either. He pressed his head into his hands, wracked with heaving sobs that made it difficult for him to breathe. Chas was stunned. She'd never seen anyone cry that hard. And she'd only cried like that herself when she'd lost Martin and her baby. She moved to sit beside him, putting her arm around him. He immediately put his head in her lap and held to her tightly while he cried himself into exhausted silence. Chas wept silently on his behalf, unable to even imagine what the rest of the story might be.

Jackson felt like a complete stranger to himself when he realized how long and hard he'd been crying. Then he realized where he was and who he was with, and he felt mortified—but only for a moment.

His embarrassment was quickly replaced by gratitude. He rolled over to look up at her, keeping his head in her lap while he lifted his legs onto the couch. He reached up a hand to touch her face where there was evidence that she had been crying as well. It was easy to say, "I am more grateful to be here now with you than I could ever tell you."

"I'm grateful too," she said.

Before he had even another moment to think about it, he hurried to say, "He won't go to prison. He's dead. He took his own life when he realized there was no way out. He did it with a bomb." Chas gasped, but he kept going. "Two of my best men had been sent to arrest him, and he knew they were coming. If they hadn't been really sharp and really fast, he would have taken them out, too. Apparently that was his intention."

"Are they all right?" she asked, finally getting a glimpse into the horror he was feeling.

"They'll live. They're both in the hospital; broken bones, burns, shrapnel." More tears came. "These men are my friends, Chas. We've worked together for years. We've covered each other, trusted each other, put our lives on the line for each other. They have families. If this . . . *cretin* chose to sell his soul and take up with drug dealers, he should have been willing to take the consequences. But he had *no right,*" he said through clenched teeth, "to take innocent people with him. *My* people."

"I'm so sorry," she said, certain it sounded trite, but he took hold of her hand and squeezed it tightly. Trying to let it all sink in, a terrible thought occurred to her. "If you had been on the job . . . would you have gone with them to make the arrest?"

"Yes."

"I hope you aren't feeling guilty that you're not in the hospital with them."

"That's *exactly* what I'm feeling guilty about," he said, still sounding angry. "But that's just added on top of the guilt I feel for not taking the bullet that took Dave last month."

"You can't do that to yourself, Jackson. Guilt is something people should feel only when they've done something wrong."

"I wonder if I *did* do something wrong."

"Did you break the law? Lie to anyone? Hide the truth from people who trusted you? Did you go home at the end of any given day without doing everything you could have done within your human capabilities?"

He thought about that for a long moment. "No," he said.

"Then you have nothing to feel guilty about."

"But these men have families. If I were taken in the line of duty . . ."

"What?" she asked when he hesitated, wanting him to finish it.

"I was going to say that no one would miss me. I can't say that any more, can I?"

"No, you can't say that."

"It's nice to know that someone cares enough to miss me, Chas, but if I had been killed the week before Thanksgiving, you never would have known. It would have made no difference to your life."

"That's just it, Jackson, you *have* made a difference in my life. But what about the men you work with who surely care for you the way you care for them? They would have noticed. And maybe you're the one capable of helping your friends put their lives back together after what's happened."

"How can I help them when I can't even stand up straight?"

"You're still in shock. You need some time. A day will come when you'll know what to do, and you'll understand why you're still alive. With any luck it will have something to do with me."

Jackson pondered the implication and felt strangely comforted. Whether or not she ended up a part of his future, the hope of that possibility gave him something to live for, as opposed to just staying alive. "With any luck," he repeated with conviction. He recounted the way she had responded to his grief and felt in awe that any person could be so good. He had to ask, "What is it about you that makes it so easy for you to be so . . . kind? So understanding? So compassionate?"

She tipped her head as if it were nothing, then she said, "Christ taught that we should mourn with those that mourn, and comfort those that stand in need of comfort. It's just the way I believe we should live."

"Your grandmother told me you're a Christian woman. She's right, of course."

She pressed a hand to the side of his face. "It's no sacrifice to behave that way when you love someone."

Jackson sat up and turned to face her. "Do you, Chas? Do you really?"

"I do, Jackson," she said, taking his face into her hands. "I love you."

He let her words fill him, then he wrapped her in his arms and buried his face in her hair. "I'm so glad," he murmured, "because I love you, too. I don't know how I ever survived without you."

Chas held him close and reminded herself that he was grieving and in shock. She didn't question his feelings or his sincerity. But she had to be prepared for the likelihood that once he found his footing again he would go back to his old life, and he would find a way to survive without her. In the meantime, she was glad to have him here, and prayed that she could help him find his way through the swamps of grief that had engulfed him this day.

CHAPTER 10

"I need to check on Granny and help her with a couple of things," Chas said, easing away from Jackson. "Will you be okay for a little while?"

"Of course," he insisted. "Thank you . . . for listening . . . for caring . . . for being wiser than I am."

"I don't know about that last part. But you're welcome on the others." She kissed his cheek. "I won't be far. Let me know if you need me."

He nodded, and she left the room. When the reality of what had happened descended over him again, he laid back on the couch and covered his eyes. He couldn't believe it. He just couldn't believe it.

* * * * *

"Is something wrong?" Granny asked Chas when she came into the room.

Chas gave her a brief explanation, then helped her get cleaned up and out of her pajamas. While Granny was in the bathroom, Chas checked on Jackson. He was either asleep or pretending to be, so she left him alone. Once Granny was dressed for the day and her hair combed and teeth brushed, she insisted that Chas help her into the wheelchair and take her into the parlor. They entered quietly, not wanting to disturb Jackson's rest, then Chas left her there while she took care of some things that needed her attention.

Jackson realized he'd been dozing and wondered how he could possibly sleep under the circumstances. But then all of that emotion had surely sucked the strength out of him. He opened his eyes and found Granny sitting in her wheelchair, watching him.

"Who let you out?" he asked, knowing that she knew him well enough to understand his humor.

"I thought maybe you could use a friend."

"I won't argue with that."

"You look terrible," she said as he sat up.

"Well, thank you very much, Granny," he said with light sarcasm. "You look old enough to be my grandmother."

"That I am. So listen to an old woman who has seen a thing or two of how ugly this world can be. Some memories will always be bad, and no matter how much time passes, if you think of those things, it will sting. But they grow more distant, and distance has a way of making things fade. Distance gives perspective."

"Is that coming from experience or—"

"My brother was killed in the war. You don't have to do much math to know I mean the first world war. He was older than me. I loved him, looked up to him. The wood box he came home in was never opened. They said we wouldn't have recognized him. I had nightmares over it for months. Couldn't talk about it for years. This world can be an ugly place, young man."

"Yes, it can."

"You know more about that than most people. You probably have a lot of memories that sting."

"I'm afraid I do, but this is a tough one."

"I can well imagine. If I had to go through losing my brother again, there's one thing I would have done differently."

"What's that?"

"I would have tried to have more faith, more hope. I would have tried to see the joy in life that I was missing because I was too busy feeling sorry for myself. One day, years after his death, I realized that I shouldn't feel sorry for him. He was at peace. He was in a better place. I've never been one to go to church much, but I believe that Jesus did what He said He did. I believe He'll take care of all the things we can't fix in this life. If I'd believed that back then, I think I would have gotten through it a lot easier." She paused and gave him a hard stare. "Chas taught me that. There's a difference in missing someone you love, and allowing grief to destroy your life and rob you of your peace. She knows that difference. You could learn a lot from her. I did."

Jackson took her frail hand and kissed it. "Thank you, Granny. You *and* your granddaughter have both been a great blessing in my life."

"And the other way around," she said, which surprised him. "It's going to be okay, but while it doesn't feel like it ever will be, you know where to find me."

"Thank you," he said again.

They talked for a few more minutes, then he took her to her room and helped her to the other chair, which was more comfortable. He found Chas in the office, and she came to her feet when she saw him. He eagerly took the embrace she offered, holding her in silence for long moments while he could almost feel her strength seeping into him.

"You okay?" She took a step back and looked up at him.

"I think I'm in shock at the moment, which is probably good. I need to make some phone calls. I should do it while I can sound rational."

"You didn't eat. Can I get you something?"

"No, thank you. I don't think I can eat right now. I know where to find food when I'm hungry. I'll be fine."

She touched his face. "I'm not going anywhere, so let me know if you need anything—anything at all."

"I'll let you know," he said. "Thank you." He kissed her brow. "Granny said I could learn a lot from you. She's right, of course. She's always right."

"Whether she's right or not, she'll insist that she is."

"Ninety-three years should earn someone that privilege."

"I suppose."

"Will there be guests this evening?"

"Yes; four rooms rented tonight besides yours. And my home teachers are coming this evening, but they usually don't stay long." At his confusion she clarified, "It's a church thing. Two men are assigned to each household to pay a monthly visit. They give a spiritual message and just make sure everything's all right. They're coming at seven. You're welcome to join us, or you can hide."

"Okay," he said and went upstairs to his room. Now that he knew what had happened, he felt the need to speak with every member of the team, and a few other people as well. He wasn't able to talk to the two men in the hospital, but he talked to others who had seen them and got a detailed report. With some of these people he knew they needed *him* to be strong, and he knew how to do that. With others he could be a little more open and tell them he was struggling to cope with this. But he realized through every conversation that there was no one with whom he could completely be himself. He was the one who had established the dynamics of these relationships. He'd kept himself closed off and independent all these years for a reason. He'd never wanted the people he worked with to know too much, or care too much. And now, during the worst tragedy that had ever occurred among this group of people, he felt incapable of communicating to them what he really felt. Only Chas, a stranger until recently, could see what this had really done to him. And her Granny, of course. On both counts he felt grateful.

When there was no one else to call, Jackson realized he was feeling nauseous again, and it would probably be wise to get something to eat, even if he didn't feel like it. In the hallway he met Chas, who was carrying a tray.

"What are you doing?" he asked.

"I was bringing you something to eat."

"I was going down to get something," he said and took the tray. "You didn't have to do that."

"I wanted to," she said.

"Thank you. If I take it back downstairs, will you keep me company while I eat?"

"I would love to," she said. "Let's take the elevator."

"There's an elevator?" She led the way around the corner, and he observed, "So there is."

Jackson felt a little better after he'd eaten and told Chas about the conversations he'd been having. The shock he felt was still intact, but he preferred it that way. He just hoped when he exploded again, he could handle it.

When suppertime came Jackson wasn't hungry yet, but he made it a point to be reading the newspaper in the parlor at seven when the home teachers came. His curiosity was a strong motivator. It also helped distract him from thinking about things he'd rather not think about right now. He heard the doorbell ring, then saw Chas go down the hall. She stopped and took a step back when she saw him.

"Oh, hi," she said. "Are you going to join us?"

"Unless you don't want me to." He set the paper aside.

"I wouldn't have asked if I didn't," she said and went to get the door.

Jackson heard voices in the hall as greetings were exchanged, then Chas walked into the room with two men, dressed casually, who both looked fairly ordinary. His immediate assessment was that one probably worked in a cubicle; very smart, but not very social. This he could tell from the pale color of his skin, the look of his hands, and the evidence that he had worked in the clothes he was wearing. He held back and didn't make eye contact when they came into the room and saw someone different there. The other was a blue-collar worker, probably in some kind of construction, and self-assured. This he could also tell by the condition of his hands and the look of his skin. And the fact that he had obviously showered and changed his clothes before going out for the evening. He stepped forward with a smile and held out his hand to Jackson before they were even introduced. Jackson came to his feet and took the firm handshake.

"Hi, I'm Ron," he said.

"This is Jackson Leeds," Chas said. "He's a guest at the inn, but he's more on a lengthy retreat than just a short getaway."

"Nice to meet you, Jackson," Ron said. He motioned to the other man who pushed his glasses up his nose and held out his hand with some hesitance. "This is Jerry."

"Hello," Jerry said, and Jackson nodded. The visitors sat on one couch. Jackson sat back down, and Chas sat beside him. Jackson was asked questions about where he was from, what he did for a living, and if he was enjoying his stay. When the subject of the FBI came up, it sparked interest and questions, as it usually did, but Jackson was used to that. Ron gave a brief spiritual message, which included a little story about a boy being saved from a terrible accident by a prompting from the Holy Ghost. Jackson listened and nodded occasionally, feeling a little dazed over such a concept. It felt like a foreign language to him. But then, his brain was naturally more foggy today than usual, so he didn't give the matter much thought. They asked Chas how she was getting along and if she needed help with anything. She assured them that she was doing fine and reached for Jackson's hand as she said it. He didn't know if she'd done it unconsciously, or if she wanted these men to know there was something romantic going on. Either way he welcomed her touch and her reassurance that he was part of her life. Before the men stood to leave, one of them said a prayer. Once they were on their feet, Ron stepped toward Jackson and once again shook his hand, saying that it was a pleasure to meet him and he hoped that his stay would be pleasant. He told Jackson that Chas was a wonderful woman, almost as if he were congratulating them on a forthcoming marriage and he was thrilled to know she'd found someone. Jackson felt warmed by the apparent acceptance and approval, but he was more interested in the fact that Jerry was talking quietly with Chas and that she looked mildly annoyed. While he was pretending to listen to Ron, his ear tuned discreetly to the other conversation, startled to hear this man say to Chas with astonishment, "You're dating a nonmember?"

He waited to hear what Chas would say, but she stepped farther away before she said it, and he couldn't hear her. After Chas had shown them to the door and locked it, she returned to the parlor to find him sitting there. She sat beside him and took his hand, saying gently, "You okay?"

"It's been a long day," he said and turned to look at her. He had to know. "Is it against your religion to marry someone outside of your religion?"

She looked alarmed, then disgusted. "You heard what he said to me."

"Only one sentence. What I want to know is what you said in return that you didn't want me to hear." She sighed and looked away. How could he not ask, "Is this something that would inevitably come between us?"

"No," she said and looked at him again. "If I believed it would inevitably come between us, I would have brought it up before now, I can assure you. I told him that I appreciated his concern on my behalf, but I am an adult and not interested in his opinions on my personal life. He's a kind man, but he's not very tactful. Mormons come in all types, just like any other religion in the world. He just happens to be a little stuffy and dogmatic. That doesn't make him a bad person. Just a little . . . annoying sometimes."

"Okay, so you told him to mind his business. Now, I need to know why he would bring it up like that. I know practically nothing about your religion. I've encountered religious issues that have come up in my work, but never with this religion. I respect your beliefs, even though I don't know what they are. I just have to know if this relationship has the potential to cause problems for you."

"And if it did?"

"I don't know. I just think that it needs to be considered while we discuss potentially life-altering decisions."

"How can we possibly begin to know at this point if we could ever create a future together?"

"We will never know if we don't discuss the pros and cons. Talk to me."

Chas leaned back and sighed again. "Like every religion, we are encouraged to marry someone who shares our beliefs. Obviously, having religious beliefs in common is a good thing. We believe in the concept of eternal marriage, that when a marriage takes place in one of our temples, by the proper authority, it will last beyond the grave. But obviously that doesn't happen if both parties are not members in good standing."

"Is that how you married Martin?" he asked, wondering if she still considered herself married to a man who was dead.

"No. I wasn't a Mormon when I married him. Ironically, he *was* a member. He'd grown up in the Church. But he didn't live his religion, and it wasn't an issue. After he died, his family and members of the Church were very kind to me. So, I investigated and realized that what they teach is true. I knew it was the right thing to make it a part of my life. It's given me a great deal of peace. It's a big part of my life. I can't deny that I would like to be married to someone who shares those beliefs. If I get married again, I would like it to be forever. But I will not force my religious beliefs on you or any other man. Embracing religion is not something that anyone should ever do for someone else, or for the wrong reasons. It has to be between God and the individual. If I have children I will raise them with the gospel, and I would expect their father to support me in that. I would prefer that he go to church with us, as opposed to sending us without him, but it's not in me to be a nag or try to rob someone of their free agency. I live my life by prayer and trying to listen to the guidance of the Holy Ghost—just like he talked about in the lesson tonight. I would never make any significant decision in my life without an undeniable affirmation that it was what God wanted me to do."

"And how can you know that? I mean really know that?"

"He speaks to us through our thoughts and feelings. Most often it's just a matter of feeling peace or the lack of it. Sometimes impressions come more strongly. It's not something you can really explain. Some people call it instinct or conscience. It's probably happened to you, and you don't even realize it."

"How so?"

"Don't your thoughts and feelings guide you in your work? Don't you ever get ideas that seem to come out of nowhere that lead you to the solution?" She didn't wait for him to answer, as if she didn't want to put him on the spot. She went on to say, "You're a good man trying to protect good people from bad ones. It's not a stretch to think that your efforts would be guided by a Supreme Being who cares about His children."

Jackson thought about that for a minute and couldn't comment. It all just felt too strange and new. He went back to the point of origin. "Could you please clarify in simple terms the answer to my original question?"

"If you ask me to marry you, I will make the decision a matter of serious prayer and do what I believe in my heart my Father in Heaven wants me to do. I would not simply base the decision on the technicality of whether or not you are a member of the Church. I would, however, greatly appreciate—if we end up together—your going to church with me and supporting me in religious activities at home."

"Fair enough," he said, more relieved than he could admit.

"Will you go to church with me this Sunday?"

"Yes," he said without hesitating, but Chas felt certain that if he felt at all that doing so was due to pressure or would prove to be an issue in their relationship that he would not have agreed to go. In her heart she believed that a man like Jackson Leeds would not make life-altering decisions quickly or easily. But she believed that when he did make them, he stood by them with conviction. She doubted that such a man could participate in certain aspects of the gospel and not have it gradually warm him to it. But that was between him and God.

"I have one more question," he said.

"Okay."

"Did you pray about this?"

"This?"

"About . . . encouraging a relationship between us, as opposed to avoiding it?"

"I did."

"Really?"

"You sound surprised. I pray about everything." She chuckled. "Well, not *everything*. Obviously I have a brain, and God expects me to use it. But I pray about things that make a difference to my life, or someone else's. Yes, I prayed about it."

"And what was the answer?"

She smiled. "That should be obvious."

"I guess it is. So . . . you believe that . . . God approves of us . . . being together?"

"Under the present circumstances, yes. I'm sure He expects me to be appropriate and smart, and take it one step at a time."

"Of course," he said, feeling more steadily drawn to these foreign concepts. But it was impossible to listen to Chas talk about such things and not respect her more deeply. Whether he could ever share her beliefs or not, he admired her for them. He thought of what Granny had said earlier. He certainly could learn a lot from Chas. He just needed to keep paying attention. "Thank you," he added.

"For what?"

"For answering my questions without getting defensive or pushy." He kissed her. "And for everything else."

"I'll do anything I can to help you through this, Jackson. I just don't know what to do."

"Just . . . keep doing what you're doing."

"I can feed you," she said brightly. "In fact, I bet you're hungry. You only had one meal today."

"Now that you mention it, I could probably stand to eat, but I am capable of making myself a sandwich or something, you know."

"I know. But I've got some great leftovers in the fridge, and it will only take a few minutes to heat some up. You go say hi to Granny while I do it."

"Deal," he said, and they both stood up.

Chas kept Jackson company while he ate; then he felt suddenly exhausted and insisted that he needed some sleep. He kissed Chas goodnight at the foot of the stairs and went up to his room. Once he had been alone for more than a few minutes, the reality of what he'd learned today descended on him, and he was assaulted with a gamut of emotions before he was finally able to sleep.

He woke up and remembered the events that were torturing him. He groaned and pressed his face deeper into the pillow. Then he remembered where he was—and who was here—and a glimmer of peace and hope soothed his torment. He wondered if that was what Granny had been talking about yesterday. Whether it was or not, being here with Chas in his life gave him great incentive to get out of bed. If he'd been home in Virginia, he'd probably be shut in with the blinds closed, drinking too much and ordering pizzas and Chinese food. He got dressed and went running, looking forward to just seeing Chas.

* * * * *

Chas was busy in the kitchen when she heard someone enter the room; she turned to see Jackson. Just seeing him quickened her heart, and she had to pause momentarily and try to accept how he had changed her life so quickly. She completely pushed away any thoughts of what life might be like again after he left. As long as she didn't do anything stupid, she could surely enjoy the moment. As usual, he was dressed in jeans and a dark, long-sleeved polo shirt. When she realized he was gazing at her the way she was gazing at him, she smiled, and he did the same. Considering what he'd been facing yesterday, a smile was a good sign.

"Good morning," she said.

"Good morning," he replied and smiled more fully.

"Is something funny?"

"Not funny," he said. "Just . . . happy." He shrugged. "Well, certainly happier than I expected to feel. I woke up this morning and realized where I am . . . and that you're here . . . and I actually felt glad to be alive. Under the circumstances, I think that's pretty amazing. I just want you to know that, because I haven't felt truly glad to be alive for a very, very long time." With this declaration he closed the gap between them, took her face into his hands, and kissed her in a way that reiterated what he had just said. She took hold of his shoulders to compensate for her weakening knees, then he wrapped her in his arms and kept kissing her.

"Good morning," he said again without letting her go.

"Good morning," she repeated, her voice dreamy.

"I *do* believe in miracles, Chas. At least I do now. I can't think of any other reason why a man like me would end up here . . . like this . . . now. And I can't think of any other reason why I could be dealing with what I'm dealing with and still feel this way."

Chas wanted to say that it would be more of a miracle if he actually *stayed* in her life, but she didn't want to shatter the mood. She wanted to make him promise that he would never leave her, but she knew he could make no such promise under the circumstances. She settled for simply saying, "Amen," then she lifted her lips again to his.

"Oh, I could get used to this," she muttered and saw him smile. She found some comfort, if not hope, in the evidence that he too at least *wanted* it to last. "However," she added, easing away, "I have guests that will be wanting breakfast any minute."

"Maybe they slept in."

"Maybe," she said and immediately heard people entering the dining room.

Jackson smiled. It was good to see him smile. "Can I help?"

"No, thank you. I'm accustomed to keeping it all under control. It's not a tough job, you know. And it's not even dangerous . . . like all that FBI stuff." She felt alarmed to hear what she'd said and hurried to add, "Sorry. I wasn't thinking."

"It's okay. It's not like you reminded me of anything that's not already on my mind. I want us to be able to say anything to each other. It's really okay."

"And how are you, really?"

"I already told you."

"Maybe you're in denial," she said with more humor than concern.

"Maybe," he said. "But when I come out of it, I know you'll still be willing to help keep me together."

"Yes, I will," she said proudly and got back to work.

"What can I do to help you?" he asked. "I mean it."

"You can take Granny her coffee and tell her I'll bring her breakfast soon. And then you can come back and eat *your* breakfast."

"I'll eat when you have enough time to eat with me."

"Fair enough. Give me half an hour, and I think I can sneak it in between guests."

He kissed her again, then cleared his throat, chuckled, and said, "Granny's coffee."

"A little cream and lots of—

"Sugar, yes I know—to keep life sweet."

Throughout the day, Jackson felt more inclined than usual to not let Chas out of his sight. He didn't feel like he was in denial, because the reasons for his grief were continually in the forefront of his thoughts. But if Chas was close by, he felt connected to some kind of buoy that might keep him from drowning. They didn't talk much, but she suggested that it was probably good for him to just let his mind adjust and sort through all that had happened.

Chas was working at the desk in the office while Jackson leaned back in a comfortable chair with his eyes closed, wondering if his friends in the hospital would be able to speak to him on the phone yet. He was glad for the excuse of being in another state in order to avoid going to see them. He didn't want to see the evidence; not yet, anyway. But he did want to talk to them.

The phone rang and Chas answered it with her usual business greeting. Then she said, "Yes, I do have rooms available tonight."

Chas opened the reservation book and heard the woman on the other end of the phone say, "They have rooms, Mama." Her accent was southern, and not subtle. She said to Chas, "I'd like to reserve two rooms. It's for me and my mother, but we'd like separate rooms if you have them."

"I do," she said. "I can give you two rooms right next to each other."

"My mother has trouble with stairs. Do you—"

"We don't have rooms for rent on the main floor, but we do have an elevator."

"Oh, that's perfect."

Chas repeated the price for the rooms, as she always did whether the guests asked or not. She got the personal information she needed and put the reservation in the name of Melinda Lafferty. Melinda and her mother had just arrived at the airport in Butte and would be arriving in an hour or so, as soon as they were able to rent a car and make the drive. Chas gave her driving directions, then Melinda asked, "Do you have a restaurant there? I know you serve breakfast, but it's hard for my mother to get around much, and—"

"We can provide lunch and supper for a standard rate, but we don't have menu options. If you can live with whatever I'm fixing, then we can make certain you and your mother are fed."

"Oh, that's perfect," Melinda said again, and Chas heard her say to her mother, "We can eat there, Mama. It's all going to work out. You'll see."

Chas then heard in the background an elderly woman saying, "He won't still be there. You should have called before and asked if he was there."

"He'll be there, Mama. Stop worrying."

Chas felt a little prickle at the back of her neck but didn't make any conscious connection. She simply asked, "Is there something else I could help you with?"

"It's kind of personal," Melinda said, "but maybe you *could* help me. You probably can't tell me whether or not a certain person is staying there; privacy laws, or something. But we're looking for my brother. He sent a Christmas card with your inn as the return address. We haven't seen him for twenty-six years, and we've just been praying that he's still there."

Chas completely lost her breath, then had to cough when she got it back. The cough barely disguised the terrified gasp she was trying to swallow. She glanced at Jackson at the same moment as he opened his eyes to investigate the strange noise that had come out of her mouth. There was no hope of attempting to be nonchalant. He picked up on her concern immediately and sat up straighter.

Melinda continued her explanation. "My mother thought it was ridiculous for us to just up and run to Montana without calling, but my soul just told me we needed to, and if he'd known we were coming, he might not be there. On the other hand, he hasn't put a return address on anything all these years. So, if he put it there, it seemed to me like he wanted us to find him." She chuckled tensely. "I know I'm rambling, ma'am. I apologize. It's just . . ." she got emotional, "we've been praying for years that we could find him."

Chas wondered what to say, but she had no doubt that this was exactly what it seemed to be. She knew Jackson would be furious. She knew this could end up being as difficult a day as yesterday had been. The only thing she didn't know for certain was how a return address label had ended up on the card Jackson had sent home. She finally cleared her throat and came up with a reasonable response. "I can't give you any specific information, but if you've been praying, Ms. Lafferty, then I'm certain everything will work out."

She'd said the name aloud to see how Jackson would react. He bolted out of his chair as if he'd been shot out of a gun. She hurried to end the call by saying, "We'll see you in an hour or so, then. Drive carefully."

She hung up the phone, and Jackson leaned both hands onto the desk, looking at her with stern eyes. "Who was that and why do you look so guilty?"

"I am not guilty of anything, Agent Leeds. But obviously the name Lafferty means something to you."

"It's my sister's married name."

"Well, then . . . that must have been your sister."

Jackson was so stunned that it took him a minute to even know what to say that was short of yelling. He was full of questions but they were too intermixed with anger to know which one to ask first. Chas took advantage of his silence to say, "Apparently you sent your usual Christmas card."

"Yes," he drawled.

"And you didn't put a return address on it?"

"I *never* put a return address on it."

Chas swallowed carefully. "Did you give it to Polly to mail?"

Jackson straightened his back and sighed. If this was nothing more than an innocent mistake, he had no right to be angry with anyone. Still, he felt so angry! "What did she say?" he asked in a voice that felt was thick with hypocrisy.

Chas repeated the gist of the conversation while he pushed his hands into the pockets of his jeans and hung his head. He tried to imagine how to handle this and realized that he couldn't. He couldn't handle it at all.

"I can't deal with this, Chas. Not now; not like this."

"I'm not going to lie for you, if that's what you're asking."

"Then I need to leave and come back when they're gone."

"Don't be absurd!" she said, coming around the desk. "It's your mother and sister, Jackson. Twenty-six years? How can a man go twenty-six years without even having a conversation with his mother? She's your mother. If nothing else, she deserves your respect for giving you life."

Jackson's anger deepened. "I already explained that to you, and you can't possibly judge where I'm coming from."

"No, I can't judge that. But I can see that you're trying to run from something that will never stop chasing you. If you just stop and . . . face it, maybe you can stop running."

"I don't need this right now," he snarled, sounding suddenly angry. "Not from you, not from them. I'm leaving. You can deal with the—"

Chas grabbed his arm to keep him from leaving the room. "They've come a long way, Jackson. Surely you can just give them an hour and hear what they have to say. It's been twenty-six years."

"It doesn't matter how long it's been. People don't change, Chas."

"You have. Stand there and try to tell me that you're the same person who left your family to join the Marines. You don't even talk the way they do."

"No, I do not."

"How does a man get rid of an accent like that?"

"It wasn't easy."

"So, you think that you've changed and everything else has remained the same? I know you're not that naive, which means you're just being stubborn. I don't know what you're afraid of, but I think it's time you faced up to it. Maybe this is a blessing in disguise."

"A blessing?" He made a scoffing sound. "This is a disaster. I *am* hiding, Chas. That's why I came here, remember? And now it's all going to be . . . tainted . . . poisoned."

"How?"

"You don't know what they're like. You don't know what you're saying."

"Are you afraid I'll think less of you when I meet your family? Do you think I'll judge you according to their behavior, or their problems?"

"Maybe," he admitted.

"Well, I won't. What's between you and me is between you and me. Just . . . talk to them." He sighed again, and she knew she was wearing him down. "Listen," she said more gently, taking hold of his arms, "they'll be having supper here. I'll tell them you'll meet them in the parlor at five-thirty, and we'll have supper with them, and then if you want to go hide in your room, I'll keep them at bay for you. If it turns out to be a disaster, I'll take responsibility for it and get rid of them as soon as possible."

Jackson blew out a long, loud breath, then he surprised Chas by taking her in his arms and holding her fiercely. "You can't leave me alone with them."

"What if I need a potty break, or Granny needs me?"

"Okay, you can't leave me alone with them for more than five minutes."

"Deal."

"Oh," he groaned, then cursed. "I can't believe this is happening. Why does Polly have to be so blasted efficient?"

"Why would I keep her around if she weren't? It's going to be okay, Jackson. And maybe it will be more than okay. Maybe you'll be glad this happened." He scowled at her. "Have a little faith," she added with a smile. "You never know what can happen with just a little faith."

CHAPTER 11

Chas sent Jackson upstairs to try to mentally prepare for this unexpected turn of events, while she went to explain it to her grandmother and do some preliminary dinner preparations. She called Polly and explained the situation, asking if she could come in just a little earlier than she'd been planning because Chas needed to be focused on the family reunion.

"I feel awful," Polly said. "Does he hate me?"

"No, of course not. It was an innocent mistake, and not really a mistake at all. He should have told you *not* to put the return address on instead of just assuming you wouldn't. It doesn't matter now. I think it's a good thing anyway, so I'm glad you did it. Even if it's a disaster, he'll have faced his family and he can get on with his life."

"That's one way of looking at it," Polly said skeptically. "I'll be there in twenty minutes. I can't wait to see these people."

While Chas hurried to get everything under control as much as possible, her mind tried to imagine how this might turn out. She fervently prayed that the outcome would be favorable, that hearts could be softened, and that forgiveness would take place. She'd felt concerned over Jackson's attitude about his family right from the start, but it had been put on her mental list of things to deal with when their relationship became more established. Now it had been thrust upon them in a way that Chas couldn't help believing had been guided by Divine Providence. She didn't believe in coincidences. And this was just way too strange to ever be that.

Feeling a need to speak with Jackson again before his family arrived, she hurried up to his room and knocked on the door. He pulled it open and asked, "Are they here yet?"

"No. Polly's here in case they come while I'm up here. She begs your forgiveness."

He shrugged and said, *"Why* are you up here? You've already talked me into doing this. Did you come to see if I'd changed my mind?"

"Did you?"

"No, but it's tempting. I really need a drink."

"You do not *need* a drink. You want a drink. There's a difference. I'll stay with you. Everything will be fine."

"You realize what you're doing, don't you?"

"What am I doing?"

"You're just shifting my dependence on liquor to a dependence on you."

"I'm better for you," she said proudly.

"But what do I do when you're not around to hold me together?"

"Just keep me around."

He took her in his arms and held her close. "Oh, how I hope that will be possible."

"Me too," she said, then looked up at him. "Are you okay?"

"No, I'm not okay. I'm a wreck. This is . . . insane."

"I know it's difficult, Jackson. Just remember to . . . be kind." He looked at her sharply and she added, "I don't understand all the hurt that's bottled up inside of you, but I do know that you shouldn't take it out on your mother or sister. Later, when it's over, you can rage and scream and vent all your anger and frustration on me if you have to. But be kind to them. Don't say something you'll regret later."

Jackson almost felt afraid of how well she had him pegged. He hadn't consciously considered what he might say to these people who had become strangers to him, but he felt certain that without Chas's warning it would *not* have been kind. "In other words, behave like a Christian."

"Yes, if you want to put it that way."

"You want me to behave the way *you* would behave." She looked unsure of what he meant, so he added, "That's not a bad thing, Chas. In fact, it's a very good thing. I appreciate the advice. I will do my best to be kind. But if they start tearing me to shreds, you have to protect me."

"I'll do my best," she said. "And one more thing. Don't tell them the return address label was a mistake."

"Lie to them, you mean."

"No, of course not!" Chas made a noise of disgust. "If one of them comes right out and asks if it was a mistake, tell them the truth, but do it kindly. If it doesn't come up, don't tell them."

"Why?"

"I just . . . it seems like . . ."

"Spit it out, Chas."

"I think they probably believe the address label was an indication that you wanted to be found, and—"

"But I *didn't* want to be found."

"Okay. Okay. Just . . . be kind. Enough said."

"I'll do my best," he said.

She turned to leave, then added, "Forgiveness is a powerful thing, you know."

"For them or me?"

"You have no control over whether they forgive you. Your burden lies in whether you will forgive them. You have no idea what life has been like through your mother's eyes."

Jackson felt stunned speechless. It's not that the thought had never occurred to him. But seeing life through *Chas's* eyes combined with the prospect of actually facing his mother made the concept sink deep into his soul.

Chas gave him a quick kiss before she went back downstairs; then she left him to ponder, glad that their monumental guests had not yet arrived. Then she heard the back door open, and her heart began to pound. She said another quick prayer that she could handle all of this in the best possible way on Jackson's behalf. As she came into the hall and neared the office, she saw two women coming through the back door from the parking lot. While the younger one helped her slow-moving mother come inside, Chas got a pretty good look at them. Jackson's mother came across as plain and simple, with curly gray hair, a dark coat, a subdued floral-print dress that hung below her knees, support hose, and shoes that looked like they might serve some medical purpose. She carried a big purse and had no makeup on her careworn face. Her daughter was the opposite in every regard. Melinda

Lafferty wore high heels that were impractical in any weather, but especially in Montana in the winter. Her jeans were tight, and the colors she wore were loud and attention-grabbing. Her blonde hair was styled big and fluffy. She wore too much makeup, and her nails were professionally done and painted bright pink. Chas would have never in a thousand years looked at either of these women and connected them to Jackson Leeds.

Chas heard Melinda say, "Let's get you settled in so you can rest, Mama, and then I'll get the bags."

Chas hurried to the old woman's side and took hold of her arm. "Here, let me help you," she said, quite accustomed to offering such aid.

She turned surprised eyes toward Chas, then offered a smile that showed a resemblance to Jackson Leeds's. "Thank you, dear," she said, and Chas guided her to the comfortable chair in the office where Jackson had been sitting earlier. "This arthritis has sure slowed me down before my time."

"How's that?" Chas asked once she was seated.

"Very nice, thank you. What's your name, dear?"

"Just call me Chas. And yes, it's my real name." She chuckled and took the old woman's hand, asking just as she would with any guest, "And you are?"

"Melva Leeds," she said. "You're a very sweet girl."

Chas smiled at her, then turned to Melinda, who asked, "Are you the woman I spoke to on the phone?"

"If you're Melinda Lafferty, then I am."

"Oh, marvelous!" Melinda said. "We're so relieved to be here. It's been a long day."

"I can well imagine," Chas said. "Now you can relax. We'll take very good care of you."

"She's a very sweet girl," Melva said to her daughter.

Melinda smiled at her mother and dug into her purse for a credit card, which she handed to Chas. "Have a seat," Chas said, and Melinda gratefully complied.

While Chas ran the card through the system and had Melinda sign for the charges, she wondered and prayed for the right thing to say at the right moment. She sensed that Melva was nervous, and Melinda looked very tired. Melva finally spoke to her daughter in a loud whisper, as if that might keep Chas from hearing, or if it might imply that Chas shouldn't listen. "This is all a waste of time. He won't be here."

"We had to try, Mama," Melinda said with the barest hint of an edge, as if they'd had this conversation a hundred times today already.

Melva countered, "We should just—"

"He's here," Chas said, glad to be able to stop the disagreement. They both looked at her in astonishment. "I assume from everything you've told me that you must be looking for Jackson Leeds." Melva gasped at the name and put a hand over her mouth. "He's here. He was in the room when you called earlier. He knows you're coming."

"And he's *still* here?" Melva asked as if the Red Sea had parted.

"I told you he'd be here, Mama," Melinda said with the same tone. "He wouldn't have given us a return address if he hadn't wanted us to find him." Chas couldn't wait to repeat *that* to Jackson. To Chas she said, "Is he well?"

"He is," she said, then corrected herself, adding, "other than some challenging things related to his job."

"What does he do?" Melva asked.

"I think you should ask him that," Chas said and hurried to get to the point. "He and I will be joining you for supper, if that's all right." Again Melva put a hand over her mouth, as if that were her standard response to news that was difficult to believe. Chas tried to imagine how she might feel to be in the place of either of these women, and she almost felt near tears. "Supper is at six, but he'll be in the parlor at the front of the hall at five-thirty," she said, pointing in that direction.

Melva broke down and wept. Melinda moved to her side and wrapped her arms around her. "It's okay, Mama. Remember what we talked about? It's going to be okay."

Chas allowed them a few minutes while she tried to be discreet. She felt hard-pressed not to cry herself, and mildly angry with Jackson for creating this heartache. Recalling his description of his childhood, however, she had to keep in mind that he'd been deeply wounded. He'd chosen to remain unfindable for twenty-six years, but he hadn't chosen the circumstances that preceded that decision. She simply hoped that healing would take place during this reunion, and that good things might happen in this family in the future. Focusing especially on Jackson's mother, Chas couldn't help thinking that she was very sweet. Of course, it was impossible to know the depth of a person's character in just a few minutes. But what she saw now was a woman grieving over lost years without her only son. Chas wanted to burst in and say, *I'm really hoping to become your daughter-in-law.* She smiled to herself at such a silly thought, then gently interrupted them since Melva had become more calm.

"I can show you to your rooms, if you'd like, and you can get settled in and rest."

"Thank you," Melinda said. "You've been so nice."

"You're a very sweet girl," Melva said again.

Chas helped Melva to her feet, thinking that this woman had to be at least twenty years younger than Granny, but she was almost as limited in her mobility. As they moved slowly up the hall toward the elevator, Chas said, "My grandmother lives here with me. I'd like you to meet her later. I'll bet the two of you would have a lot to talk about."

"Oh, that's very nice," Melva said, "but I'm sure she doesn't want to be bothered with—"

"She likes it when guests visit her. Most people are in too big of a hurry, but if you want some company later, I'll take you to meet her."

"Oh, that's very nice," Melva repeated, and they stepped into the elevator.

* * * * *

Jackson sat at the top of the stairs on the third floor, where he knew he couldn't possibly be seen from the floor below. He'd heard the distant, subtle noises of guests arriving, and voices that he couldn't discern, as the guests got into the elevator. Now his heart pounded as he heard the elevator door open on the second floor. He only heard Chas's voice at first, giving the usual spiel about breakfast, snacks, Internet, and where to find her if they needed anything. Then she said, "This is your room, Melva," and he squeezed his eyes closed. The last time he'd heard that name spoken, it was being yelled by his father in a drunken voice.

"Oh, it's lovely!" Melva said, and Jackson put a hand over his mouth to keep from whimpering. And that was the moment when he realized how much he had missed his mother. He also realized that the reasons he'd left home were not the same reasons he'd stayed away. Maybe he'd been afraid to feel what he was feeling now. Maybe he'd been afraid to acknowledge exactly what Chas had accused him of. *How could a man go twenty-six years and not call his own mother?* He felt like a fool. His anger melted into raw sorrow and regret, and tears trickled down his face while he wondered what he would ever say to them. The feelings only deepened when he heard his sister's voice as well. He heard doors close and knew they were both in their rooms, but he wasn't prepared to have Chas come up the stairs. She stopped when she saw him, but he didn't have time to hide the tears. But she'd already seen a great deal of those from him. How was it possible to find the woman of your dreams at the exact time when your life was falling apart and you couldn't keep yourself together? He couldn't decide if that was a blessing or a curse. Then she sat beside him and took his hand, and he couldn't deny it was the former.

"They both seem very sweet," Chas said. "Your mother broke down and cried like a baby when I told her you were here."

Jackson nodded, and more tears came. "Must run in the family." He coughed to try to get some control. "I've been such a fool," he said. "I don't know what to say."

"Say, 'Hello, it's good to see you; I'm so glad you came.'"

"What if they can't forgive me? What if they're angry?"

"Apologize and take it like a man. Listen with some humility and compassion to what they have to say. I don't think we can ever go wrong with humility and compassion."

Jackson pushed Chas's hair back off her face. "Your grandmother told me I could learn a great deal from you. I didn't know I would learn so much in so short a time."

They heard a door come open, and Chas whispered, "I think Melinda is getting the luggage."

Jackson thought about that for a second, wiped his face on his shirtsleeve, gave Chas a quick kiss, and hurried down the stairs. "Come with me," he said. "You promised."

"I'm right behind you," she said, and they followed Melinda discreetly and at a safe distance out the door and to her car.

Chas held back a little as Melinda opened the trunk. She was lifting a suitcase when Jackson stepped beside her and said, "Let me help you with that." He took the suitcase and set it on the ground by his feet while Melinda watched him, her mouth open, her eyes filled with disbelief, her expression revealing her realization that this man was her long-lost brother.

Jackson made eye contact with his sister, fearing she could hear the pounding of his heart. "Hi," he said, fearing they would both stand there and freeze to death otherwise. She threw her arms around his neck and started to cry. He hesitated a moment before he returned the embrace, and then he hugged her tightly, feeling a little teary himself.

"It's really you," she said, taking his face into her hands. She touched his hair and chuckled. "The last time I saw you, your hair was black as coal and you were covered with pimples."

"Well, thank you for remembering the important stuff," he said.

"You've lost your accent." She sounded astonished.

"Yours is thicker," he said.

"Arkansas'll do that to you," she said as if she were proud of it.

"You look . . . exactly the same," he said, startled by how true it was. Beyond subtle signs of aging in her face, she had the same hairstyle, same makeup, same jewelry.

"Thank you," she said.

Sensing that it was going to get awkward, Jackson took the other suitcase out of the trunk and picked up the one at his feet. "Let me get these for you," he said and headed for the door.

Chas held it open for him, wearing a complacent smile. "Pimples?" she whispered.

"Very funny," he whispered back.

With the women following him up the hall, he had a moment to think, and realized he needed some time alone. He set the luggage in front of the elevator and pushed the button. "Listen," he said to Melinda, "I know Mom's resting, and you probably need to do the same. I know we need to talk, but there's no point talking about things now that will just have to be repeated later. I just wanted to say hi and let you know I'm here, and . . . that I'm glad you came. We'll talk later."

"Okay," she said, looking disappointed. He turned and tossed a glance toward Chas that he hoped she understood, then he took the stairs three at a time, barely getting through the door of his room before he was overcome with helpless sobbing. He cried for the lost years since he'd left home, and for the lost years before then. He cried for his horrible childhood and his adulthood that hadn't been much better. He cried for the grief he'd caused his mother and sister. And swirled into all of that was the anger and betrayal he felt over the horrors that had happened among his coworkers.

Jackson lay back on his bed and stared at the ceiling, trying to reckon with the fact that his mother was here. He didn't have to wonder why his father wasn't here. There were only two possibilities. He was either drunk or dead, the latter being more likely considering how much of his life he'd spent drunk. But perhaps it was time to forgive *both* of his parents.

Jackson made certain he was in the parlor at five-twenty. A few minutes later Chas came and sat beside him, holding his hand. "You okay?"

"I don't know." They heard the elevator bell, then distant voices, and he muttered, "Oh, help. I can't believe I'm doing this."

"Would you have ever gotten on a plane and gone back to Arkansas?" she asked.

"Probably not."

"Then it's good they came here. This is a good thing, Jackson."

"We'll see about that," he said, hoping she was right, but feeling more skeptical on that count. If Chas could see the memories of his childhood, perhaps her outlook might be a little more realistic.

The distraction of the conversation left him a little taken off guard when he looked up to see Melinda and his mother standing in the doorway. He came to his feet, grateful to have Chas standing beside him. His stomach tightened, and his heart beat hard and fast. She'd changed so much. But so had he. She looked old and frail. She only took a glance at him before she put a hand over her mouth and started to weep. Chas nudged him, and he glanced at her to see a nod of encouragement. He stepped closer to his mother, who looked up at him and took his face into her hands, just as Melinda had done. "Oh, my boy. My boy!" she cried and wrapped her arms around him.

Jackson took a deep breath, reminded himself that the past was in the past, and returned her embrace. While she clung to him and cried against his shoulder, he felt his heart softening and his embrace tightening. He glanced at Chas and Melinda and saw them both wiping tears. He felt grateful to Chas for her perspective and guidance that had allowed him to come to this moment without anger or resentment.

"It's okay, Mom," he said, taking hold of her shoulders to look at her. "It's okay. I'm glad you came, and I'm so . . ." his voice broke, "I'm so sorry."

She gave a wan smile and again took his face into her hands. "There's something I need to say, Jackson, my boy, and I hope you'll hear me out."

He nodded and said, "Let's sit down, Mom."

"Not yet," she said. "I've wanted to say this to you for more than twenty years, and I'm not waiting another minute. You hadn't been gone long when I began to realize how dreadful it must have been for you. I understand why you left, and why you didn't want to come back. He's dead now, and none of us were too sorry to see him go, but I know it wasn't just him who treated you bad. There's no excuse for bad mothering, Jackson. I can only say that I just didn't know what I was doing. My kids were grown and gone before I figured out that the way my mama and papa had treated me just wasn't good enough, and I'd done it all wrong. I just need to tell you that I'm sorry." She started to cry again. "I'm so very, very sorry."

"It's okay, Mama," he said and heard himself thirty years younger in his own voice. He was amazed at how easy it was to say those words with sincerity, "It doesn't matter anymore, Mama. It's all in the past, and we're together now."

At this she lost complete control of her emotions again, and Jackson just held her and let her cry, noting that the other women were crying again as well. He shed a few tears himself before his mother quieted down enough for him to look at her and say, "Forgive me . . . for waiting so long. It wasn't right. I can see that now."

Melva laughed through her tears and touched the moisture on his face. "As you said, it doesn't matter anymore. It's all in the past."

He noted that she seemed a little unsteady, and he insisted, "Come and sit down." He guided her to one of the couches and sat beside her. She took his hand into hers, and the other women sat down on the other couch.

"There's one more thing I need to say," Melva said to her son. "I need to thank you for the money." Jackson stole a quick glance at Chas, noting her pleasant surprise. He hadn't really wanted her to know about that. But perhaps he needed to accept that there was no keeping secrets from Chas. "It helped more than you'll ever know," she added.

"I just figured it was the right thing to do," he said and changed the subject. "How long has Dad been gone?"

"Going on twelve years now. It was liver cancer that took him."

"Not a surprise." He couldn't believe how easy it was to talk to her now that the hard things had been said. "And how are you, Mom?"

"I've got this nasty arthritis that makes it hard to get around. It's given me grief for years, but other than that I do okay. I live with Melinda. She takes good care of me."

"It's a good thing somebody does," he said with self-recrimination, but Melva patted his hand as if to say, *We already had that conversation.*

"Tell me what you've been doing all these years," Melva said to Jackson. "You said you were going to join the Marines. That's all I know."

"I spent several years in the Marines," he said. "Mixed in with that I got a four-year degree from a good college in New England. Now I work for the FBI."

"Serious?" Melinda said.

"Isn't that dangerous?" Melva asked.

"Yes, I'm serious, and yes . . ." he exchanged a glance of irony with Chas, "it can be dangerous."

"Marines?" Melva said. "FBI?" She made a concerned noise. "No wonder I've been so worried all these years. Were you ever hurt?"

Chas tightened her gaze on Jackson, wondering the same thing—now that it had come up.

"Clearly I'm fine," Jackson said.

"Do you have a woman in your life?" Melinda asked with a mischievous smile.

"I do," he said with joy in his voice, "but you've already met her." He motioned toward Chas, and Melva's eyes lit up with pleasure. Melinda just looked pleasantly surprised.

"Oh, she's a very sweet girl," Melva said.

"Yes, she is," Jackson said, winking at Chas.

"You're living here, then?" Melinda asked.

"No," he said, "just an extended stay. I hope to . . . one day." Chas smiled at him. "We'll just have to see. Chas and I only met the Sunday before Thanksgiving."

Chas broke a stretch of awkward silence. "He needed a break from his work and came for some peace and quiet."

"Oh, that's nice," Melva said, and Chas heard the timer from the other room.

"That's dinner," Chas said, coming to her feet. "Jackson, why don't you show these ladies to the dining room and I'll have it on in five minutes. And no," she said as she smirked at him, "you can't help."

Chas left the room and peeked in on Granny to see that she was dozing, then she hurried to the kitchen to get the chicken and rice out of the oven and the salad out of the refrigerator. She was putting food out on four plates when Jackson came into the kitchen.

"Look at you," he said, putting his hands on either side of her against the counter so she couldn't move, "all smug and proud of yourself." She smiled, and he chuckled. "If I didn't know better, I'd say you put that return label there on purpose."

"I had nothing to with it, but I'm glad it happened."

"Yes, so am I. Thank you. And don't ask what for. Without you, it would have been a disaster."

"You're welcome," she said. "Now let me go so I can get supper on."

"In a minute," he said and kissed her. Then he let her go.

Supper went well, with good food and pleasant conversation. Chas listened as they talked about people back in Arkansas, and Melva and Melinda asked lots of questions about the Marines and the FBI. Jackson was typically vague and cryptic about personal details, but great at sharing generalities that were very entertaining. Chas slipped away to take some supper to Granny now that she was awake. She came back to serve dessert, and Melva told her again how sweet she was. The conversation continued, and Chas couldn't help but notice how happy both Melva and Melinda seemed. But remarkably,

Jackson did too. She was proud of him. And happy for him. And she loved him. She wanted to be a part of this family, and wanted him to be a part of hers, as small as it was.

When Granny had finished her supper, Chas suggested that Melva come and meet her. While Melva was coming to her feet, Chas said quietly to Jackson, "Why don't you just visit with your sister for a while. I'll watch out for her."

"Thank you," he said and took her hand to kiss it.

Alone with his sister, he asked, "You still married to Lafferty?"

"I dumped that idiot years ago," she said. "But I kept the name because my children have it. Obviously I haven't married again. But I'm doing okay."

"I'm glad to hear it. Tell me *how* you're doing okay. Tell me about the kids. How many? How old are they? What are they doing?"

"One question at a time, little brother. First off, after the divorce I was waitressing and barely getting by. Then one day I thought that I should go into business for myself. I started with a room in my house and soon was able to rent a shop. It's like that thing they say, that one man's junk is another man's treasure. Or woman's, in this case. I take in things women don't want any more and give them a little money for it, then I turn around and sell it to other women. The business is called 'Junk and Treasure.'"

"Catchy. So, it's working for you?"

She laughed softly. "I now have twelve shops and nearly a hundred employees."

"Really?" He chuckled. "That's amazing. Good for you! And I guess that answers one of my questions. I was wondering how you and Mom could afford to fly all this way and stay in a place like this."

"A place where you can afford to stay for weeks?"

"I've done well enough. I've made some good investments, and I haven't had anyone to spend it on."

"Now, that's not true. Mama was always very grateful for the money. I've been able to help her more since the business took off, but there were some tough years in there. The money you sent made a big difference."

"I'm glad I was able to do it," he said. "Do you have what you need now? Does Mom?"

"Oh, we're great," she said, "although I know it means a lot to Mom when she gets help from you. So don't stop on my account. It was always the card that made her cry, but the check inside made her believe you loved her."

"I always loved her," he said. "I was just . . ."

"Angry?" she said. "Yeah. I've been to a lot of counseling to get past angry. Mom's had some counseling too."

"Really?"

"It's helped us both. And since you asked about my kids, they actually turned out pretty good. Sasha is married to a nice guy. They have three kids."

"You're a grandma?"

"I am," she said proudly. "Brian's got a good job, and he joined the Reserves. You'd be proud of him. That's it. They're all grown, and my business is practically running itself, so I try to keep Mom busy. I've been getting her away on little excursions like this every month or so. Well," she motioned toward him, "not like *this.*" She became more serious. "It's good to see you, Jackson."

"It's good to see you, Melinda. I don't mean to beat a dead dog, but I really am sorry I didn't bridge this gap sooner."

"Just keep in touch from now on, okay?"

"Okay," he said firmly. "And you let me know if there's anything you or Mom need. I mean it."

"I will if you give me your phone number."

"Of course," he said, then he took his sister to Granny's room where they all sat and talked and laughed until it became late. Jackson enjoyed just sitting back and observing these four women, wondering how such a moment as this had come to pass. He silently thanked God and figured that Chas being in his life surely had something to do with the presence of miracles in his life. He knew for certain that she was on a lot better terms with their Maker than he was.

CHAPTER 12

The following morning, Chas was surprised to see Jackson arrive in the dining room earlier than usual, wearing slacks, a button-up shirt and tie—much as he'd looked when he'd shown up for Thanksgiving dinner.

"Where are you going?" she asked after he'd given her a brief kiss in greeting.

He looked puzzled. "It's Sunday. I told you I'd go to church with you." Chas was so thrilled and pleasantly surprised that she couldn't come up with a response. "Is there a problem?" he asked.

"No, of course not," she said. "I'd love to have you go with me. I just thought that . . . with your family here, you would . . ."

"They're sleeping in. I told them we'd be gone for a while today. When do we leave?"

"As soon as you eat your breakfast," she said.

While Jackson ate, Chas made certain everything was under control for leaving Polly in charge. She was taken off guard by the multiple assaults of butterflies in her stomach at the thought of walking into church with a man, and having him sit beside her in a setting where she was so accustomed to being entirely alone. She couldn't tell if she was nervous or excited, then concluded that she was excited for herself and nervous on Jackson's behalf. She wondered what he might think, and how he might be received. For a man who had never given a thought to religion prior to his coming here, she hoped the experience wasn't too overwhelming.

When they left the inn, he drove, and she gave him directions. "Something wrong?" he asked, pulling into a parking place at the church building.

"I guess I should warn you."

"About what?" He put the car in Park and turned it off.

"There are a lot of really nice people here, but . . ."

"But?"

"But some of them might be a little *too* nice. They just get really excited when nonmembers show up. Just . . . don't be put off."

"I promise," he said and got out. He opened the passenger door for her and took her hand to help her out, keeping hold of it as they went inside.

Chas saw many curious eyes turn in their direction as they entered the chapel, but Jackson appeared completely relaxed as a few people approached and introduced themselves. Chas kept introductions simple, telling people he was a very good friend. Once they were seated, Jackson put his arm on the bench behind her and asked, "You okay?"

"I'm fine," she said and smiled at him. "It's nice to not be alone." He smiled in return and pressed a quick kiss to her brow. "Oh, I don't know if you should have done that."

He looked alarmed. "Is it against the rules to kiss in here?"

"No." She laughed softly. "But now these people will *really* think there's something romantic going on between us."

"Is that a problem?"

"If it were, I wouldn't have invited you to church." She took hold of his hand. "But what do I tell them when you're not here any more and people ask where you are?"

"Tell them he has every hope of returning . . . permanently."

Chas inhaled his hope, and the meeting began. She discreetly noticed that Jackson was taking in the experience with cautious observation. The talks were focused on being charitable, and he listened attentively. When the meeting was over, they were greeted by a few more ward members, and the bishop approached and introduced himself.

"I'm Bishop Wegg," he said to Jackson, offering a firm handshake and a smile. "I'd heard a rumor that Chas had a man in her life. I'm glad to know it's true. It's nice to have you here."

"A pleasure," Jackson said.

"We hope to see you here again," the bishop said.

"Oh, I'll be back," Jackson replied with a smile.

They chatted comfortably for a couple of minutes before the bishop moved on. By then everyone else had gone to Sunday School classes.

"Now what?" Jackson asked.

"I usually go to a couple of classes, but I'd already decided I was going to skip them today. I think we should spend some time with your mother and sister."

"They're not going anywhere," he said. "We can stay if you want."

"Okay," Chas said and led him to the Gospel Doctrine class where they found a couple of chairs near the back of the room. During the discussion of a New Testament text, Jackson again seemed attentive rather than bored; however, when that was over, Chas felt it would be best to go home and save the experience of sending him off to priesthood meeting without her for another time when he was better prepared. When she told him that the men and women separated for the next hour, he was more eager to leave.

"Thank you," Chas said when they were in the car.

"For what?"

"For going with me."

"Not a problem," he said, driving toward the inn.

"Have you ever been to church before in your life?"

"Only for funerals and weddings," he said.

"Then it all must seem very strange."

"Not very," he said. "In fact, it wasn't nearly so strange as I might have imagined a Mormon church meeting to be."

"You told the bishop you would be back. Was that based on religion or me?"

He chuckled and took her hand. "I'm mildly curious about the religion. I want to spend the rest of my life in the same room with you, wherever that may be. I hope that's the right answer, because that's the honest one."

"I would never want you to be anything but honest with me."

"And vice versa."

They returned to the inn to find Melva and Melinda in the parlor. Polly had fed them a good breakfast, which they'd just finished because they'd slept very late. Chas watched Jackson greet both women with a kiss on the cheek, then he pulled off his tie while he sat on the couch beside his mother to chat. It was truly a day of miracles.

Melva and Melinda stayed three nights at the inn, and Chas thoroughly enjoyed being a witness to the miracles of healing and forgiveness taking place. Jackson said more than once to her when they were alone together that he deeply regretted not bridging this gap sooner. She told him that regret accomplished nothing because the past couldn't be changed, and she suggested that perhaps the intensity of feelings throughout the long separation had helped the healing to be more deep and complete. Chas was also a witness to Jackson surprising Polly with a big hug.

"What was that for?" she asked with a giggle.

"For being efficient with those address labels," he said, and she giggled again.

During the days that Melva and Melinda were in town, Chas had Polly and Jen put in extra hours to cover for her so that she and Jackson could take them out on the town to see some local sights. They took a drive through Washoe Park, which looked lovely in the winter, but Chas told them they should all come back in the summer when they could walk through it and enjoy an entirely different kind of beauty. They also went to the library, which was a beautiful old building that had been well preserved. Chas discovered that Jackson really liked old buildings—another thing they had in common. The following day they went to a movie at the Washoe Theater, which was also a beautiful building. The building definitely caught Jackson's attention more than the movie, but Chas had seen the building before. She enjoyed sitting next to Jackson and sharing his popcorn. She also enjoyed seeing him so happy, especially considering the current challenges in his life.

When it came time for Melva and Melinda to leave for the airport, they all cried a little—except for Melva, who cried a lot. But there was more joy than sorrow in this farewell, since Jackson had given all of his contact information to both his mother and sister, and he promised to call them both every week, and even to pay a visit as soon as his work allowed. From the way he said that, Chas knew that his mind was drifting toward the need to return to Virginia and to his job.

Jackson felt a stark letdown after his mother and sister left. Their being here had made it easier to push aside all that was going on back in Virginia with the people he cared for there. The intensity of his grief and shock had settled, but he felt concerned and unsettled over the matter. Once again he made calls to several people, just to touch base with them and learn all he could about what had happened and where things stood now. He was able to talk with the two men who were in the hospital, and felt much better after he did. They were both coming along nicely and were in good spirits. One would be going home in a couple of days, and the other a few days after that. They both told him they were grateful to be alive, and that the plus side to all of this was they would get to spend more time with their families through the holidays while they were recuperating.

Jackson didn't want to, but felt that he needed to call the widow of the man who had taken his own life. He talked it through with Chas, and she helped him see the perspective that Ken's wife was probably struggling with more grief and heartache than Dave's wife, Mary, because Dave had at least died an honorable death. In both cases, the wives were innocent victims. He appreciated Chas's feminine perspective on the matter, and took her suggestion to send flowers to both widows. But first he called them. He'd spoken to Mary a few times since Dave's death, but he felt the need to connect with her again. She was doing as well as could be expected, but she told him more than once how much she appreciated his calls. And she told him something she hadn't shared with him before, that Dave had often told her how much he admired and respected him, and what a privilege it had been to work with him. Jackson could only say, "The feeling was mutual."

The call to the other widow started out a little rough, but once he was able to say that he wanted her to know he'd been thinking about her and hoped she was doing well, they were able to have a straightforward conversation. She admitted that her husband hadn't been himself for a very long time, and she'd been worried. She confessed that she was struggling with guilt over feeling some relief that he was gone. She worried over what other damage he might have caused if he were still alive. Jackson was able to say that he was struggling with the same feelings. They both cried a little, which felt strange, since they had met only briefly on a few occasions. He apologized for not having been at the memorial service since he was out of state. She told him that she'd been amazed at how many people from the agency had come, and how kind they had been. He was glad to hear that. He wished her well and gave her his contact information, making her promise that she would call him if there was anything he could ever do to help.

After the calls had been made and the flowers ordered, Jackson sat in the parlor while Granny slept and Chas was in the office with Polly. He tried to read the paper but couldn't focus. He wondered if the feeling he had that he needed to get back to work was simply habit, which had been motivated by connecting with the people he knew there, or if he really needed to be there. The thought of leaving before Christmas felt horrid. At Thanksgiving he had believed that he'd be home long before Christmas, even if it had meant spending Christmas all alone. He'd now received multiple invitations to spend Christmas Day with families who would include him in all the fun and fineness of a good holiday. But he wanted to be here with Chas. At Thanksgiving he'd been concerned about imposing himself on their family celebrations. Now Chas and Granny felt like family to him, and he knew they felt the same about him. He knew that Chas's friends would also be a part of the celebrations, but he'd grown fond of Polly and Charlotte, and her children, and the whole prospect seemed delightful.

But he wondered if staying would only prolong the inevitable— the need to go back and face what he'd left behind. Or did he need to face it at all? He could call right now and tell them he was retiring. The work would get shifted to someone else, and he could go back later and clean out his apartment. There wasn't much he owned that couldn't be sold or given away. He could ask Chas to marry him, and then take up his new life as an innkeeper—provided she said yes, of course. He could start taking more of an active role in the running of the inn, and he could be happy here for the rest of his life. He knew he could. He didn't even have to question it. And yet he felt drawn back to Virginia. Was it habit, or his gut telling him that he needed to be there? Perhaps his spending Christmas there could help his friends who were struggling with the same emotional whirlwind that he was facing. He felt confused and uncertain, and thought of what Chas had told him about the way she made decisions. He'd never made prayer a part of his life at all until he'd met Chas. And since then it had been nothing more than a silent expression of gratitude here and there. Now he wondered if God would answer his prayers the way He did for Chas. Could he be given divine guidance on the matter at hand? Deciding that there was nothing to lose, he closed his eyes and simply asked God to help him make the right choices at this crucial time in his life. He'd barely finished the thought when Chas came into the room.

"You okay?" she asked.

"Just thinking," he said, holding out a hand for her. She took it and sat beside him. He put his arm around her, and she tucked her feet up beneath her, resting her head on his shoulder.

"Tell me," she urged. He hesitated, and she said, "You're wondering if you should be going back."

"How do you do that?" he asked.

"I just know you, but I was still guessing."

"Well, you're right. I admit it. I hate to even face it or bring it up, but . . ."

"I know, Jackson. I understand." She wrapped her arms around him, and he heard her voice quaver. "I don't want you to go, but I understand."

He blew out a harsh breath. "I could retire right now," he said, "and I'm certain the work would go on without me just fine. There are some loose ends on a few cases that I would like to take care of myself, but the world wouldn't end if I turned them over to somebody else." He went on to explain in more detail all of his thoughts and feelings, realizing as he did so that it had become clear to both of them that he needed to go back. He just didn't know when or for how long.

"You don't have to decide right this minute," she said. "I can understand why it might be good for you to be among friends there for Christmas, but I'm not going to pretend that I don't want you here for the holidays. It just won't feel right without you. However, I'm not going to whine and try to manipulate you into staying for the wrong reasons. You have to do what you feel is best."

Jackson heard courage and determination in her voice. It made him feel loved, and it made him feel torn. He wanted to expound on those feelings, but he settled for saying, "My mother's right about you. You are a very sweet girl." He pressed a kiss into her hair. "And I was right about you, too."

"How's that?"

"Falling in love with you is the best thing I ever did."

"Amen," she said, and they both chuckled.

The cordless phone she always carried with her rang, and she reached for it, saying, "I've got to get it. Polly went on an errand." She pushed the button and answered, "Dickensian Inn. How may I help you?" Jackson thought of when he'd called here, not so many weeks ago—the first time he'd heard her voice. If he'd only known how she would help him! "Yes," she said brightly, "I do believe we have at least one room available." She was up and on her way out of the room. "Just give me a second here and I'll see."

She came back a few minutes later, and he said, "You owe me dinner out."

"Do I?" she asked, and he knew that she knew where he was going with this.

"I've gone *more* than a week without a drop of liquor, and Granny even offered to share her brandy with me more than once."

"I'm *very* impressed," she said, sitting beside him again. "You did it. What I'm wondering is why."

"Why what?"

"Why were you willing to take on my challenge and win? Is this some kind of Marine-slash-FBI kind of willpower? You just need to prove it for the sake of proving it?"

He looked into her eyes. "You really don't know, do you?"

"Know what?"

"I thought you could read me."

Chas laughed. "Sometimes. And sometimes you are like a stone, Mr. Jackson Leeds. I *do* know that you dumped out the liquor *before* we had that conversation . . . when you took on the challenge."

"How did you know that?"

"I clean your room, remember? You don't call me Detective for nothing."

"That's true," he said. "I suppose I *did* prove something. I proved you wrong. I can clearly live without liquor if I choose."

"I'm impressed. And you didn't freak out or throw a fit or anything."

"I think you have a short memory. It wasn't an easy week."

"No, but that had nothing to do with what we're talking about."

"It most certainly does. Under any other circumstances, I *would* have been drinking. Instead I've become addicted to you. But I'm glad you're impressed, because my main goal in life is to impress you."

"Since you put it that way . . . I'd be even more impressed if you would just stop drinking altogether—forever. You don't need that stuff. When you go back I would hope you could remember what you've proven. Dump it all out and don't buy any more. There're all kinds of wonderful things to drink in this world that don't rot your guts out and impair your judgment. But hey, you're changing the subject. I want to know why you did it."

"You asked me to."

Chas chuckled. "You're not trying to start one of those meaningless relationships here, are you?"

His expression didn't hold even a hint of the humor she was attempting to feed into the conversation. In fact, his seriousness was so intense and his silence so drawn out that her heart began to pound. Just when she thought he would never speak, he said, just one decibel above a whisper, "If I thought it was meaningless, I wouldn't have stopped drinking." He took her hand. "You inspire me, Chas. I told you that a long time ago. That's why I did it. And for you, I will dump it all out when I go home. If I feel like having a drink, I'm going to call you instead."

"Deal," she said firmly, then gave him a kiss. "I love you, Jackson. And I'm glad you love me. But don't do it for me. Do it to make your life better."

"Okay, point taken . . . but it still doesn't hurt to have a woman in my life who inspires me."

"I won't dispute that . . . at least the part about being in your life." Silence made her thoughts drift, and she finally had to admit to them. "I don't want you to leave, Jackson."

"I don't *want* to leave, but I think it's inevitable."

"When?"

"I don't know. I don't want to talk about that. Let's talk about how you owe me dinner, although that's entirely ridiculous because you give me dinner every day."

"This is different, although I confess, when I said that I would take you to the finest restaurant in town and buy you a meal you will never forget, I was actually talking about here. I just thought I could fix you something really special."

"That's very noble," he said, "but I think it would be nice for you to get out and *not* have to cook. And when you get right down to it, I think that I owe *you* dinner, since you're the one who inspired me. So, what do you say tomorrow we go out . . . for something really special?"

"Deal," she said. "You talked me into it. And how about this evening we watch a movie?"

"Where? In Granny's room?" It was the only place he could think of that had a TV, except for their private rooms, which would not have been appropriate for a woman like Chas. She stood up and opened what he'd always assumed to be some kind of cupboard or armoire that looked authentically Victorian. Inside was a nice television and video equipment. "Tah dah!"

"Very clever," he said. "You talked me into it. What are we watching?"

"My favorite Christmas movie, of course."

"And that would be?" He motioned with his hand.

"Scrooge, of course."

"Of course," he said and chuckled. "And will the ghost of Charles Dickens be watching it with us?"

"Maybe," she said, sounding much like her grandmother.

After supper, Chas made certain that Granny had everything she needed, and left her to watch a couple of programs that were her favorites. While Jackson built a fire in the parlor fireplace, Chas made popcorn and Kool-Aid. With the Christmas tree lights adding a sparkle to the room, they settled onto the couch, and the spirit of Christmas unfolded through a quality rendition of *A Christmas Carol*. Jackson was touched to see that Chas actually cried a little.

"How many times have you seen this?" he asked. They had remained where they were with the fire burning low and the Christmas lights twinkling.

"At least once every year, but it always makes me cry. It's such an amazing story. Dickens was truly inspired."

"I can't dispute that."

"And the message is so powerful."

"What is that?" he asked, mostly because he wanted to hear *her* interpretation of its theme.

"That people can change. Many people are given opportunities to make their lives better, but they choose not to act on them. Scrooge was given a marvelous opportunity to change, and he took it. And through the changes he made in his life, he was able to affect many other lives for good."

"You're saying that even people like me can change for the better?" he asked, his tone mildly facetious. "Say, for instance, that I stopped drinking, or . . . forgave my mother. Stuff like that?"

"Exactly stuff like that," she said and kissed him.

He smiled, and she settled her head comfortably against his shoulder, not wanting to think about what it would be like when he left, and praying for the hundredth time that he would choose to at least stay for Christmas. And she prayed for at least the thousandth time that when all of the current challenges in Jackson's life were settled, he would choose to spend the rest of his life with her.

Out of the silence, Jackson said, "I have a confession to make." He put his head in her lap and stretched out on the couch so that he could look up at her.

"Ooh. I can't wait."

"Charles Dickens saved my life."

Chas took a moment to gauge his expression. "You're serious."

"Of course I'm serious. Do you think I would joke about something like that in a place like this?" He chuckled. "No, seriously. One of the only good things that happened in my youth was this teacher I had in junior high. I guess she saw something in me besides the white trash kid that even Social Services couldn't save. She had a way of getting through to me with the way she taught, and then she sent me home with a Dickens novel. It was *Great Expectations*. I remember reading late at night with a flashlight. I loved it. I became completely lost in it. And then I wanted another, and another. I read them all. They gave me hope and perspective. That's why I chose *this* place when I was Googling a bed-and-breakfast."

"Really?"

"Really. I put the word Victorian in my search, because I love Victorian decor and architecture—probably a side effect of my love for Dickens and his time period. But yeah, it was the Dickens thing that brought me here."

"Wow! That's amazing." She let out a delighted little laugh.

"Yes, it is. I guess that means Mr. Dickens brought us together."

"So he did. You'd better tell Granny this story."

"I already have," he said, "but I needed to tell you, too."

"It's a great story. But how did he save your life, exactly, besides giving you hope and perspective? I can tell there's more by that look on your face."

"Very good, Detective. Yes, there's more. As I got closer to being eighteen, I wondered what to do with my life. I didn't have a good GPA or the money to go to college, so that didn't seem possible. I knew I couldn't stay in my parents' home, or even my hometown. I hated everything about it, and as you've figured out, I was full of a lot of anger. I was afraid of joining the military, even though it offered some solutions. I knew it would take hard work and sacrifice, and of course, there's always the concern about the danger involved. And then I felt drawn to rereading *A Tale of Two Cities*. Then I read that last line . . . 'It is a far, far better thing that I do, than I have ever done; it is a far, far better rest that I go to than I have ever known.'"

Chas was amazed at how he quoted it perfectly, and she knew that he did because she knew it well. "That's very impressive."

"I've lived by those words, Chas, because they changed my life. I was so in awe of the concept that Sydney Carton could go to the guillotine on behalf of Charles Darnay in order to give the woman he loved a better life. And that's when I knew that my life could have value in the military. That, if nothing else, I could sacrifice and serve on behalf of my country to make life better for someone else; then my life would have meaning and purpose. It wasn't just a way to get out of town. It became a way of life. I lost my fear of dying when I came to believe that something good could come out of it. But I think it was that very way of thinking that's kept me alive, and made it possible for me to . . ."

"To what?" she asked when he stopped abruptly.

"I was just going to say something that I've never said out loud before. It sounds . . . arrogant, perhaps."

"Just say it. If it sounds arrogant, I'll be sure to let you know."

He chuckled. "I'm certain you wouldn't be afraid to do that."

"So, just say it."

"I was going to say that I think my attitude and determination had a lot to do with being able to achieve a higher rank at a young age, and to receive the commendations that I was given. And because of that I was able to go into the FBI with a better position and better pay. My philosophy has carried over into the work I do there, and I think it's served me well. That's all."

"That doesn't sound arrogant in the slightest. It makes me proud of you."

"I've never really cared much what people thought of me or what I do, but I have to admit that knowing *you* are proud of me feels good. That's because I respect your opinion. And *that* is how Charles Dickens saved my life. His writings have had an impact on me, over and over again. I can't count the times I've been confronted with a difficult situation, and then I would remember what one of his characters did, and it would give me a new idea or a different perspective."

"That's remarkable," she said. "It's almost like we're soul mates, or something."

"Yeah," he said, tightening his gaze on her. "That is one of *many* reasons I believe we're soul mates."

She looked intrigued. "What are the other reasons?"

"I know better than to think that you haven't noticed the commonalities between us."

"I've noticed, but I want to know what *you've* noticed."

"You married a man who joined the military at a very young age. I've wished that Julie would have had the conviction and commitment you did, but then it probably would have ended in divorce anyway."

"Maybe not."

"Or maybe."

"I do think that you and Martin have a lot in common," she said.

"I'll take that as a compliment, as opposed to a reason to be jealous of your feelings for him."

"He's been dead for twelve years, Jackson. And yes, it's one of the highest compliments I could give. He wasn't perfect, but he was a good man, and his patriotic convictions are much like yours. What else do we have in common?"

"We both love Granny," he said, and she laughed.

They talked a long while about the things they had in common, ignoring the things that they didn't—most specifically the clash of homes and careers and religion, and how it seemed inevitable that those things would come between them. Chas chose not to think about that now, and knew that he was choosing to do the same.

The following day Jackson had a longer-than-normal visit with Granny, enjoying her stories and antics. She was perkier than usual, and Chas joined them a little way into the conversation. The three of them talked and laughed until Granny was tired and it was time for Chas to get back to work.

That evening, they left Polly to care for Granny and the inn so they could go out to dinner. She'd decided to just stay the night since she hated to go home to an empty apartment after dark. When they were on their way out, Polly said, "I'm just thinking of moving in here. I spend more time here than I do at home, and I bet you'd give me a better deal than my rent."

Chas chuckled and said, "It's worth considering. Thank you, as always. We won't be late."

"Have fun," Polly said.

Dinner out proved to be a delightful experience, one that Chas would always cherish. Looking at Jackson across the table while they talked so much that their meal dragged on far longer than normal, she wondered how he could have changed her life so quickly, and how she had ever managed without him. She knew she'd been lonely, but she'd never been able to acknowledge just how much until now. Oh, how she dreaded having him leave! She wanted to beg him to stay for Christmas, but didn't even want to bring it up.

They returned to the inn to find Polly and Granny playing Rummy. All of the expected guests had arrived and were settled into their rooms. The breakfast and cleaning schedules for the following day were all prepared, and everything was in order. Chas and Jackson sat to watch the end of the game and cheered when Granny won.

Polly pretended to be hurt and went to bed. Jackson and Chas stayed when it was apparent Granny was still in a talkative mood. When she began to wind down and admitted to being tired, Jackson gave her a tight hug and a kiss on the forehead, something that had become a habit between them. Then she took his hand into both of hers and said, "You're a fine young man, Jackson. It's been so wonderful having you here. I hope that when you have to leave, you'll always know that you can come back."

"I *do* know that, Granny," he said and kissed her brow again. "You sleep well, and I'll see you tomorrow." She smiled and patted his hand.

Chas kissed Jackson goodnight at the foot of the stairs and thanked him for a wonderful evening. He kissed her again and went upstairs to read a little and go to sleep.

While Chas went through the usual routine of helping her grandmother get to bed and make certain she was comfortable, she thought of what a privilege it was to have this precious woman in her life. She recalled the tenderness between Granny and Jackson that had become habitual, and her gratitude deepened.

"What are you thinking about?" Granny asked as Chas sat on the edge of the bed to tuck the old woman in and kiss her according to years of habit.

"I was thinking how lucky I am to have been raised by you, and to be able to take care of you now."

Granny squeezed her hand tightly. "I'm the lucky one, honey. You've been such a joy to me."

"But?"

"But what?"

"I see a 'but' in your eyes, Granny. You can't fool me."

Granny patted her hand. "You need more in your life than an old woman to care for."

"I have the inn, Granny. I'm very happy."

"Happier lately, I've noticed."

"You *are* a shrewd old woman, just like Jackson said."

"Shrewd or not, listen to an old woman who sees more than you might think she does."

"What do you mean?"

"There's something I need to say, and it's important."

"I'm listening," Chas said, becoming especially alert.

"He loves you, Chas," Granny said.

She felt only mildly surprised. Granny had seen them holding hands, and she knew that they were spending a great deal of time together, but their feelings for each other hadn't actually been discussed.

Granny went on. "I've seen it in his eyes from the first time he sat down in this room. He loves you, my dear girl. Don't let him go. Don't let this opportunity pass you by."

"We're very different, Granny. He has a life far away from here, and you know I could never leave the inn. I love him too—and he knows it, but I don't know if something permanent is possible."

"Geographical differences can be worked out. They're not so important in the grand scheme of things. You would have followed Martin anywhere. Would you really choose an old house over the love of a good man?" Chas honestly couldn't answer that question. The house was stable, predictable; it wouldn't die on her. For that and many more reasons, she doubted she could ever leave here. As if Granny could read her mind, she added, "He's a good man. Don't close your heart to him because you're afraid of getting hurt again. Promise me." Chas hesitated, and Granny insisted, "Promise me."

"I promise," Chas said, knowing her heart was already a lot more open than it had been a few weeks ago. But she wondered if she had been steeling herself for an inevitable end to this relationship, as opposed to *truly* hoping that it could work out. Or perhaps she'd believed that the only way it could work out would be for Jackson to give up *his* life and come here. Whatever the case, Granny's words struck her deeply and gave her much food for thought.

She kissed Granny again and told her how she loved her, then she went to her own room and pondered the situation and her feelings for a long time before she was actually able to sleep. She woke up with a determination to enjoy the present and not worry about the future, because there was so little she could do about it. And yet her underlying prayer was that Jackson would decide to retire and spend the rest of his life here with her.

* * * * *

Jackson was barely out of the shower and dressed when the phone on his bedside table rang. It took him a moment to get his bearings and pick it up, simply because he'd never heard it ring before.

"Hello," he said.

"Jackson." Chas sounded so upset that his heart immediately pumped with adrenaline.

"What's wrong?" he demanded.

"I need you. I'm in Granny's room."

That was all he needed to hear before he went down the stairs so fast he nearly fell twice. Entering the open doorway, he didn't know what he'd expected, but it wasn't to find Chas laying in the center of the bed on top of the covers, her arms wrapped tightly around her grandmother, who was beneath the covers, the top of her silver head barely showing.

"Is she ill?" he asked, crossing the room to stand beside the bed.

Chas looked up at him with red, watery eyes. "She's dead."

Jackson's stomach tightened, and he went to his knees, instinctively putting his fingers to the old woman's throat to check for a pulse. He knew he wouldn't find it when he felt the temperature of her skin. It was cold enough that he knew she'd probably been dead for hours.

"You don't have to check," Chas said through an ongoing deluge of tears. "She's obviously gone."

"Sorry," he explained. "Habit."

Chas pulled her attention away from her grief long enough to consider the implication of his words. "You've found many dead bodies?"

"Far too many," he said, then he touched Granny's face with tender reverence, and his voice betrayed a rustle of emotion. "But they never looked like this. She looks so . . . at peace."

"She is," Chas said through copious tears. "Someone came to get her from the other side."

Jackson met her eyes, but she could see more intrigue than skepticism. Not many weeks ago she felt certain it would have been the other way around. "Who?"

"I don't know. Maybe Walter; my mother perhaps. Or her parents, or . . ." She let out an unexpected chuckle that seemed so out of place at the moment that she couldn't hold back another.

"You're laughing?" Jackson asked.

"I was just going to say . . . or maybe it was Charles Dickens."

"Maybe," Jackson said with a smirk, but it was a kind smirk. More seriously he asked, "And how do you know that someone came to get her?"

"I just know. They were still here when I came in the room and found her. I can't explain how I know. I just know." This brought on an explosion of tears, and she pressed her face into her grandmother's hair and wept. Jackson felt helpless and too close to the grief to remain objective. He'd grown to love the old woman in the short time he'd been here. But even more so, he'd grown to love the woman grieving for this loss. And he didn't know what to say. He'd lost count of the people he'd had to inform of the death of a loved one, and he'd witnessed all levels of grief. But he'd been detached, more concerned with watching for clues in their behavior. Now all he could see was the stark evidence of how much Chas loved this woman, who was the only mother Chas had ever known, the only real family she'd ever had. Jackson just held her hand and let her cry, shedding a few tears of his own. He thought of how the situation had been reversed from not so many days ago, when he'd been falling apart and she had held him together. He hoped that he had learned enough from her support of him at the time to be the strength that she needed and deserved, now that the tables had turned.

CHAPTER 13

Chas was amazed at Jackson's efficiency as he informed Polly of what had happened. Then he started making necessary phone calls with just a little guidance from her, while Polly called Jen in for extra help. During the preparations for the funeral, as she dealt with the shock and grief of losing her grandmother, the inn ran efficiently with Chas hardly lifting a finger, and Jackson was never far away with an ear to listen and a shoulder to cry on.

When Bishop Wegg and one of his counselors came to help with the funeral plans and offer any assistance they could, Chas noticed that they talked with Jackson for a long while after their business was completed. He told her later that he thought they were good men and he was impressed. He was also impressed with the visits from the Relief Society sisters, and with the help they offered.

Polly insisted that she was just going to bring some of her things and move into the room that was rented the least, and stay there for the time being. She didn't want Chas to be alone, and they all knew it was better to have her there for many reasons. Having Polly under the roof to help keep the business under control was a tremendous blessing. And Chas had never before dealt with the issue of being romantically involved with a guest at the inn, but with her grandmother gone, she felt it was more appropriate to have someone else staying there, especially on nights when no other guests were there. She told Jackson it was more a matter of principle than any real concern, and he seemed to understand, even though he didn't comment.

Jackson called his sister's home and spoke to both her and his mother, telling them about Granny's passing and everything that was going on related to it. His mother was down with a terrible cold; otherwise, she insisted, they would have come for the funeral. He assured her that there was no need to be concerned over that. She thanked him for calling, and the next day a beautiful floral arrangement arrived for Chas from his mother and sister. She called to personally thank them, and he noticed that she visited with his mother for more than an hour.

Two days after Chas had found her grandmother cold and unmoving, she felt no incentive whatsoever to get out of bed. She knew that her work would be taken care of, and she felt exhausted from all the tears she'd cried. She heard a knock at the door and forced herself close enough to reality to call, "Who is it?"

"It's Jackson. Can I come in?"

"It's not locked," she called back and heard the door open, but she didn't turn to look at him.

"I brought you some cocoa," he said, and she heard the cup being set on the bedside table.

"Thank you," she said and stuck her hand out from beneath the covers.

Jackson slid a chair next to the bed and sat where he could comfortably hold her hand. Chas squeezed it tightly and turned over enough to peer at him over the edge of the covers. "Why are you so good to me?"

"That's like asking why I exist." She raised a brow, and he added, "I just do." He leaned closer and pushed her hair back off her face. "How are you . . . really?"

"I'm awful, as you can see." She started to cry and couldn't believe how endless the source of tears could be. "I don't have any trouble with knowing it was her time to go. She was old and tired, and she's in a better place with people she loves. I just . . . miss her. She's all I had."

Jackson pressed a hand to her face, wanting to tell her that she had him, but he wasn't naive enough to think that he could sit here in the midst of her grief and make promises about a future that was still vague and uncertain.

Chas felt so lonely and starved for his company that she said without thinking, "Come closer. Hold me."

Jackson had to lean back in the chair and put his strongest willpower in check to keep from immediately heeding her request. He *wanted* to hold her, all day and all night. He wanted to give her all his strength, anything that might help her get through this. But he needed to be rational. *One* of them had to be. Trying to keep it light, he said, "Now, that doesn't sound like the woman I know. Inviting a man into her bed."

"That's not what I meant."

"I know it's not what you meant, but we both know it's too close to the edge of a cliff. I may not see everything in life the way you do, but I'm smart enough to know that a person should never compromise their own rules—especially when they're not thinking clearly. And no human being who is grieving should be making decisions that go contrary to their rules. You wouldn't respect me if I actually got any closer than this right now." He squeezed her hand to remind her that he was still holding it. He couldn't tell if that was disappointment or respect in her eyes. He chose to think of it as respect, if only to aid his own convictions, then he lightened the mood. "Besides, what would Granny think if she knew you were breaking her rules already? What was it? All four feet on the floor? She's probably in the room with us right now, making sure we mind our p's and q's."

Chas laughed and then cried. "I thought you didn't believe in angels."

"I believe in Granny. And I believe in you. If you believe in angels, then I believe it, too. If anyone had the right to be an angel, it would be your grandmother. And if anyone had the right to be watched over by such an angel, it would be you."

He saw new tears in her eyes, but there was more hope than despair in their glimmer. He touched her face and kissed her brow, then he leaned back in the chair, keeping hold of her hand.

"I'm so grateful you're here," she said.

"Well, it's nice to be good for something for a change."

"I need you."

He squeezed her hand. "And I will be right here, holding your hand, for as long as you need me."

"There's something I want to tell you," Chas said.

"Okay." He leaned forward and kissed her hand.

"The night before Granny died . . . when I think about it now, it was like . . . she knew she was going. When I tucked her into bed, she said there was something important she needed to tell me. The more I think about it, the more important I think it must be."

"Why?"

"It was about you."

"Did she tell you to steer clear of me, that I was no good for you?"

Chas wasn't affected by his attempt at humor, even if he had been at least partially serious. "No, quite the opposite, in fact." She took a deep breath. "She told me that you love me." Jackson raised his brows but didn't comment. "Of course I already knew that. But I never told her that it had been spoken between us. And I have to know if you told her."

"No." He shook his head. "We talked a little about you, but it was never about our relationship."

"She said she had seen it in your eyes the first time you walked into her room."

Chas checked his expression for a reaction but found him more unreadable than usual. She hurried to get to the point. "I just wanted you to know what she said, and I need to tell you what else she said . . . about me. I just have to say it."

"I'm listening," he said when she didn't say anything at all.

"She told me not to . . . close my heart . . . because I might be afraid of getting hurt again. She made me promise. I *did* promise. What else could I say? I've wondered how exactly to go about keeping my promise, and I've realized that I can't do it alone. So, I want you to know that whether anything permanent comes of this or not, I want to learn how to open my heart. I don't want to be afraid anymore. I'm trying to say that . . . *you* told me a long time ago that I was afraid to feel. I'm telling you that you were right; you were both right. Maybe that's why you came here . . . to teach me to open my heart again."

Jackson studied her eyes for a long moment, then said, "I don't think I could ever teach you a tenth of what you've taught me, Chas. I will never be the same . . . whatever happens. And for the record, I've seen your heart open a great deal since I said that. I recognize the signs, because I've felt the same thing happening to me. I *do* love you. Don't ever forget it."

"I love you too," she said, but she still had to wonder if her opening heart might be broken when their lives took separate paths.

After a minute he said, "Granny *was* a shrewd old woman."

"So I've heard," Chas said.

He chuckled and shook his head. "She knew. She knew even before I knew."

"Knew what?" she asked, if only to hear him say it.

"From that very first day, I just wanted to be in the same room with you. And she could see it. She knew that I was falling in love with you." He laughed softly and added, "I wonder what else she knew that she didn't tell us. Maybe she could have foreseen our future if we had bothered to ask."

"She did mention something about that."

"Really?"

"She told me that geographical differences could be worked out, that they weren't so important in the grand scheme of things. She reminded me that I would have followed Martin anywhere, and she asked me if I would give up the love of a good man for an old house."

Jackson let that sink in for a minute. "I could never ask that of you," he insisted. "This is more than an old house. It would break my heart to see you leave all of this behind. I could never live with it."

"But you have the work you love somewhere else; it's *your* life."

"It's temporary, Chas."

"For how long?"

"I don't know. But neither of us knows at this point whether or not being together permanently is right. And neither of us should be worried about such things under the present circumstances. Let's just get through the funeral and take it from there, okay?"

"Okay," she said and sat up to drink her cocoa, terrified that once the funeral was over he would be gone and she would be left to face the holidays without her Granny. The thought seemed too much to bear.

* * * * *

The night before the funeral, Jackson found Chas sitting in her grandmother's chair, wrapped in one of the little blankets that Granny had often had over her lap. He pulled a chair close to her and took her hand.

"I know you've heard it a hundred times," she said, "but I still can't believe she's gone. I thought she would get sick, or something. I thought I would have some warning that it was coming. I'm glad she *didn't* get sick. It's how every person wants to go, right? Just go to sleep and wake up on the other side? I'm glad for her. I just feel so . . . unprepared."

"Your feelings are completely understandable, Chas, and you can repeat them to me as many times as you need to."

She looked at him and squeezed his hand. "I don't know what I would have ever done without you. I've thanked God over and over for sending you here . . . now. I didn't know it was her time to go, but God did, and He sent you to help me through."

"Funny, I was certain he sent me here so that *you* could help *me* through."

"It's been eventful for both of us."

"Yes, it has," he said and kissed her hand.

Jackson watched her eyes take on the distant expression that had become typical in the days since Granny had left them. They had talked and cried together many times in between all of the preparations that had to be dealt with. But occasionally she just zoned out, and he allowed her the silence to try to accept this altered reality. He knew the feeling well, even if for him it had been less personal; more traumatic perhaps, but less personal.

When the silence dragged on longer than usual, he felt compelled to tell her something that he'd been meaning to for a couple of days, but the moment had never seemed right. Without preamble he said, "I'm staying for Christmas." She turned toward him, her eyes showing surprise, then relief, then tears. "If that's all right with you." She threw her arms around him and cried.

Chas knew her tears in that moment were more from relief than sorrow. When she had calmed down, she looked at Jackson and said, "I just didn't know how I could face Christmas without her when there's so little time to get used to having her gone. Now I think I can actually look forward to it, instead of dreading it."

"Me too," he said.

"But I didn't want to say anything, because I didn't want you to stay because you feel sorry for me, or—"

"I'm staying because I want to be here—and because I know you need me. But it's nice to feel needed." His voice turned facetious. "And since you invited me to Thanksgiving dinner out of pity, I can stay for Christmas for the same reason. Even if that's just a tiny bit of the reason."

"I don't care why you stay, just as long as you're here."

She kissed him and he said, "You're going to be okay, Chas. I know you miss her, and you'll probably never stop missing her. But you're strong, and you're going to spend your life in this home she left for you, honoring her legacy." She nodded, and he kissed her again.

Jackson saw her zone out again and looked for something to say to distract her from her grief. "You know," he said with some degree of exasperation, "the awkward thing about spending Christmas in someone else's home is that they think they have to buy you gifts, and you wonder if you should buy them gifts. And nobody knows what to get, or how much to spend, and everybody's worried and it's just . . . awkward. So, I'll make you a deal. I'll stay for Christmas if we can just . . . enjoy the holiday and forget the gifts. Although . . ."

"You're reneging before you've even made the deal."

He chuckled. "So I am. You're as shrewd as your grandmother. I really would like to get you a gift. I just don't know what to get. But I don't want you to get me a gift, because just being here with you is gift enough."

"Oh, no, you can't do that. Fair is fair. Let's just . . . set some rules."

"Rules?"

"Yeah. One gift. Ten-dollar limit."

"Deal," he said, liking that idea thoroughly and immediately.

"That way it has to be either sentimental or silly, and either way it works."

"Agreed," he said.

The following morning they had breakfast as usual, except that Polly cooked it, and Chas was so somber that she didn't say much. After they'd eaten they each went to their rooms to change their clothes. Jackson waited in the parlor for Chas, and looked up from his paper to see her dressed in black, looking beautiful and elegant— and very sad.

"You look great," he said and stood, "but you told me it wasn't a requirement to wear black to Mormon funerals."

"It's not. It just . . . seemed like the right thing to wear."

"I would agree." He took her hands and kissed her. "You're beautiful." She tried to smile. "You okay?" he asked.

"Considering what day it is, I'm holding it together. Just hold my hand and help me through this day. I can fall apart later."

"An excellent plan," he said, and they left for the church where the funeral would be held.

Jackson was intrigued by the differences in a Mormon funeral compared to any he'd ever been to. He'd taken keen notice of all the people from Chas's church who had been in and out of the house the last few days, bringing food and flowers and compassion. People had come to help with the funeral plans, and simply to check on her and see how she was doing. And Jackson had been impressed. Now, sitting through the service, he couldn't recall a funeral ever having such a positive mood to it. More than grief and heartache, he heard hope and peace. It was more a celebration of this woman's life, as opposed to sorrow over her death. Of course, it was mentioned more than once that she would be missed, and the difficulty was for those left behind. It was mentioned by Bishop Wegg that the woman they were honoring had not been a member of the church he represented, but that her granddaughter, who was, had requested he take charge of the funeral, and he considered it an honor. It was obvious he'd met Granny on more than a few occasions and knew her well. His tribute to her was touching.

At the cemetery it started to snow just as soon as the prayer spoken there was finished. Jackson stood with his arm around Chas next to the casket, holding an umbrella over them. Everyone else left, but she just stood there, and he was more than willing to stay there with her for as long as she needed. She finally blew out a long sigh, touched the casket, then headed toward the car, leaning into him while he kept his arm around her.

"I miss her so much," she said in the car.

"I know. It's going to be a tough adjustment, especially since you've been taking care of her. I worry about you. You've got to find something to fill in the hours you used to spend helping her, or you're going to get depressed."

"You're an expert?" she asked.

"No, just an observer of human nature. You're entitled to grieve and to miss her, but if what they said at the funeral today is true, you should be able to go forward with faith, find peace over this, and be happy, because you know that's what she would want."

Chas took his hand. "Listen to you telling me to have faith."

"Hey, I've learned a lot from you and Granny." He kissed her hand, then drove in silence back to the church building where a luncheon was being provided by the women of the Church. But Chas didn't want to stay long. She told him she was tired of hearing condolences—and just plain tired.

Once they'd eaten and exchanged brief words with a few people, especially appreciation to the bishop and the ladies who had put on the luncheon, they were on their way home. Back at the inn, Chas said she was going to change her clothes and check on the work Polly was doing. But Jackson went to the office to talk to Polly long enough to be able to assure Chas that it was all under control. Then he found her in Granny's room, her shoes on the floor, still wearing the same clothes, curled almost into the fetal position on the bed, holding her grandmother's pillow. Jackson sat down and told her, "I've talked to Polly. Everything is under control and it will be until you feel ready to get back to work; however long it takes, she said."

"Thank you. I didn't want to deal with it."

"I know, but you would have if you'd had to."

"I'm glad I don't have to."

"Do you want to be alone?"

"No."

"Anything you want to talk about?"

"No," she repeated, so he just sat there in silence for more than an hour, while Chas stared at the wall and didn't make a sound. She finally closed her eyes, and when he knew she was asleep, he covered her with one of Granny's blankets and went to change his clothes and take care of a few things that might help ease Polly's responsibilities.

He was back in the chair when Chas woke up. She reached out a hand when she saw him. He took it and kissed it and reminded her of how strong she was, and that they were going to get through this together.

"I like that together part," she said and actually smiled.

The next morning Chas and Jackson were eating breakfast when Polly sat down at their table and said, "I don't want to stress you out, Chas, and I'm willing to do whatever you need me to do, but I have to remind you that the open house is the day after tomorrow."

"Oh, good heavens!" Chas said and hit herself in the forehead with the palm of her hand. "I can't believe I forgot."

"I think it's reasonable that you forgot," Polly said. "And I can take care of most of it. But other than what you asked Charlotte to do, the plans are in your head, so I need to know what you've got."

"Oh, my gosh!" Chas said. "I can't believe I forgot."

"We got that already," Polly said, completely calm. "It'll be fine. Just tell me what you need me to do. Jen will help, and so will Michelle." Jackson knew these girls were the maids who cleaned the rooms, but they were competent and hard working, and Jen had helped cover other things here and there many times. "Charlotte will help as well. If we can just sit down and go over some details, we'll be set."

"Okay," Chas said, breathing deeply, as if she'd just avoided a near collision.

"What are we talking about?" Jackson asked.

"It's been a tradition ever since we opened the inn," Chas explained. "We had our grand opening at Christmastime right after the renovations were completed. We opened it for tours and served refreshments, and it helped get the business off the ground. After that, people around town started asking if we were going to do it again because they had such a good time, so we made it a tradition."

"With the house already decorated," Polly said, "all we really need to take care of are the refreshments, right?"

"Right," Chas said.

"And Charlotte will be doing most of that, right?"

"Right," she said again.

"And we'll all just pitch in to help that day, and we can all play waiter that evening, and we'll help clean up. It's not a big deal."

"I can do that," Jackson said proudly.

"Do what?" Chas and Polly both asked at the same time.

"Be a waiter. I went undercover as a waiter once."

"Really?" Chas said, and Polly laughed.

"It's not funny," Jackson said, pretending to be offended. "I was very good at it."

"That's pretty cool," Polly said. "What else have you learned to be for secret missions?"

"It was not a secret mission; it was just a little undercover work."

"Whatever your FBI definition might be," Polly said, "it sounds secret to me. What else did you do?"

"Oh, exciting stuff," Jackson said. "Janitor, pest control, bartender, store clerk a few times. But the most exciting was ticket taker at a theater."

"That's hilarious," Polly said.

"So, how often do we encounter FBI agents passing themselves off as normal people?" Chas asked.

"Rarely if ever, I'm sure," Jackson said. "Did you just say I wasn't normal?"

"Ordinary," she corrected. "I meant ordinary." She took his hand. "You are far from ordinary."

He made a disgruntled noise, then insisted on being present while the women discussed the open house and their plans. He was pleased when there was actually something he could do to help, and that Chas was willing to let him do it. The next day he was given a list of errands and a list of things to get at the grocery store. He was glad to see Chas keeping busy with something that kept her from thinking too much about Granny's absence, although she still spent far too much time just sitting or resting in Granny's room.

"Maybe you should just move into this room," he said that evening when he found her there again. "It's bigger than yours, and you spend more time here anyway."

"Maybe I will," she said and changed the subject.

The following day was very busy, but Chas was relieved to see how smoothly everything came together with the help of her friends. When guests started arriving, she was amazed to see that Jackson had been serious. He had no trouble being completely comfortable with inviting people to look through the house, and answering questions about it. And he was often seen carrying around trays with food, or making certain the punch bowl remained full. She wandered around, mingling with guests, some of whom she knew and some of whom she did not. The scented candles that were burning throughout the house, along with the soft Christmas music playing in the background, gave her a sense of anticipation for the holiday that she hadn't felt since Granny had left her. She also loved the chatter of people having fun in her home, and realized that she loved this tradition as much as, if not more than, anybody else.

"You're pretty good at this," she said to Jackson during a quiet moment while they hovered where refreshments were set out on the sideboard in the dining room. "Maybe I should hire you."

"You can't afford me," he said and chuckled. "Maybe you should just marry me."

"Is that a proposal?" she asked.

"It's a wish," he said and kissed her quickly before he went back to work.

After the last guests had left the inn, Chas found Jackson in the kitchen, wearing one of her aprons folded down and tied around his waist. He was washing the baking sheets that Charlotte had used to bring her variety of baked delicacies, while Polly and Charlotte were packaging the majority of the leftover food for the freezer. Jen and Michelle were combing the house for stray garbage and dishes and making certain all was in order.

"Thank you," she said, sidling up next to Jackson with a clean dish towel that she used to dry the pan he'd just washed.

"A pleasure," he said and kept washing.

"Did you go undercover as a dishwasher?"

"Yes, actually, but it only lasted a few hours."

"What a relief for you," she said, and he laughed.

With the open house behind them, the holiday was fast approaching, and Chas put all her efforts into creating the best possible celebration. She missed Granny every hour of every day, but she found strength in imagining her close by, observing all the preparations with a sparkle in her eye and a smile on her face. During the moments when she felt tempted to grieve over Granny's absence during this most precious time of year, Chas turned her thoughts instead to Jackson. Having him in her life didn't replace her grandmother's presence in her home, but his being here for the holidays gave her more to look forward to. His company assuaged her sadness and made her losses more bearable.

The countdown to Christmas began with a day in the kitchen, where everyone was involved. Chas always purposely scheduled this day on a Monday or Tuesday when there were few if any guests at the inn. There was only one couple staying in the Carol on Tuesday evening, and there were no guests on Monday, so there was no one to take care of Tuesday morning. As always, Chas had scented candles burning and Christmas music playing quietly. She considered that creating the perfect atmosphere was one of her gifts, and she took it very seriously. Charlotte always supervised the baking projects, giving her children special assignments, and Chas supervised the making of fudge and caramels and chocolate-covered pretzels. Polly was patient about stirring candy that had to get to the perfect temperature, and the children were mostly occupied by cutting out batch after batch of sugar cookies. Chas loved watching Jackson. He was wearing one of her aprons, guiding the children, and covering himself with flour. At moments it seemed he had a great deal of experience with children and was perfectly patient with them; at others he seemed like a child himself, and she wondered what his Christmases had been like when he was young.

By suppertime phase one was completed, and the countertops in the kitchen were covered with a variety of candies and baked treats, waiting for the finishing touches to be done during phase two on the following day. They ordered pizza for supper and worked together to wash all of the dishes and put everything in order before it arrived. After they'd eaten, they all gathered in front of the TV to watch a Christmas movie while they strung popcorn and cranberries, which were added to the already-decorated Christmas tree for a homey effect.

After Charlotte and her children had left and Polly had gone to her room to read, Chas and Jackson sat near the Christmas tree, holding hands while they looked into the flames of a fire that he had kept burning throughout the evening. Chas took the opportunity to ask him something she'd been wondering all day. "Tell me what Christmas was like when you were a child."

He made a disgusted noise. "If you want the day to remain cheerful, we shouldn't talk about that."

"Was it really that bad?" she asked.

"It really was," he said. "My mother tried; I'll give her credit for that. But a holiday was just another excuse for my father to be drunk, and since he spent all of his money on booze, there wasn't much money for anything else. Enough said. What was Christmas like when *you* were a child?"

"Almost like today," she said. "Granny taught me and Charlotte everything we know. Until the house was renovated, some of it was in pretty bad shape, but it always felt like home. Granny loved Christmas and worked hard to make it wonderful, even if there wasn't a lot of money."

"You live her legacy well, then."

"I try," she said and got a little sniffly. "I miss her."

"I miss her too," he said. "I can't imagine how much *you* must miss her."

"Having you here helps," she said. "I'm grateful for that."

He kissed her hand. "I'm grateful too," he said and smiled.

The following morning, Charlotte and the kids arrived after breakfast, and they all spent the day frosting and decorating cookies with artful details. The kids made a glorious mess with the different colors of frosting and the variety of sprinkles and decorations. After lunch, having given the cookies time to dry, lovely gift plates were assembled with some of everything they had made. And everyone sampled a little bit of everything, along with hot chocolate, just to make sure it all was good enough to share. That evening they went caroling and distributed the goody plates to many friends and neighbors and people that Chas went to church with.

The next day Chas and Jackson watched Logan and Karlee while their mother did some errands and finished her Christmas shopping. They decided to build a snow fort in the backyard, and had a great snowball war, boys against the girls. They had to really bundle up because it was so cold outside, but after the girls won, they went inside for hot chocolate by the fire and another sampling of Christmas goodies. That evening, after the children were gone, Chas and Jackson shared a nice dinner with Polly, then they all watched another Christmas movie. They had to pause it twice for carolers that came to the door with music and home-baked offerings, but then they had different goodies to sample during the rest of the film. Chas kept Jackson's hand in hers as much as possible, silently thanking God at regular intervals for bringing him into her life and for allowing him to stay through the holidays. She simply pushed away any thought of his inevitably having to go when the new year came.

The following morning Jackson went into town in search of the perfect gift for less than ten dollars. The only good thing about his shopping excursion was how much he thought of Chas and how she'd warmed his life while he looked with apparent futility for something that would be appropriate. He had to go home for lunch, since he knew Chas was expecting him, then he went out again, being purposely vague, even though he knew that she knew what he was up to.

He *did* find some simple gifts for his mother and sister that he mailed off while he was out, and some silly ones for Charlotte and Polly that were cheap and meaningless but would provoke a good laugh. He enjoyed finding something for the children, since kids were easy to buy for and he'd gotten to know Logan and Karlee well enough that he could get them gifts that were not ostentatious or presumptuous, but would still be fun. Still he struggled to find something for Chas, but when he *did* find it, he knew it was perfect. The little porcelain statue of an angel had a Victorian look to it, and for some strange reason it reminded him of Granny. He held his breath and looked at the price, thinking he would cheat if it was beyond the limit. $9.99. Perfect! He had it wrapped so that there was no chance of Chas seeing it before Christmas, then he took all of his purchases back to the inn. When he came in the back door, he became aware of Chas in the parlor visiting with some women. He took his things upstairs, including the wrapping paper he'd purchased, and wrapped the gifts. When he saw from the window that the ladies were leaving, he took his wrapped packages downstairs and put them under the tree, loving Chas's curiosity as she read the tags.

"Who was here?" he asked.

"My visiting teachers," she said, and he responded with silent confusion. "Like home teachers, only it's women visiting women. You know how we women need someone to talk to."

"Yes, I do know that," he said with a chuckle, then he noticed a *very* large package beside the tree with a tag that indicated it was for him from Chas.

"That cost less than ten dollars?"

"It did," she said proudly.

"Can I get it in my luggage when I leave?"

"If you can't, you might have to leave it here . . . and then you'll have to come back and get it." She let out a mischievous chuckle. "I guess you'll just have to wait and see."

"This isn't one of those tiny little gifts with lots and lots of packing is it?" he asked, and she just laughed. He silenced her laughter with a kiss and refused to think about the day he would have to go back to Virginia without her.

Amidst the Christmas preparations, while Chas was busy doing other things, Jackson took note of some minor repairs that needed to be done around the inn. He went into town and found the hardware and other materials he needed, then he took it upon himself to fix two slightly dripping faucets, some broken baseboards in the hall, and a cupboard door in the kitchen. He replaced some light bulbs that required a ladder in order to reach them, and some that didn't. And he kept shoveling snow from the walks and steps whenever it fell; with the series of storms they were having, that was almost daily. Chas was ridiculously grateful for his efforts, and told him more than once that she was impressed with his handyman skills. He told her it was the only thing he'd gotten from his father that was of any value. The man could fix anything, and Jackson hadn't hired anyone to do a repair on his behalf in all his adult life. Chas told him he'd make a perfect innkeeper. He agreed and kissed her, and they both ignored the uncertainty of whether or not that would ever come to pass.

On Sunday they went to church together, where they enjoyed a lovely Christmas program during sacrament meeting. Jackson went to Sunday School with Chas, and then Ron, one of her home teachers, invited him to come to priesthood meeting with him while Chas went to Relief Society. Jackson gave her a glance that was somewhere between amused and panicked, but he said to Ron, "I'd love to. Thank you." At least he liked Ron; that was a good thing. Chas prayed that it would go well, then focused on the Relief Society lesson. Afterward, Jackson made no comment beyond, "It was fine." She just left it at that and thanked him for going to church with her.

The last night of the year that Chas kept the inn open was December 23. The final guests left the morning of the twenty-fourth, and the remainder of the day was spent preparing for tomorrow's great Christmas feast and putting together some charity baskets that would be delivered secretly after dark to some struggling families in town. They wrapped gifts and sorted food according to lists that Chas had been compiling and planning for days. Charlotte and the kids came over for supper, and they all enjoyed soup and cornbread and a Jell-O salad layered in white, red, and green. After they had eaten supper and cleaned up the dishes, they made their deliveries and were successful at not getting caught. Charlotte took her kids home to try to get them to bed, and Polly made popcorn so the three of them could watch *It's a Wonderful Life* before they went to bed themselves. Chas cried at the end of the movie, then she had trouble stopping when she was struck with a wave of missing Granny so much that it hurt. But Jackson allowed her to use his shoulder and offered words of comfort and assurance while she got it out of her system. They finally kissed goodnight at the foot of the stairs, and the next morning they awoke to falling snow. Chas fixed waffles and bacon for breakfast while Jackson went out for his run in spite of the weather. Then they sat to eat with Polly, and Jackson teased her and Chas for wearing funny flannel pajamas.

"Oh, we'll be in them all day," Polly said. "It's tradition."

"I see," Jackson said and chuckled.

A little while later Charlotte and her kids showed up, all wearing funny flannel pajamas. "I would have gotten you some," Chas said to Jackson, "but it was over the ten-dollar limit."

"How tragic," he said with sarcasm.

Karlee and Logan had obviously been up very early and had already opened their Christmas gifts at home. They eagerly showed Jackson, Chas, and Polly what Santa had brought them before the group all gathered in the parlor to open the gifts under the tree—except that the one Chas was giving to Jackson wouldn't fit *under* the tree.

The gifts were all a big hit, and Jackson enjoyed the silly gifts that Polly, Charlotte, and the children gave him. He assured them that a pair of Christmas socks with reindeer on them and a tie with Charles Dickens on it were exactly what he'd always wanted. The ten-dollar gifts that Chas and Jackson exchanged were saved until last, and he noted how Polly and Charlotte seemed to magically distract the children and usher them from the room when it came time to open them.

"They thought we might like a private, romantic moment," Chas said to him.

Jackson glanced at the huge box with his name on it. "Is that meant to be romantic?"

"Use your imagination," she said.

"Okay, but you go first," he insisted and handed her the beautifully wrapped package. "It was wrapped at the store," he said, as if she might not know. "I could never do something like that with a bow."

"It's lovely," she said and removed the tag. "But I like this part better." She held it up, pointing to how he'd written, *To Chas, with all my love for Christmas, Jackson*. "I'm going to save it forever."

"You do that. Just open the present."

He wasn't disappointed by her reaction, and he didn't even have to explain it. She took one look at the little angel statue and said, "It's Granny."

She got tears in her eyes and cooed over it, declaring that she would put it in her bedroom to watch over her always. Then she put Jackson to work opening the huge gift. And sure enough, it was a package, inside of a package, inside of a package. They laughed together as he kept unloading wads of newspaper and other packing materials only to find another wrapped gift, and another. When he finally came to a small box that was wrapped with more care and beauty than the others, she put her hand over his so he would hesitate. "I have to explain," she said. "I didn't actually go out and buy this. It's something I came across in a drawer last week; something we used to sell here at the inn, and yes, it sold for $9.95. I actually had some made especially for the inn as a marketing thing at one time, but this was the only one left. I knew it was perfect, so I hope that's okay."

"It's more than okay," he said and kissed her before she made him open the package. In it he found a key ring. Attached to the ring was a silver oval with an engraving on one side of an image of the Dickensian Inn. On the other side were the words, *God bless us, every one.*

Jackson was surprised at how emotional he felt when he looked at it, and when he thought of being able to carry it with him wherever he went. As if she'd read his mind, she said, "Keys are something that go with a man nearly everywhere he goes. I want you to always be reminded of your time here, and your time with me, of course. And every time you look at it, I want you to remember that there's always room at the inn."

Chas was surprised to have him look up, a glisten of moisture in his eyes. "Thank you," he said and hugged her tightly. "It's perfect." He slipped the key ring over one finger and took her face in his hands to kiss her before he murmured against her lips, "It's been a perfect Christmas; everything has been perfect—especially being with you." He kissed her again. "The only thing that could make it better would be having Granny here with us."

"Yes," she said, "but somehow I think she is."

"Yes, I think she is."

Hearing the children nearby brought them back to the moment, and they worked together to clean up the mess from the wrappings and put all the paper and boxes into the recycling can outside. They all worked together to put on Christmas dinner, although it wasn't much work with all the preparations they had done previously. After sharing a beautiful meal in the family dining room, then cleaning it up, they all gathered around the table to play games until it was time to pull out leftovers for supper. After eating and having some hot chocolate along with remnants of their Christmas goodies, Charlotte and the children went home, and Polly went to visit some friends. Chas and Jackson sat down together to watch one of the many versions of *A Christmas Carol.* Again Chas cried, then they talked until late about the depth and magnitude of the story, and what an amazing miracle Dickens had been a part of in writing it.

"He *was* an amazing man," Chas said.

"You inherited your grandmother's admiration for him," Jackson said. "Although I agree completely—speaking from his writings, that is. I think the writings are a testament of a great man, even though I know very little about him personally."

"They say that *David Copperfield* is highly autobiographical. Some things are right out of his life, and some things seem to be how he would have liked his life to turn out. I've read a few different biographies, actually."

"That's impressive," he said.

"I figured if I was going to run an inn with his name on it, I should know something about the man. I wanted to read multiple biographies so I could see what the different viewpoints might be, and what facts appeared in all of them. I think I got a pretty good overview of the man."

"Really?" Jackson turned more toward her. "I'm very interested. Tell me."

"Well, obviously it's late and there's far too much to tell in one conversation, but I can let you borrow the books—or perhaps just the best of the three."

"I'd like that," he said, "but I want to hear your summary of Charles Dickens."

"I believe he was terribly unhappy. His childhood was difficult, and I believe it traumatized him emotionally in ways from which he never recovered. He wasn't perfect, by any means, and I don't agree with all of the choices he made, but I can understand why he made them, given his baggage, so to speak. What I believe is truly remarkable is that he actually devoted an enormous amount of time and energy to promoting the causes he wrote about. His influence effected a great many changes in prisons and schools and workhouses. No matter what mistakes he may have made in his life, he did a lot of good. As you said, his writings stand as a testament to the man. But he did a lot of writing for periodicals that had nothing to do with his novels, and he did a lot of good through that and many other avenues. He truly is one of my heroes."

"As he should be," Jackson said. "Who are your other heroes?"

"I don't have many."

"Tell me."

"Martin," she said.

"Of course. He's one of my heroes, too."

"Really?"

"He took good care of you, and you loved him. He died a hero's death."

"I didn't look at it that way until you said what you did when we first talked about him. I've been grateful for the perspective you've given me."

"Who else?"

"Joseph Smith," she said.

"Ah, the first Mormon Prophet."

"In the latter days," she corrected. "You *have* been listening at church."

"A little," he said. "Anyone else?"

"You," she said, and he looked at her with dubious surprise. "I'm serious. I think you're an amazing man."

"Maybe you don't know me well enough to know whether or not I'm a hero."

"If you ever do anything to fall from hero status, I'll be sure to let you know."

"You do that," he said.

They talked more about Dickens, and recounted what a great holiday it had been. Then they both reluctantly said goodnight and went to their separate rooms about the time Polly came home.

During the following week, they stayed busy with outings and projects, trying to drag out the holiday mood as long as possible, especially while the inn was closed and there was no business to attend to. Chas dreaded the new year as much as she knew Jackson did, but neither of them voiced their thoughts. They just spent every possible minute together, collecting memories to carry them through their inevitable time apart. And for all that Chas dreaded his leaving, she could not go an hour without feeling gratitude for the time that he'd been able to spend with her. Whether he believed it or not, he truly was one of her heroes.

CHAPTER 14

Not a word was said about Jackson having to leave until New Year's Day was behind them and the inn was once again open for business. The bomb was dropped at breakfast.

"I have to go back," he said.

"I know."

"I have a flight booked the day after tomorrow."

Chas set her fork down and took a deep breath. She was determined to not complain. She'd known it was coming, and she'd had him here far longer than she'd hoped for or expected. In truth, she had to wonder if a part of her had been in some level of denial all along. They had helped each other through some tough things, and they had helped each other heal old wounds. But perhaps permanent just wasn't feasible, and never would be. She wanted to beg him to stay, but in her deepest self she was convinced that this was the end, and she would be a fool to expect anything more once he left the inn and returned to the life from which he'd been hiding. She needed to prepare herself for that, whether she wanted to or not. She found some peace in believing that they would probably always keep in touch, and perhaps her influence on him would leave enough of an impression that he might one day be led to embrace the gospel. If such a thing were possible, she could never begrudge anything else.

Recalling that he was still here and she needed to make the most of it, she tried to sound positive as she said, "So, what do you want to spend your last two days here doing?"

"As long as I'm with you every waking moment, I don't care."

They filled those days with good memories, long conversations, and even a few tears. It was impossible to ignore any longer the imminent separation, nor the dark cloud that hung over their time together as they counted the remaining hours. They speculated over the possible outcomes of the situation, but neither of them could say for sure that marriage was the best choice, even though neither of them could even consider the possibility that it wasn't. But Chas felt certain that for all of his hopeful speculations on the future, he just wasn't being realistic, and it wouldn't take long for him to merge back into his life in Virginia and realize that this had all been just a dream.

On the morning that Chas knew Jackson was leaving, they shared breakfast as usual while Polly was already at work in the office down the hall. They had very little to say to each other, and it felt to Chas like a death in the family all over again.

After the meal, Chas worked in slow motion to clean up the kitchen, knowing that Jackson was finishing his packing and saying farewell to the room where he'd stayed for weeks. She felt desperate and terrified when she heard him coming down the stairs, then she could tell that he was setting his luggage near the door. A moment later she found him standing in the doorway to the kitchen, looking exactly as she felt. The fact that he shared her grief was somewhat of a comfort.

"I should stay, Chas," he said, and she wanted to hit him for making this more difficult. "I'll call and cancel the flight. I'll cancel everything. There's no reason I ever have to leave here. Ever!"

"Stop it! Just stop it!" she shouted and slammed the refrigerator door.

"Stop what?" he demanded.

"Stop . . . pretending that . . . some . . . permanent happily-ever-after is going to automatically happen for us. You're a city man, Jackson. And your work is in your blood. We both know it."

Jackson felt astonished. "What are you saying?" She couldn't answer. "Don't you *want* me to come back? To stay?"

"I do," she said. "But it's . . . not realistic. Maybe you just need to be in the city, and I need to be here."

"I'm tired of the city, Chas. And my work stopped making me happy a long time ago. Being here is what makes me happy. Suddenly the things I thought I needed to do there don't seem so important."

"It *is* important, and you're kidding yourself if you think it's not."

Jackson was hearing a side of her he didn't understand, but he felt the need to defend himself. "Do you really think I'm so coldhearted and stubborn that I couldn't leave all of that behind and—"

"Stop it!" she said again and turned her back to him. "You're not coldhearted; not by any standard. But you're living in a fantasy world here, Jackson. You're miles away from the reality of your life. The time that you've spent here is just like . . . some Hallmark movie. It's sappy and sweet and tender, and even the commercials make you cry. But ten o'clock comes, the movie ends, and real life goes on. Don't stand there and tell me that you can give up everything for me, when you don't even know what you're giving up." She turned to face him. "You can't make a decision like that while you're here like this." She shook her head, and tears trickled down her face. "You can't stay here when you've run away from home and left all kinds of holes in the life you were living. Those holes would start to eat at you, Jackson. You would never find peace."

Jackson took a step back and looked at the floor. He had to swallow hard and cough to keep from crying. The silence beyond her sniffling became torturous until he said with a quaver in his voice, "You know what? You're right. I hate it. But you're right."

He looked up to gauge her reaction. She shook her head again, and her tears increased. "No," she muttered, "you're not supposed to agree with me. You're supposed to argue and convince me that . . . you should stay, that you should never leave me."

"How can I when you've just given me such a convincing argument, Chas? You're right. We both know you're right. I have to go back. I have to face what I left behind."

She nodded and started to cry so hard she couldn't speak. He put his arms around her, and she clutched his shoulders tightly. "And then what?"

"I don't know, Chas. I thought I knew what I wanted; now I'm not so sure. Maybe I'm not the right man for you, but maybe I've convinced you that you need a man in your life."

"Not unless it's you," she muttered and lifted her lips to his.

Their kiss was long and full of fear. He took her wet face into his hands. "I love you, Chas. I *will* come back, but whether that is to visit or stay, I suppose I need time to tell."

She nodded and kissed him again, then she turned her back and said, "Go. Go or you'll miss your flight. Call and let me know you made it home safely."

"I will," he said and left the room. Then she heard him come back. "I *will* come back, Chas."

"Maybe," she said. "And maybe you'll decide one day that it's best to just enjoy the memories for what they are and move on with your life. One day, when you just stop calling, I'll know that it's time to move on with mine."

"I love you," he said again and left the room. She heard him pick up his bags, then the door opened and closed again. Chas moved to a chair and cried as if someone she loved had just died. She knew the feeling well.

Throughout the remainder of the day, Chas tried not to watch the phone or think that every time it rang it might be Jackson. Determined as she was to keep her focus elsewhere, she still held her breath each time it rang, and was always disappointed when she glanced at the caller ID. And he'd only left hours ago. She was just checking doors and lights before going to bed when the phone in her hand rang. She looked at it, letting out a squeal of laughter as she read the little screen: *Leeds, Jackson T.* In a voice more calm she answered, immediately saying, "It's you."

"It *is* me," he said, and just the sound of his voice soothed her.

"You made it home safely?"

"I did," he said. "Is everything okay there?"

"Everything except . . . it is pretty quiet. No guests tonight. Polly's on a date." At the risk of gushing, she added, "I miss you already."

"I miss you, too . . . a lot. Can I admit that I've never felt as lonely being alone in this house as I do now?"

"Oh, yes. You can admit that. Can I admit that I know exactly how you feel?"

"Oh, yes."

"I wish I could take it back," she said. "When you said you would stay, and I talked you out of it. I wish I could take it back."

"But you can't, and you wouldn't. I thought a great deal about what you said. In fact, I don't think I thought of anything else during the flight. You're a very wise woman, Chas. It's one of the things I love about you. And I think you hit the nail right on the head. I'm ashamed to say that I couldn't see it myself. But I know you're right. If we're going to be together, it can't be with any doubts, or with unfinished business that might end up coming between us. Given that, and all the time I've spent thinking, there's something I need to say."

"Okay," she said and steeled herself.

"It's not easy to say, Chas, but it has to be said. I want to be with you, but I have to make sure I'm in a position to give you what you deserve, and I'm not sure I'm the man to do that." Chas put a hand over her mouth to hold back her emotion, glad that he couldn't see the tears rolling down her face. Was he trying to break it off completely? Even though a part of her had been trying to accept that it would probably come to this, she wasn't ready. Had it only taken this many hours for him to decide that it was over between them? Her relief was indescribable when he added, "I need time, Chas, because if I'm going to commit my life to you, I don't want it to ever go bad. I would rather have you love me in memory than come to hate me because I couldn't give you what you deserve." He became silent, but she couldn't answer without letting on to her emotion. "Are you there?" he asked. "Chas?"

"I'm here," she finally said.

"You're crying."

"Yes, I'm crying. However wise or practical this might be, I hate it. I want you in my life, Jackson."

"I want you in my life too," he said earnestly. "And with any luck, it will end up that way. But you were right about not making decisions under such circumstances. We just need time. All I was trying to say is that . . . given some time to think, I've figured out *why* I need time. Be patient with me."

"Of course." She sniffled. "Does this mean we officially have a long-distance relationship?"

He chuckled. "It would seem that way."

"Okay, I just . . . need some parameters here. If you see another woman socially, or romantically—at all—I need to know; I need you to be completely honest with me."

"Chas," he said gently, "I said I needed time. There's isn't going to be another woman. I'm not trying to choose a flavor of ice cream,

Chas. I already know which flavor is right for me. I just need to decide if I'm the kind of man who should have ice cream at all." He chuckled. "That is the most ridiculous metaphor I have ever come up with."

"It made perfect sense. And I'm glad to know I'm the right flavor."

"What about you?"

"What about me?"

"What if some other guy comes along who—"

"Have you seen the town I live in?"

"Yes, but you run an inn. You never know when some mysterious man will show up and change your life."

"Such things only happen once in a lifetime, Jackson. And it's already happened. I love you. I will always love you. And until I have solid evidence that you're not going to pursue a life with me, I'm going to be counting on that. I would just prefer that when you figure it out, you tell me straight—as opposed to just . . . not calling me . . . or avoiding my calls, or something equally male and immature."

"I would never do that."

"I know. I'm just paranoid. Can I admit that I'm paranoid?"

"Yes, because I'm paranoid, too. I'm afraid that when you pray for the answer, God will tell you I'm not the right one, after all. But until that happens, I'll be calling you . . . a lot."

"Oh, good. I hope you have a good phone plan."

"I do, and I intend to use it. Email has its uses, but I prefer hearing your voice."

"Amen."

"And maybe you could come and see me one of these days."

"In Norfolk?"

"That's where I live. I was thinking that since I've become so familiar with your life and your territory, maybe you should at least get a glimpse of mine."

"That sounds fair."

"But don't think that means I'm suggesting you should ever leave your life for this one. It would never work; you would hate it here."

"You sound so sure."

"I know you. You would hate it here."

"But you don't?"

"I'm used to it." He paused and sighed. "I guess I should hang up. I've got an early day tomorrow."

"So, here we begin a long-distance relationship."

"I guess so."

"If you were in the Marines we would have a long-distance relationship."

"That's true." A stretch of silence made it evident that neither of them wanted to hang up, but they both knew they had to. "I love you, Chas," he said with such sincerity that she started to cry again and made no effort to hide it.

"I love you too, Jackson. Take good care of yourself—and be careful. I hear it's a dangerous job."

"I will. You too."

Chas cried long and hard after she'd hung up the phone, then she went to the computer to look through the digital photos from Christmas that she had downloaded there, evidence of the time she'd spent with Jackson. The next day she got some high-quality prints made and framed them, putting two on her dresser and one on her nightstand. And she sent framed copies of the same ones to Jackson, along with a letter and some of Charlotte's cookies. When he called to tell her he'd received them, and to thank her profusely, he also gave her a lengthy update of the situation at work. The men who had been injured were back on the job and both had been through some counseling. Security was tighter in some respects, and there was a little bit of a dark cloud hanging over the office, but work was going on as normal. He was tying up some loose ends on old cases, and was also working on a new case that had come up. And he was also looking into finding more information on the scumbags, as he called them, who were responsible for the disasters that had occurred.

"Drug dealers, you mean," she said.

"That's what I mean."

"Be careful," she insisted. "I've invested too much in you to let you get killed by an angry drug dealer."

"Don't worry. I'll be fine."

Chas wanted to believe him, but she had no illusions over the kind of work he did.

They quickly established a routine. He usually called her on his way in to work so she could help him get through the traffic stress while she worked in the kitchen on mornings when guests were there. She only mentioned once that her neck was hurting from holding the phone on her shoulder while she worked, and two days later a phone headset arrived by FedEx with a note that said she was going to get a lot of good out of it, and he didn't want her neck to hurt. This way she could put the cordless phone in the pocket of her apron and go anywhere in the inn and do anything she needed to do.

Most of the time he called her at least once during the day when he had a break, but that call was always brief. Sometimes he was in the office, or even on a stakeout, but more often he was out somewhere, driving to and from odd places. And Chas's favorite time of day became the bedtime call, when both of them had timed it to have everything taken care of and be ready for bed so they could talk until they got sleepy. She enjoyed hearing more about his work, although he was vague about much of what he did. He mostly liked to tell her funny things about the people he worked with, and she came to know many of them by name and by their individual quirks.

She suspected that he had a fair amount of authority in his particular branch of the agency, but he wouldn't admit to anything. He'd talked to her in detail of his difficult feelings upon initially returning to work, and the awkwardness he'd felt in some respects. But everyone had been kind, and after a few days he said it all felt like things were back to normal—except for the conspicuous absence of a man he had become accustomed to working with closely over many years. He talked to her about visiting Dave's widow, and how *her* kindness had also soothed his own wounds. She and her children were going to be moving to the city where she'd grown up so they could be near family, and he believed that was a good thing. He also talked about Ken, the man he'd been acquainted with who had done such horrible things, and how his absence in the office felt strange in a horrible way. He had also visited Ken's widow and was pleased to find her doing relatively well.

For Chas, life at the inn went on as it had for years, except that Granny's absence was difficult every day—and so was Jackson's. But his phone calls, and simply knowing that he was out there and he loved her, kept her going and made it possible to feel some joy in spite of her loneliness. Polly's presence didn't hurt any, but it just wasn't the same.

About a month after he'd returned home, Jackson called to say, "Could I speak to someone in bookkeeping, please?"

"That's me," Chas said.

"Can you explain to me why there has been no charge on my credit card for the Dickensian Inn?"

"Maybe you missed it."

"Don't get sassy with me, Chas. Fix the mistake and run the charge."

"How can I charge you for becoming my best friend . . . or holding me together through my grandmother's death, or—"

"Those things are irrelevant to the fact that I came there as a customer and I used the services of the inn every day for weeks. You need the money and I know it. You might think you're pretty clever in getting me to believe that it's a thriving business, but I recognize the signs of making ends meet. And I will *not* contribute to the burdens in your life. Give me a discount if it will make you feel better, but run the charge or I will never speak to you again."

"That is *not* funny."

"It's not intended to be. I need integrity in this relationship. I need to know that I wasn't some charity case that you took in like a stray dog."

"That's pride talking, Jackson."

"You bet it is!"

"You're really angry."

"You bet I am! And you don't want to find out what I might do to get even for something like this. Just . . . run the charge and we'll drop it now."

"You're threatening me."

"Call it what you like. Just do it."

"I'm not some terrorist suspect, Agent Leeds. I'm not going to be bullied or intimidated into anything. If you don't know me any better than that, I just might charge you double."

"Fine, you do that. Do it today. Do it now."

Chas realized what she'd just said and almost hissed at him, "That's what you *want* me to do. You're just trying to get *me* angry so

I *will* charge you. Well, forget it. I love you and I'm not going to charge someone I love for staying in my home. For most people it's an inn; for you it's my home. It felt good to open my home to someone I care about and to know that you found joy here. Are you going to deny me that?" He didn't answer. "If you can't understand why I didn't charge you, then maybe I won't talk to *you* anymore."

"Is that a threat?"

"Maybe."

"You couldn't do it any more than I could. Just run the charge and we'll drop it."

"Just keep your stupid money," she said and hung up.

For the rest of the day Chas was afraid that he *wouldn't* call, or if he did, that he would still be angry. But he called at bedtime and was more calm. He didn't say anything more about the issue, but she wondered how he would feel when he realized in a few days that she wasn't going to run the charge. He was right. She *did* need the money. But she couldn't bring herself to charge this man for anything. It just didn't seem right.

* * * * *

Jackson waited three days to see if Chas would bill him anything at all. When she didn't, it took another two days of calling the inn in the middle of the day before Polly answered the phone.

"Hey, it's me, Jackson."

"Hi, Jackson!" she said with ridiculous exuberance. "The place isn't the same without you."

"I'm not the same without the place, either."

They exchanged some small talk, and he learned that Chas had gone on some errands. "But you can call her cell phone. Do you want the—"

"I have the number. I want to talk to you. Could you please tell me where Chas sends her mortgage payments for the inn?"

"Why?" she asked with a suspicion that didn't surprise him.

"None of your business. And I don't want you to tell Chas that I asked you."

"Why?" she said with more fervor.

"Just answer the question, Polly."

"I don't know if I should."

"I can find out, you know. I'm in the FBI."

"Then why did you call me?"

"This is more legal."

"Intimidating your girlfriend's friends? Is that what you mean?"

"No law against that. Just tell me which bank."

"Don't you need a warrant, or something?"

"I'm not asking for anything but the name of a bank, okay? I want to surprise her. It's a good thing, Polly. Think of it as conspiring for a surprise party . . . only better."

"Okay," she drawled, still suspicious but more calm.

"Come on, Polly. Just give me a name."

"I would know you're FBI even if I didn't know."

"Yeah, it shows. Give me the name."

"Fine," she snarled, and told him.

"Thank you," he said. "Now, don't go spoiling my surprise."

"It had better be good," she said, and he hung up without a good-bye.

* * * * *

Chas went to the office to go over the usual details with Polly and found her wearing a strange expression. She looked both nervous and delighted.

"What?" Chas demanded.

"I think you'd better sit down."

"Why?"

"Just . . . sit down."

"Okay," Chas said and did.

Polly handed her a piece of paper that had two folds in it. "This came in today's mail."

Chas looked it over and gasped. "What *is* this?"

"It appears to be a notification that your mortgage has been paid in full."

"Well, it's a mistake."

"Not a mistake. I called them. The payoff amount they received was just a little off. You'll be getting a bill for eleven dollars and forty-two cents. Of course, they wanted us to know that it has been a pleasure doing business, and they regret that they couldn't have dragged the payments out for many more years in order to soak as much interest out of you as they possibly could." Chas listened to Polly, feeling dazed and completely baffled. "You should really close your mouth," Polly said. "You could trap flies with the way it's hanging open."

Chas closed her mouth and swallowed hard. "I don't understand."

"Oh, I think you do," Polly said. She leaned over the desk and spoke in a stage whisper. "I think it was your boyfriend."

Chas sucked in her breath and had trouble letting it go. "That . . . that . . ."

Polly chuckled. "Since you have a rule about not swearing, you can't think of anything to call him, can you."

Chas just groaned and rushed out of the office to find a place where she could call Jackson without being overheard. Although she suspected Polly would be impressed when she responded to his hello with, "You are a dirty rotten conniving manipulative creep!"

"I love you too," he said.

"It's okay to keep *your* pride by wounding mine?"

"Is that what you think I did?"

"How else should I interpret this? Remember that deal we made over Christmas gifts? Well, you went way over budget."

"You broke that rule first. So don't start lecturing me or comparing this to a ten-dollar gift limit."

"You have no idea what—"

"Why don't you shut up for a minute and—"

"Don't tell me to shut up."

"Fine. Will you please be quiet for a minute and listen to me? I made the decision to pay off the mortgage before I ever left the inn. I suspected you wouldn't charge me, and I was just using it as an excuse to get even."

Chas was so stunned that it took her a long moment to speak. "So, you're admitting that you're conniving and manipulative?"

"I don't have any trouble admitting to that. Don't forget that I'm a dirty rotten creep."

"I can't accept it, Jackson. It's too much. It wouldn't be right."

"You can and you will."

"You're awfully bossy, Mr. FBI. And what was all that . . . angry stuff?"

"Hey, a little stimulating disagreement over matters of principle keeps people on their toes. Isn't that what you told me?" She didn't answer. "Do you still want to live with me?"

"I can't live without you."

"I'm sure you could."

"I don't want to."

"But I'm a dirty rotten creep."

"Only when it comes to money. And if we let money come between us, we're just fools."

"I agree with that."

"I still don't feel like I can accept this, Jackson."

"If something happens to me before I get a chance to change my will, I'll know that I did something to help make certain you're taken care of." What little was left of her anger melted into fear at the mere mention of such a thing, but he treated it so nonchalantly that she couldn't comment. "No strings attached, Chas. Consider it a donation to preserving the historical value of the Victorian era. Whether I marry you or not, Chas, I want to help take care of you. I'm not going to miss the money. I don't have much to spend it on, so it's just sitting there. I've had a good income, and I made some good investments. It felt good to do something worthwhile with it. Granny would be pleased."

"How do you know?"

"She told me."

"You've been talking to Granny?"

"I haven't been hearing any voices, if that's what you mean. But I sure couldn't shake the feeling that I was supposed to pay off your mortgage. It was like if I didn't do it, I would never be able to sleep peacefully again. Isn't that what you Mormons call inspiration?"

"Something like that," she said. "I don't know how to argue with that."

"You can't."

"If you paid off my mortgage, you should be my partner, or something; you should be getting a share of the profits."

"All I want is room and board at the inn whenever I might be able to come, and however long I might stay."

"There will always be room at the inn for you, Jackson. Always. And it has nothing to do with money."

"Good. Now I can cross one big concern off my list."

"*What* concern?"

"I don't ever have to wonder if *you* wonder if my marrying you was just an easy way to a comfortable retirement because you live in a really great house."

"Oh, if you marry me, I intend to put you to work."

"And what exactly would you have me do when everything runs so smoothly without my lifting a finger?"

"I'll fire the snow guy," she said, and he laughed. "And the gardener," she added. "You haven't been here in the summer. It takes a lot of work to keep the lawns and flowers looking good."

"I know absolutely nothing about such things, but I'd be willing to learn."

"It would be like training to go undercover . . . as a gardener. If you don't figure out how to do it yourself, *you* can pay the gardener—and the snow guy."

"It's a deal."

"Is this a proposal?"

"It's hypothetical planning."

"Fair enough," she said. Then silence. "Jackson?"

"Yeah?"

"Thank you."

"You're welcome. Thanks for the room and board."

"You're welcome," she said and hoped that it wouldn't be too long before he took advantage of room and board again.

CHAPTER 15

It took Chas a few days to get comfortable with what Jackson had done. She made it a matter of serious prayer and pondering for a number of reasons. Uppermost in her mind was the question as to whether this was a sign of some undesirable character trait in Jackson that she should be wary of. While his efforts had every appearance of being genuine and motivated by love, she wasn't naive enough to believe that a man couldn't use such appearances to be controlling. He'd said there were no strings attached, but his definition of strings might be different from hers. She couldn't possibly know with her limited perspective whether or not this man might one day use the fact that he'd paid off the mortgage on the inn to manipulate her into decisions about it that she might not agree with. But God knew. He knew Jackson's heart and his motives, and by trusting in God and listening to the still, small whisperings of His Spirit, she could know for certain whether accepting this tremendous gift was a good thing. She reminded herself that just because it was right didn't mean that it might not still become an issue in the future. But with the confidence of knowing she'd done the right thing, she could take on the challenges with equal confidence.

Chas also felt the need to ask her Heavenly Father if her difficult feelings over accepting the money were simply related to pride. She'd accused Jackson of such pride and he'd not denied it. Apparently he was proud of being proud. But she suspected that his interpretation of the word had more to do with being strong and responsible and serving his country. He'd been a Marine, for heaven's sake. *The few. The proud.* He would have no understanding of the meaning of pride as it was discussed among those who shared her religion. And in that context, she couldn't deny that she had much evidence of his humility and sincerity. He had a sharp edge of arrogance that she suspected had also come from his profession, as did his stubborn refusal to be bullied or intimidated. But even given that, he'd never tried to elevate himself above her—or anyone else, for that matter. He wasn't perfect, but neither was she. And it was the beam in her own eye she was searching for now.

Chas continued to pray, and even fasted, knowing this was no small matter. She'd learned not to expect answers to be big and overwhelming. She'd learned to recognize feelings of peace versus the lack of it. And she listened carefully for those feelings. She was entirely unprepared for the sudden and overwhelming feeling that she had to get a priesthood blessing. She phoned one of her home teachers, and they both came over that evening. They went into the private dining room where they visited for a few minutes, then one of them offered a prayer. She didn't tell them anything specific to the problem; only that she needed some guidance and had felt prompted to ask for the blessing.

Chas had been given many blessings during her years as a member of the Church, for a number of reasons. But this one left her barely able to breathe as she was told that her Heavenly Father loved her and was pleased with her example and charity to those who came into her home. She was told that she should always remain humble and be gracious in accepting the help of others in times of need, and that her reliance on others could bless the lives of those willing to give, even more than her own. She couldn't hold back tears as she heard that she needed to trust in the Lord as He carefully molded precious lives to achieve their greatest potential. She was also told that His ways might not make sense to mortals, but by living close to the Spirit and keeping the commandments, she would be an instrument in His hands to bring souls to Christ through her charitable nature and humility. Her tears increased as she was reminded that the Lord was mindful of the grief she'd suffered from the losses in her life, but she was assured that her loved ones on the other side of the veil were progressing in the gospel and watching out for her. There was no vagueness about being informed that difficulties lay ahead in her life, but that through her righteousness she would be sustained and comforted.

That night Chas lay awake long after she'd crawled into bed, pondering the wonder of such personal communication from God, and what it meant to her at this time. She knew that she shouldn't try to speculate over what difficulties might lie ahead, or who she might help bring to Christ. But there was no doubting in her heart or mind that angels existed in her life, and that she knew the course she needed to take, a course on which she was already firmly embarked. And she had found peace—perfect, undeniable peace.

When sleep continued to elude her, Chas got up and wrote a long, handwritten letter to Jackson to share her feelings regarding this evening's experience, keeping in mind his minimal knowledge of gospel principles. She was purposely vague on some things, but made it clear that she believed he had been inspired to help her; she also told him that money had been tighter than she had been willing to admit. She thanked him for being a great blessing in her life, and apologized for anything unkind she might have said, and also for her pride over the money. She closed the letter by telling him how much she loved him, and how grateful she was to have him in her life. She didn't wonder any more then than she ever had if she should be reticent about her feelings. She and Jackson weren't the kind of people to play games, and he needed to know that she hoped and prayed every day that this story would have a happy ending for them, and that they could be together forever. She felt sure he wouldn't catch the same implication of *forever* that she'd intended, but maybe someday he would understand.

The next time they talked, Chas told him she'd sent a letter, and asked him to please let her know when he got it. Then they talked about other things. He called her a couple of days later to tell her that he'd just read the letter. He thanked her, said it was remarkable, and then he asked her a couple of questions. They talked of other things, and the money issue didn't come up again. Chas felt grateful as the financial freedom began to settle in over the coming weeks. She was able to take care of some repairs that were overdue, and to start putting some money away for future needs.

All in all, she felt that she was adjusting fairly well to Granny's absence and her long-distance relationship with Jackson. She missed them both, but she was coping. Polly and Charlotte helped fill in the gaps, and as always, she loved running the inn. It was a good life. She just hoped and prayed that Jackson might not settle too comfortably back into his life elsewhere, and that one day he might choose to share this life with her.

Chas reached a day when she not only felt ready to go through all of Granny's things, she felt eager. Prior to that, she had kept the room exactly as it had been, often going there for solace. But suddenly the room felt as if it had become some kind of unhealthy shrine that needed purging. Perhaps Granny was nudging her along from the other side. During a few days at the beginning of a week when no guests were scheduled at the inn, Chas started emptying the drawers and the closet. She stripped the sheets from the bed where her grand-mother had died, and with Polly's help she rearranged the furniture. Most of Granny's things were given to charity, while Chas just turned a blind eye to her lingering sentimentality and reminded herself that, after all, they were just *things*. She carefully put any belongings of Granny's that had *true* sentimental value away in the cedar chest where Granny had kept things that were precious to *her*.

With that much accomplished, Chas started cleaning out her own room and moved her things into Granny's old room, taking it over completely. With Chas's old room cleaned out and cleaned up, Polly moved her things there, and the room she'd been staying in was once again made ready for guests. Chas was grateful for Polly's friendship as well as her companionship, and wondered what she would ever do without her. They joked about running the inn together as a couple of old spinsters. Chas laughed over the idea while inside it broke her heart. She far preferred to imagine herself growing old in this house with Jackson by her side, raising a family. But whatever happened, Polly would always have a place with her.

Throughout the course of the project, Chas spoke with Jackson on the phone several times. He helped talk her through the process, and they shared many tender memories. She felt so grateful that he had known Granny, as opposed to just being told about her. In fact, she marveled at how well he had known her. He knew all of her little idiosyncrasies and eccentricities, and he had been a recipient of her generous heart. Their bond was deepened by the mutual love they shared for this great woman who would remain alive through their mutual memories.

With her project completed, Chas felt more comfortable in the house than she had since Granny's death. When many weekend guests arrived, she became caught up in her work and felt grateful for all she'd been blessed with. She was thrilled to get a funny card in the mail from Jackson, and not many days later, she got a sentimental one. In turn she started looking for cards to send him, and it quickly became a little game back and forth. She looked forward to receiving his cards as much as she enjoyed sending them to him. And occasionally she sent a little care package with something silly in it, and always some of Charlotte's baked goods.

Jackson laughed out loud to see a card from Chas appear in his stack of mail. The regular appearance of cards and packages was one of the highlights in his life, second only to their daily phone calls. He immediately broke the seal on the envelope as he moved to a chair to sit and read. On the front of the card was a photograph of the inn that had been artistically altered to give it an ethereal effect. And printed with it were the words, *It was the best of times, it was the worst of times . . .*

"Wow," he said aloud and opened the card. He could never beat that. Inside there was nothing printed, but Chas's handwriting filled the entire thing, and he eagerly began to read. *My dearest love, I came across this card in a drawer and thought of you. It was one of those things I'd had made at one time as a marketing tool, but now it seemed perfect to send, if only to remind you of your other home, and hopefully to manipulate you into missing me and the inn as much as we miss you. While I was thinking about the words printed on this card, and the meaning they must have surely had for our friend Mr. Dickens, I thought of the time you spent here. For both of us it was surely the best of times and the worst of times. I am astounded to think of the life-altering challenges we both faced during that time, and the grief we had to deal with, each in our own way, but at the same time, there are so many wonderful moments and so much joy mingled into those memories. You changed my life and opened my heart. You gave me strength when I needed it, and you blessed my life by allowing me to help you through some of the worst of times for you. Whatever the future may bring for us, we must always*

remember that we have shared the best and the worst of times, but as time
passes and life moves on, I hope that we can remember more fully the best
of times, the times that are close to my heart as I know they are close to
yours. May God be with you, and bless and protect you every hour of
every day, and may we yet share more and more of the best of times. All
my love and then some, Chas.

Jackson had to blink back tears as he read, then he read it all the
way through a second time. He sat for a long time with the card in
his hand, pondering the state of his life. Every day he felt torn
between letting go of this life to take hold of a new one, and seeing to
what felt like unfinished business in Virginia. He had trouble
defining what exactly felt unfinished. The only thing that really
bugged him was the elusiveness of the drug dealers responsible for
Dave's death, and for other deaths as well. But they were at dead ends
in every direction, and there was nothing to be done that other agents
couldn't do. Still, he felt hesitant to leave, and he didn't know why.
He concluded that he just needed more time.

Chas was thrilled when Jackson called to thank her for the card,
saying that it was the best card he'd ever received in his life. He told
her that he'd set it on the nightstand next to a framed picture of the
two of them in front of the Christmas tree. Then they talked until it
was time to go to sleep. With the difference in time zones, it was a
good thing that Jackson was accustomed to going to bed later than
Chas.

Every once in a while Jackson suggested that she fly to Norfolk
for a weekend. He even offered to pay all of her expenses, but she
assured him she could afford it. He told her there was a fairly nice
hotel not far from his apartment, and he would take very good care of
her. After it had come up a number of times and she'd managed to
mostly avoid the subject, he finally asked, "What is it, Chas? Tell me
why you won't come."

"I was wondering when you'd see through me."

"It's not easy to see through you when I can't even see you. Tell
me why. If there's a reason that makes sense, then tell me, and I'll
drop it. Do you not want to see me or—"

"Oh, it's not that! I *do* want to see you."

"Are you worried about leaving the inn?"

"Yes and no. It feels strange to think of leaving it, but I know Polly and Jen could manage. And of course Charlotte would help."

"Then what?"

"It scares me a little. Does that shock you?"

"No. I've wondered."

"I've never been to a city that big."

"It's not *that* big, compared to some."

"Bigger than I've ever been to."

"It would be good for you to leave your little world for a few days. I will pick you up at the airport, and will take very good care of you."

"I have no doubt of that."

"Then come. I miss you. And I can't get away long enough to make my coming there worth it right now. I think it's your turn to come to my house."

"Is this a role reversal test?"

"Maybe," he chuckled. "Do I need to call Polly and Charlotte? Do your friends even know this has come up?"

"No. If they did, they'd kick me out of my own house."

"So, just gather all your courage and do it. This weekend would be good. I can get an extra day off."

"This weekend?" she asked, wishing she hadn't sounded so astonished.

"The weather is beautiful, Chas. It's spring. Come and see me."

"Okay, okay," she said. "I'll do it."

After she hung up the phone, Chas wondered what she had agreed to. Then she thought of seeing Jackson and nearly squealed out loud. She got busy making arrangements, and the enthusiasm of her friends helped make it easier. She talked to Jackson several times through the course of making certain that everything was in order, and before she knew it she was in the air on her way to Virginia. She felt butterflies at the thought of seeing the man she loved, which helped compensate a little for her mild nervousness over the experience of traveling so far.

Chas did as Jackson had instructed and called him from her cell phone the moment the plane landed. Without even saying hello, he said, "You are going to hate me."

"What?" she asked, immediately panicked.

"Now, there's no need for alarm. I just . . . got hung up here. It was important and I couldn't get away."

"Okay," Chas said, trying to be reasonable. "I'm sure I can survive here at the airport until you get here. Lots of people do it."

"You don't have to. I've sent two of my best men to pick you up."

"Your best men?" She laughed. "It sounds like witness protection, or something."

She'd meant it to be funny but Jackson was completely serious as he said, "Yeah."

"You mean . . . they really do that kind of stuff?"

"Yeah."

"Okay," she sighed. "How do I find these great secret agents?"

"They'll find you."

"How?"

"They're FBI, Chas. Since you're not actually being pursued by the mob, or something, I don't think I need to give you any code words or signs. I'm sorry about this, but I'll see you soon. I love you. I've got to go."

Chas sighed again and put her phone in her purse. She was finally able to get into the plane aisle and get her bag from the overhead compartment, grateful for a kind gentleman who helped her. Once in the airport, she worked her way toward baggage claim according to the signs, even though she didn't need to claim any baggage. She didn't have time to even stop and look around or wonder where her escorts were before she found a man on each side of her; both were wearing dark suits and sunglasses.

"Chas Henrie?" one of them said.

"Yes?"

He then opened his wallet to show her his ID, saying, "I'm Agent Ekert, FBI. And this is Agent Veese. We'll take you where you need to go."

"Thank you," she said, a little surprised by their seriousness. She recognized the names the same moment she recognized vague scars on both their faces. These were the men who had almost lost their lives in an explosion. But she thought it best to pretend she didn't know about that, aware that it was still a sensitive issue.

"Do you have luggage?" Agent Veese asked.

"This is it," she said. "I'm ready."

The two men flanked her as they left the airport, and they guided her into the backseat of a black sedan that had been parked in a No Parking zone. Agent Veese was driving, and once they were beyond the airport, she noticed that he drove very quickly, but she tried to focus her attention elsewhere and not indulge in feeling nervous. The silence between the agents ended when Ekert said to his partner, "You'd better take it easy there, buddy, or Leeds'll have your head."

"He told me to hurry."

"He'd appreciate getting the car and the passengers all there in one piece."

"Amen," Chas said quietly.

"I apologize for my partner's reckless driving," Ekert said over his shoulder. "He is very good at it, however. The boss always lets him drive when we need to get somewhere in a hurry."

"Don't speed on my account," she said. "Take as long as you need."

"There's no need to be nervous, ma'am," Veese said.

"About your driving?" she asked.

"That too. But I meant whatever you've been brought in for."

Brought in for? "What exactly did Agent Leeds tell you?" she asked.

"Normally, that would be classified information, but it's not, because he didn't tell us anything. I'm sure there's nothing to worry about."

"I'm sure there isn't," Chas said, smiling to herself. Clearly these men had no idea that she had a personal connection to the man who had sent them to get her.

"Except for Veese's driving."

"Hey," Veese chuckled, "he said to hurry, and I always do what the big man tells me."

The big man? Chas had suspected that Jackson was being humble about his position. Now she had proof.

Attempting to distract herself from Veese's driving, she focused on the scenery passing by. Everything just looked way too big and busy and overwhelming. She *was* glad to be in the care of competent professionals who knew their way around the city. She lost track of the time it took to get to their destination, but when they were getting out of the car she had a repeat episode of the butterflies that had consumed her when the plane had been landing. *He was so close!*

Again the agents flanked her as they entered the building and went up the elevator, Veese carrying her suitcase. They stepped off into a busy area with many desks and a lot of noise. A woman looked up from her work for only a second and said, "Leeds wants her in his office."

"Why?" Ekert asked.

"I don't know. Because he said so. Since when do we need any more reason than that?"

"His office, really?" Ekert asked.

"He made it very clear," the woman said with mild impatience. She glanced at the clock. "He said he'd be out of that meeting by four, so he should be there soon."

"Okay," Ekert said, and they went down a hall, away from the noise, and through a door that said *Jackson T. Leeds* on it. "Have a seat," he told Chas, and Veese set down her bag. But the two men left the door open and remained near it in the hallway. She ignored them, glad their backs were turned, while she remained on her feet and took in her surroundings.

The room's size and its fine furnishings were an indication of his status. She briefly perused the things on top of his desk, which indicated a very busy man. She smiled to see one of the framed photos she'd sent him sitting there. She wondered why the men who'd come to get her hadn't recognized her from it, but noticed that it was facing Jackson's chair, not the other chairs across from his desk.

She was amazed at the number of framed certificates and awards behind the desk, including his college diploma. But she was more intrigued by the other wall that was covered with framed photographs. Most of them had Jackson in them with other people. Some appeared to have been taken at important events. Many were military, with a mixture of formal and casual. She thought of Martin, but with less pain than she'd become accustomed to feeling over thoughts of him. She liked seeing Jackson younger, and with his hair much darker, but she concluded that he had aged well, and he was definitely a man who had improved with maturity.

She was studying a picture of him and three other men looking as if they had literally just survived a battle, standing in front of a helicopter, when she heard his voice in the hall. Her stomach flip-flopped and her heart quickened.

"Thank you," she heard him say. "Don't forget that I want those reports on my desk Monday morning when I get here."

"Yes, sir," one of them replied.

"Have a great weekend, boss."

"You too," Jackson said and stepped into the room.

In the few seconds it took him to close the door, Chas took him in visually and felt utterly giddy. He wore dark slacks, a light blue button-up shirt, and a striped tie. And a leather shoulder holster with a pistol. For a long moment they just looked at each other, then he showed that rare full smile that lit up his eyes. "Wow," he said and chuckled. "It is really good to see you."

"You too," she said. "Are you just going to stand there, or are you going to kiss me?"

He smiled again and stepped slowly toward her, as if he were savoring the anticipation. Chas knew her heart had rarely if ever pounded so hard as he took her face into his hands and pressed his lips to hers.

"Oh," he said, looking into her eyes, "I *do* believe in miracles. It is *so* good to see you."

"Amen," she murmured and urged him to kiss her again, then she wrapped her arms around him, holding him tightly while she settled her head against the warm familiar spot on his shoulder. The only thing that felt unfamiliar was the leather strap of the holster. But it suited him so well that it took no effort to become accustomed to it. He held her tightly and pressed a kiss into her hair. The warmth and secure familiarity of their embrace soothed and filled her.

"I'm sorry I couldn't pick you up," he said. "I had great fantasies about a romantic airport reunion."

"Me too. But it's okay." She looked up at him. "They took very good care of me."

"They'd better have."

"And now I know how it feels to be in FBI custody. I was wondering if you did that on purpose."

"What?"

"Sent agents to get me without telling them we had any personal connection?"

He chuckled. "No, but now that you mention it . . . it was pretty clever of me. I just don't need these people knowing my personal life. All they would do is razz me about it."

"At least you *have* a personal life. That's a positive development, right?"

"Very positive," he said and kissed her again.

Chas eased away as she said, "So, apparently you're a pretty important guy around here. I think you've been holding out on me."

"There's nothing I could have told you that would have impressed you," he said as she sat in his chair and he sat on the edge of the desk. "There're many people I have to answer to. I'm just somewhere in the middle."

"But getting here . . . to the middle . . . can't have been easy."

"No, I suppose not."

She turned in the chair to look again at his awards and photos. He noticed and said, "It's kind of vain, I know. But everything on the walls is a piece of evidence that reminds me—and the people I have to face— that I've earned the right to sit in that chair. It gives me perspective."

"I like that about you, Agent Leeds."

"You like what?"

"The way you appreciate perspective." She spun his chair like a child so that it went around several times. "I'm getting a whole new perspective on you."

"It's still me."

"Yes," she said, stopping the chair, "it only took about thirty seconds to realize that." She smiled, and he smiled back. "So, I'm here."

"Yes, you are."

"I did it. I drove to Butte, got on a plane, got an FBI escort, and I'm here. No panic attacks or anything."

"Remarkable! I told you I believe in miracles." He laughed softly. "It is *really* good to see you. This office has never looked better, and next week when I come back to it, it's going to be really drab."

"Don't think about that now. I just got here. What are we going to do?"

"We're going to stop by my place long enough for me to change my clothes, then we'll check you in at your hotel, and then I have reservations at my favorite restaurant. Tomorrow we're going to see the sights and spend the entire day holding hands while we do it."

"Sounds great so far."

"On Sunday . . ." He used a dramatic voice to indicate he had a great surprise. "I found a Mormon church and figured out what time they meet."

"You're taking me to church?"

"I am," he said proudly. "And then I thought we could cook dinner at my place and watch a sappy movie, or something. And Monday . . . well, I don't want to talk about Monday. We have time to go out to breakfast before I take you to the airport, and then I have to be back at my desk by noon."

"You're right. Let's not talk about Monday." She stood up. "Come on, Leeds. I want to see where you live. Fair is fair."

He picked up her bag and opened the door, motioning her into the hallway. They walked side-by-side toward the elevator, and she took another good look at all of the people working here, and the activity taking place. It was a lot more complicated—and noisy—than running an inn.

In the elevator, Jackson kissed her again since they were alone, then he smiled at her as the doors opened and they walked to a dark blue SUV. He pushed the button on the remote and the back opened, where he put her bag. Then he opened the passenger door for her and she got in.

While he was driving she could only stare at him. "I can't believe I'm here . . . with you."

He took her hand and kissed it. "I can't believe it either." He stopped at a traffic light and gave her a quick kiss. "It is really good to see you."

"You too."

He pointed out some things about places they were passing, but she felt indifferent to anything but being with him. His apartment turned out to be one floor of a four-story home that was connected on both sides to a long row of similar homes. They were beautiful and classic, and it was obviously a nice part of the city. But she didn't know how he could handle the closed-in feeling. When she mentioned that, he only said, "I'm not home much, and when I am, I'm on the phone."

The apartment itself was fairly tidy, but then he'd known she was coming. She knew, however, from his staying at the inn, that he was a fairly tidy man. The apartment was simple and practical, and looked like a place where a man lived alone. He gave her a brief tour, then he went into the bedroom and closed the door, telling her he'd only be a few minutes. She looked around more carefully, and everywhere she looked, she found cards she had sent him, along with pictures of the two of them together. He came out dressed in the way she was most accustomed to seeing him, wearing jeans and a dark polo shirt. He gave her another kiss, and they went to the hotel where she was staying. He checked her in, then carried her bag for her as they went to the room to make certain everything was in order. Then they left to get to the restaurant where he'd made reservations. Dinner was wonderful, and being with him was heavenly. The sparkle in his eyes strengthened her hope that one day he might choose her over his job. But she couldn't think about that too deeply at the moment.

The remainder of the weekend was everything Chas had been hoping for. They had a wonderful time, and being together helped fill the reservoir of loneliness for both of them. But saying good-bye at the airport was excruciating. She was aware of him lingering while she went through security, then once she was past the metal detectors, she waved and blew a kiss. He returned the gesture, and she had to turn and walk away in order to keep from sobbing in public.

On returning home, Chas was glad to see the inn and to be back within its secure walls. She and Jackson quickly settled into their old routine of exchanging phone calls and cards. She began to wonder if she was being stubborn about her resistance to leave the inn, and she made it a matter of serious prayer, along with the question of whether she should continue to remain invested in her relationship with Jackson. If he wasn't the right man for her, then this was just torture for both of them. With time she got her answers very clearly. She *did* need to remain at the inn, and she needed to be patient with Jackson. But her convictions had deepened. She knew her place in Jackson's life, and she could only hope that he could come to the same conclusion.

Weeks later, while she was struggling to hold on to the answers she'd received, Chas felt impressed to read her patriarchal blessing. She hadn't done this for a long time, probably a year or more. In actuality, she'd probably only read it a handful of times in the years since she'd received the blessing. It had always left her feeling like something wasn't right in her life, like maybe the promised blessings were not meant to be hers at all. She'd never been able to read it without missing Martin and feeling that he had been her one chance at having certain things in her life. She was surprised now to have her mind filled with an entirely different perspective, and the warmth in her heart verified that these promises were not related to Martin, but to Jackson. She read the phrases through five or six times, asking herself if she was putting Jackson into it simply because she wanted him there. But deep inside, she knew it was him. The answers she had received before were reaffirmed now. They were meant to be together, and she knew it.

With that conviction fresh in her heart, she read the specified sentences again, overcome with joy and peace. There it was in black and white, that in this mortal life she would kneel at a temple altar with the man of her choosing, and together they would bring children into the world and do much good with their arms linked in living the gospel.

While the feelings were still strong, Chas wrote them down in her journal. She'd hardly touched her journal since Jackson had come into her life, and then she'd lost her grandmother. Now she started spending some time with it every day until she was able to fully record the events that were close to her heart; some wonderful, some sad, all a part of the woman she was becoming.

Months passed with nothing changing in either of their lives, but Chas kept reminding herself to be patient with Jackson, and to accept that she couldn't possibly comprehend the grand scheme of life from God's perspective. She simply had to trust in Him.

Jackson came to the inn for a weekend late in the summer. It was so wonderful to have him there that Chas was almost delirious. They settled immediately into a comfortable routine, although Chas left most of the work to Polly and Jen so that she could enjoy Jackson's company. His stay was way too brief, but Chas tried to focus on how grateful she was to see him at all. She didn't know if it was a curse or a blessing to have his presence at the inn renew her deep desire to have him there permanently. She'd been praying for an opportunity to bring it up, and as the time drew near for him to leave, she knew she couldn't put it off. During a quiet moment, she took his hand and said, "I don't want to keep living like this, Jackson. If this is going to be a permanent long-distance relationship, I . . ."

"You what?"

"I want more. I think you want more as well."

He sighed. "I do, Chas. I just . . . need time."

"Time to what? Become more settled into your work? Time to get yourself into a dangerous situation and never come back to me at all?"

"I don't know." He sounded frustrated. "I just . . . feel like something is undone, like there's something I need to do."

"You can't track those drug dealers down single-handedly."

"No, but I know more about them than anyone else."

"Then teach someone else what you know."

"It's not that simple. My gut tells me I need to stay . . . at least for now. And even if I were ready to retire and leave it all behind, how do I know that you're going to pray and get the answer that it's all right to marry a man like me?"

Chas looked at him firmly. She wanted him to know the conviction she felt. "I already have. I've known for months."

Jackson couldn't respond to that. The silence became loud while he pondered the implication in light of everything he knew about her.

"Does that make a difference?" she asked.

"Maybe. Why haven't you said anything?"

"I was trying to be patient and give you the time that you need. I'm not feeling very patient. I'm feeling more like . . . if something doesn't change for us soon . . ."

"What?" he demanded.

"I don't know. Maybe I'm just paranoid. I feel like something bad is going to happen to you. Or there's the old fear that you're just going to realize you don't want to marry me after all and you'll just stop calling."

"I would never do that."

"I know, Jackson. This is fear talking, and I should learn not to be so paranoid . . . but I just can't shake this feeling."

Again there was silence until he said, "I just need a little more time. Let me think it through, and . . . I don't know. I'll make a decision."

"Okay," she said. "Thank you."

It didn't come up again before he left, but when they embraced as he was leaving, Chas felt a horrible sense that she might not ever see him again. She told him twice to be careful, and he insisted that he would. But she still couldn't shake that feeling.

CHAPTER 16

Jackson rose from the chair behind his desk when one of his superiors entered the room with an unmistakable air of determination and purpose. He was wearing an expression that Jackson knew well. Something had upset him, and something needed to be done about it. He started out by bringing up a particular group of drug dealers that Jackson had been tracking for years, using a number of unfavorable words as adjectives. Jackson knew well the people he was referring to; they were responsible for the deaths that still haunted him and everyone else in this office. Jackson was then informed that they had obtained an incredible lead about something going down in a third-world country with these people, and Jackson was the only one who knew them well enough to go undercover and be the spearhead for a plan to bring them down. His Marine experience was crucial to the plan that had apparently been formulated by his superiors in the last ten minutes. Hearing that made him nervous.

"Okay," Jackson said, "what do you need me to do?" His heart was pounding while his mind swirled with a combination of thoughts. Maybe this was what he'd been waiting for. And now it could all be over and he could retire in peace and get married.

"We're leaving now," he was told.

"Now?"

"This minute."

Jackson felt a little panicked. "Okay, I just need to make one call and—"

"No calls." The director took his phone, turned it off, and threw it into a desk drawer. "No one can know where you are or that you were even planning to leave. We have to go now. If everything goes as planned, you'll be back in a few days."

What could Jackson do but follow him out the door and down the hall? His lifetime allegiance to duty and his deep desire to see these undesirables go down fueled his determination to follow orders. He could only pray that Chas would forgive him. He couldn't even imagine what she might think if he didn't call. He hoped it would be over quickly.

* * * * *

Chas only waited about ten minutes past the time that Jackson usually called before she tried to call him. She only got voice mail, both at home and on his cell phone. She left messages, then waited. An hour passed; then two. She prayed and told herself there could be all kinds of reasons why someone in the FBI wasn't reachable by phone. But when she was still awake hours later and he hadn't called, her mind had gone wild with imagining things that might have happened to him. She dozed on and off throughout the night, but never got any good sleep. All through the following day she kept trying to call, and felt more frantic every hour. She wondered more than once if this was his way of letting her know that it was over, but he'd told her he would never do that to her, and she believed him. Something was wrong and she knew it. By evening she had worked herself into such a frenzy that Polly and Charlotte had to talk a long time to get her to calm down. They convinced her that no phone call didn't necessarily mean something was wrong; maybe it just meant that he had gone undercover or something. She liked that idea. But she wasn't sure what to think when Polly said, "If he had died, the FBI would surely check the numbers on his cell phone, or something, and call you. They would surely call his mother."

Chas nearly called Melva, but didn't want to worry her. Jackson only called his mother once a week. Until that time came, she thought it best to keep the concern to herself. But that night she had to take something to help her sleep. She couldn't function without sleep, and she couldn't sleep wondering what was happening. Her recent feelings of paranoia on his behalf didn't help any. In her heart, she wondered if she would ever see him again.

* * * * *

During the long flight on a cargo plane, the plan was discussed in detail, and Jackson stepped off with a new temporary identity. He knew where to go and what to do, taking into consideration several possibilities of how it might go down. But he was prepared to do whatever it took.

Within twenty-four hours, he was acclimated to the country and culture enough to feel fairly confident that this was going to work. He found himself praying and knew he had Chas to thank for that. He prayed for Chas as much as for himself—that she wouldn't be worrying, that she would forgive him, and that whatever the outcome of this, she would be all right. He found it ironic that he was concerned for his own safety more than he'd been in years. The thought of being able to go home to a woman who loved him had given his life more value and meaning. Knowing that his mother and sister would miss him added to that feeling, and he prayed that all would go well and he could be home and retired before the end of the week.

When the time came to complete the deal, Jackson went into the situation in place of a drug dealer who was now in FBI custody. Their target had never met the man before, but many weeks of communication over the pending deal had been taking place between them. An arrest had been made, information had been confiscated, and communication intercepted. Now Jackson only had to hope that no one was on to him, and he could be in and out in a hurry, giving the local police all they needed to bring this guy down for good. With the grief this drug lord had given *both* countries, they were in this together, which made everything a whole lot easier.

Jackson was amazed at how easily it came together. Years of watching and waiting paid off, and it was over in minutes. With his mission accomplished, Jackson went to bed in a dirty motel, anticipating being on his way home early in the morning. He would be especially glad to call Chas, to hear her voice, and to reassure her that he'd had no choice in being unable to call her. He drifted into sleep, while thoughts of her soothed him like a lullaby.

Jackson was yanked out of his sleep so abruptly that he was consumed with terror. He knew there were at least three men dragging him out of his bed by the way he was being held too tightly to do anything about it. A dark sack was put over his head, assaulting him with images of terrorist executions. He'd encountered fear countless times in his career, but he had *never* been so afraid in his life. He'd never felt so helpless as he was bound, dragged, and shoved into a vehicle where he endured a long and painful ride in some kind of confined space. He realized he must have fallen asleep when the vehicle came to a jolting stop and he was startled back to the awareness that this was really happening.

After being dragged into some kind of foul-smelling structure with hollow-sounding passages, he was thrown onto a concrete floor, and the sack was pulled off of his head. But he couldn't see his captors due to the bright light in his face. He'd encountered many moments in his life that had felt like some sick twist on a bad movie, but this definitely topped the list. While he was wondering what exactly this was about, and if there was any possible hope of escape, the questions and accusations started flying. He was grateful for his fluent Spanish, which made it possible for him to understand and answer. He was certain they would have beaten the language into him had he not already known it. But as his understanding of the language made the situation alarmingly clear, he began to doubt that he would ever get out of here alive. The identity he'd taken on to get rid of a drug lord was apparently someone these people had good cause to be angry with. They wanted information that Jackson couldn't give them, and he knew these kinds of people well enough to know that there was only one possible response to not getting what they wanted.

* * * * *

Every hour that Chas didn't hear from Jackson was torturous. She knew something was wrong; she just *knew* it. She desperately wanted to talk to his mother and sister, knowing their grief and concerns would be the same. But she held off, knowing that when Melva missed her son's call, Chas would hear from her.

When Melva *did* call, Chas could only try to reassure her, but she knew she didn't sound very convincing. Melva got her daughter on the other extension, and the three of them discussed the possibilities and all they were feeling. By the end of the conversation they were all crying. But at least she had someone to cry with, Chas concluded. The following day Melva called her again. And the day after that. By the time Chas had not heard from Jackson for a week, she had become dependent on over-the-counter sleeping pills to get any rest, and her days were spent aimlessly going through the motions of her work and her life. She prayed constantly, and did a twenty-four-hour fast every few days. It didn't feel like much of a sacrifice when she could hardly bring herself to eat.

On the day that she was supposed to go to the temple, she almost didn't. Then she realized there was no better place for her to go when she so desperately needed God's help in giving her hope that Jackson would be all right. She came home feeling more calm, but she feared that the peace had more to do with her acceptance of Jackson's death than with his being alive and well. And the worst of it was the not knowing, the helplessness, the wondering. She missed him so much! She ached for his company. Even across the miles, he had become her best friend, and she had grown to rely on his companionship every day. She loved him! She needed him! But all she could do was pray.

* * * * *

Jackson came awake to the horror that he was still in the same place. Nothing had changed. The stench of his surroundings was still there. The growling pain of hunger hadn't left him. The floor where he slept was still hard and cold. And the slightest movement brought to mind the repeated torture he'd endured. These people didn't know who he was, but the man they believed him to be apparently was a great threat to them. The problem was that he couldn't give them information he didn't have, and they were too sadistic to just kill him and get it over with. And with every waking moment, he felt continual heartache while he wondered what Chas was thinking. And his mother and sister. The internal torment was equal to his physical suffering.

He felt sure that being in hell itself with Satan as his warden could not be worse than this. There was the tiniest bit of satisfaction in knowing that before he had ended up in the wrong place at the wrong time, he *had* been instrumental in bringing down the evil scum he had been hunting for years. These thoughts gave him some tiny degree of sanity. Arrests had been made, and he had felt vindication on behalf of Dave and everyone else affected by what had happened. That gratification had quickly disintegrated, however, during daily sessions of tortured questioning, and the rations he was being given couldn't sustain a cat. What little food and water there was tasted bad and was making him sick. He could only pray that it would end soon.

* * * * *

Chas was flipping through channels and paused when she saw the letters FBI. She watched for a minute as men with those letters printed boldly on bullet-proof vests entered a building with guns poised. Then the shooting began, and she changed the channel. After a few minutes on the Food Network and a brief look at *Little House on the Prairie,* she cruised through channels again until she stopped on the scene of a drama taking place in a busy office, with a couple of nice-looking guys wearing guns in shoulder holsters. Not as nice-looking as Jackson, she concluded. The next channel was news from Iraq, then she ended up back at the same movie where the FBI swat team was now arresting the bad guys and putting one of their own into a body bag. Chas flipped off the TV. No wonder Jackson hated watching it. She actually screamed as she threw the remote at the wall, grateful to know that she was alone in the house. Then she sobbed uncontrollably before crawling into bed, even though it was only nine o'clock.

A little before nine-thirty the phone rang. The caller ID told her it was either Melva or Melinda. She sighed, wondering how she could give these women hope when she felt none at all. Melinda had barely said hello before Chas could tell that something was wrong.

"What's happened?" she demanded.

"The FBI called."

"Is he dead?" She had to know.

"They don't know," Melinda cried. "Mama's so upset; we both are." Chas couldn't believe what she was hearing. She felt like she was going to throw up even before she got any more information. "Ironically, they called because Jackson had Mama down as next of kin in his file when he was first hired. She's living with me, so she's not at the number he put down, but they found her through her Social Security checks. They *are* the FBI. If we hadn't seen him in December, it would have been the first we'd heard of him in all those years."

Chas appreciated the irony, but she was more concerned with the present. "What did they tell you? What's happened?"

"They would hardly tell us anything. They said he had to go out of the country on very short notice and he couldn't let anyone know he was going. But he disappeared in the middle of whatever they were doing, and they can't find him. They're looking, they told us. But they wouldn't tell us which country, or anything else. Now you know everything I know, Chas. I just don't know what to think."

Melinda started to cry so hard she couldn't speak, but Chas was crying too. They cried together on the phone for a few more minutes until they realized it was pointless, and Melinda promised to let her know when they heard anything, no matter what time of day or night. Chas threw the phone at the wall and it landed near the remote. A deep, unfathomable pain rose from within her, and she howled with anguish before she curled around her pillow and cried so hard that she ended up having to dash into the bathroom to throw up. The possibilities of where he might be if he was still alive were as nauseating as the possibilities of how he might have died.

Chas was curled up on the bathroom floor, still sobbing uncontrollably, when Polly found her there. "What's happened?" she demanded. "Tell me, Chas. Calm down and tell me." Chas tried but couldn't speak. Polly sat on the floor beside her and wrapped her in a sisterly embrace. Chas continued to cry, but Polly just held her. When she calmed down enough to speak, Chas muttered, "They don't know if he's alive or dead. The FBI doesn't know where he is, or what happened to him. They won't even tell his mother what country he's in. We only know it's not this one."

"But he could still be alive?" Polly said.

"Under what circumstances?" Chas countered and started to cry again.

"Let's get you to bed," Polly insisted and helped her to her feet. "Have you taken anything yet to help you sleep?"

"No," Chas said. "I don't want to sleep. I want to . . ."

"What? Cry your heart out all night? You need some sleep. It's just the two of us here tonight, and we'll talk it through in the morning." She handed Chas a pill and glass of water.

"Don't leave me, Polly."

"I'll stay right here until you go to sleep," she promised, "and then I'll be in the next room with the door open. I'll be here if you need anything. Now rest."

Chas was grateful for the numbing effect of the pill that lulled her into sleep, but her dreams were littered with images of Jackson being shot down in the streets of some third-world country—or worse. She knew she'd watched way too much TV when visions of what could be happening became all too clear in her mind as she drifted in and out of sleep, caught between the terror of her dreams and the horror of her thoughts.

* * * * *

Jackson was grateful to spend more time unconscious than awake, but he wondered if that meant he was nearly dead. He hoped so. He'd lost his sense of time, but he knew he'd been there at least three weeks. His mind had started playing tricks on him as memories and fears all mingled with the present and he couldn't tell what was dreaming and what was hallucination. More than once he heard a voice; a comforting voice, familiar and warm. But he couldn't quite tell what it was saying. Then he heard the voice and thought he felt a hand on his face. He jumped at the sensation and found no one there. Then the voice became more clear. Whether it was in his mind or he actually heard it with his ears, he couldn't be sure, but he distinctly heard the words, *Hold on a little longer, young man. You have much to live for. You're just getting started.*

Jackson drifted again into oblivion, and his next awareness occurred as he was being dragged to his feet, as much as that was possible when he was too weak to stand. He was literally being dragged by two men holding his arms. The pain such movement provoked was excruciating, but he didn't have enough voice to protest. He hoped this was the end, and prayed that it would be quick and painless. And he prayed that the three women who loved him would forgive him, and be comforted. He could barely see shadows and glimpses of blurry light through his swollen eyes, but he knew they were going the opposite direction from where he was taken for the usual torture routine. This increased his hope that death was coming. He felt fresh air and knew they were outside. It was dark; nighttime. He was shoved into a vehicle, and he groaned. He heard an engine start, and a second later he was pulled out of the vehicle through the other door. He heard whispered words near his ear, "We're going to drop and roll, buddy. Just hold on to me."

Jackson's heart began to pound. The voice was familiar! The words were in English! It only took him a few more seconds to recognize that he was rolling on the ground with another man holding onto him. It all felt familiar. Marine training. Rescuing the wounded. He found enough adrenaline to assist in the efforts of his rescuer. A split second after they stopped moving, an explosion occurred; presumably the vehicle they'd gotten in and out of.

"Okay, buddy," he heard near his ear. "We're going to stay right here and not move for a while. With any luck they'll think you're dead."

"Got it," Jackson managed to say. "Thank you." Then he lost consciousness. When he came around again, he still couldn't see more than shadows, but he knew the sound. He was in a helicopter. He moved slightly and realized he was strapped to a rescue gurney. There was an IV in his arm. A soothing male voice said, "Don't try to move. Just relax. You're going to be fine."

"Okay," Jackson said. "Water."

"You bet," the voice said, and his head was lifted so that he could drink. And it was *real* water. He couldn't believe it! He was really going to survive this.

The next words out of his mouth were, "Phone. I need a phone."

He heard chuckling. "Give us another hour or so, Agent Leeds, and you can use my phone."

"Okay," Jackson said again. "More water, please."

"You got it," he was told, and Jackson pulled the water into his body like he pulled hope into his spirit. It was over!

* * * * *

Chas was practically inconsolable, and she was so upset that Polly finally called the home teachers, who came to give her a blessing. She was offered comfort and peace, and she was able to rest better. But there was no promise of the outcome, and her heart ached for Jackson in ways she couldn't comprehend. At least when Martin had died she had known he was dead. She had known how and when it had happened. She had known that it was quick; he hadn't even known what hit him. This was pure, unrefined agony.

Two and half days after Chas had received news that she felt certain she would never recover from, Polly told her she needed to go out for twenty minutes, and as Jen hadn't arrived yet, Chas would need to man the phone.

"Are you okay with that?" Polly asked. "Or do you want me to have someone come over and—"

"I can answer the phone," Chas said. "It's not likely to ring, anyway. I'm not completely crippled, and I'm going to have to get a grip sooner or later. Just go, but hurry back." She knew Polly had meant that she was more afraid to leave Chas alone than she was of leaving her to answer the phone. She'd never felt so traumatized in her life. At least when Martin had been killed, Granny had been here. And Granny had been here when the baby had died. And Jackson had been here when she'd lost Granny. Now she couldn't imagine what she would do without Polly, and she didn't want to be alone.

Polly hadn't been gone five minutes when the phone rang, and Chas wanted to curse, except that she had a rule about that. She looked at the caller ID. Out of area. That didn't mean anything. She cleared her throat and struggled for an even tone of voice, answering as she always did, "Dickensian Inn. How may I help you?"

"Chas?" she heard through a horrible mass of noise in the background.

"Yes," she said, her heart pounding with hope that it was him, and dread that it wasn't. She sat up straighter and clutched the phone more tightly.

"Thank God it's you," the voice said, and with those four words she knew it was Jackson, even though his voice sounded gruff and unnatural.

She resisted the temptation to start sobbing when she feared barely being able to communicate with him at all. "Where are you?" she demanded.

"What?" he asked.

"Where are you?" she shouted. "I can barely hear you."

"I know. It's insane here. I can't tell you where I am, and I don't know when I can call you again. I only have about a minute—literally—so listen carefully."

"Okay, I'm listening," she said, tears rolling down her face.

"There's a reason I didn't call, Chas. You need to know that. But I'm okay now."

"Now?"

"I don't know when I can call you again, but please don't worry. And don't think it's because I don't care. I love you. Are you hearing me?"

He was shouting and she could barely hear him, but she replied firmly, "Yes. I hear you. I love you too."

"I'll be in isolation; I don't know how long. They'll be treating me for PTSD, and there's the whole debriefing thing, and . . . I'm rambling. It doesn't matter. Just know that I'm okay, and will you call my mother and . . ."

The phone went dead and Chas yelled into it, "Jackson? Jackson?" as if she could make it reconnect. She turned the phone off, then hung her head and sobbed every bit as hard as she had when Melinda had called a few days ago. Then she sank to her knees and thanked God for giving her a miracle. She couldn't imagine what Jackson had been through. But he was alive! Oh, he was alive! In the midst of her prayer, a question popped into her mind. *"PTSD?"* she repeated aloud. What kind of horrible disease had he contracted? Was that it? He'd gotten sick somewhere? Maybe it wasn't as bad as she'd been believing. She hurried to the computer and googled the letters. She gasped when the list came up. She put a hand over her mouth. *Post traumatic stress disorder.* "Oh, help," she muttered and started to cry again.

Polly came in and startled her. "What are you doing?"

"He's alive, Polly. He called."

"Oh, my *gosh!*" Polly squealed. "I'm never here when the drama hits!"

Chas repeated the gist of the conversation, then pointed to what was on the computer screen. "Oh, dear," Polly said. "That doesn't sound good."

"No, it doesn't, but . . ." Chas hugged Polly tightly, "he's alive. Oh," she said, "I need to call his mother. I've got to do it now."

"I'd say," Polly said.

Chas dialed the number with trembling fingers. Melinda answered, and Chas said, "It's me. Put your mother on the other extension." She whimpered. "Jackson just called me. He's alive."

Melinda let out an excited shriek and said, "I'll get her. Hold on."

With Melva and Melinda both on the phone, Chas repeated what had happened, and they *all* cried. After she got off the phone, Chas took a nap. It was the first sleep she'd had without drugs since Jackson had stopped calling. That evening Melinda called to tell her that the FBI had called to inform *the next of kin* that Jackson Leeds was alive and in a military hospital, which they would not name, and they weren't sure when he would be able to make any calls. When Melinda had inquired over his condition, she was told that he was stable and he would recover; nothing more. The two women talked for a long while and concluded that they just had to be patient and settle for the relief of knowing that he was alive and that he *would* recover. And they didn't even want to talk about what it might be that he needed to recover *from*.

For more than a week none of them heard anything. Chas fought to keep busy, and now that she knew he was alive and in a hospital, it was easier to focus on something besides her grief and fears. Still, she felt afraid—and haunted. Haunted by things she didn't know and could only imagine. She started having nightmares about him, and had to call the home teachers again to ask for another blessing. Ironically, Ron had a brother-in-law who had been through some horrible things in the military, and had been treated for PTSD. Ron reported that it took some time, but he was doing well. That information, combined with the blessing, helped Chas feel more calm, and she stopped having nightmares.

Chas woke up one morning with the determination to find out what was going on with Jackson, and if possible, to at least hear him assure her with his own voice that he was okay. She was fed up with this FBI covert excuse for keeping this man's loved ones from being involved in his recovery. Even his own mother hadn't been informed of anything that gave her any consolation.

Chas started with a prayer, then she called the office where Jackson had worked and asked to speak with either Agent Veese or Agent Ekert. She said it was urgent but remained vague. She hoped they might believe she had information regarding something they were currently working on, which would encourage them to call her back sooner rather than later. Only twenty minutes passed before she got a call from a wireless number, and heard a male voice ask to speak to her.

"This is me," she said.

"This is Special Agent Veese calling from the FBI. I was given a message to call you."

"Yes, thank you for calling me back." She told him exactly who she was, calling herself "the woman in Jackson Leeds' life, the one whose picture is on his desk and all over his apartment," and that she needed more information to go on. She expressed concern for Jackson, and a desire for him to know his loved ones were there for him. She also expressed frustration on behalf of herself and Jackson's mother and sister. Even with her careful explanation, she was still expecting to be diplomatically brushed aside with the same old answers. But Agent Veese said kindly, "You're Chas. You're the one I picked up at the airport."

"That's right," she said eagerly.

"In that case, you call this number back when you have a flight to Norfolk, and I'll pick you up at the airport and take you to see him."

"You can do that?" she asked, suppressing the urge to squeal loudly into the phone.

"Yes, but I can't promise you'll get more than a few minutes with him; an hour if we're real lucky. He's heavily sedated, and an agent is required to be with him all the time, especially when any visitors or medical personnel are in the room."

"Why?" she asked, aching for answers, anything to help her understand this.

"It's protocol, ma'am, under the circumstances. Because of the work he's been involved with, we need to know what he says when he doesn't know what he's saying."

"Okay." That made sense to her. It was nice to finally have something actually make sense.

"And what about his condition? Can you tell me how he's doing . . . really?"

"I can tell you that on the drive to the hospital. But I have to warn you, ma'am, I'm willing to do this because I think Jackson needs to see somebody that can give him some hope. However, you might want to reconsider. He still doesn't look very good; not at all like himself. He might belt me in the jaw after he comes around for letting you see him like that."

Chas thought about that for a second, managing to keep silent the tears that came. She asked quietly, "Can he talk on the phone if someone could help him?"

"Maybe, but I doubt it would be very effective."

"You've worked with him for years, Agent. What do you think I should do?"

"I think you should be on the next plane and make sure he knows that you love him no matter what's happened. If you're the kind of woman who can do that, I'll do anything I can to help you."

"Why?" she asked, wiping more tears.

"He would do the same for me." His voice picked up traces of warm pride and fierce determination. "He's put his life on the line for me more than once, and if it weren't for him, we never would have brought down the drug-dealing scumbags who nearly got us *all* killed."

"He did it?" she asked, feeling the same warm pride.

"He did. But I shouldn't say anything more."

"I understand. I'm going to get a flight. I'll call you back soon. And thank you. Thank you so much!"

Chas had everything arranged in less than an hour, including making arrangements for all of the business at the inn and letting Melva and Melinda know where she was going. They all agreed that it was best for Melva *not* to try to see Jackson in this condition, and Chas reassured them that she would call as soon as she could and tell them everything.

During the drive to the airport, Chas cried intermittently. But there was hope and joy mixed with her tears. She was going to be able to see him. And while she was steeling herself for how bad it might be, she was grateful to be the one that Agent Veese would be willing to help, because he believed that she could help Jackson. And that was all she wanted right now—to help Jackson.

The flight felt far too long, and by the time she landed she had to continually will herself to remain calm. She didn't want to be a sobbing idiot with Agent Veese. She could save that for being with Jackson. He'd already seen her as a sobbing idiot.

Veese and Ekert found her at the same place as they had before, but this time, the drive from the airport was more calm. A few minutes into it, when nothing had been said, Chas interrupted the silence. "I'm waiting, Agent Veese."

"I know," he said. "I'm stalling." He sighed and turned to look at her over the seat while Ekert drove. "We don't know why it happened. Apparently the undercover identity he'd assumed in order to get the people we were after got him into trouble. Apparently someone else was real angry with this guy, and they thought that Leeds could give them information, which of course he didn't have." Chas nodded and fought for her composure. If she started crying, he was more likely to stop talking. "He was in their custody for three and a half weeks before we found him and were able to get him out. They roughed him up pretty bad," he said, but he said it gently. "There were no broken bones, and no internal injuries; nothing that won't heal with time."

Chas nodded and let out a sigh of relief that couldn't disguise the little sob that came with it. "That is very good, then."

"Yes, it's very good," Veese said, and Chas realized that knowing nothing had truly let her imagination wander into horrible territory.

"The worst of it now is just how sick he's been."

"What do you mean?"

"Apparently he picked up some kind of nasty parasite, and it's made him really sick. I have to be straight with you and tell you that . . ." He paused and met her eyes. "Do you want me to be straight with you?"

"Yes, of course," she said, cautioning herself against discounting the horrible territory where her imagination had wandered. "They didn't feed him much, and what they gave him was wretched. That's probably what made him sick, and whatever he's got, it's bad. He's been in a lot of pain, so they keep him pretty much sedated, just because he's utterly miserable otherwise. Between the injuries and the illness, he's just been a mess. That's all. But they're treating both, and he's showing improvement, and he's going to be just fine. Nothing permanent."

"Oh!" Chas said and put both hands over her quivering stomach. There was no stopping the tears that trickled down her face.

"It's okay, ma'am," Veese said, facing forward again but passing her a tissue over the seat. "We've both had some of that since we dragged him out of that hole."

"You?" Chas said. "You're the ones who rescued him?"

"Yes, ma'am," Ekert said. He hadn't previously said a word.

"He would have done the same for us," Veese added.

The remainder of the drive allowed Chas time to take in what she'd learned, and to vent her tears silently so that she could hopefully be more calm when she saw Jackson. The only other thing she said was, "Could I have a couple more of those tissues?"

"Yes, ma'am," Veese said and passed them to her.

At the hospital she took every step with hope and dread. She prayed that she could handle this well, and that her being here could make a difference on Jackson's behalf—and her own. She knew when they were approaching the right room because a man in a dark suit with an ear wire was sitting outside the door. He came to his feet when he saw Veese and Ekert approaching.

"Any change?" Veese asked him.

"Nothing other than they say his vitals look better today," the man said.

"Take a break," Veese said. "I'll cover for a while."

"Good, I'm starving," the agent said and walked away. Ekert sat in the chair he had been occupying, and Veese pushed open the door, hesitating a moment to check Chas's expression. She nodded firmly and followed Veese into the room. He closed the door behind them.

Chas approached the bedside, holding her breath. She felt immediate relief to see that he didn't look as bad as she'd expected. Again she had allowed her imagination to run wild. But perhaps that wasn't all bad when she felt more relieved than shocked. He still looked bad. His face bore evidence of many cuts and bruises, but they were clearly in stages of healing. He looked a little swollen in places, but she suspected that too was improving. The only medical equipment hooked to him was an IV in his left arm, and monitors that showed he was very much alive. She set her purse on the floor and quietly slid a chair across the floor so she could sit and hold his right hand. She felt a subtle flinch in his hand when she took it, but he remained asleep, no doubt aided by the medication.

She was glad to have him unconscious while she cried again, consumed once more with a combination of horror and relief. Veese handed her a box of tissues that had been on the opposite side of the bed. She thanked him, and he made himself comfortable on the other side of the room, discreetly reading a newspaper to give her as much privacy as possible. She sat there for a few minutes, adjusting to the reality of being with Jackson, and the evidence of what he'd been through. She knew that once he recovered physically, he would be treated for PTSD. And his healing on both counts might not go quickly. Once again, she was faced with needing to be patient.

A nurse came in, said hello to Veese, and started checking Jackson's vital signs while Veese gave her a one-sentence explanation of who Chas was and why she was here.

"Don't be afraid to talk to him," the nurse said to Chas, "even while he's asleep. They say it helps. Although," she glanced at the clock, "he should be coming out of it soon. We like to bring them around a little between doses, just to see how they're feeling and responding. I'll just give you some time with him, and you let me know when he needs something for the pain."

Chas nodded and thanked her as she left the room. "Once he wakes up," Veese said, "I'll give the two of you some privacy. I'm not worried about him divulging any great national secrets when he's conscious."

"If he does, I'll be sure to pass them along and then conveniently forget," she said, mildly facetious.

He smiled at her and turned the page on the newspaper. "No wonder Leeds likes you."

"I like him, too," she said and kissed Jackson's hand. Recalling the nurse's advice, she ignored Veese in the room and eased closer so that she could speak in a low voice near his ear. "I'm here, Jackson. I love you. I love you so much. We're going to get through this . . . together." He remained as he was, and she impulsively started rambling about the good times they'd had together, the holidays they'd celebrated, the things they'd helped each other through. She knew Veese was in the room, but also knew he couldn't hear what she was saying while she whispered. She just hoped that Jackson could hear it. She needed him to know that she loved him. She loved him so much.

CHAPTER 17

Jackson felt himself merging into consciousness. It still took him a long moment each time to be assured that he was surrounded by the sounds and sensations of a hospital room in the blessed United States of America. Once he knew that, the rest was just a temporary inconvenience. He'd been assured often enough that the pain and illness were temporary, so he was beginning to believe that was true. And he knew from experience that he didn't need to be awake long before he'd be given something to help him remain in oblivion while the healing took its course.

He'd been promised that he would soon be able to actually make a phone call, and he was greatly looking forward to that moment. The nurses and agents who came in and out had offered to help him make a call, but he didn't want to speak to Chas and sound as horrible as he felt. And for reasons he couldn't explain, he was a little afraid to talk to her. He'd been haunted by her words when they'd last parted, that she was afraid something bad was going to happen. Maybe if he had listened to her . . . He couldn't go there. He'd told himself a hundred times not to go there. But he couldn't avoid the regret he felt for the choices he'd made that had led up to this disaster. And the thought of how close he'd come to leaving Chas to face life alone—again—enhanced the chronic nausea he'd been dealing with.

Jackson came more fully awake but found it difficult to open his eyes. That was nothing new. He found some comfort in a vague sense that his dreams had been good, as opposed to what he usually experienced. He couldn't remember *what* he'd dreamt, but it had left him feeling less alone, less frightened, more prone to believing that this was going to end. Then he moved his hand and became aware that someone was holding it. He squeezed and felt the gesture returned. His heart quickened while he attempted to convince himself that this had to be his imagination.

Chas's heart sped up when he began to stir. She saw his expression change and knew he was conscious and that his thoughts were deep. She remained quiet and allowed him time to become more awake before she made her presence known. She felt him squeeze her hand, and her heart beat hard and fast.

Jackson turned his head on the pillow and forced his eyes open. It took him a long moment to focus, and another long moment to accept that he wasn't hallucinating. He felt tears slide over his temples and felt her hand wiping them away. "You're here," he said, his voice raspy.

"I am," she said, and he made a noise of disbelief.

As they made eye contact with an intensity that was familiar, she felt such an enormous combination of sorrow and joy that she couldn't speak. His eyes reflected her own emotions perfectly. He seemed to understand without a word spoken that the unfathomable joy of being reunited under such circumstances would not be felt without the horror that had preceded it. She finally leaned over and pressed the side of her face to his, whispering near his ear, "It is the best of times; it is the worst of times. . . ."

"Amen," he muttered and lifted his other hand to the back of her head, holding her close to him with a strength that surprised even him. She looked at him again, and he said, "I didn't want you to see me like this."

"It doesn't matter." She touched one side of his face, then the other, as if she could heal the wounds. "I had to see you. I had to. Veese helped me."

She nodded toward him, and Jackson turned just as Veese put down the paper and came to his feet. "I'll give you a few minutes alone," he said and opened the door.

"Veese," Jackson said.

"Yeah, boss?"

"Thank you."

"You'd do the same for me," he said and left the room.

Jackson turned his attention back to Chas. She felt the need to say, "I won't be able to stay long. They said I could only see you for a few minutes, and my flight leaves in a couple of hours. But I figured a short visit was better than no visit at all."

"I can't believe you're here," he said. "I never thought I'd see you again."

She whimpered, unable to hold back her emotion. "I thought you were dead . . . or worse."

"It *was* worse. I wanted to die. But now . . . now I'm so grateful to be alive."

"Oh, me too," she said and couldn't resist putting her lips to his. "I hope it isn't catching," she said, but kissed him again as if it didn't matter.

"It's not," he said and urged her into another kiss. "Oh," he murmured, "I wish I could get up out of this bed and leave with you now."

"I wish you could too," she said. "But it's okay. When you're better, I'll be waiting."

"Then I'm going to have to hurry and get better," he said, and she kissed him again. "Is everything okay?" he asked.

"I'm better now," she said. "Not knowing was the worst. I'm just so . . . grateful."

"You were praying for me," he said. "I know. I felt it."

This provoked fresh tears from Chas. "I *was* praying for you . . . constantly."

"And you need to know . . . I believe in angels, Chas. I do."

"What are you saying?"

She saw fresh tears in *his* eyes. "Granny was with me," he said in a whisper, and Chas took a sharp breath, marveling at both the concept and his conviction. "I don't know how I know, but I know. I often felt like I wasn't alone; there was a comforting presence. But more than once I heard her voice . . . in my mind. I didn't realize it at the time. It was after I came back that I remembered, and I knew it was her. She called me 'young man.'" He chuckled, and she could tell it hurt. "No one called me that but her."

"What did she tell you?"

"She told me to hold on, that there was much to live for."

Chas laughed through a gentle sob. "She's right about that."

Jackson could feel the pain coming on more, taking over, and he felt himself having to choose between being with her and being racked with what he knew would become difficult to bear without drugs. He felt compelled to say what he'd wanted to say a thousand times. "I'm so sorry, Chas," he said as he became increasingly emotional.

"For what?" she asked, and he was surprised. He felt certain she must have been angry with him all this time.

"You didn't want me to go back. You had a bad feeling. I should have listened."

She swallowed carefully. "It's over now, and you're going to be okay. It doesn't matter anymore. Nothing matters except that you're going to get better, and we're going to be together. Do you hear me?"

He nodded, but had to say, "I'm not the same man, Chas. I feel . . . broken . . . and scared. I don't know how long it will be before I can even . . ." He couldn't finish the sentence.

"It doesn't matter," she said and kissed him again. "I love you. Whatever may have changed, you're still you . . . and I love you."

"I love you too, Chas, but . . ."

She put her fingers over his lips. "You're the man God told me to marry, Jackson. When you're ready, you know where to find me."

He nodded, and she could see that he was too emotional to speak. Then an alarm went off in the room and startled her, but he seemed used to it. "What is it?" she asked.

"I'm fine," he said. "It's nothing." But she sensed he was holding back. Watching him more closely, she could see that he was in pain and trying to be brave.

The same nurse came into the room, turned off the alarm, and said, "Your blood pressure is up again. It happens every time we let the pain meds wear off."

"Or maybe it happened because this beautiful woman kissed me," Jackson said, keeping his eyes connected to Chas's.

"Now, that's a much better reason to see it go up. But we still need to get it down."

Jackson turned to see her putting the medication in his IV, then he turned back to Chas, feeling desperate. "I love you," he said, not caring that the nurse was still in the room. "I'm so glad you came. Keep praying for me."

"I will," she promised, and the nurse slipped out. "Promise me you'll get better every day."

"I'm trying. I don't know how long it will be, but don't give up on me."

"Never. As soon as you can call me, you do it."

"I will," he said, already feeling the headiness taking over. "You'll call my mom . . . and Melinda?"

"I will. I talk to them nearly every day."

He nodded, and his eyes got heavy. Chas wanted to shout at him and tell him to stay with her. Instead she pressed her lips to his and felt him respond before she whispered, "I love you too, Jackson. Don't forget it. Don't ever forget it."

A moment later he was asleep, but Chas remained by his side, crying a steady stream of silent tears while she held tightly to his hand. She was aware of Veese coming back into the room, but he just sat down without comment and started to read the paper. She remained where she was, counting her blessings and praying on Jackson's behalf until Veese said quietly, "I need to get you back to the airport if you're going to make that flight."

"Okay," she said, wiping her eyes, "thank you." She stood and bent over Jackson, squeezing his hand while she whispered in his ear that she loved him. She pressed her lips to his and allowed Veese to escort her from the hospital. She took several tissues with her.

During the journey home, Chas pushed away every negative aspect of this situation and focused instead on her gratitude. Jackson was going to be okay. She'd been able to see him. He knew that she loved him, and she knew that he loved her. She felt renewed and filled with hope, and with that she could press forward with great anticipation for the day when they could be together again.

Once she was back at the inn, she updated Polly and the others on what had happened, then she called and talked separately to Melinda and Melva, while they indulged in their recent habit of crying with her over the phone.

Chas went to bed early, exhausted from a long day. She marveled that she had flown to Virginia and back in a matter of hours. She woke the next morning determined to stay busy and not watch the phone—or the calendar. It was several days before Jackson called her. The joy she felt just to hear his voice was indescribable. He told her that they were keeping him awake more, but that was just making him more aware of being miserable. Knowing how sick he'd been helped him understand why he still felt so lousy, but it was discouraging. He was being moved to a different part of the hospital where they would continue to monitor his physical condition closely, but the focus would shift to the therapy for PTSD. And he got emotional when he admitted to how much he knew he needed it.

"I'm a wreck, Chas. I'm having nightmares and panic attacks. I feel like I don't even know who I am."

"You need to be patient with yourself," she said. "And remember that I love you. It will get better with time." Her words reassured him, but Chas felt discouraged herself, wondering how long it might be.

"I don't know when I can call you," he said. "They'll be keeping very close tabs on me, and the rules are ridiculous. I can only say that I'll call when I can."

"I know," she said. "I understand."

They shared their good-byes and "I love yous," then he had to go, and Chas cried for half an hour.

Throughout the next few weeks, Chas got only a few more phone calls, and they were brief. She knew that he was also calling his mother with the same brief reports. She was overjoyed to finally hear him call and say, "I'm home now. I'm officially an outpatient. But I hate being alone."

Chas already had a premeditated answer. "You should come here, Jackson, no strings attached. Just . . . come. I'll take care of you. I'll come and get you if you need me to. I've already checked into some things. You can do counseling over the phone with your therapist there, or we can find a good therapist in Butte—or both. We can work on it together."

"That sounds more wonderful than I could ever tell you, and I think we can work up to that, but I need to be here for a while; I don't know how long. They've still got me in therapy—both kinds. I need time. I can't even think beyond one day at a time right now. I hope you can understand."

"Of course," she said, fighting to keep her emotion silent.

"If everything goes well, I'm hoping to be there for Christmas." Chas couldn't speak as joy leapt out of her throat, and she had to put a hand over her mouth to keep from squealing in his ear. "Is that a problem?" She didn't answer. "Chas, if there's a reason you don't want me to come for Christmas, then—"

"No," she said and sniffled. She laughed, then sobbed, then laughed again. "Nothing could make me happier than to have you here for Christmas." She sniffled. "Do you really mean it?"

"I really do. We'll just plan on it, okay? It'll be just like last year."

She laughed, feeling the hope surge into her, mingling with precious memories. "Ten-dollar limit?"

"No promises there," he said. "I think our relationship warrants a little more thought and effort than that for something so wondrous as celebrating Christmas together. It's not about the money, Chas. I just want to get you something for Christmas this year that will let you know how much you mean to me."

"Amen," she said.

The next day she sent him a card, but didn't expect she'd get one in return for a while. He probably wasn't up to card shopping. But that was okay. She'd just keep sending them. If nothing else, it was a way to let him know that she loved him and she was there for him.

Through the following week Chas heard from Jackson only once more. He told her that he actually hadn't been home very much. He'd been spending time at the office, not working but more as therapy in being able to be among people who gave him a comfort zone and helped him merge his pre-trauma life with the present. He'd also been spending time at the homes of some of the same people, and everyone had been very kind. The counseling was still going on every day, but he said it was going well, and that physically he was much better. He would be on some medications for the parasitic problem for a long time, but he was now mostly free of the symptoms. His wounds were healing, and he hadn't taken anything but Tylenol for the pain in several days. Chas was grateful to hear the report. She just missed him desperately. Then she woke up on a snowy morning and realized what day it was. After a good, long cry it took a great deal of willpower to get out of bed. *The Sunday before Thanksgiving.*

Chas took care of the usual business and left Polly in charge while she went to church. The snow had stopped, but it was still very cloudy. As she sat through the meeting, she realized she was tired of being there alone, and she missed Jackson desperately, but she focused her mind on prayer, especially gratitude that she was anticipating his arrival for Christmas as opposed to trying to cope with his death, or having to wonder if was dead or alive. It could be *so* much worse, and she needed to keep perspective.

Chas came home from church, trying to hold on to the peace she'd felt there. Polly reported that all guests had checked out, and no one was coming in the rest of the week. The maids would come the following morning to clean the four rooms that had been used. Chas had known that, but the report was part of the routine.

"I know you know this too," Polly said, "but I'm having dinner with friends. Why don't you come with me? You shouldn't be alone; not today."

"No, thank you, Polly. I *want* to be alone. I'll be all right."

Polly tried to protest again, but Chas escorted her to her car, noting that the clouds were growing heavier. She wondered when they would let loose again. How could she not think of a year ago today when a horrible storm had escorted Jackson Leeds into her life? She went inside and went into the kitchen where she opened cupboards and the refrigerator multiple times and stared. But nothing inspired her to actually work up enough appetite to motivate her to cook. She ended up just sitting in Granny's chair, wondering what would become of her now. Jackson was coming for Christmas, but that felt so far away. And that didn't necessarily mean that he would want to marry her. Or maybe he would want to, but he might still feel like he needed time to make that decision.

When the silence began to eat at her, she grabbed the remote and pushed the buttons, wondering how many times she would watch the same movie that Granny had been in the middle of when she'd died. She nearly threw the remote at the TV screen when it quickly came to the scene where young Martin came home. Then she could have sworn she'd heard something in the house. She pushed Pause and stood up to go and see if someone was at the door. As she came into the hall, she lost her breath and felt light-headed. She had to reach out a hand to take hold of the doorjamb to steady herself. Jackson really had just come through the back door. Unaware of her presence, he set a bag at his feet and hung up his coat and scarf. Taking in his appearance she had more questions than answers, but she couldn't speak at all.

He took two steps away from the door, then stopped abruptly when he saw her, and he became as frozen as she felt. He looked good, she thought. At this distance she never would have known that anything was any different than it had been the last time he was here. It was a miracle! He stuck his hands in the pockets of his jeans and said, "I don't have a reservation, but I heard there's always room at the inn."

Chas still couldn't speak, but she had no trouble closing the space between them and wrapping him in her arms. He returned her embrace, and she relished the strength she felt in him. She started to cry and realized he was doing the same. He buried his face in her hair and murmured her name over and over. She put her hands on his face and took a long look at him.

"Oh, you look good!" she said, noting that the physical evidence of his ordeal was minimal. He had a little scar on his cheekbone and one next to his lip. Beyond that he almost looked the same.

"Yeah," he said, "remarkable, isn't it. Even the scars aren't as visible as I thought they would be." He touched her face as well, wiping her tears with his thumbs. "You look just the same, just as I've imagined you all this time." He kissed her and laughed softly.

"Oh, it's you," she said and kissed him again. "It's really you." She took a step back and took both his hands into hers. "But what are you doing here?"

"That's a long story," he said and scooped her into his arms, walking toward the parlor. "I think we'd better sit down."

Chas let out a startled laugh, then said, "Apparently you've gotten your strength back."

"Apparently," he said and sat down, easing her beside him with her legs over his lap. "You see," he said without any more urging from her, "they told me I'd achieved a big breakthrough, that I was doing well, but I felt depressed, and I had trouble figuring out what to do about it. I went shopping . . . for a card. And then I was sitting in my apartment after I'd gotten the card ready to mail, but I couldn't find a stamp. And that's when I looked around and wondered what I was doing there . . . when I could be here. So, I just decided to forego the stamp and bring it myself." He reached inside his jacket and pulled out a card in a lavender envelope.

"Ooh," she said, taking it from him. "Can I open it now?"

"Oh, you have to. It's a card that must be opened today, which added to my incentive, because mail doesn't get delivered on Sundays. The only way I could be sure you'd open it today was to bring it myself."

Chas pulled the card out of the envelope, so filled with happiness that she wondered how she could hold it all in. On the front, in various fonts and colors, there was a list of events and dates, with the heading at the top, *Important Dates in History*. On the list was the day man had stepped onto the moon, the days the world wars had ended, the day the Berlin wall had come down, the day the smallpox vaccine had been discovered, and the day the Declaration of Independence had been signed. Inside was printed, *And most of all, the day I met you.* He'd written in parentheses, *The Sunday before Thanksgiving.* And printed below that it simply said, *Happy Anniversary.*

"Wow," she said, wiping her tears. "How long did you have to look to find that one?"

"A long time." He chuckled. It was so good to hear him laugh, to have him here, to see him looking so much better. She hugged him tightly.

"It's perfect. Thank you! And thank you for bringing it yourself. That was very thoughtful!"

"Purely selfish," he said.

"Is that any indication of how we feel about each other?" she asked. "If it feels selfish to you and so good for me, it must be good, don't you think?"

"Yes, I agree completely."

"When did your flight come in?"

"I didn't fly."

She leaned back a little to check his expression. "You drove?"

"I did."

"When did you leave?"

"Three days ago. I made a few stops so I could get my rest. And I did some shopping."

"So you just . . . got in your car . . . and came?"

"There was a little more to it than that. First I had to officially submit my resignation." Chas put a hand over her mouth, not wanting to interrupt, but feeling stunned to realize what that meant—or at least what she hoped it meant. "I packed up my clothes and what little I own that has any personal value. If it didn't fit in the SUV, I left it behind. Veese is going to oversee selling the place, *and* the stuff. I'm not going back."

Chas wrapped her arms around his neck and cried for a few minutes before he facetiously said, "If you're that upset about it, I *could* go back, or—"

"You *know* I want you here," she said and kissed him.

"I'm sure glad, because I'm a man without a job and without a home."

"And you think you can just show up here without calling and I'll give you both?"

"You will, won't you?"

"You're taking a lot on faith . . . Jackson Tobias Leeds."

"You taught me that," he said and kissed her again. Following a kiss that changed her life, Chas looked into his eyes and hit him in the shoulder.

"Ow! What was that for?"

"For not calling to tell me you were coming."

"And spoil the moment of that look on your face? Never! It was worth it."

"Worth getting hit?"

"Yes," he said and kissed her again. "After what I've been through, getting hit by you is nothing." She checked his expression carefully. "What?" he asked.

"You can talk about it . . . just like that?"

"No, not just like that. I've been through weeks of intense therapy to be able to make a joke about it."

"We need to talk about it," she said, and felt him bristle.

"No, we do not need to talk about it. I have talked about it thoroughly with trained professionals who are not personally involved. If I need to talk about it anymore, I will talk to them. There are some things I will never tell you."

"Why not?" she sounded hurt.

"Because I'm not going to pollute your mind with it. It's over and done, and I'm grateful. Enough said."

"I understand what you're saying . . . at least I think I do. But . . . do we just pretend it didn't happen?"

"Not at all. We just don't need to discuss the details. I have no problem telling you or anybody else the bare facts."

"Which are?" she asked as if she were testing him.

"I was kidnapped by drug-dealing terrorists in a third-world country and held hostage for nearly a month. They treated me very badly, and it took weeks in a hospital and even more weeks of therapy to recover. But I survived and I'm grateful. Other men have been through worse and have gone on to lead normal and productive lives. I intend to do the same."

Chas shook her head and touched his face. "It was so terrible."

He laughed. "It was pretty bad."

"Then why are you laughing?"

"Because it's so good to see you." She saw moisture glisten in his eyes. "I was really afraid I never would again."

Chas hugged him once more, understanding his fear completely. "It's good to see you, too." She tightened her embrace and admitted, "I don't ever want you to leave again."

"I was hoping you'd say that, because I wanted a good reason to give you your Christmas present early."

She looked at him but kept her arms around his neck. "This is *really* early."

"Okay, so call it a pre-Christmas anniversary gift. Call it whatever you like." He reached into his jacket pocket and pulled out a little box that he flipped open with his thumb, as if he'd practiced it several times. "Just say yes."

Chas let go of him so she could take the box and touch its contents. It was the only way she could be completely certain that it really was a diamond ring. Then she made eye contact with him just before he said, "I'm not running away from anything this time, Chas. I'm not hiding or pretending or lost in any kind of temporary fantasy.

I've come home. There's nothing in this world that has any value to me if I can't be with you. I've served my country and I've done my part. I'm putting that life behind me, and I want you to be my wife. I only wish I had asked you months ago and we could have just skipped the adventures of the last few months. Although, I've had to wonder if I'm just stubborn enough that I needed torture and starvation to realize what a fool I was being. Forgive me, and say yes. Say it now because I can't stand the suspense."

"Yes," she said and kissed him. "Yes, yes." She kissed him again. She laughed and cried as he took the ring out of the box and slid it onto her finger, where it fit perfectly.

"How did you know what size?" she asked.

"Granny told me," he said. She looked surprised. He just laughed and added, "Well, I just knew. What other possibility is there?"

"It sounds perfectly logical to me."

He kissed her again and said, "Now that we're engaged, can we make a sandwich or something? Once I got to Montana I couldn't bring myself to stop anywhere. I'm starving."

Chas laughed and came to her feet. "I'm starving too. I was too depressed to eat."

While they were working in the kitchen together to prepare a simple meal, Chas kept looking at the ring on her hand, and the man at her side, trying to convince herself that this was real. While she was considering the fact that she couldn't take in any more happiness, he said, "I have a favor to ask."

"Go for it," she said.

"Could we invite my family here for Thanksgiving?"

"Oh, that would be wonderful!" she said and laughed.

"I talked to Mom just a while ago and told her I was on my way here. She's waiting to hear whether or not you said yes, by the way. I should call her. She said that she and Melinda would just be having dinner there. Melinda's son Brian might be there, but he could come too, right?"

"Of course."

"Sasha and her family will be with the in-laws this year, and Melinda was saying that it was going to be too quiet. What do you think?"

"I think it's perfect," she said.

"Good." He stopped what he was doing and turned her to face him, taking both her hands into his. "And then they would be here for the wedding."

"What wedding?"

"Ours, of course. How about Friday? The day after Thanksgiving is a great day to get married, don't you think?"

"You're serious."

He chuckled but said, "Of course I'm serious. What do we have to do but make a few phone calls? I bet I could talk Charlotte into making us a cake. What else do we need that we can't take care of before Friday?"

Chas laughed and threw her arms around him. "Nothing," she said. "It's perfect."

He tightened his embrace and lifted her feet off the floor. Again she felt the evidence of his strength, and his love, and she felt utterly and perfectly happy.

They made plans over a quiet dinner, then Polly came home. She squealed with excitement when she saw Jackson. She hugged him and told him how happy she was that he'd survived—and that he was there. Then Chas showed her the ring, and she squealed even louder. When they told her they were getting married Friday, she nearly hyperventilated.

Later, after Jackson had put some of his things into the Dombey, he and Chas snuggled on the couch while they watched *David Copperfield*. Chas had never felt such perfect contentment, such sublime hope. She'd long ago come to believe in miracles, but now she could never dispute it. These were truly the best of times.

CHAPTER 18

Chas woke up Monday morning feeling as if the previous day had been a dream. A glorious and marvelous dream. Then she felt the ring on her left hand and knew it had been real. She prepared for the day with extra vigor and felt such pleasure and gratitude to be making breakfast for Jackson that she had trouble controlling her emotion. Just knowing he was in the house, and that the waiting was over, she realized that the proverbial glass wasn't just half full; it was over-flowing.

Chas chatted with Polly when she came to the kitchen for a quick breakfast, then Polly went to the office, and Chas heard the once-familiar sounds of Jackson coming in the back door after his morning run. She heard him go up the stairs and knew he'd be down for break-fast in about twenty minutes. She went over a few things in the office with Polly, and she was back in the dining room when he arrived.

"Good morning," they both said at the same time, and exchanged a smile and a kiss.

"How did you sleep?" she asked.

"Great," Jackson said, keeping to himself that his measurement of a great night was getting through it without any bad dreams. Wondering why there was a subtle awkwardness between them, he poured himself a cup of coffee and attempted to make small talk. "The bed is every bit as comfortable as I'd remembered. But then, anything beyond cold concrete is great." He heard her gasp and wished he hadn't said it. He couldn't even make casual conversation without bringing up things he didn't want to talk about. But when it was still so prominent on his mind, it was difficult to not let it slip into his words. "Sorry," he added.

"Don't apologize for being honest with me," she said.

He turned to look at her and leaned against the sideboard while he took a sip of coffee. "I told you I didn't want you to have to deal with those images, and I meant it. Sometimes it just . . . slips out."

"I understand your concern," she said, "but I don't want you to feel like you have to be on guard with me. If something slips out, let it slip. We'll deal with it."

"Okay," he said, and they made eye contact, but it still felt awkward. "What?" he asked when she just stared at him.

"You really had to sleep on cold concrete?"

"Yes."

"The entire time?"

"Yes," he said again and bit his tongue to keep from adding a snide comment about how little they'd actually allowed him to sleep. "Can we change the subject now?"

"Sorry," she said. "It's so good to have you here."

"It's good to be here," he said and glanced at her hand. "And it's good to see that ring on your finger, especially since I know I put it there."

"Yes," she said and laughed softly, "it's marvelous, isn't it." She cleared her throat and hurried into the kitchen. "Sit down. Breakfast is ready."

While they shared a meal in a way that had once been common and comfortable, Jackson had trouble believing he was really here. But he hated the way that difficult memories regularly intruded upon his happiness. It was as if he couldn't fully appreciate the miracle of being alive and reunited with Chas unless he recalled the horrors that had taken place since he had first come here and fallen in love with this incredible woman. He forced the ugly memories away, but they hovered uncomfortably close while he shared breakfast with his fiancée, and they lingered during the day as he and Chas made calls and ran errands to arrange everything for the wedding. Chas called Bishop Wegg at the bank where he worked to be certain he could perform the ceremony, which she considered the most important thing. Once he assured her that he would be thrilled to do so, the rest was easy to put into place. That evening, Charlotte and her children came over for supper. With Polly there as usual, they all discussed the upcoming event, and it seemed that everything was under control. Jackson kept watching Chas as if through a haze, hoping that he'd made the right decision on her behalf. He couldn't help wondering whether bringing his problems into her life was good thing. Still, he felt so perfectly happy at the thought of their upcoming marriage, and there was no disputing that Chas was equally happy. How could he not want that?

When the day came to a close, Jackson kissed Chas good night at the foot of the stairs, loving the memories of previous kisses and his hopes for the future. He read in his room until he fell asleep blanketed by the comfort of his surroundings. His next awareness was coming out of a nightmare that had replayed in detail the most horrific events of his life. Heart pounding and wet with sweat, he told himself that everything was all right. But he still felt panicked, as if one part of himself wasn't willing to believe what the other part was telling him. He could hear his own strained breathing as he pressed his hands over the bed where he was laying in an effort to convince himself of his present surroundings. But even that wasn't enough. He groped for the lamp on the bedside table, needing light to assure himself that he wasn't hallucinating. In his desperation, he almost knocked the lamp over and barely managed to steady it while he found the switch and turned it on. The evidence of his surroundings bathed him with relief, but he sat on the edge of the bed for several minutes before his heart and his breathing started to slow down. He consciously went through every mental exercise he'd been taught to counteract these episodes, but such things always made more sense in theory than in their actual application.

An hour after he'd turned on the light, the sun was coming up and his hands were still shaking. He didn't have the strength to go running or the motivation to take a shower, but the room suddenly felt like it was closing in on him. He splashed cold water on his face and wiped it dry before he got dressed and went down the stairs. He wandered around quietly, and finally ended up in the dining room, appalled to realize that his hands were still shaking. And with the evidence of how bad off he really was, he began to doubt the course he was taking. He wanted Chas to show up to help him keep perspective, yet he hoped to avoid her indefinitely. He felt scared out of his mind. When he heard her in the hall and saw her come into the room, his heart rate increased again, and the shaking worsened.

Chas opened the drapes in the dining room and turned around to see Jackson sitting at one of the little tables, as if he'd been there a long time. His presence startled her.

"Sorry," he said.

"How long have you been up?"

"A long time," he said, knowing he needed to be honest.

"Is something wrong?" she asked, sitting down across from him.

"Nightmares," he said, avoiding her gaze.

Chas considered his body language as much as what he'd said. "Does this happen often?" she asked.

"Yes," he admitted, then said what he knew he needed to say. "Since we're getting married, I assume we'll be sleeping in the same bed."

"That's the way it usually works."

"Then you should know that I don't sleep very well. Everything is worse at night. Sometimes I'm scared of the dark."

"We'll leave the light on."

"Sometimes I wake up and don't know where I am, and I have a panic attack."

"Maybe if you don't wake up alone it won't be so bad," she suggested.

"Maybe," he said and finally looked at her. "Maybe not. Maybe you're being way too optimistic because you don't know what you're dealing with. Maybe we're moving too fast. Maybe you should reconsider."

Jackson expected her to be taken aback by the suggestion and stammer over what she might say in response. But without missing a beat she said with conviction, "Maybe you should have more faith in me and remember that when I told you I loved you no matter what, I meant it. For better or worse. That's the way it works, isn't it? I told you that I prayed about this. I know God wants me to marry you."

"But you got that answer a long time ago," he countered.

"I've kept praying all along, Jackson. Do you think I'm naive enough to think that what happened to you is just going to magically go away? I *saw* you in that hospital bed. I may not know all the details, but I can put pieces together. You don't call me *Detective* for nothing. I've spent hours studying parasites and PTSD and . . ." Her voice broke, and she swallowed hard to keep from getting emotional.

"Then maybe you could explain this," he said and lifted his hands to show her how they were trembling.

"Are you okay?" she asked.

"No!" he said, setting his hands flat on the table. "Obviously I'm not okay."

"Is it the nightmares or the prospect of marriage that's making you shake?"

"I don't know," he said.

"Has this happened before?"

"Yes, and I assume it will calm down as it has before. But it's still evidence of something I don't think either of us is prepared to handle under the circumstances."

"But you said you were doing better."

"I *am* doing better, Chas. But better is relative. And I wonder if I'm jumping the gun a little to be thinking I should get married this week."

"Listen to me," she said, putting her hands over his. "I have some idea of what we're dealing with, but the operative word here is *we*. Me, you, and God—because I *know* you and I are supposed to be together."

"How can you *know*, Chas?"

"How did you know Granny was with you in that prison?" she asked, and he could only look at the floor. "I just know," she added.

"Okay, so *you* know. But *I* don't know. I don't get answers the way you do."

"Or maybe you're getting them and you just don't know how to recognize them."

"What's that supposed to mean?"

"Would you be critical of me for not being a good FBI agent? Would you think I should be critical of myself?"

"Of course not."

"It's only been a year since you've even stopped to consider whether or not you believe in God. You don't have as much practice as I do. God knows that, and so do I. You shouldn't be so hard on yourself. And it's not been so many weeks since you survived something that most people could never imagine, let alone live through. So give yourself a break and let me help you through this."

Jackson sighed and shook his head. "It's what I want, Chas. I want to be here with you, and I know it's what you want, too. But maybe that's not enough."

"I *know* it's right," she insisted. "But neither one of us should be naive enough to believe that such knowledge means the road is going to be easy. It's about commitment, and trust, and respect. We have to trust each other enough to work through whatever comes up, and the commitment has to be stronger than the challenges."

Jackson sighed again, not knowing what to say. Chas stood up and took his hand, leading him to the parlor where they sat on the couch and faced each other. "Talk to me," she said. "You don't have to tell me details, but I need to understand what you're feeling."

Jackson took hold of her hand and played with her ring. He noted that his shaking had almost stopped. "I thought I was a lot tougher than this. I've been trained for stuff like this. And even though they tell you that all the training in the world can't really prepare you for the reality, you think you can handle it. I started praying for death the first hour. After a week I couldn't believe that the human body was capable of enduring so much and *not* dying. I became angry with God for keeping me alive. Now I'm grateful that He did, but it's not black and white."

Jackson saw tears on her face. "What is this?"

"When I think of how you suffered, I . . . I . . ."

"That's why you mustn't think about it."

"How can I not? Sometimes I think my imagination is worse than whatever you might tell me. When I was told that they didn't know where you were, my mind went wild with possibilities. Now I know that some of them were true, and it's just so . . . horrible."

"Yes, it is," he said gently. "That's why my feelings are complicated. Sometimes I'm still angry, and I wonder if it would have been better if I hadn't survived."

"I don't know how you can sit there and hold my hand and wish that you were dead. Do you have any idea what that would have done to me?"

He looked her in the eye. "I'm not unsympathetic to your grief, Chas. But there are things worse than death. I don't want what haunts me to haunt you, too. You say that you know this is right. I'm not sure that *I* know. Maybe I should have thought things through a little more before I showed up here with a ring."

"And maybe you need to trust the decision you made when you were thinking clearly, as opposed to doubting it when you're over-whelmed with the memories of what you've suffered." He was thoughtfully silent until Chas asked, "What are you thinking?"

"I'm thinking that I could really use a drink."

"No, you don't need a drink. You've come this far without it. You don't need to take up drinking again now." He said nothing, and she added, "You *have* come this far without it, haven't you?"

"I haven't had a drop since the day I told you I would stop drinking, but that doesn't mean it hasn't been tempting."

"All the more reason for you to be living here with me, as opposed to somewhere else by yourself. You need me."

"I won't dispute that."

"Then what's the problem?"

"Whether or not I should be a burden to you."

"I think you're blowing this all out of proportion. You think I can't handle some nightmares and panic attacks?"

"I don't know, can you?"

"Try me," she said, then kissed him before he could argue any further. He took her face into his hands to prolong the kiss. Then she whispered, close to his lips, "You need me. I need you. This is right. Now, why don't we have some breakfast. We need to drive to Butte to buy something for you to wear to our wedding." She was going to be wearing her grand-mother's dress; but she needed a veil, and Jackson needed the perfect suit.

Keeping hold of her face, he asked, "Are you sure?"

"Yes, I'm sure. Trust me."

"Okay," Jackson said, thinking he still had a few days to talk her out of it, even though he was hoping with all his heart and soul that she wouldn't bend. He didn't know what he'd do without her, but he wasn't sure that was basis enough for marriage.

By the time they were on the road to Butte, Jackson felt more calm and realized that he *did* need to keep perspective. He still felt concerned, but it didn't feel so overwhelming. He took Chas's hand and said, "Your patience means a lot to me."

"It's not so hard to be patient when you love someone," she said, and they exchanged a warm glance before he put his attention back to the road. "It's really nice to have you back."

"It's nice to *be* back," he said. "I just hope that my brain will catch up with the rest of me before too long."

"I'm sure it will."

"That's what my therapist says."

"What else does he say?" she asked.

"She," he said. "It's a she, and she's almost old enough to be my mother. She said that getting married and starting a new life was probably one of the best things I could do, *only* because we have an established relationship that was in place before the incident. I hate that word. It's always referred to as *the incident.*"

"So call it something else."

"I can't think of anything else that I would dare say in mixed company, so I'll just have to refer to it as *the incident.*"

Following some minutes of silence, Chas said, "May I ask what else she said? And does *she* have a name?"

"Her name is Marie, and her specialty is working with military PTSD. I can't imagine the horror stories she must hear."

"I'm only interested in what she said about *your* horror story . . . only if you want to tell me. But maybe it would help if I knew what kind of guidance she's giving you."

Jackson blew out a harsh breath, preferring to avoid this, but knowing it was inevitable, and necessary. If there was any real hope of the two of them getting married and making it work, she had to know what they were dealing with. "Marie believes that I'm having trouble letting go of certain aspects of *the incident* because they're linked into traumatic memories associated with my father. And I can't dispute that. I thought of him way too much while . . ." He stopped himself, cleared his throat, then said, "What kind of man was I raised by if being beaten by sadistic drug lords reminded me of him?"

Chas wanted to ask what his father had done. She wanted to ask what exactly had happened to him that had made such a connection in his mind. But she wasn't sure she wanted to know, and she *was* sure that he would likely never tell her. She only said, "I thought you had come a long way with your feelings about your father."

"I thought I had too," he said. "Apparently I was wrong."

"You're still struggling with that, then?"

"Every day," he said. "I think it's time to change the subject now. I can only handle so much talk of *the incident* per hour."

"Okay," Chas said. "Have I told you in the last hour how much I love you and how grateful I am that you're alive, and that you're here with me, and that I get to be your wife?"

Jackson smiled at her and kissed her hand. "Not in the last hour, but that's okay. Hourly reminders won't hurt." He kissed her hand again. "I love you too."

Their errands in Butte went well, and they were able to find what they wanted without too much trouble. On the return drive, Chas reminded Jackson that the bishop was coming over that evening to visit with them. "Since he's going to marry us on Friday," she said, "he just wanted to have a little chat with us."

"Okay," he said. "You told me that already. Is there a problem?"

"I'm just wondering if you're okay with that."

"I'm fine with it. As I recall, he's a very nice man."

"He is."

"I just wonder if he has a problem with you marrying outside the Church."

"I already told him that I'd prayed about it and I knew it was right. He respects that completely. He likes you. Not that it would matter if he didn't. I know what I'm doing is right."

"I sure hope so," Jackson said and chuckled, "because we just spent a fortune on that suit."

"Worth every penny," she said and laughed with him.

Through miles of silence Chas prayed for guidance in being able to do the right thing, for herself as well as for Jackson. She didn't question whether marrying him was right. Her answers had been clear and firm all along. But she wanted him to feel the same peace that she felt, and she wanted him to feel hope over the possibility of healing from all that currently plagued him. With his limited understanding of gospel principles and the workings of God, it was difficult, if not impossible, for her to explain the hope she felt on his behalf that he could eventually come to terms with *the incident,* as well as his feelings toward his father. But they had to move one step at a time, and with a man like Jackson, they had to move slowly. *What's the next step?* she asked her Heavenly Father over and over, knowing that He knew what she meant.

She prayed and pondered in silence for many more miles before a thought came to her. A simple, quiet idea that would fit perfectly into their plans for the evening—provided that Jackson would agree to it.

"Have we ever talked about priesthood blessings?" she asked.

Jackson roused himself from his thoughts enough to hear what she'd said and then process it. "I think so. Remind me."

She gave him a brief summary of the power of the priesthood, its purpose, and how blessings could be given for reasons of health, guidance, and comfort.

"Okay," he drawled. "And the point would be? You *are* trying to get to a point, aren't you?"

"So I'm transparent. Remind me never to play poker with you."

"You don't play poker."

"If I did, I wouldn't play it with you."

He chuckled. "Nor would I with you."

"Touché," she said. "The point is that the bishop is coming over this evening to talk with us about the wedding, and I think it might be a good idea for him to give each of us a blessing." She watched him closely for a reaction. "If you're okay with that."

He was quiet for a minute. "So . . . you believe that God can speak through a man who holds this priesthood power?"

"I do."

Chas expected him to say that he *didn't* believe it, but he only said, "I'm not a member of your church."

"The only requirement to receive a blessing is some measure of faith." Chas allowed some long moments of silence for him to think about that before she asked, "Do you believe that God exists, that He hears our prayers, and that He might answer them through a chosen servant on our behalf?" He looked at her, then shifted his gaze back to the road. She could see his mind working and knew that he would never be anything less than completely honest with her. She added firmly, "And don't say that you believe it if I believe it. That's not good enough."

"I realize that. But is it okay to say that the things you've taught me, and the way you live, have made me believe it's possible?"

"Yes, that's okay," she said and smiled.

"I don't know that such things are true the way you do, and as you've pointed out on numerous occasions, I can't just take your word for it. But I believe in God, and I believe in miracles. Is that faith enough?"

"I'm certain it is," she said and squeezed his hand. "You also believe in angels."

"Yes, I do," he said.

"But you haven't really answered my question."

"What question?"

"Are you okay with having the bishop give you a blessing?"

"If you think it would help," he said, "I'm okay with it. I'm not sure what to expect, but . . . I'm okay with it."

"All you have to do is show up and listen . . . with a little faith."

"Okay, I can do that," he said, and Chas felt a deepening hope that everything would be all right. In her opinion, Jackson wasn't nearly so bad off as he thought he was. She suspected his panic over the issues was due more to opposition attempting to keep them apart, rather than being an accurate indication of his mental state.

When Bishop Wegg arrived that evening, Chas answered the door and ushered him into the parlor where Jackson was waiting. The two men shook hands, and they all took a seat. The bishop told them that he was pleased with the decision they'd made, and honored to be able to perform the ceremony. He explained how the ceremony would go according to Church and legal guidelines, and said that he'd be happy to answer any questions they had for him. But before he stopped talking long enough for either of them to ask a question, Bishop Wegg said, "I hope I'm not being presumptuous, but there's something I'd like to say."

"Of course," Chas said at the same time as Jackson motioned with his hand for the bishop to go on.

"I've been thinking a great deal about the two of you since you called and asked me to perform the ceremony, and you've both been in my prayers. I realize that it's not up to me whether the two of you get married, but . . ." Jackson held his breath, waiting to hear this man say that he felt it would be best if Chas didn't marry him because he wasn't a member of the Church—or because the man had been inspired concerning Jackson's mental issues. The bishop took a breath and said, "I want you to know that I've felt a great deal of peace and happiness on your behalf. If I *did* have a vote, I would give it heartily in favor of this marriage. I'm certain the two of you are going to be very happy together, and bless each other's lives a great deal."

Jackson felt Chas squeeze his hand while he basked in the relief of the bishop's statement. It didn't erase his every doubt, but it helped to know that Chas's ecclesiastical leader was supportive of the union.

"I also had the impression," the bishop went on, "if you're not opposed to it . . . that I might give each of you a blessing."

Chas and Jackson exchanged a lengthy glance then looked back to the bishop, who seemed alarmed. "Unless there's a problem with that," he said. "As I said, I don't want to be—"

"There's no problem," Jackson said "Whatever you feel is best."

Chas felt a miracle at work as the bishop laid his hands on her head and proceeded with the blessing. In it she was told that her Heavenly Father was pleased with the way she lived her life and with the choices she had made, and that the Spirit would be with her continually, to protect and guide her and her loved ones through whatever challenges might lay ahead, so long as she remained faithful to her covenants.

Chas sensed some mild nervousness in Jackson when it came his turn, but only because she knew him so well. She felt certain the bishop wouldn't have noticed. His blessing was much longer than hers, and she had trouble holding back tears as she listened. He was told that he was a choice son of God who had devoted his life to an honorable cause and had done much good. He was also told that his Heavenly Father was pleased with the place he had come to, and that he would continue to be guided so long as he continued to exert simple faith and trust in God. Chas nearly gasped aloud when words came forth about the severe injustices of the world and the harm that they caused to the human spirit at times. He was told that few people could understand the extreme depths of such depravity, but that God understood and had perfect empathy for his suffering. Jackson was promised healing in accordance with his faith, and great blessings through the trials that lay ahead as he united himself with the woman of his choosing and sought to be anxiously engaged in a good cause with her by his side.

After the amen had been spoken, Chas met Jackson's eyes and saw wonder and amazement there. If he believed that what had just been said was true, and had indeed come from God, it could be a huge step toward his eventually embracing the gospel that was so precious to her. *One step at a time,* she reminded herself as they exchanged a serene smile.

After they had all returned to their initial seats, Jackson said to the bishop, "Were you aware of the recent challenges I had related to . . . my work?"

The bishop looked confused, and Chas said to Jackson, "I spoke with my home teachers when I was going through the worst of it, but the bishop was out of town at the time, and . . . I didn't tell him."

"I'm sorry," the bishop said. "I didn't know. Is it something I can help with?"

"Perhaps something you should be aware of," Jackson said. "Or maybe you already are."

Their eyes met firmly, relaying a silent message, and the bishop chuckled. "Forgive me, but . . . I often can't even remember what I say when I give blessings. However personal it might have been, it really didn't have anything to do with me."

"Okay," Jackson said, as if accepting that fact was not a problem. "But since you're going to be my bishop too, in a roundabout way, I think you should know that I have been officially diagnosed with PTSD."

Chas took his hand, feeling proud of him for being so open about it, and she intended to tell him so later.

"Post-traumatic stress?" Bishop Wegg asked.

"You know it."

"Know of it," he said. "It's hard not to these days. But you haven't been in the military for many years, or—"

"I was held captive for three and half weeks during an undercover assignment with the FBI. It hasn't been terribly long, and I must admit that I've wondered if I should burden Chas with the problem. It happened since the two of us met, and I believe I've changed a great deal because of it."

"Obviously God believes the two of you should be together," the bishop said, and Chas waited for Jackson's response, not certain how he *really* felt about what had been said in the blessing.

"That would seem apparent," Jackson said. "I suppose I just want to say that . . . I'm glad that you know so . . . if problems come up, you can be aware . . . for Chas's sake."

"I'll be happy to do anything I can," the bishop said with evident sincerity. "Don't hesitate to call if there's ever a problem; anytime—day or night—I mean it."

"Thank you," Chas and Jackson both said at the same time.

The conversation lightened with some small talk that eased any residue of awkwardness over the difficult topic. After they walked the bishop to the door, Jackson went back to the parlor and sat down. Chas sat beside him and waited for him to say something. When minutes passed and he didn't, she finally said, "Well, what do you think?"

She was aching to hear his thoughts regarding the entire conversation, and the outpouring of spiritual information. He just smiled and said, "Will you marry me?"

"I already said yes."

"Then, I guess we're set."

He made no further comment, and she didn't bring it up again. She knew that the blessings and the bishop's kindness and compassion had left a deep impression on him, but he was keeping it to himself. Perhaps he feared that if they talked about it too much, she might get pushy with religion. Perhaps he just needed time to mull it around in his mind. Whatever the reason, she respected where he stood and knew that he would do the same for her.

The following morning at breakfast she felt the need to clarify thoughts that wouldn't leave her. She reached across the table and took his hand before she said, "I need to make something perfectly clear."

"Okay," he said and took a sip of coffee.

"We talked about it a little when we started seeing each other, but a lot's happened, and I don't ever want discord between us over it."

"It?"

"Religion."

"Did you think there would be?"

"I hope not, but I want to be clear where I stand."

"I know where you stand," he said. "And you made it clear that you wanted your children to be—"

"Our children."

"*Our* children to be raised in this church, and that you would appreciate my being actively involved, as opposed to not being involved at all. I'm fine with that."

"I'm grateful for that. I really am. That's just it. I want you to know that I *am* grateful. I respect your beliefs, except that I'm not quite sure what they are exactly."

"I'm not quite sure myself, but I've got a lot to think about."

"I guess what I'm trying to say is . . . I'll be happy to answer any questions, or talk about anything you want to talk about . . . and I promise to never be pushy about it or make it an issue in our relationship. I won't pretend that it wouldn't mean a great deal to me to see you become a member of the Church for many reasons, but you will never get pressure from me. Never."

She saw him thinking about it, then he smiled. "I know," he said, "but I appreciate the clarification. Truthfully, if I'd had the slightest notion that you *would* get pushy about it, I don't know if we could have made it work."

Chas thought of how many times she'd felt strongly about holding back; now she had to believe such feelings were inspired. "It would really bother you that much?"

"I'm afraid it would," he said. "It's probably residue from my childhood in one way or another; most of my issues are. But I have to do things in my own time and in my own way. It's just who I am."

"I know," she said. "It's one of the things I love about you."

"Then I guess we should get married."

"I think we should," she said, and he stood up to lean over the table and kiss her.

Later that day, with all of the plans for the wedding completely taken care of, Jackson and Chas drove to the airport in Butte to pick up his mother and sister. His sister's son, Brian, was also coming.

"I could get used to this," Chas said, holding Jackson's hand.

"What?"

"Being with you . . . all the time."

"Yeah," he said and kissed her hand. "I could definitely get used to this."

"So, you really think you're ready to take up the life of an innkeeper?"

"I am so ready," he said and chuckled.

"Good, because I fired the snow guy; he's had his two-week notice. Next week you'd better go buy something you can drive to move all that snow."

He laughed at the thought of such a task in contrast to his former life. "I'd be happy to . . . but not next week. After I get back from my honeymoon I'll take care of it."

"Deal," she said. "And then I have a whole list of things that need to be done around the house. Guy chores, you know. Just pretend you're going undercover as a fix-it man, and we'll be set."

He laughed again. "How delightful."

She laughed too. "That's easy for you to say. You haven't seen the list."

At the airport, Melva and Melinda both started to cry when they saw Jackson. After a ridiculous amount of hugs, Melinda introduced them to her son, who had been born after Jackson had left home twenty-seven years earlier.

"I understand you're in the Reserves," Jackson said to him.

"Yes, sir, I am. I understand you were in the Marines."

"I was."

"I'd love to talk to you about that, sir."

"Not sir," Jackson said. "And yes, I would love to talk to you about that."

The drive back to the inn went quickly with all they had to talk about, and the evening went well with a festive anticipation in the air. Thanksgiving Day proved to be one of the best Chas had ever enjoyed. If not for Granny's absence, it would have been perfect. But in her heart she knew that Granny surely had to be aware of the joy Chas was feeling.

During the meal Melva suggested they go around the table and say at least one thing they were grateful for. She got emotional as she volunteered to start, and expressed her gratitude to not only have her son back in her life, but to have him safe and well. By the time everyone had taken a turn, they were all emotional. Jackson concluded that it was great to be alive.

The following day Polly helped Chas into the dress that had been pulled out of storage just a few days earlier. When Chas had married Martin, Granny had suggested that Chas wear the gown she had worn when she got married. At the time, Chas had been unable to appreciate the antique beauty of the gown, or how much it would mean to her grandmother, who had taken great care to preserve the gown well. Now it had been professionally cleaned, and the fit made it evident that Granny had once been exactly the same size as Chas was now. Chas looked at herself in the mirror and knew it was the perfect dress for her, and for a wedding at the Dickensian Inn. She felt taken back in time, certain that Granny was looking over her shoulder, telling her she looked dandy.

When she was ready, Chas stepped into the hallway and found Jackson waiting for her, wearing a classic black tux, with a tailcoat and an old-fashioned cut to it. They both smiled while appraising each other. She said, "Mr. Dickens would definitely approve."

"Yes, he would," Jackson said and took her hand. They walked together into the parlor where a small group of family and friends was gathered for a simple wedding. Bishop Wegg made some lovely comments prior to the ceremony, and the vows were spoken with conviction. The moment that Jackson kissed her to seal their marriage, she knew in her heart they would be together forever; that the joy she felt now was only the beginning. She wasn't naive enough to believe that the years ahead would be perfect or free of struggle, but she knew they were on the right path, and they were on that path together.

When the ceremony was over, they had a formal wedding portrait taken in the parlor, which Chas intended to have enlarged in brown tones and hung over the fireplace as part of the decor. They spent their wedding night in the Carol, and Chas admitted to her husband that it was about time *she,* of all people, was able to enjoy a romantic getaway at the Dickensian Inn.

The following morning, Jackson came awake to daylight and felt the same relief he felt each time he woke up with no memory of bad dreams. He felt rested and content, then he remembered that he was married, and his contentment deepened. He turned over to find his wife sleeping beside him, and he watched her for several minutes, in awe of the miracle she was in his life. When she came awake and saw him there, she laughed softly before she eased closer and kissed him.

"Is something funny?" he asked.

"No," she said, "I'm just . . . happy."

"Amen," he said and kissed her again.

Following a honeymoon in Florida, they settled into a life they'd shared briefly the previous year, except that now as husband and wife the fulfillment and joy of that life was greatly magnified. Jackson loved being an official part of running the inn, and each day seemed to put the horrors of *the incident* further behind him. Occasionally he did have nightmares or panic attacks—always at night—but with Chas there it *did* make it easier to calm down more quickly and not allow it to affect him so deeply.

Preparations for Christmas were even more magical than they had been the year before. Jackson felt as if he'd come home, and realized that never before in his life had he enjoyed such a feeling. He'd never felt so content or fulfilled.

They spent Christmas Eve in the Carol, deciding to make it a tradition. They were, after all, celebrating nearly a month of wedded bliss. Jackson had settled so naturally into life at the inn that Chas couldn't imagine what those weeks and months without him had been like. Now that he actually lived there, he worked himself easily into being involved with the business, helping in the kitchen here and there, and working away at the list Chas had made—even though she kept adding things to the bottom as he crossed things off the top.

It snowed hard on Christmas Day, not unlike the day when Jackson had first come to the inn. But they stayed inside and enjoyed the storm, reminding each other frequently that neither had ever had a Christmas so fine. With a bottle of sparkling apple juice and two beautiful goblets, Jackson told his wife that he would like to propose a toast. With the lights on the Christmas tree twinkling, and the fire ablaze, Jackson clinked his glass to hers and said, "God bless us, every one!"

"Amen," Chas said and kissed him.

Epilogue

The Sunday before Thanksgiving

Chas woke up to see snow falling outside. She groaned and rolled onto her back, wishing she'd gotten more sleep. Jackson eased next to her and snuggled up close. "You okay?" he asked.

"I'm fine. What about you?"

"I'm fine," he said, wanting to ignore the nightmare he'd had that had awakened them both. They didn't happen often these days, but often enough to be upsetting. It was a perfect distraction to rub his hand over her rounded belly and ask, "How's my son?"

"He was kicking me all night, if you must know." She then let out a little gasp and said, "Hey, I just remembered what today is."

Jackson wanted to say that it had been fourteen years ago today that she'd gotten news that her first husband had been killed. But she smiled brightly and said, "We met two years ago today!"

"Yes, we did," he said and kissed her. "And after church we're going to celebrate."

"How are we going to do that?"

"I don't know. We could turn off the lights and pretend the power is out and make a sandwich, or something."

"How romantic," she said and giggled.

"Okay," he said and got out of bed, "I'll check with Polly and Jen and make sure everything's under control. You get yourself ready for church. We'll go as soon as we get some breakfast."

"You're so good to me," she said, certain the remaining weeks of the pregnancy were going to kill her. She felt so fat and awkward and useless. But Jackson had been nothing but doting and helpful, and the girls kept everything under control. She got to a sitting position on the edge of the bed before Jackson had his shirt buttoned. And a moment later she said, "I think you'd better rework our plans for the day."

"Why?" he asked, wondering what she might have forgotten.

"My water just broke," she said, then she laughed at the way he panicked. She might have felt panicked herself, except that they had known for certain many weeks ago that this baby had a good, strong heart, and all was well. With every reason to believe they were going to have a healthy baby, what she had to go through today didn't seem so bad. And Jackson would be with her. The last time she'd done this, the baby's father had been dead, and the future had been difficult to face. Now she had nothing but happiness in front of her.

It was snowing hard by the time they got to the hospital, and the storm settled in deeply during the course of Chas's labor. But with the help of modern medicine, her pain was minimal, and the process went smoothly. The sun was going down when she gave birth to a healthy boy with dark hair.

"Happy anniversary," she said to Jackson when the baby was laid in his arms and their eyes connected. She saw tears there and silently thanked God for giving her so much.

Later that evening a nurse came in to check on Chas and motioned toward the baby that Jackson was holding. "He sure is a cutey," she said. "What will his name be?"

"Charles," Jackson said matter-of-factly, "after his mother."

About the Author

Anita Stansfield began writing at the age of sixteen, and her first novel was published sixteen years later. Her novels range from historical to contemporary and cover a wide gamut of social and emotional issues that explore the human experience through memorable characters and unpredictable plots. She has received many awards, including a special award for pioneering new ground in LDS fiction, and the Lifetime Achievement Award from the Whitney Academy for LDS Literature. Anita is the mother of five, and has one adorable grandson. Her husband, Vince, is her greatest hero.

To receive regular updates from Anita, go to anitastansfield.com and subscribe.